FIRE DRAGON STREET THEATER
1962 – 1967

Also by Jeri Hilderley

Mari

Time Traveling with Sappho

FIRE DRAGON STREET THEATER
1962 – 1967

Jeri Hilderley

DEDICATION

I dedicate this book to everyone who understands that only through struggle, steadfast hope and tender revolutionary solidarity can we create the humane, just, compassionate, and non-violent world required to sustain our planet and all its living creatures—and to all oppressed people who have found ways to express this unalterable truth with their own words.

Finally, my book is dedicated to the act of collective-supportive-activism, where each person's precious and unique abilities and needs are recognized and integrated to struggle for change. Twenty-four years of teaching my curriculum, "Learning the Language Arts through Music," to students with special needs solidified my instinct that individual and group development thrives in a caring, creative supportive environment. We are all connected!

"One cannot live with sighted eyes and feeling heart
and not know or react to the miseries of the world."

— Lorraine Hansberry

CONTENTS

Prologue
Tavern on the Green
May Day 1966

"Why are we there, killing Vietnamese?" Louis' voice reverberated like a trumpet call from an improvised stage area on the restaurant's patio. A huge swarm of park revelers pulled by the street theater's hypnotic parade through Sheep Meadow—the gyrating dragon puppet, colorful banner, snappy drum beats gathered around the compelling voice. "As we take you into the life of Sam, a twenty-one-year-old American about to receive his draft notice, ask yourselves: 'Is it our war to fight? Does he have to go?'"

Two cops suddenly slashed through the growing crowd. "That one! The beard and cape guy. Commie kike!"

They yanked Louis from his soapbox, ripped off his silver cape and hurled it across the flagstone. Lucina dropped the red drum and rushed to him. "Get off him, you bastards!"

Someone from the crowd shouted, "Hell, no he won't go!"

"They're real! Not actors! Stop them!" she shrieked.

"Hey, peaceniks—where's your crazy fire dragon puppet? He'll stop them!" someone snickered.

As one cop grabbed Louis' belt and hauled him through the jarred and baffled crowd, more voices rang out: "Hell no! He won't go!" They bumped Louis' prone body across the rough stones to the roadway where their squad car idled, a silent accomplice.

"Louis! Louis! I'm here!" Lucina tore after them, with Marin, Jenny and Al racing after her.

Al grabbed her arms. "Stop it, Lucina. They'll get you too!"

She wriggled away and made for the cop jabbing his stick into Louis' ribs. "You're killing him! Monsters! I'll kill you!"

She clawed at his back as he rammed Louis into the back seat. The other cop shoved her aside. "Lady, back up. We got room for two!"

Al, Marin and Jenny surrounded her as the car sped off. "C'mon, Babe," Jenny yelled above the chants and shouts. "We know our rights! We have to find the pig pen!" Marin turned to the agitated crowd. "Is there a lawyer in the house?"

PART I
THE SCULPTOR AND THE POET

1
Lucina Builds *Rune*
April 1962

Lucina Holzer, with twenty-three years and an MFA under her belt, stalked the alley next to the old factory building in Hell's Hundred Acres, New York City, her studio's home. A dumpster squatting in the shadows spilled out renovation discards: split two-by-fours, warped sheet rock, buckets of hardened plaster. This stuff did not interest her.

But when she sighted a large, ornately shaped wooden object leaning against the scarred metal bin, she pulled it to her with the hunger of a lover. Her fingers explored the oak treasure, then pressed in deeper to find a memory: a similar newel post had marked the stairway leading to her childhood room, her place to dream. Her eyes flashed; she was giddy, expectant. The muse had struck again.

Lucina needed to wrestle with wood. She needed to reshape things previously formed by machines and men into an image that fed her. She was a woman sculptor. She dragged the newfound wonder to her studio and set to work.

The top sphere would be the head. Her mallet whacked on chisels, quickly shaping high cheekbones. Two curving ridges made the mouth. Incised lines suggested a nose. The chin should not be prominent. There would be no sockets to suggest normal sight, but above the nose, she scooped out a third eye. Newel post gave way to sentient being.

"The forehead must be grand," she murmured. "And don't the great ones sport some sort of crown?" When her drill met knots in the top of the skull, she tensed. She had to go with the grain. Now as she twisted wooden rods into fresh holes, they bent together, forming cone, not crown. A witch's cap? "Of course! My lady's not a queen. She's like me, a genuine crone!"

Evening after evening, whatever the weather, Lucina haunted Spring Street, Prince and Broom, seeking arms, collarbones, breasts, and a spine embedded in chairs, inlaid trays, a door panel and frame. They could all be used. When she spotted a small maple table huddled by garbage cans in front of her building—the stout legs carved in an acorn pattern brought to mind her parents' Duncan Fife dining room table, used only for holidays—she saw her Lady standing upright, bolted to this table, now altar and base.

"I know what I'll do next," she exclaimed aloud. "I'll make a xylophone so my crone can croon and be a spinner of tunes." Why the root cellar in her parents' basement, with its grouty smell, came to mind just then, she couldn't say; or why the words *Rune Keeper* took over her mind. But she was off scouting for a dictionary: "Rune, a magic incantation, a charm, a spell; one of the characters of the runic, or the Orkhow, or the Szekler alphabets; a Finnish poem (as the Kalevala); an old Norse poem; song. Related root words: rün, rüna, rünen, rumor, a secret whispered, a secret revealed, slowly."

It was settled: she would call her new piece *Rune*. An enigma was definitely present. The sculpture was a kind of protector of beautiful, sacred, secret things, like feelings. The name really fit.

"Maybe a long time ago an ancient Rune figure was tossed to the dung heap," she conjectured. "And I'm keeping her memory alive."

A force—call it intuition—now guided Lucina. With the newel post as backbone, she also had support for shoulders and arms—carved from parts of an Adirondack rocker, found tottering on the curb at Broome and Wooster Streets—and breasts cut in expressive curves from the inlaid trays she'd found. Her creation would be outrageously, courageously female. When hands shaped from redwood bookends bent together in prayer and touched the one mysterious eye, she had a new thought: *What if someday my woman will not keep secrets, but reveal them? At any rate, my figure's pose ought to suggest searching and introspection, not the contented, all-knowing stance of some Buddhas I've seen.*

Blowing sawdust off *Rune*'s headpiece, she mused aloud again: "I've groped in the root cellar of my mind to find another piece of the puzzle called Art. Someday I might even know why I needed to make you, *Rune*."

With saber saw she made a square hole in the tabletop and inserted her torso-post there, bracing and bolting it to the table's four legs—*like Aunt Margaret's thick legs, only doubled*—to give sturdy support. A skirt of molding slats flared out from the post and over the sides of the table-base, adding lightness and grace. Next, she attached a sturdy, stylish frame—plucked from the corner of Spring and Greene Streets—to the altar table around *Rune*'s torso and head. *To protect her?* Lucina wondered. Immediately, she imagined a lightweight panel of pressed wood hinged to this frame, a swinging door as entranceway to *Rune*'s secrets.

When Lucina attached caster wheels to the table legs, she chuckled: "A portable *Rune* with shrine, always poised to move. And what about that xylophone? Whoever plays it will enter my ritual." She would cut the instrument's keys from cherry wood, making four octaves to extend across the figure's mid part.

Sawing, shaping, chiseling, drilling, bolting, screwing, sanding, and varnishing went on for nine months. Every Sunday night she made a pot of vegetable soup and baked a whole chicken with apple dressing to last the week. Her social life stayed shuttered to give time and passion to her work. No listening to Pacifica Radio or reading newspapers. On the days she reported to her temporary office job, she washed up, taking care her fingernails were clean and pearls hung from her ears. As the gray corduroy suit replaced blue jeans and work shirt, she went on automatic pilot until she could be back in her studio again—a woman possessed like a mad scientist, convinced she and the world would change dramatically when *Rune* was complete.

Maybe this is what a pregnant woman feels as new life grows inside her, she thought. *Birthing is always anxiety and awe, side by side. And painful, I hear.*

In fact, she bruised her thumbs, scraped her legs, wrenched her back, and gashed an arm, needing six stitches. Lucina was not naïve; she knew that her sculpture was challenging her former professors, retrograde teachers who preached laws of balance, armatures, and longevity that were very different from her own. Max Brodsky, her graduate advisor, had decreed: "For a large sculpture to last at least a hundred years, it must be built like a tank." Lauding technique over expression, he'd nearly kept her from the Master of Sculpture degree. Her concern was not longevity, but something else: Had she expressed her own truth? Had she made something new? Brodsky would not feel comfortable with the rugged and handsome, yet fragile female person she'd wrestled out of her mind and forged with her hands. Even with the solidity of Aunt Margaret's legs, the construction—now the size of a walk-in closet—looked ready for takeoff. But Lucina was not done yet.

Her hands were tired, though not tied like her mother's; her shoulders ached; she had to be ambidextrous, coordinated as a juggler, and terribly strong, with an athlete's endurance to keep going until…*when? Until* Rune *said, "I'm done!"* She still had to attach the swinging door and the xylophone.

Bracing the lightweight door panel with her right arm to *Rune*'s frame, she used her left hand to attach brass hinges with tiny screws. Twisting the delicate screws into hard oak took considerable muscle, concentration, and a solid stance, as she struggled to keep the door in place. *Damn it! Screws need to go in straight for the proper tight fit.*

"Take a break now, kiddo," she urged herself. "You aren't done yet. Still need to attach the xylophone with bolts and nuts to the altar table!"

Her arms fell as she strode toward a tarnished full-length mirror on the wall near her studio workbench. Did she dare confront herself now? She'd never been sure how she felt about that person gazing back at her—tracking her in store windows, catching her off guard in the restaurant bathroom, spotting her shy and uncertain in a lover's bedroom. Looking in a mirror was always startling, like confronting a taboo presence.

Yet those stolen glances had the power to bring her to the present. Now she saw herself in her workplace, fully responsible for each and every decision made; every piece sawed, carved, shaped, and sanded; every nail, screw, and bolt applied—all to forge a new invention. She felt powerful. The small, pretty, brown-haired woman whom others saw was a pleasant wrapping. But the mirror spoke truth: she was the boss, the inventor, and the creator. She was also a vulnerable, mysterious, and longing woman going about her business—being a sculptor! And maybe at last she was allowing and embracing all the beautiful strangeness that she knew was her true self.

She pursed, puckered, and winked; threw her head back and whooped. Yes, that was she, momentarily caught somewhere in the mirror's rough maple frame by a patina of tarnished gold. Her tightly wound presence, awkward and serious, couldn't rest into a single reflection. She was changing shape as objects and people and nature did in the ripples of lakes and ponds. And in her dreams. The young person in the mirror was held by wonder—eyes open with surprise and purpose, mouth tight, angular body hovering between male and female. That woman in the mirror was focused and alive when chisel scooped out wood; muscles flexed and sprang into action; vocal cords stretched and quivered in song; and drawing pencil sharpened images on paper. That woman in the mirror was Lucina.

Then the brightness was gone and a glazed melancholy settled in, as her body receded into the only world that gave her even obliquely back to herself. She turned to view her *Rune* again. *Was it self-portrait? Doppelganger? Stalking golem, renegade priestess, or reclaimed crone?* This thing of hers, taking up more space than she could imagine claiming for herself, seemed to be directing its own creation with a sly and playful flair.

Giving a final twist of her wrench to the bolts holding xylophone to *Rune*'s altar, Lucina flung herself eagle-spread on the ground and looked skyward at the thing she'd made. Her mother wouldn't understand the work. She heard her father groan, "The money I've spent sending you to the good schools!" Gallery owners would dismiss it curtly: "Sorry, Ms. Holzer, our clientele wants small, dustable pieces this year."

But she was filled with compassion for the gangly, imposing thing balancing on tiny silver wheels. There was a strange mix of rawness and whimsy in the figure looking down on her. Her thoughts turned maternal. Who would take care of the old girl after she was gone? No museum would offer her a permanent home. Would *Rune* be hustled off to attics and sheds, root cellars, and uninhabitable basements? She wondered.

The large middle eye, catching a splinter of light, seemed to wink. Lucina gasped, "I don't know where the hell you came from, my *Rune*. But I think you have a lot to teach me."

*****

Lucina couldn't explain to her actress friend how she knew her creature was complete. She and Marin sat with other artists at The Gay Palette on the corner of Prince and Mercer Streets, chugging beer and grateful to be done with another week of menial jobs.

Marin hollered over the din, "I hope you're going to take a break from your obsession."

"Hold on, babe," Lucina broke in. "I'm thinking of a toast to *Rune*. Will you join me?" She clinked her friend's mug. "It wasn't an easy birth, but I'm so glad she's with me."

Marin sighed, "Well, *Rune*, I'm glad Lucina is done with you. Now maybe I get my friend back." She glanced at Lucina. "It meant a lot to me, you know—when you came to my improv group's honoring of the Freedom Riders at Judson Church. You said you wanted to know more about them—do you remember that? But you've been focused on *Rune*."

"Marin, I know what you're saying."

"We can't stick our heads in the sand and pretend people aren't being beaten and jailed. And for what? Fighting for the right to sit where you want on a goddamn bus!"

"I read the *Times*; I do know some things. It's just taken all my energy and time to finish making her. And *Rune* deserves to be seen."

"I understand, Lucina—I do. But there must be something we can do to support them. Robert Kennedy's been trying to cool things down in the South. Yet good people are getting smashed every day for protesting all kinds of racist hatred."

"Please be patient with me, my friend. Don't give up on me. I wish I could be more open to what's happening, like you are."

2
Sculptor and Poet

Lucina Holzer squatted on the rough cement floor and focused on her next task: loosening the steel bolts securing *Rune* to an altar base. *A Sculptor's Theater* was finally over; she was dismantling all her pieces for the trip back to her studio.

A voice startled her like an electric shock. "You not only make the damn things, you take them apart, too!" She swiveled to confront it and nearly toppled.

A young man was eyeing the xylophone on the front of her sculpture with amusement. She wanted to ignore him and get her work done; she was exhausted. But his probing eyes—dark one moment, then swirling with flecks of light—caught hers. His solid bearing and warm, handsome face were appealing.

"My musicians were going to help me dismantle the show," she offered, wondering why this stranger deserved an explanation. She stood up. Though he was not even six feet tall, she was conscious of herself as smaller.

He tapped on a wooden key, then ran his fingernails up and down the instrument. "Mellow and tinkly at the same time," he said.

The long loft tunneled away from them into shadow. It was almost midnight and the rest of the building was empty. Was she safe with this guy?

She watched his delight in the sounds he was producing. He had expressed some awareness of the work it took to put together one of her theater-sculpture Happenings. Yes, she would be friendly. She should tell him just how much effort was involved—working with cocky musicians and dancers to incorporate her pieces into ceremonial scenes was no joke! Three weekends at the Bleecker Street Theater and a few hundred audience participants made her eager for the peace of her studio again.

"You need some help?" A Brooklyn accent poked through the kind voice.

She handed him two pliers and pointed to the bolts she'd been undoing. "Thought you'd never ask," she said, too bluntly to be interpreted as coy.

He eyed the tools with interest. "It's amazing—you did all this!"

"Did you like my show?" She saw the soft mouth that showed vulnerability, even as he smiled. His top lip curved gracefully over the lower one, the line of a bird in flight. She was drawing him.

"You used stair posts, trays, table legs—"

"Maybe I should make furniture instead."

"You didn't make the xylophone?"

"I made everything." Lucina grasped the panel door, now unhinged from the piece, and placed it on the floor.

"The cut-out shape in that swinging door—" He hesitated. "It's like a memory. Or like some aspect of your *Rune* is too secret to reveal. That's the name of this piece, right?"

Perceptive, but no handyman. She showed him how to hold a nut firmly with one pliers and grip its square-headed bolt with the other. "Now turn the bolt counterclockwise," she instructed.

"Tinklow," he mused, as he twisted the wrench.

"Tinklow?"

"Tinkle and mellow together—the sounds of your xylophone."

"That's nice," she said and felt her shoulders relax.

While he loosened bolts, Lucina dismantled the arms, the slat-skirt, and the xylophone.

After he withdrew the last bolt holding the figure to the table enclosing it, she lifted the figure free and placed it on the floor. What had been a primitive rendering of a female now rested prone and unrecognizable beside them.

"Only eleven more sculptures to go," Lucina said. She was sure he would excuse himself politely.

"Which one next?"

She grinned as his eyes fastened again on hers.

"By the way," he added, "my name is Louis Altman."

"So, Louis, what do you do to live?"

"You could have asked your *Rune* that. Doesn't a rune have magical powers? But I guess he's out of commission now."

"It's a *she*!" Lucina headed to her next piece, a figure breaking through a stained glass window.

"I write poems," he said and followed her.

3
Explorations

Falling in love with Louis meant falling in love with the city he knew as well as the back of his hand. As they wandered the neighborhoods in early summer, Lucina felt a strange nostalgia. She was going back in time with him, marveling at the careful craftwork even in the architecture of the old factory buildings. Her hometown in Illinois was focused on the future—neat malls, drive-in banks and sleek, pristine homes, with a slight Frank Lloyd Wright cast. Not once since she'd moved to New York had she really examined the rounded cobblestones in the streets of Hell's Hundred Acres—how each stone was a different shape. And the elegant arches set over the top-floor windows of the buildings in her neighborhood now appeared as sacred entranceways. Louis was opening her eyes to new beauty.

When they sat on a park bench by the small handball court at the corner of Spring and Thompson Streets entranced by the pigeons circling above them, Lucina felt herself swirl up with the birds as they flew around the huge water tanks squatting on every rooftop. Louis said the tanks looked like ancient monuments to sky gods. To Lucina they evoked the silos of midwestern farms, which brimmed with fodder every fall. Far away, a full moon was still visible in the day sky.

His renewed awareness that she was not a city girl, that the huge buildings surrounding them seemed to frighten her, provoked her to confess, "They make me feel so tiny, overwhelmed actually. I'm very affected by my surroundings, Louis. Those midwestern vistas I grew up with—so flat and boring. That's what pushed me to imagine grand sculptures to liven things up a bit."

"Your tornadoes aren't boring," he protested. "They can drive a straw through a telephone pole." She marveled at the wonder in his voice.

They enjoyed walking through Washington Square Park, where young folks, sheltered by hawthorn and black locust trees, strummed gutsy songs on worn guitars and held out cups for contributions. But she would never forget the change in Louis when they first walked on nearby Washington Place. He stopped suddenly, staring up at a huge gray building.

"That's where it happened! Young women, immigrants, flung themselves to their deaths out of those top-floor windows—their only escape. The owners had locked them in—forced their suicide!"

Lucina froze; she recognized the building. Her college history professor had made it mandatory to write an essay about workers' rights, and she'd picked the Triangle Shirtwaist Factory—*this very building!* "It was the eighth, ninth, and tenth floors—that's where they jumped from on March 25, 1911, Louis. I had to write about it. One hundred and forty-six workers were killed. They sewed women's blouses, called shirtwaists. Twelve-hour days, seven days a week for pennies. The reports said their bodies struck the pavement like bombs." Right then she thought of Marin. She should tell her about that essay! She'd gotten an A on it.

"Yes, and the owners weren't found guilty," Louis spat out. "No laws protected sweatshop workers. It took all those deaths to start a revolution in workers' rights!"

They clutched each other's hand tightly as they walked solemnly on in silence, she wondering: *What about the people who once made metal toys in my loft? Were they also treated with such cruel indifference?*

*****

Sometimes the two made dinner, either at Lucina's loft on Spring Street or in Louis' small flat on Avenue C. They also discovered an Italian restaurant near Chinatown. Though always crowded and noisy, Puglio's Restaurant on Hester Street became their place. Here Aldo, seventy years old and debonair, strummed "Arrivederci Roma" on his guitar. Rosie, his younger and stouter partner, rocked with her accordion and belted out the words, her cheeks reddening as the night wore on and friends supplied her with cheap Chianti.

They wanted to be brave and try an inexpensive dish served to regulars. But when the waiter suggested roasted goats' heads, complete with eyes and brains, they decided pasta and escarole, sautéed with olive oil and lots of garlic, suited them better.

Young love in that spring of 1963—they were both twenty-four—was thrilling and terrifying. When Louis cried openly one night after vigorous lovemaking, Lucina knew he came with heavy baggage. He seemed haunted. When he took her hand, she fought the impulse to run.

"How do you go on when you feel like you've hurt people you've loved, and will love the rest of your life?"

"Like what people, Louis?" she managed.

"I'm recently separated, Lucina, and I have a little boy." His face tightened, as if his child were there with him, pressing against his chest.

She wanted to scream, drown out his words. Why couldn't love be simple? And why, if he'd loved mother and son so much, had he left them? Would they always be with him—with Lucina—staring into their faces when they made love? She had no comforting words for him.

He grasped her shoulders roughly: "Miriam didn't want me to be a poet. She needed a bread winner, not a dreamer, in her words. Wanted a guy in a business suit—not me. We fought all the time. Believe me, Lucina, I want her to find someone she respects—and I need to be me! I can hold a job, but I need to write! That's how I make sense out of man's injustice to man. You think this is easy?" His fingers tightened uncomfortably on her. "First I say, *I can't go on—I just can't*. Then something clicks in my brain and I say, *I must go forward!*"

"But, Louis—are you getting a divorce?" She hadn't seen this depth of sorrow before.

"I want to, but I don't want to lose my son, Joel."

She pulled away. This man was like a dark storm cloud. She wanted to run to her work space, feel the chisel and hammer in her hands.

"Poets and part-time bookstore clerks aren't great parent material," he said.

Louis obviously loved his child terribly.

"Lucina, my compassion for Miriam does not translate into 'still being in love with.' We were kids when we got married."

Lucina couldn't bear the clamping in her head any longer. She fell into his lap and sobbed.

"Trust me, Lucina," he said. "You and I have met equal passion."

These words thrilled her. *Didn't people have the right to sit across from a person they were in love with day after day?* She would blink away that face of a small child weeping for his absent dad.

When Louis confided that Miriam, still legally his wife, was negotiating clandestine meetings between him and their little girl even though her mother had forbidden such meetings, Lucina's emotions did another flip-flop. She saw him with safety pins in his mouth, changing diapers.

"Then you do see them!"

Louis looked through her and said nothing.

*****

She confided in her girlfriend, Marin. "I never expected a bed of roses, but this? A poet, yet! Who knew?" *She already sounded like him.*

Always quick on the draw, Marin responded, "What difference does it make, Lucina? We go to trouble or trouble comes to us. You love each other, don't you? Besides, there's no escape from pain. And there's no escape from facing the uprisings in the South. Look, I'm glad you found your poet, babe. He sounds more political than you. Anyway, just keep in touch, will you?"

4
Confrontations

By midsummer Lucina knew Louis was solidly in her life, for better or worse. As she made her way one stifling night to his flat on the Lower East Side, she reminded herself to look for a bakery; he wanted fresh Jewish rye bread. So fussy—like when he wanted bagels, and only onion bagels would do. For her family it was bland whole-wheat bread. They didn't know about bagels. Her mother called them *bag-ells'* anyway, as if they were French. How would she tell her about Louis? Her daughter shacking up with a married man who'd abandoned his child! Edith Holzer would get the police, accompanied by a minister and screaming sirens, to knock down his door and arrest him. She must protect him. His divorce would soon be settled, though there was still no paper to show her.

Louis didn't have a steady company job like her father and her brother did. He didn't talk about corporate mergers or profit-driven expansions. Louis didn't even own a suit. He wore the same blue jeans and work shirt all winter, along with the same Navy Pjacket and blue woolen cap. In the spring, he bought a new pair of blue jeans and several white Tshirts. She admired his simple style. His focus was on writing. He always had a book in hand and a notebook for the jottings of his next poem. When he had money, he spent it or gave it to needy others. When he lacked money, he asked a friend to help him out. She was still encumbered with rules her mother had pinned on her—particularly about relationships and money. Just when Lucina needed kind support, Mother Edith would pull out a maxim from her somber Lutheran upbringing: "Neither a borrower nor a lender be" was frequently cited.

She would not tell her family about Louis until they were really a pair. But how would Louis handle his deep attachment and guilt for his child? He had to help out with her support! And what would Lucina do about his fierce passion for justice? *Wasn't that trouble waiting to happen?* Whenever he witnessed an unfairness he spoke up, no matter who the perpetrator or victim. She warned him that interfering in other people's business was dangerous. *Was that her father talking?*

When a young man with twirling payess shuffled past her on Eighth Street, she definitely heard Dad size him up: "Now that's a funny-looking geezer!" His out-of-touch smugness always stung her ears.

There was no escape now; in Louis' words, she had met her passion.

The only breeze came from the crowds streaming by her. Saturday night and everyone was hungry for an adventure. She'd never looked so closely at the people passing her on Main Street in Belmont, Illinois. If only she could draw each of these incredible faces.

Screeching tires! Only a few yards away, an elderly woman stood frozen in the middle of Third Avenue. A taxi running a red light was about to smash her against the pavement. Lucina must dash in front of the car and push the woman to safety.

The cab jerked to a halt two feet from the woman. She was untouched.

A saxophone wailed from the entrance to The Cooper Union School of Art, mourning the tragedy that wasn't. Lucina clutched at herself: *A woman had almost been obliterated right in front of her!* Uncontrollable sobs shook her into the moment. As Marin had said, there was no escape from pain. Death could be waiting at any corner, whether it was New York City or Jackson, Mississippi.

By the time Lucina approached Second Avenue, her parents had faded.

The gaunt trees along St. Mark's Place—*were they maples or oaks?* —usually made her sad; now they affirmed life. She would be a survivor like them. She wouldn't let the city break her. When she passed the Gem Spa, where Louis had treated her to her first egg cream, her spirit lifted. Only in New York could a run-down candy store become worldwide famous.

Happy shouts sailed toward her as she neared Tompkins Square. She imagined pressing her lips impulsively on the cheek of a young man loping toward her. Or was he a young woman? Louis, the first person she'd allowed herself to embrace fully, was inviting her to fall in love not only with him, but with these strangers on the street. With possibility.

*****

The buildings on Avenue C were pressed together as if to hold each other up. She felt her body tense. *No trees could breathe here*, she decided. Of course, poorer people were always deprived of space and nature. Heat always brought out sharp new odors on his block. As she began the climb up to the fifth floor, she smelled fried eggs. On the second floor, spicy chicken. The third floor offered burnt something or other, and the fourth, garlic and onions. At last she reached the fifth floor, with its odor of fresh paint. A man was in the dimly lit hall, rolling a psychedelic color on the walls. Louis' apartment was to the left, in front. Luckily he had windows opening to the street, not to the airless shaft in back.

She rapped their special knock on the door and waited. His muffled yet expectant voice slipped under the door. "I'm coming, I'm coming."

Her adrenaline rose—in moments, she would see her poet again. *My unknowable Sephardic Jew.* These words held the secret to some mysterious world. His mother's maiden name was Avisar. Whenever she announced to friends, "Louis is a Sephardic Jew," he would grin at her appreciatively. He hadn't comprehended yet just how far she'd have to travel to escape her parents' fears and ignorance to be with him. But she heard the childlike awe in her voice; she imagined herself saying, *Louis is King Arthur*, or *Louis is my very own Jesus.*

The door opened and there was Louis, shirtless. The hair on his chest and shoulders seemed like a soft, velvety garment, caressing him, protecting him. She loved his hairiness. The men in her family seemed bare in comparison. He was her animal, her beast. She had begun to sketch his face—always changing, always intriguing her. Drawing was her way to grasp what she had no words to express.

"I was taking a shit," he said ingenuously.

"Such a kid," she crooned. She felt Louis' gaze take in not only her body but her thoughts as well. Should she tell him about the woman who'd almost been struck near Cooper Union? Their hug ended in a long kiss, which gentled her fears and brought her to the present—to him.

Then he was questioning her: "Did you bring the bread I asked for?"

A sudden cramp tightened her chest. She'd promised to stop at the bakery on Seventh Street and Third Avenue to add to Louis's menu of Italian salami, hot peppers, and celery soda. *How could she have forgotten the rye bread he loved?*

Louis chastised her, saying, "You forgot," and Lucina felt herself shrink. Kind Louis was gone. Some austere and judgmental person stood over her.

"How could you forget?" he said accusingly, as if she'd betrayed him in some essential way. He sank down on a chair by the kitchen window, where he often kept watch over his block, and groaned.

"I'll go right back," she said quickly.

"Forget it. It'll take too long. We just won't eat!"

"Louis, I can go get it. It'll take me ten minutes."

"It'll be dark soon. It's not safe. The cop cars are patrolling up and down the streets. That's why I said, 'come by at seven.' The world turns upside down after dark."

"What do you mean, Louis?"

"You have to stay awake in the streets."

"I was thinking about you all the way here."

"About what?"

"How much I love you."

He looked up at her. Some proof he needed was there in the softness of her eyes. "It's okay, Lucina; I'm not mad."

"I'm terribly, terribly sorry, honey." She sank into his lap; eyes closed, she reached for his head. His dear, huge head that was like a baby. Her baby.

Her mother's words, "they aren't accepted," came to her again, words spoken when she was nineteen and falling in love for the first time. She'd screamed back: "Maynard Epstein is not accepted? He's the top student in his class! And I love him." How could she be real with her mother again! Prejudice was forcing silence and walls between them.

She couldn't look at Louis. *Had she forgotten the bread on purpose? To hurt him?* He was the stranger, the feared other. Her heart was ripping apart.

"Are you crying?" Louis was impatient. "I said it's okay. It's okay, Lucina!"

His tongue was inside her mouth, filling her and making her feel alive and hungry at the same time. His aroused penis thrust inside his jeans against her hand. "Let's fuck, Louis!" she cried out with defiance and need. She wanted him: opening her up; unleashing the juices, the sensations that made them cry out like animals together.

"Okay, my sexy one. Then let's go out to eat. I didn't eat all day. I was waiting for you."

"I thought you were working on your poem about the Brooklyn Bridge?"

"I was."

"Then you weren't waiting."

"I'm always waiting for you."

"But I'm here, Louis."

"I'll turn the lights out." Louis, his pants off now, charged for the kitchen, where the light switches for the apartment were lined up in a row—the peculiar brainchild of some previous tenant.

In the abrupt darkness, Lucina remembered again the old woman on Third Avenue—how she'd clutched at her bright red vinyl purse as if it might save her. She must tell Louis what had happened. *That's why she'd forgotten the bread!*

Lucina pulled him to the mattress covered with the tie-dyed bedspread she'd given him the week before, her nude body embracing his with no restraint atop its vivid, kaleidoscope-like designs. That artist-activists had sewn the bedspread made it a safe haven for them.

Suddenly, a blitz of voices slapped at them in the dark, coming from the street below. Louis' hand clamped her shoulder.

Damn! She should have gotten those curtains up the last time.

Then a volley of gunshots exploded near the window, and Louis wrapped his body around hers.

"Should we run?"

"Shh."

A man's angry voice shot loudly through the open windows, as if coming through a megaphone. "Those windows on the fifth floor."

Another man's voice broke out. "Where the lights are?"

"No—to the right. Somebody just turned the lights out."

"God, Louis!" Lucina felt his sweat covering her. "They're talking about us."

Angry beams of light stalked the ceiling. Drumming footsteps approached.

"They're going to kill us," Lucina whimpered.

Louis's hand was over her mouth. "Quick, put on your shirt. Where's mine?"

"The bathroom."

Within seconds, the two lovers sat frozen—like fawns stalked by a jaguar—on wooden chairs in the front room, their hands twisting frantically at shirt buttons.

Harsh banging. A rattling doorknob.

"It's locked!" came a harsh voice. "Should I break it down?"

"Knock again."

"Police! Open up or we're entering." They were the same staccato voices that had shouted from the street.

Lucina clutched at Louis' arm. He pulled away. "You don't fool with cops. I'm going to let them in."

In the sudden light, Lucina saw two uniformed men, angry and determined, behind Louis in the open doorway.

One of them, apparently the spokesperson, charged toward Lucina, jabbing his thumb toward the front windows. "You threw bricks down on our squad car!"

"What are you talking about, Man? My wife and I were in bed making love." Louis' bravado made Lucina gasp.

The other man, still in the kitchen, swung his head in every direction as if checking for accomplices.

"Who are you guys looking for?" Louis demanded.

"Look, we'll ask the questions," the spokescop said. "You give the answers."

"Okay," Louis said.

Lucina stood abruptly, forcing a smile as the silent man now edged into the room. "Let the lady sit," he said quietly.

"Is this your apartment?" The spokescop barked. "Let's see your identification."

Lucina's heart sank. Why had Louis said, "my wife?"

"Sure." Louis reached into his back pocket for his bill-fold, and then nodded to Lucina to get hers from her purse. He gave a few cards to his interrogator, a short, paunchy man with a round face.

"So, what do we have?" the man snarled. "Hmm, Louis Altman. Any relation to the Altman Brothers?"

"Cousins," Louis said, not missing a beat.

"How about driver's license? Social Security card? Union card? You do work, don't you?"

Lucina saw disgust pouring from the eyes of the gaunt, silent man peering over the shoulder of his partner, who was shuffling through Louis' cards. *And she'd thought, at least that one's decent.*

"Don't have a car." Louis pointed to his plumber's union card. He'd told her about being his father's assistant for a sum-mer—before college; before poetry and politics had taken him over; before he'd turned to clerking in bookstores for money; before he'd married Miriam; before he'd torn himself away from his son. He'd known it would serve him someday—when he needed its protection.

"So, a plumber," the stout cop was saying.

"I'm a plumber. My wife's a teacher."

The gaunt cop—he had a fuzzy red mustache and blood-shot eyes—was thumbing through Lucina's cards: a bank card, a driver's license, a card saying she taught art classes at the Henry Street Settlement. "Lucina Holzer?" He spoke for the first time. "Not Lucina Altman?"

"Female artists don't change names so easily," Louis answered quickly, shifting his glance back and forth between the two armed men.

"That's news to me!" the bully cop snarled.

"Look, Officers." Louis tried a less aggressive tone. "We didn't do anything. Isn't that obvious? What happened, anyway?"

"What happened?" the spokescop shot back angrily. "Somebody threw a brick down from this building and broke our front windshield. That's what happened. It's not safe for anybody around here anymore. Decent people should consider moving to a nicer neighborhood."

Lucina nodded in agreement, as if she might be considering such a move. "We don't keep bricks here," she offered meekly. Louis' look shushed her.

"We aren't going to take it anymore," the stout cop went on. He began fussing with his nightstick in a funny way; Lucina saw a schoolboy about to burst into tears. She eased back into one of the chairs.

"They look okay," the gaunt one added softly, as if completing some mental checklist of his own. "I think it came from the roof. Let's take a look."

"Okay." The stout man flipped Louis' cards on the table, as if it were beneath him to return them directly.

When the gaunt cop handed Lucina her cards, his face showed a cocky grin. "Lucky you didn't have your heads out the window when we drew our guns."

Lucina bristled. "What do you mean? You fired at us! And we didn't do anything."

His eyes locked with hers. "By the way, ma'am, your driver's license has expired. Don't want a ticket, do you?" Then he followed his partner out the door, brusquely pulling it shut.

Louis shook his head as Lucina began sobbing.

Later, after they had made love, it seemed to her that Louis' arms and legs were attached to her body.

*****

The raucous crowd at Rappaport's Dairy was comforting after the shocking intrusion by the police. And blueberry blintzes had never tasted so good.

"What do you think, Lucina?" Louis put his hand over hers after a grumpy waiter slapped down the check.

"Grumpy waiters I can handle," Lucina laughed, hearing Louis' way of talking in her comment. "And you know what, Louis? I was proud to be your 'wife' tonight."

"I mean about us," Louis said. "Is there room for a poet in your loft, maybe?"

<h1 style="text-align:center">5</h1>

<h1 style="text-align:center">Circle Man</h1>

"For you, Lucina!" Louis shouted from his desk into the grinding sound of her saber saw. The huge, raw space still showed evidence of a factory. Ugly fluorescent lights lined the ceiling; metal filings embedded in the floor sparkled like bits of ice. "Pietro Tambourine—or something like that."

She whipped past him to the wall phone near the kitchen area. "Oh, good. It's Tamborcini," she whispered, sheltering the phone with her hand.

While Lucina chatted animatedly, Louis surveyed the top of his desk, swamped with papers. Lucina, not he, had decided his desk should be in the back of the loft, by the kitchen. They should be at opposite ends of the long space, she'd said. He liked to play the radio when he worked, and she was always making noise—sawing, chiseling, and pounding. So he'd agreed: he would be in the back where the windows overlooked the fire escape and the neighboring lofts. He had not considered the phone and its interruptions.

Lucina had teased him, "You can get an eyeful of naked women, Louis. Lots of artists use their roofs for parties and sunbathing." He liked her references to his sexual appetite. When he'd told her, "Since I'm with you, women find me irresistible," she'd laughed and looked pleased. Good, he thought. She was confidant in his love. Jealousy would not eat at her! Neither he nor she had mentioned his ex-wife for weeks. Soon he would have the divorce papers and could get on with his life, here on Spring Street with Lucina.

After ten minutes of Lucina's enthusiastic responses to the caller, Louis was feeling irritated. He didn't know any Tamborcini.

When she got off the phone, he was shoving papers from one side of the desk to the other. "So, what did that guy want?"

"I met Pietro at Virginia's gallery show last week. He invited me to be in a group show at St. Mark's Church, November 24 through December 8. He's an organizer."

"I thought they're called curators?"

"No, he organizes artists to be in his circle." Lucina cast a critical eye at Louis. "Honey, you have to deal with those papers, not just push them around. Everyone who comes here will see your study. It can't look messy."

"Oh, I forgot. You come from God is Cleanliness country. Well, like you said, it's my study. Remember, I'm sharing the rent. So, is this Pietro coming here?" He already disliked the guy—she'd never talked about messy papers before.

Lucina slipped into his arms. "You're jealous!"

Now she was goading him. "Stop it, Lucina."

"I'll leave you and your desk alone, Beast. Just make neat piles. Pietro's show is called *Breaking Out*."

"Sounds like acne. Besides, I don't like how he's affecting you, woman. Now I'm a beast!"

Lucina settled on one of the kitchen stools, painted bright yellow. "He wants to challenge the Abstract Expressionists."

"Guys like Pollack put energy back into painting, Lucina. What's this guy do?"

"Pietro is called the Circle Man. He makes, well, circles, both on paper and with groups of people."

"Just circles?"

"He's got this whole philosophy. Artists from Houston Street to Canal have to become a community. Uptown galleries suck our energy, time, and money. So he wants to start a series of shows by artists in their own studios. The Saint Mark's show would kick that plan off. You might like him. He's certainly intense, anyway. I said yes. So could you help me cart *Arrival* and *Poet* there?"

"What about *Rune*?"

"I'm giving her a rest."

"He sure didn't give you much notice," Louis growled, still shifting papers to bug her.

"I can rent a van and do it myself!"

He watched her retreating figure; each step said she wasn't playing. "Don't get huffy, Lucina. Okay, I don't want you to get big muscles. When's the show again?" He was shouting over the bookcases that divided them. "I'm working at the Strand, remember? And Wednesdays I have SDS meetings—Students for a Democratic Society. I might do a journal with—"

"Oh, good, you'll help me," sailed back to him. "I told Pietro I'll bring them on Wednesday—November 21."

"But Lucina, I just said—oh forget it." The sound of her saber saw chewed up his words. He stood up, hands planted in his pockets mumbling, "I can do both," and went to face her. "Can you fix us some lunch soon, Lucina? I'm working at my desk."

She stopped the saw. "If you throw out some of your old newspapers. Why is it so hard? Didn't your mother make you help with housework?"

"Work, shmirk. Make some lunch! I said I'll help you on Wednesday."

6
Man-made Images

On a chilly Wednesday afternoon in November they loaded two of Lucina's sculptures into Al's pickup: *Arrival* portrayed a carved female figure smashing through a church window of stained glass; *Poet* incorporated lively figures leaping, flying, and running through interconnected door frames. Sections of the sculptures were secured in the back of the truck with tarpaulin and ropes. She would not show *Rune* again until she had a one-woman exhibit or another show of *A Sculptor's Theater*. Her "womanwhole"—definitely not "masterpiece"—deserved a showcase.

Louis and Lucina squeezed into the front with Al, a midwestern writer. They'd had Al over for dinner the week before, and Lucina had been touched by his response to her *Arrival* sculpture.

"Geez, you've got guts, Lucina," he'd said. "I bet you won't show your Illinois family a photo of this."

"No way, Al. They still think I'm doing little bronzes of dancing women—to use as bookends."

"It's great you'll have two pieces in that St. Mark's show. I told Louis, me and my pickup are at your service."

When she'd started to make excuses for Louis' study, visible from the kitchen area, Al had set her straight. "Poets need to be free to flex our minds, not be tied down by a nagging woman. Come on, Lucina. You've got your space, let Lou have his!"

As she'd busied herself filling up plates with salad and barbecued chicken, the tension had fallen from her shoulders: *A poet needs another poet. But what is Al like with a woman,* she'd wondered. *Definitely, a little macho, I bet.*

Al enjoyed portraying himself as a hayseed, a tough guy who'd come to New York to "git cultured." He'd met Louis at a reading of Neruda's poetry and they'd quickly become friends. That Al's midwestern background resembled hers, while Louis was obviously fond of his no-nonsense manner, gave Lucina comfort. She felt Al could have been her cousin.

As they headed to the East Village via West Houston Street in Al's truck, Louis questioned, "Does Tamborcini know how large these things are?"

"I'm not stupid, Louis." Lucina put her hand on Louis' knee so Al wouldn't think they were about to quarrel.

"They take up a lot of space," Louis said. "That's all I meant."

"They're supposed to." Lucina turned to Al. "I'm really grateful for this help."

"Glad to help. You're good people," he replied.

She liked that he didn't drill his way into people's emotions as Louis did, yet he spoke up for his friend. She patted him on the shoulder, then rested against Louis.

"Al's a good friend to both of us," Louis said, as if intuiting her thoughts. "We should just keep driving to New England, the three of us."

"Hey—any time!" Al said cheerily. "You guys are my best buddies. I wish I'd had pals like you in Ohio. Growing up on a farm doesn't prepare you for city slickers, but it made me resourceful. I mean, you learn to confide in your cows when everyone else thinks you're whacko. I swear, when I recited my poems to my Holsteins and my Guernseys, their milk came out sweet and creamy."

"And I bet you know how to fix things, like city slickers don't," Lucina laughed.

"Yeah, well, if your dad's got arthritis and your mom and sister are into cooking, cleaning, and canning, who's going to fix the leaks? That's why my hands are so rough and cracked. But I just kept reading Whitman, Ginsberg, Corso—those guys kept me going."

"And you went to college," Louis added.

"Thanks to scholarships and my mom's guidance. But, now I'm in the big evil city and I love it. Do you guys know about St. Mark's Church, where we're headed? Rumor has it that Stuyvesant's ghost hangs out there and steals money from Sunday collection plates."

"I never heard that one before," Lucina giggled. "I see you are gittin' cultured, Al."

Al gripped the wheel and suddenly let out a stream of "fuckin' cocksuckers" as he braked. Lucina was at the edge of her seat. "Three yellow cabs cut right in front of me," he snapped. She fretted; had they secured her pieces tightly? But she could see that Al knew how to handle crazy New York drivers. She relaxed against Louis again and closed her eyes.

"Let me know when we get there," she murmured, feeling a little nauseous. "Just help me carry my sculptures in, you guys. Then you can pig out at Ratner's and wait for me."

Louis directed Al through the crowded East Village to the gates of the church on Eleventh Street. Lucina was struck by the huge beech trees dominating the courtyard. They looked like the haunted forest in her favorite childhood book, Maeterlinck's *The Blue Bird of Happiness.* City trees kept her from feeling locked in by brick and cement.

The men took the bigger pieces, while Lucina hauled the lighter ones into a large room off the yard. Many works were already in place for the show. Some hung from the ceiling; some hugged the floor; others crawled across the floor and climbed the wall. The objects were definitely breaking out and challenging the confines of a rectangular room.

Pietro came up to them and introduced himself brusquely. Lucina shook his hand, then watched the three men interact. Louis was describing the size of her works. "The *Poet* piece needs an area fifteen-by-fifteen-by-fifteen," he was saying. *How dear,* she thought. *It's as if he made them.*

Pietro, smaller than Louis or Al, jerked with impatience. He was older, probably in his late thirties. His skin was olive color and his black hair was slicked down, *like a greaser's*, Lucina decided.

"Not enough room," Pietro said. "I told her she could bring the ten-by-four-by-three piece." He pointed to *Arrival*, still lying on the floor in three sections. "It could fit right here." He stood in a spot next to a series of plastic shapes swinging on ropes attached to the ceiling. "Miss Holzer, I thought you said the other piece was five-by-fifteen, a wall piece!"

Lucina faltered, "I—I don't do wall pieces." She was shocked by Pietro's reinvention of their phone agreement.

Louis stepped toward Pietro. "Hey, man, find a place for it!"

"She should be happy to get one piece in." Pietro was glaring at Louis. "I didn't take a lot of artists."

"You said I could bring both works," Lucina shot out. "Pietro, I described them to you in great detail over the phone. You can't do this to me!"

As if energized by Lucina's firm retort, Louis motioned to Al. They immediately wrenched the pieces of *Arrival* together.

Then Al headed toward the door opening onto the churchyard. "So long, you guys," he shouted. "I'm out of here!"

"Just wait a second, Al," Louis shouted back. "I also need help with *Poet*."

"I need some air. You two can handle this." Al stood in the doorway wringing his hands.

"Louis, you go with Al," Lucina instructed as she inched toward Pietro. "I'll take care of this."

"I'm staying." Louis pointed to a separate space set off by giant screens. "What about that area? It's empty. C'mon, man! She needs a space that size for the *Poet* piece."

"Sorry, my work goes there," Pietro said.

Louis was incredulous. "Everybody else gets leftovers?"

"Look, buddy." Pietro's hand went instinctively toward Louis and then froze. "Your wife is in the show, not you."

"She's not my wife! She's Lucina Holzer, and she's a damn good sculptor. You invited her to show these two pieces."

"Louis, I better deal with this." Lucina stepped between the two men. "So, how are we going to work this out? Obviously, I can't take *Poet* home. You did say I could bring both sculptures. Otherwise…why would…" Her words slowed with the effort to stay calm.

Pietro pulled nervously on a section of *Poet*, his glance shifting back and forth between the couple. "Well—what does it look like when it's together?"

"It's fuckin' brilliant!" Louis snapped. "Better than dead chickens!" He jabbed a finger at three abstract shapes covered with bird feathers and hanging from giant hooks jutting from the ceiling nearby. Then he went about rapidly bolting the frames of Lucina's work together.

As Louis continued bolting, Pietro was examining the action figures that were to be suspended within the frames.

Al watched the scene from the doorway. An unlit cigarette hung in his mouth. Moving past a glimmering metallic sheet, he abruptly struck a match and called out, "Okay, guys, I'm really outta here. Louis, give me a call!"

Lucina waved goodbye to the smoke wafting against the silvery thing that trembled beside the empty doorway.

Pietro shrugged. "So, those figures are frozen within their frames?"

"No!" Lucina rejoined sharply. "Obviously they're in motion, breaking out."

"Okay, okay. Breaking out of frames," Pietro yapped back. "That fits into my theme. So does the color. You know Stendhal's novel *The Red and the Black*?"

"Yeah—she can even read, jerk," Louis mumbled, his hands clamping pliers as his eyes probed the man pawing at his sweetheart's animated figures constructed of metal and wood.

"Revolutionary colors," Pietro mused, indifferent to the couple nearby. "Yes, my black circles can be seen through the red frames. Okay. I could probably put this piece in my area."

"That would work," Lucina said flatly. She was praying that Louis would stay quiet. After Pietro disappeared around one of the giant screens setting off the semi-enclosed area, she quickly sidled up to Louis. "Let me deal with the egomaniac, honey. Trust me, he's going to take *Poet*. He's just difficult."

Louis, still grimacing, followed her into the large semi-enclosed space, where sheets of oatmeal-colored paper plastered the floor. A crude black circle—executed with one continuous, rapid brush stroke—leapt from each sheet.

"Wow, circles," Lucina chirped softly. "I do love the circle form."

*****

Louis' attention stayed on Pietro, fussing with a row of the endless, repetitive renderings of circles at the far end of the space. To Louis they seemed the outpourings of a madman.

42

The man was laying more sheets of circles on the floor. Louis heard the self-congratulatory banter: "I'm capturing dynamic evolution. I'm the force of change—" *Why was Lucina buying this crap,* he wondered. *The guy walks around in circles and sloshes paint on pieces of paper. So what? Takes about as much imagination as collating.*

"Hammer the image into people's minds," Pietro pontificated in rhythm as Lucina nodded along. "Revolving wheels."

Oh, Jesus, Louis fumed. *Just like Hitler did with the swastika!*

"Americans are locked into boxes of thought. So is the Madison Avenue art world. We have to start motion—a movement."

How did Lucina get hooked up with this creep?

"Artists have to form socialist communities. You know the meaning of communism, don't you?"

Louis watched as Pietro suddenly whirled around, piercing Lucina with a maniacal, all-knowing beam. *Now the asshole is going to fuck her with his Marxist rhetoric.*

Lucina offered, "Communal?"

"What about Lucina's sculpture!" Louis shouted out, shattering their conversation.

"Now, you just take it easy." Pietro spoke with icy calm. "What did you say your name was?"

"Louis. My name is Louis."

Lucina moved nervously toward her lover.

"Okay, Louis." Pietro spoke offhandedly, keeping his distance. "Your girlfriend's piece can go here in this area. Satisfied? Put it together so I can place it where it enhances my circles. I have other work coming in soon."

Lucina's eyes closed, as though imploring Louis not to say anything more. He understood and kept silent.

*****

Under Pietro's clipped directions, the couple carried *Poet*'s sections into the semi-enclosed area. After bolting them together, they placed the completed sculpture precisely where Pietro pointed. Louis fumed: *Pietro doesn't care how Lucina's piece looks. Just how the frames interact with his damn circles.*

After this work was completed, they finished setting up *Arrival* near a swing made from bicycle chains and used tires. Close by hung a piece composed of baked tiles and thin metal spoons suspended by copper wires. When you blew on the spoons, they struck the tiles, causing faint metallic sounds.

While Lucina and Louis were examining these works, Pietro climbed a ladder and began taping some drawings on the wall near *Poet*. By the time they were ready to leave, he'd filled all four walls with his work.

Lucina stared, as though noting what Louis had already observed: no circle was rendered whole.

"So, they aren't circles after all," he heard her muttering. "Just pretend circles."

Pietro was tracking Lucina from his ladder with gyrating eyes. "These aren't machine-made circles. I made them. Each one of them is man-made."

Lucina was looking drained. "We're going, Pietro." She pulled Louis toward the open doorway. Giant beech trees beckoned like old friends. "Take care of yourself," she managed. "We'll be back for the opening."

*****

The exhausted pair shuffled down Eighth Street in silence, headed for the bookstore. Louis wanted the latest book of Neruda's poems, but Lucina burst out suddenly, "I should have challenged Pietro—'Circles are okay, but the infinity form has more motion—'"

Louis faced her. "The guy's a fascist, Lucina. I know—you were humoring him for your sculptures' sake. He distorts Marxist theories and his fuckin' circles to intimidate and drug people."

"Maybe we're too suspicious of him, Louis."

"I thought you agreed with me."

"He's self-absorbed, like most artists."

"Lucina, he's an asshole. I don't trust him. Stay away from him."

"Louis! I can take care of myself, thanks. You saw how I handled him." She jerked away and then fell in two paces behind him.

"Aren't you coming in with me?" He motioned impatiently for her to follow him into the bookstore.

"I'll wait outside, Louis. I need to clear my head."

"I helped you at the church!"

"Don't bawl me out, Louis. I help you, too. We just have to be independent sometimes, or we won't know who's who."

"Bullshit!" Louis stormed into the store alone, barking out, "I know you, Lucina! And you can't be suckered by some asshole's propaganda."

7

Breaking Out

"That piece, *Arrival*, with the broken church window? It was in a Happening at the Bleecker Street Theater." The young man shouting out to Lucina at the *Breaking Out* opening seemed in constant motion, grabbing at the hors d'oeuvres floating by on trays carried by small, pretty girls.

"Good memory. It was in my show, *A Sculptor's Theater*, last April." She couldn't find his eyes.

"I loved it. But I can't remember your name." Tiny morsels flew from colored toothpicks into his mouth.

"Understandable—lots of artists in New York. So, standing before you is the one and only—Lucina Holzer." She snatched up a shrimp, then an olive.

"Any relation to Baby Jane Holzer?"

"Who's that?"

"A model with Andy Warhol's crowd. A real looker if you like that type."

"What type is that?"

"A toothpick with lipstick."

Lucina laughed giddily. "What's your name?"

"Hugh Levin—I go to openings to eat. Sorry, I don't have much money—musician, you know. I hardly ever meet the artist." He was already scouting for another tray.

"I'm always looking for musicians to work with." A tray of wine drifted by. Plucking two glasses, she handed one to Hugh. "I'm more like a carpenter—always shaping stuff with my hands."

"Groovy—I really dig it. Like what you did with that stained glass. Was it broken when you found it?"

"Unbroken—part of an old abandoned church on Riker's Island."

"You're kidding! Isn't that where convicts are or something? You just took it out of a church?"

"When I see something I need, I'm fearless," she said proudly.

"Do you do that with guys, too?"

Lucina shot Hugh a quizzical look, then explained, "Oh, my boyfriend picked *me* up!" The memory of her first meeting with Louis—his laboring with her to pack up the sculptures—made her lower her eyes. She really wasn't good at boy-girl bravado.

"Same with my girlfriend," Hugh returned. "She snagged me. She's a writer—doesn't like the noise at openings. It's really great how you caught the moment of impact." He paused to consider. "That woman—why is she crashing into a church window, or out of it?"

"She's seeking love that embraces all beings. You saw my theater-sculpture Happening in April?"

"Yeah, with the procession and the coffin."

"You saw Jesus getting buried in a coffin, covered by a black cloth? And then the flames around him? For me he was a revolutionary, a real human being seeking justice for all people."

"I think I get it. The Phoenix. Rebirth." Hugh wiped his hands on his jeans and let them hang loosely at his sides. "I studied Eliade at Bennington, about myth and how symbols—"

"I think we need to bury the religions that allow murder and war," Lucina broke in. "We need female spiritual guides."

"I guess you aren't into Christmas and mangers?"

"No. Not the same old, same old." Hugh's interest in her work felt good. "When I was a teenager, I thought if a boy kissed me I would get pregnant. And then when I was taught in Sunday school that Mary was a virgin giving birth to Jesus, boy did that confuse me even more. No hocus-pocus virgin birth stuff for me. An unreal metaphor like that." She gestured toward her sculpture as if it somehow helped clarify her comments. "Plus, I don't want to worship a crucifixion. Too violent. So—tell me about you."

"Oh, I'm a secular Jew. I don't worry about virgins—just exterminations of my people."

"Yes." Lucina nodded compassionately and gulped down the rest of her wine.

"Hey, I hear you. My girlfriend talks like that sometimes. But crashing through glass isn't exactly loving."

"Change has to begin somewhere, Hal."

"Hugh! Hugh Levin."

"Sorry. I've had four glasses of wine already. I hate openings."

"Even when you're in them?"

"People don't look at the art—well, except for you. That's why I usually put my pieces in a theatrical event, a the-ater-sculpture Happening."

Hugh's attention had clicked off. She found herself talking to a tray of fat oysters and his fingers, stuffing one, two into his mouth. She really should socialize with some of the others huddled by her piece.

Hugh was scribbling on a paper from his pocket. "Hey, Holzer, I live in the Village. When you have another Happening give me a call." He handed her the scrap. "Oboe, flute, also guitar," he called out.

"Beautiful. I will call. Thanks for…"

The young man was eaten up by the mob.

*****

Lucina pushed her way into the restless crowd to look for Louis. She needed him. She needed to touch him to feel grounded. A clash of voices rose above the mob like a heavy black cloud. It came from the area where Pietro's circles and her *Poet* piece were nearly obliterated by the pack of bodies. "You can't force an image on someone!" That was Louis' voice. She must find him.

"The Americans are duped, drugged. You have to show them the way, over and over." That sounded like Pietro's speechifying.

"I say, speak to the best part of people. Show respect!" Yes, definitely Louis. She forced herself into the framed space of her own sculpture. Interesting how no one had barged into this sacred area. Someone called out to her, "Hey, lady. Stay out of there!" She nodded to the directive but stayed put.

Louis was off to her left. She could see his face through the frame that held a broken mirror and the skeletal figure in flight. Pietro's voice was coming from the far right. A hand gestured in the air above the crowd—was it his?

Lucina imagined two boxers without gloves; half the crowd rooting for Pietro, the other for Louis. She looked for Louis again. There he was, surrounded by a group of young people.

"Kiss Mad. Ave. admen on the ass." Pietro sputtered like a honking goose.

"Go, man, go," someone encouraged.

"Promises, promises," said another.

"Drugged people can't see visionary art." Pietro's words sliced at the air.

Louis was right—the man was a pain. "Louis! Louis!" she called out. What was going on? A full moon?

"You got to make them change," Pietro harangued.

"Feed us first!" a woman shouted.

Why couldn't Louis hear her? "Louis…" But instead of shouting, she was just whimpering. She tried again. "Louis!" This time a woman with a sweet, expectant face smiled at her for a second, then disappeared behind a thick mass of shoulders and heads.

"…have to drive a symbol into the hypnotized mind, before they'll get it." The honking grew louder.

A kid, barely fifteen and directly in front of Lucina, cupped his hands to his mouth. "LSD is good for me," sputtered out.

Then Louis was screaming, "You sound like Hitler, man. Art is complex. People are complex. You aren't going to reach the human spirit spouting cliché dogma about circles."

Lucina tightened her fists. Louis had hit below the belt. Pietro moved in front of Louis' supporters. She could see him clearly now. Her sculpture's shiny red frame cut across the man's wiry shoulders, so that his head seemed suspended like a cartoon portrait, eyes bulging and his tongue slapping at his lips.

She should tell them to stop. They were ruining the opening. Why did Louis bother?

Louis was talking again. "Hey, you better wake up. There's a lot of really smart kids doing a lot of thinking about America now." The roar had become a soft droning. People were listening. Louis intoned, "Make it more humane, not less, man. Make it more humane!" His supporters were grinning and nodding. A boy in an army jacket chanted back, "Right on—move left. Right on—move left!"

Lucina felt a cry rise up in her. She wanted to shout out with the boy.

"Participatory, man. That's what I'm talking about." Louis was unstoppable. *What a fighter he was.*

A tall Black girl behind Louis shouted, "Talk about really breaking out. Look what's happening in Alabama, Mississippi. My brothers and sisters are rising!"

A man's thick voice rose up behind her. "She's right! What about the Mississippi Freedom Party? SDS is a bunch of white kids."

Pietro was a couple of feet from Louis now. Sleek black hair, olive skin, gnashing teeth. "Yeah. Too many SDS brats out there with rich daddies," he sneered. "They'll go back to daddy and get a job in his corporation!"

A mean, nasty animal, that Pietro. Lucina wanted to claw him.

The tall Black woman took him on. "Hey, big talking white man—at least the SDS kids are trying."

Lucina's mouth soured with the tension and cheap wine. *When would the shouts stop?*

A gray-haired man near the back wall gestured toward Pietro's drawings. "How long did it take to make these bull's-eyes, Tamborcini?" His tone was harsh. "Five, six minutes?" The crowd hushed.

Lucina felt her chest cave in. *Even a crowd knows when something's too much. Pietro's eyes are spinning circles, just like his drawings.*

Pietro yelped, "Get out of here!" He jerked at Louis' arm as if he were the one who'd just trashed his artwork. "This is my art show. I let your wife in and her work sucks!"

Louis shot back, "Lucina's art is a gift, asshole. You're a pompous creep!"

Pietro turned away. Louis was screaming now. *She must protect him as he was protecting her. Or should they run away from this nightmare? She had to get out before she barfed.*

She shouted, "Louis!" sharp and clear. He couldn't hear her. He was clamped to his supporters. Suddenly Pietro jammed himself into the mound of bodies and stood nose-to-nose with Louis.

Black circles spun free of the walls. Lucina closed her eyes to steady the swirling room. *They're going to fight, right by my sculpture. Nobody will stop them.*

Good thing she hadn't brought *Rune* here.

"Help! Somebody?" Her screams felt impotent. Pietro must be choking Louis now.

Shrieking voices. Open her eyes—open them! So dizzy. No, not screams—sirens. Get Louis out of here fast!

*****

He stood a few feet from her, holding onto one of the frames of *Poet* as if to keep from flying off. Only a few people, motionless yet somehow connected, remained in the room. Sirens disappearing, sucked up by the black night. No Pietro anywhere.

She looked at Louis again, a dark, haunting presence. He looked back at her. No, he looked through her, staring intensely. She smiled at him, but he did not smile back.

Louis is one of the old ones. His all-seeing gaze. He's one of those old souls that keeps coming back, revolving, evolving. No wonder he hates Pietro's faux circles. Next to Louis, the guy's a frantic child scribbling desperately to be noticed.

It was the surreal quiet after the storm. Had there been a brawl or not? And where was Pietro? At least she and Louis were okay. She couldn't wait to be back safe with him in the loft.

8

Two Heads Are Better Than One

Lucina loved her studio in the early morning. The street below was quiet. Light made its way miraculously through the jumble of buildings in Hell's Hundred Acres and entered her giant windows, forming lemon rectangles on her west wall. The cement floor, a soft blue, turned luminescent. When sunlight found her space, it was a blessing. She was alive and well.

She would not put her energy in a group show again! Time to make a new piece. No more Pietros—what a terrible night. Louis could've ended up with bruises or in jail. Those two hated each other from the get-go. No more situations where he felt called on to protect her. He was as vulnerable as she was, and more out-there. An easy target. How they'd made it safely out of that frenzy, she wasn't sure—though she managed to laugh about it the next morning.

When she wasn't sculpting, Lucina was plagued by dissatisfaction; heavy, lost, longing again for elation, as when *Rune* had looked down on her, a finished piece.

An image had been gnawing at her imagination for weeks: a head with two faces suspended in the top window of a heavy wooden door. *Was she remaking the front door to her parents' house?* When an image stayed with her this long, she had to pay attention. She must give in to it, work with it. Obsession was central to the creative act. But not Tamborcini's kind of obsession. That was hate.

She began a sketch of two profiles, looking in opposite directions and merging at the ears. They would be an interpretation of her and Louis. His features would be rendered with sensuous curves—waves or petals—while her features, more angular and fixed, would seem like arrows or forces. She wanted his face to be strong yet yielding, hers to be delicate yet piercing. Together their faces would make a complex statement, like a dialogue.

She taped the completed drawing to the wall behind the workbench and contemplated how she might begin: draw the main shapes on wood with charcoal. A block of oak was ready and waiting.

Within minutes, simple lines covered it. She could make the first cuts with the large saw blade, then sculpt planes and curves with chisels. The finer chisels and blades would detail features. But before she got started, she needed a short break on her three-legged stool by the windows.

It was ten o'clock on Saturday morning. Louis should be up by now. The night owl and the early bird—opposites attracting. How different they were in so many ways. She, upper-middle-class, midwestern-Protestant, a mix of English, French, Dutch, and German. He, working-class, Brooklyn, Sephardic and Eastern European Jew. She'd come up with words like *sacrificing and stalwart comfort to* describe her home atmosphere. He'd come up with *fear* and *generosity.*

He belabored an insight on class differences: "Those who have nothing, give. Those who have too much, take more."

"You sound like Pietro," she chided. "I hope you're not talking about my family."

Her parents were hard working, she defended. Her dad, a chemical engineer, was dedicated to his company, DuPont. Her mom, the overseer of a family and a spacious home, did her own housework. He might include them in the haves, but they'd certainly earned it! They'd raised two children, herself and her brother, and put them through expensive colleges.

Louis held up his parents as *real* workers. A plumber father and a secretary mother gave him and his older sister solid proletarian roots. And he'd been blessed with cultural riches! Yiddish singers and storytellers gathered every Saturday night in his parents' apartment to perform.

"Why are we sparring, Louis?" she questioned. "You'll never be a ruling class husband, and I'll never be a truck driver's wife. We're more alike than different. We're certified rebels!"

Then they'd hugged and affirmed how, in spite of harsh criticisms from their families, they'd both become artists. That their job was not to squabble, but to make a more just world through their work.

Lucina sat by the large windows overlooking Spring Street. *Just a little longer*, she told herself. *Then I'll get to work.* A delicious breeze sailed through the open window and caressed her arms, her face. Sobering thoughts of her parents eased away. She liked how the large casements swung open like doors, inviting breezes, sounds, and smells into her work space. Never again would she cramp herself into small rooms, those boxes called apartments. Here she was, in this airy loft with Louis. This space, this quiet, where she could think. *Be thankful,* she instructed herself.

The comforting chatter of starlings—they nested under the eaves of her building—was interrupted by a dissonance of sounds. Trucks grunting from the Holland Tunnel were delivering food wares to local restaurants; shopkeepers called out to each other as they swept their sidewalks; hand trucks scraped the rough sidewalks as artists lugged refrigerators, lumber, plumbing fixtures to renovate their lofts. Everybody was up early this morning—except Louis.

A sudden aroma of freshly baked bread filled her space. The bakers were at work! Maybe Louis would go out with her to Kasts for breakfast—later. Now she too had to get to work.

What drove her so? She had explained it once, or Dylan Thomas had: "The force that through the green fuse drives the flower…" A natural drive to create. And a burning desire to understand her experiences and turn them into art.

Back at the workbench, saber saw in hand, she made her vow and the first rough cuts: *In this block of wood I must form the faces that haunt me now.*

*****

He sat on her director's chair and watched her work. *She has the focus of a pointer,* he thought. *She's following an inner voice. There's no hesitation in her movements.* He thought about how he fussed over every word like a nervous Nelly. He'd look out the window, light a cigarette, and tap on his desk. Over and over again, he'd utter a word, a phrase, and then try variations until something stuck, jelled. *Lucina said she could hear those words bounce on the metal ceiling.* He wished he could saw and sand his words as she did her shapes, and then fit them into the puzzle of his poem.

Look at her over there! No stops and starts for her. Maybe a divine force guided her hand. But she did make sketches before she began, trying out her ideas, like his word explorations.

"You're a creating machine!" He addressed the small, taut body he loved so dearly. The grinding of the saw stopped. Silence rang in his ears, then Lucina's voice penetrated him. "What did you say, Louis?"

"I was just sitting here minding my business."

"When out of an orange-colored sky—"

"You know what I really like about you?"

"My sexy bod?"

"That too, but I was thinking…"

"So early in the morning?"

"…how you're too engaged with being yourself to worry about impressing others. Or fitting into somebody else's image."

"I try, honey. I just try."

She came to him and rubbed his shoulders, then worked into his neck. He gave her each of his hands to be massaged as well. "More," he cooed. "That feels so good."

"Did I wake you up, Louis? You were up half the night again talking to Roy. I'm sorry I cut out on you guys. You know me—I get so restless just sitting there. Words and me don't mix. Did you get a plan worked out about the journal?"

Louis stood up suddenly. "Roy is going to run a print shop for SDS on Prince Street. We'll print the journal over there. Of course, I'll need a place for the paste-ups, collating…"

He saw the frown scurry across Lucina's face. "Louis, are you thinking what I think you're thinking?"

"No, Lucina." He turned away from her to the windows. A flutter of starlings caught his eye. "I know this is your studio," he said softly.

She watched with him until the last bird skimmed past the windows.

"So, what're you making now?" he spoke abruptly.

"A two-headed monster."

"Oh, really?"

"No, O'Reilly."

"Come on, Lucina. What is it?"

"Portraits of you and me. Who else?"

She pulled him to sit down again. Then she was kneeling beside him and her head was on his lap, her arms hanging limply over his legs.

"I love it when you draw me, Lucina. I feel like I'm really being seen."

This awe he had for her and her work! Had he ever spoken so openly like this to his ex, Miriam, or to his older sister?

Her eyes had moistened. She was stretching upward to press her cheek into his.

"What can I say? Your face takes my breath away. I'm not good with words, but I can sculpt!"

He bent to her and tentatively pulled his fingers through her hair. "You told me once that your mother spoke in monologues." She closed her eyes and leaned into his touch. "And when you tried to talk, she cut you off, told you to set the table or something."

"It's amazing, Louis. You remember everything I tell you. I just don't trust words. They don't mean what they say." She pulled away, as if clinging to him had tired her. Her eyes found the block of oak again. "Know what I mean, jelly bean?"

"I say what I mean," Louis said.

"Maybe too much."

"What are you implying, Lucina?" He pulled his hand from her shoulder.

"The way you spoke up to Pietro last week."

"Were you really scared for me, like you said?"

"Circle Man had you by the collar."

"No, he didn't! He's a faker."

"How, Louis?"

"He's a scared bully."

"You know all those kids surrounding you? I had the feeling they were gasping to hear you, like you were their oxygen. And then everyone took off when they heard the sirens. It was crazy when the cops rushed in."

"Somebody must have called 911," Louis said.

"I think I blacked out for a while. I mean, I was really dizzy." She nudged him: "So, honey, you think Pietro is a fake?"

"The only thing Tamborcini cares about is himself and the media. He was keeping our confrontation going, not me. It made everybody focus on him and his artwork. If nothing else, the guy's a control freak. I don't think he'd want it to leak out that he can't control himself."

Lucina was back to him, her arms about his neck. "I've got to confess something, Louis."

"You're in love with him."

"Oh, god. Louis! Never! I'm jealous, that's all."

"Of what?"

"Of you. How articulate you are. How you can speak up. I'm jealous and thrilled at the same time."

"I am a good talker. Well, what did you like best about what I said?" He grinned as she tousled his hair, pulled at his ears.

"Oh, Louis, I can't remember."

"Yes, you can! Lucina, tell me."

"Louis, let's go to Kasts. I'm hungry."

"Just tell me. What did you like?"

"Okay, and then breakfast." She hesitated. "Like how you said, 'It's not always comfortable to act upon a vision. But it's more uncomfortable not to.' That was brilliant!"

"I also said, 'Your vision better be worth the act.'"

"Oh, Louis—" Her voice caught. "Maybe you should run for some office. We need good politicians—probably more than good poets."

He smirked. "You know what William Carlos Williams said?"

"Something about how much depends upon a red wheelbarrow?"

"That's not what I'm referring to."

"Sorry."

"Williams taught me that it's hard to get news, and he meant truthful news, from poetry. Yet people die from that lack. Well, my poems tell the painful truths…"

She was losing patience. "Listen. Can you hear my stomach? It's growling for lack of what isn't found there."

Louis let himself be pulled up from his chair. "What's in the frig?"

"Nothing, Louis. You didn't buy groceries yesterday."

"Why me?"

"Never mind. I don't want to argue."

"We're talking."

"Sure, and my parents were 'talking' at one thousand decibels about who didn't do what." She was pushing him toward a half-wall made of bookcases that marked the entrance to their shared space.

"I know. Your mother always shouted at your father to take out the garbage."

They halted in the living area, which was comfortable enough to the casual eye but certainly not out of *House Beautiful*. He wanted her to push at him, needed to feel his body resist her. "Did you hear Roy talking about what SDS is planning?" he asked.

"What aren't they planning?" She had her arm about his waist. "Do you mean those ERAP Projects? Students working so hard to organize poor communities and living in communal houses? I can just imagine those kids fighting over who takes out the collective coffee grounds."

Her glib remark annoyed him: "Okay. Let's go to Kasts. But you can't wear that!"

"What? My work clothes?"

He poked mischievously at her worn work shirt. "There's a hole in the front and your tiddy shows."

"Okay, tease. I'll put on a different shirt and wash up, if you insist."

*****

First she returned to her workbench to clean up. With the hand sweeper she brushed sawdust into a large pail, then put chisels and saw in their cubbyholes. There, that was better. Order. Tools had to be cared for, cherished. She might work again in the afternoon, after they'd walked over to Grand Union for groceries.

She heard him shouting from the other end of the loft, then the heavy metal door scraping shut. She thought she heard, "Meet me downstairs in ten minutes."

Her glance shot to the wall behind the workbench—to the photograph that had first inspired her to make a sculpture of their two heads. Greg had taken the picture. Of course he'd shot them on the Brooklyn Bridge, Louis' favorite spot in New York City. What a fierce, ecstatic relationship Louis had with that bridge. "The graceful cables express man's potential to soar and reach," he'd said that day. "That bridge was built to transform us." While he'd effused about its colossal monumentality, she'd seen a giant stringed instrument, waiting to be played.

But what was it about that photograph that touched her so? It wasn't the bridge or its cables—their faces pulled her! How they leaned into each other, two creatures hungry to be one. Yet each stared firmly out toward the photographer, their friend Greg, not smiling but caught in some momentary sad feeling; maybe that melding was just that, a longing. There was something so haunting, so fragile in their expressions—beyond words. There was no bravado, none of the smugness young people often showed in snapshots, believing they would live forever. Was it acceptance or unease? Or what Louis called "quiet desperation"?

She couldn't say exactly what she meant. That was why she must make the sculpture. That's how she could express her feelings.

Then she heard herself commenting as if from some future time: "This was the young Louis and Lucina in a photograph taken by Greg on the Brooklyn Bridge in 1964." She spoke as if talking about strangers.

Another scene flashed in her mind: a photo her mother kept in the rosewood chest in her living room. It was she and her brother Thomas sitting on the front porch steps, dressed up for an Easter Sunday church service. She was three, he eight. She was smiling out on the world, but he was glaring at her as if he wished she'd never happened.

But Louis and herself? They were glad with each other. They were born again in each other's love. She should be more careful of him.

Both tenderness and fear grabbed at her. What if something should happen: A truck coming too fast down Spring Street? Someone with a knife lunging at them? She looked at her hands; they were holding the Brooklyn Bridge photograph. She'd torn it from the wall. The emotions were too much. She shoved the photo into an open drawer in the workbench.

"I'll work from my imagination," she fumed. "That's the only way I can handle this unknown stuff." She closed the drawer with a defiant snap.

Her glance flew to the sculptures lining the far wall. They looked like primitive guardians waiting for some signal from her. They were definitely her offspring, her brand of kachina dolls.

Rune, cramped in the furthest corner by the window overlooking the fire escape, was the only sculpture she had covered. It looked almost ghostly now, like a giant half-formed person or some monster swaddled in white bedsheets. "Dear *Rune*," her voice cooed as a mother might to her child, "you're waiting for me to play on your xylophone again, aren't you?" She laughed outright at herself. She'd never even talked to her dolls like that!

As she walked through their living area, a sudden movement startled her. It was her own reflection in the mirror by their bed. "You better hurry up, Sister, or Louis is going to have a shit-fit," she barked at the puzzled face staring back at her.

*****

Louis was waiting for her with a bouquet of daffodils.

"What are these for, honey? It's not my birthday, not Valentine's…"

"They're for you, Beautiful One, and your incredible creative spirit." He eyed her quizzically. "Don't you know what day this is? We met a year ago today at your show—I was ready to be your devoted slave, but you were wary of me."

"Oh, Louis, I remember."

As they walked down Spring Street, she clutched his arm and her bouquet proudly, wanting to call out to an older couple approaching, both wearing paint-spattered overalls and eating hot dogs: *This is the first time he gave me flowers*! She blinked away the tears clouding her eyes, not seeing the sudden smiles she and her bouquet had brought to their faces.

9

The Ink Drawing

On the night of June 23, 1964, a haunting young man's voice driven by guitar and harmonica rose up from the radio at Louis' end of the loft. Lucina recognized "Blowing in the Wind" by the new rage, Bob Dylan. Her entire body swayed in rhythm to the music as she worked, drawing abstract shapes with brush and ink on large sheets of paper tacked to the wall.

Then a Pacifica Radio commentator suddenly broke into the song: "We have just received the news. Three civil rights workers missing in Philadelphia, Mississippi—the students Chaney, Schwerner, and Goodman—are feared dead, presumably murdered by—" The speaker broke into sobs. Another voice went on: "They were working with the Student Nonviolent Coordinating Committee during Freedom Summer to help African Americans register to vote."

For a moment Lucina was propelled by the stirring music; then Marin's haunting eyes accused her, and she stood frozen with the news. *This violence must be connected to the Freedom Riders that Marin told me about. Damn! Now it's two years later and I'm still sticking my head in the sand—shutting out any violence bombarding my dreams. Not Marin and Louis—they're political artists. What's the matter with me!* She felt small and pinched, like a scared kid. That's why she'd been avoiding her friend for so long! It wasn't enough to hide in silence and make things—they both understood that. But there was no escape; she was witness to something so brutal, so shocking—young people working for fairness, for justice; real, courageous young men working to make our country truly democratic—murdered!

The names Chaney, Schwerner, and Goodman kept chaffing her ears. She must mourn them! How? Draw them.

By the time three figures emerged on the paper, she was coated with sweat.

Louis was beside her, his eyes fixed on her drawing. "Holy shit, Lucina. You caught their spirits as they were bludgeoned out of this rotten world."

"I don't know how I did it. I just felt them with me."

The two stared at the black lines darting in front of them, as their hands locked.

Louis was somber. "James Farmer was murdered a year ago. Now this. King's march last August enraged those bastards. I told you, Lucina—his 'I Have a Dream' speech to two hundred and fifty thousand people marked him as the most dangerous Black man in our country."

"Why didn't we go to that march, Louis? I read it was the most important civil rights demonstration that there's been. Marin sent me so much literature about it, I just haven't—"

"You were sick, Luie. Don't you remember? Your parents wanted you to visit them—and that made you nuts. I was worried about you—I couldn't leave you alone like that."

"I won't be like that again, Louis. Tell me! Who do you think killed those three men?"

"The white racists—KKK hate mongers."

"Why are they murdering students there?"

"Why? Because students are rising up to fight a terrible sickness in this world, Lucina. Racism is a disease. Calling our country democratic! That's the big lie. We've got to help fight this disease. That's our job!"

Her ignorance was shameful. She should know what was going on.

"Today, hate is winning. Henry Cabot Lodge, ambassador to South Vietnam, supports the South Vietnamese coup. The US wants chaos in that country; they want to perpetuate the war there."

"How do you know all this, Louis?" It was that gang he belonged to—Students for a Democratic Society, that SDS group. And Vietnam? She hardly knew where the small country was located. "I feel ashamed," she murmured, "making things when innocent people are getting murdered. We could have gone down to Mississippi to help people with the voting. It could have been us, sweetheart." She wanted to cry, but her tears were too far away.

Louis gripped her shoulders. "Say 'help our brothers,' Lucina, like SNCC does." His look penetrated her uncomfortably.

"That's the group those guys were working with." She looked at her drawing again. The electric black lines looked like a ganglion of nerves, like frenetic energy. "And shouldn't we talk about our brothers and sisters in Vietnam as well?"

He went back to his desk to listen to further reports.

She grabbed the brushes from her workbench. She must clean them! They looked like weapons coated with dried blood.

*****

For Lucina, that night was marked with a similar painful sorrow as an afternoon nine years before, when she'd heard that her school chum had died suddenly of polio. There'd been no goodbye between them. She'd run up and down the driveway screaming, "Ginny, Ginny," oblivious to the burning hot cement scorching her bare feet. She'd tried to explain her feelings to Louis: "I needed that pain to remind myself I hadn't died, too." But she couldn't really explain her feelings of loss. She'd just decided she could never be really happy again, knowing that a friend could be obliterated in a flash.

But these young men's deaths were very different. They didn't die of a disease you could look at in a microscope. They were murdered! Yes, that old sadness had been awakened, but other disturbing feelings rose up. Outrage. Horror. And the resolve to avenge their deaths somehow. Though she'd never met them, they were her brothers.

10
Louis in Flames

A few weeks later, Louis gave a reading at St. Mark's Church, in the same space that had housed Tamborcini's show. Although Lucina was disturbed to be in the *Breaking Out* space again, she quickly welcomed the huge silk-screened posters lining the walls, with their anti-war themes and images of Black and White people working together to end poverty. It was a fundraiser for the political arts journal Louis would be putting out with the SDS students, part of the *Poets Against the War* series. The area was magically transformed from gallery into reading room with comfortable wooden folding chairs and colorful tapestries of animals and plants hanging on the wall behind the lectern where Louis would read.

Among his longer poems, including a joyful incantation to the Brooklyn Bridge and a re-enactment of a pulsating ride on the D train, Louis read a lush, heartrending ode describing a visit to his son. That he'd invited Lucina to read it the week before—"so you'll be ready for my emotional outpouring of sadness and joy"—was a kindness she needed. As he poured out his feelings for Joel to the attentive audience around her, Lucina closed her eyes and remembered the young boy's innocent, expectant look in a photo he'd once shown her.

He also read several new, short poems, gathered under one title, "My Heart Bears Witness." They exposed and raged at the events of the past few weeks: the murders in Mississippi and the military step-up in Southeast Asia.

As his voice exhilarated her, she realized something: he didn't read, he cantillated (his grandfather had been a cantor), but with a richer, more expressive force than the rabbi and cantor showed at that synagogue Louis had once taken her— "to share his childhood." His complex images seared her visual center and stayed. At one moment he could evoke a bridge, a face, even an entire city, then give voice to the horror of a child maimed by a bomb.

She marveled at how artfully and carefully he incised his images within strong, clear-cut narratives; she was awed at how he forged clarity from confusion. His poems, giving witness to the ceaseless, senseless inhumanity manifested by humans, did not offer ease or use clever humor. He fought back by proclaiming his love, his awareness of miracle, in breathtaking imagery. When Louis delivered his poems, he was transformed, transfixed. He became who he was meant to be.

It was hard to put the two versions of Louis together: the one who sat at his desk day after day, struggling nervously for the right word or phrase; and this Louis before her now, a grand orator, an ageless priest chanting out his wisdom. Loving Louis meant embracing his complexity. It would take endless drawings and sculptures to do that!

Poet Louis snapped her whole body to attention. Her soul rocked with his giddy rhythms. Yet—and she had to own this—at times his pressing beat rubbed at her uncomfortably, like a masseuse whose hungry fingers worked too deeply into already-sore muscles. His voice pulled across her nerves like a cello bow. Or was it a file? At one moment the feeling was sensuous, the next it veered toward pain. The sensation was so stimulating she wondered if she might have an orgasm right there in St. Mark's Church.

When a poet cried out like that, driven by the terrible beauty of words, did it help him? Or did it hurt him? How could his heart take on such intensity? But there was Louis at the lectern, entranced. Louis was in flames.

Everyone in the room was smitten with him. He was speaking for them, crying out for them, wailing for them. His voice was the gripping voice of Whitman or Ginsberg or Lorca, of Crane, Neruda, Roethke. He brought all the ecstatic poets into the space. Louis would never go gently into that dark night. Louis would exhort himself and others to find a way to make it better, even when he exited this confusing and fragile world.

She'd never been close to someone so in love with language, with images, with the power of his own voice. His voice was his instrument—his sax and his trumpet—which he played to the hilt. He knew how to punctuate each word, ride each morpheme to its full sonorous beat. He played on your eardrums until you were transfixed by his charged music. *Look how he excited her. He called up the poet in everyone, even in her!*

Lucina understood, more fully than before, that when Louis performed he inhabited a ritual place of his own making. For him the poem became real space, real time. That's what it meant then to be an artist. It meant to lose yourself in your creative act, so you could find yourself there. It meant giving back what had come into you—with full force, with your soul stamped on it.

As he stood before her, Louis was pouring out his heart and soul, a libation to heal the world. Louis was already his own person.

She was awed and sobered by the new awareness. If he could shine so brightly before others, eloquently expressing his way of seeing and being, giving complete attention to his soul's manifestation, what then were the moments he spent with her?

And then she saw something else. Louis needed his listeners to succumb, surrender to his voice and vision, and receive what he gave. He could only flame if you breathed back acceptance. Poet and listener made a holy pact: if you resisted his voice, wanted something less strong, less humane, less emotional, you must leave the room, you must leave Louis. There was no halfway place; you must share the ecstasy. If you resisted Louis yet remained in his presence, he could break you. Yes, it was hard to say this, but Louis had the power in his voice and mind to bow you down.

She looked away from him for a moment to the wall of posters. Then she noticed, between two posters depicting Martin Luther King's "I Have a Dream" speech in Washington, a black circle or almost circle. Was it supposed to be there, or had Tamborcini twisted somebody's arm to get it there? Thank God! That man didn't write poems. Who could stand that loveless voice, that joyless yapping? There was no love or humor there to make even some real observations palatable. Listening to Tamborcini was more like allowing a sledgehammer to come down on your head.

The guy was confusing and disturbing. He was passionate about justice and change, just like Louis. He clearly wanted a world where the workers were not exploited; he wanted to turn things upside down by any means necessary. But how did that fit in with King's nonviolence policy? Or didn't it?

She closed her eyes. Not seeing Louis for a moment allowed deeper entry into herself. What kind of a journey was she really on with him? Where would all this awareness of her country's injustices lead them? Would they have to take up arms someday? Would she be able to keep up with his anger and passion? Would she be able to stay focused on her own work?

Her hands ached. She'd been gripping the seat of her chair. She was on a roller coaster, screaming into the darkness, the darkness that Louis illuminated with his hermit's lantern. Louis was like *Rune*; both were charged with an inner force. But Louis could erupt like a volcano, while *Rune* stood back from the fray, watching, keeping silent, and listening for her own voice.

11
Our Baby

The political arts journal demanded more and more of Louis' attention. They hadn't gone to a movie for weeks. His requests all summer that Lucina help out with the editing confused and frightened her. How could she become an entirely different person overnight?

She pushed him away. "I don't have a good relationship with words, especially published ones. Frankly, I don't trust them. Besides, I think with my hands."

He listened with seeming patience, then countered, "Bullshit! No one understands my poetry like you do."

By late October, with material for the first issue flooding his desk, he appealed to her creative sensibility. "Lucina, a journal needs to look good. If we want to attract the intellectual student population, we need drawings, beautiful layouts, and clever covers. This can be our baby!"

Our baby. The two words gnawed at Lucina. He really wanted her help! Her glance flew out the window of Fanelli's back room, where they sat eating hamburgers and French fries. There were no yellow or red-leafed trees there to remind her that dreamy Indian-summer days lay ahead. But the dried corn and pumpkin decorations on each table signaled that Halloween was coming soon, and her life, like the season, was changing quickly.

A part-time job at the *Socialist Book Review* had recently fallen into her lap—a contact through Louis' buddy Roy. As part of the marketing team, she was now the subscription coordinator for their monthly periodical. Despite her resistance to joining in Louis' work, she was trying to educate herself in current left-wing political analysis by reading books published by her company. Louis saw her new job as an ally in his agenda for her.

The ideas of Karl Marx, Rosa Luxemburg, Emma Goldman, and Ché Guevara swam in her head. As she consumed such texts as *Monopoly Capitalism*, *The New Imperialism*, *The Cold War*, *The Revolutions in Latin America*, *Castro's Cuba*, *Chavez and the Unionization of Farm Workers*, she tried out nuggets of newfound information on Louis. Questions about the philosophy behind the New Left's mission sparked long conversations. But should she bring up a topic while he was eating? When Louis ate, the rest of the world disappeared.

She watched him as he attended to his meal. She might as well not even be there; he hardly looked at her. The way he zoomed in on his food was his meditation, like drawing was for her. His mind was always fretting, turning over disparate ideas, meshing complex realities—the way poets' minds did. But when he ate, he was a body as well as a brain. He could stop worrying. He could just be. When she'd first understood this about him, she'd cried.

How could she interject conversation in their meals, so he would not feel toyed with, yet she would not feel lonely? Conversation and food were a happy mix for her. Not looking at him, she began mumbling: "I'm just wondering what the true value of my sculptures might be."

After a few seconds, he lifted his eyes: "Don't worry, I can focus on two things at once—you and this hamburger. So, do you mean value to you or to others?"

"I'm trying to see if Marx can help me get clear about this. Like what value my work might have in the marketplace, and is that value different in a capitalist society than in a socialist one?"

"Oh, so that's why you've been reading *Capital*?"

She smiled broadly into his questioning look. It was rare that he would talk to her while eating. Love filled her.

He flashed a beautiful smile and ordered a second hamburger.

She picked up her untouched burger in both hands and stared at it. "Isn't something valued by its usefulness to other people? And how is art's usefulness measured, anyway?"

Louis stopped pouring catsup on his burger, "Or is its value measured by how much labor went into the object?"

"I know of some artworks that took a long time to finish but sell for less than a doodle some famous artist made on a napkin." Lucina watched the stocky man at a nearby table working his pen in a small notebook. Was he a famous artist or a regular person making a list?

"A well-known artist's work has more value than an unknown person's, regardless of the amount of time put into it." Louis chomped on his burger then continued. "Because it has selling value in the market."

"So that's why it's useful? Because it can bring in money? I should forget about reading *Capital*. Just talk with you, sweetheart."

"Just keep drawing me, Lucina. Maybe we'll both be famous someday."

"Seriously, how can I put a price tag on my pieces that in any way compensates for the hours of labor I put into each one? I don't expect to be famous, but I'd like some pay for my work. That's why I show them in *A Sculptor's Theater*. I'm comfortable about charging people to see them, but I'm not comfortable about selling them yet."

"Maybe reading Marx can help you understand use-value, Lucina. If you increase the ways people can make use of your sculpture, you can increase the demand for them, thus increase their value."

"You'd make a good capitalist promoter, honey. But Marx isn't about that. His concern is how the labor force can be paid their true value for the work they do and not be exploited by owners. I'd like to be paid my true value. Something like that."

"First you say you don't want to sell your work, then you imply that you do."

"I just don't know how to put a value on the work I do. It's not only about the thing itself, it's about how it affects other people, inspires them, and makes them think. I should get paid for exercising people's minds."

"You're not going to be able to exercise anybody's brain if you don't eat, Lucina. Can't you enjoy your food? These are great burgers."

"I'm not hungry, Louis. But my brain is."

"Well, you can't live on Marx alone, babe. Eat your hamburger!" He continued watching her, waiting for her to dig in.

Lucina chewed mechanically at her food as if it were a chore, not a raison d'être, as it was for Louis. "I'm eating, Louis. I'm eating." She felt like a little kid.

Louis was still into their topic: "Marx believed workers should own the companies they work in—that's what's important about him. No white-collar–blue-collar separation." As he spoke, the last brittle fry disappeared into his mouth. "That's how I see our journal being operated, by a collective. Any money we bring in gets divided among all the workers. You would make Marx and me very happy if you'd agree to that." He grinned impishly and motioned to the waitress.

"What about me, Louis?" Lucina sorted through her fries for the less-well-done ones. "Shouldn't I be happy, too?"

He ordered a second coke while she obsessed: People didn't buy big, ungainly sculptures like hers that easily. Her sculptures couldn't be dusted or moved about at whim. Obviously they weren't the kind of useful commodities Marx talked about. What were they then? Her totems? Her creatures? At the very least, weren't they meant to help her understand her own mystery, the moments of change in her? Maybe they helped other people, too. Commodities for the soul—something like that? Lots of people said they were whimsical and fun, toys for adults. But only a few people saw how serious they were. Artists ought to be paid for their services, as priests and doctors are. At least Louis understood. He always said *Rune* was praying that the world would see a better way.

"I'll give you my decision tonight, Louis," she said suddenly.

"About what?"

"About 'our baby,'" she said testily. "What else have you been talking about for the last year?" Her voice had risen into a whining sound, and the waitress was at the table with a questioning look. "Oh, no," Lucina apologized. "Just the check, please."

She saw how her fluctuating emotions confused him. He rose abruptly from the table with a questioning look, then waited patiently while she pecked once more at her fries.

PART II
POLITICAL ARTS NEWS JOURNAL

12
"Yes," She Said

Louis was in his swivel chair later that afternoon, his radio on full blast. He seemed to be staring out the window. But when Lucina heard his mutterings from their makeshift kitchen, she realized he was reading his latest poem aloud, over and over, testing every line. It was amazing how quickly he could switch gears—from eating hamburgers to talking about Marx, and now to exploring words and rhythms.

He sensed her restlessness. Maybe she should take a nap, he suggested. She wasn't sleepy, she said. Exercise was what she needed! She would go out again—walk off lunch.

Several people were on the street selling odds and ends, from old books to picture frames. The humble wares were displayed on temporary stands or blankets. A rack of T-shirts with circular designs—were they dyed or painted?—caught her eye. Would Louis like one? Probably not. His taste in clothes was boring. The same blue jeans and white T-shirts, day after day. Enough of street shopping! What she needed was to move her limbs.

Lucina didn't want to leave her neighborhood, so she headed east, then turned left on Wooster Street and headed for

Prince. The quiet, canyon-like feel of the street, lined by empty factory buildings, was comforting. She needed to think, not be terrorized by speeding cars.

Even as a kid, she'd needed calm places. When she couldn't take her parents' arguing, she would run out of the house to the backyard, or walk around the block, peering into neighbors' yards, looking for quiet people. Silence, so she could hear her own thoughts, was a necessity. As was taking little trips away from home to find calmness.

At Prince, she made her way quickly to West Broadway. The few shops—a deli, hardware, and paint store servicing artists—made a mini-Main Street. There were some cars, but it felt safe to be in familiar territory again near her building. She'd gone around the block, just like she did as a kid! The bar at the corner of Spring and West Broadway caught her eye. A cold beer would taste good.

It can be our baby. She sure needed a cold beer and to sit alone and think about that.

Good—the bar was quiet. Only a few people sat on stools exchanging friendly comments with the bartender, a good-looking mustached fellow, probably an actor. A potted palm tree edged her small table by the window. Through its delicate, flat leaves, she could watch the flow of passersby on the street. She liked watching others go about their business; her concerns momentarily lightened as she mused on what theirs might be.

The bartender must have been standing over her for some time. "Oh, I'm sorry. A draft, please." She sounded to herself like a little girl.

"Dark or light?"

"Light, light," she repeated, as if the word itself might influence her mood.

It can be our baby! She could not escape Louis' voice. He always spoke with such intent and so much need to be heard.

She thought of his little boy, whom she'd never seen, Joel. Was she four or five now? In upstate New York, was he learning to talk, think, and play—without a father, without Louis? She knew how painful the situation was for him; his missing son was the one subject he would not, or could not, talk about easily. He could, however, write a gorgeous poem about a visit to him. It made her sad how he seemed to accept the brutal criticism his ex-wife's parents had laid on him. Yet in his poem about his son, he was transformed by the real love he had for that child. Maybe his obsession with that damnable magazine couched his real obsession, his guilt for not parenting Joel daily. He definitely did not want another child with her, Lucina. But the magazine could be their *baby*.

Did she want a child with him? She'd never questioned herself before—her thoughts were so focused on his fatherless child. She was overwhelmed with the changes in her life—it was a relief not to puzzle over having kids, with all the responsibilities that would bring. Imagine, a magazine baby! No painful pregnancy. No diapers to change.

She thought of her family, how her mother's discontent with her was a noose around her neck. She should tell her mother to stop wrestling for her daughter's soul and get a life. Her mother's problem was her own wretched loneliness! Everybody was lonely. Everybody had to find the work that could fill up loneliness; it was not another's responsibility. The day she could say that straight out to her mother would be the day of her liberation. She would take Louis out to dinner on that day. Caviar, steak, and champagne—the whole bit. If only Louis could find peace with his child; if only she could find peace with her mother. But how did you make peace with your past?

For every evil under the sun, there is a remedy or there is none. One of her mother's mantras came to mind. Where was it from? *If there be one, seek and find it...*

What about all the years she'd spent as a sculptor? If she joined Louis in his work, what would happen to her own work, her struggle to be a good artist? She thought of *Rune* waiting patiently under her white cover to be seen again; *Door*, with its two heads suspended in the frame, not yet a finished piece. And *Arrival*, *Poet*, if they could all speak, wouldn't they protest her abandoning them?

It wasn't just the matter of working many hours a week on the magazine; it was the commitment to work with a whole new group of people in a new medium. How would she get along with the talky students Louis was always bringing to their loft? Like Roy, so damn articulate. Always analyzing "The System." She'd first seen him hovering near Louis at Pietro's show, mouthing back Louis' words as in a choral response. What a wild event that had turned out to be. Artists were crazy. But better crazy artists than those talky, smart-aleck politicos.

For every evil under the sun, there is a remedy or there is none.

If there be one, go and find it.
If there by none, then never mind it.

That was how her mother got rid of problems! But this wasn't about evil. This was about Louis and *their baby.*

Her beer sweated in front of her. She hadn't seen the waiter put it there. Focus on her drink. As Louis would say, "Enjoy what you're drinking, Lucina. It's better for your indigestion and your art." With all his practice in food meditation, he knew some things about enjoying the moment.

A group of oil paintings hanging on the wall near the bar area caught her eye. Impressionistic figures had been worked into the surface of the canvas among thick, colorful landscapes. The paintings were Diebenkorn-like. They reminded her how the California-born art professors had opened her up to new textures and sensations in graduate school. Except for Max

Brodsky, the doubting Thomas of the Art Department. So cynical and dogmatic, he'd just never impressed her. Wasn't it ironic? Though her parents couldn't really understand her sculptures, they'd encouraged and paid for her graduate work in Berkeley. Perhaps they'd hoped she would wake up one day and stop taking herself so seriously—yet still have the Masters to fall back on. Parents were so hard to analyze. Sometimes they really did do the right thing.

As for the visiting artists from New York, they'd encouraged her to let her imagination take off. In New York City, you had to imagine your way past the drab skyscrapers. In California, by contrast, you were always surrounded by blue sky, sunshine, lush colors. Still, she wanted to be here, in this dirty and incredible city. People went deep here.

Yes, she'd made some sacrifices to become part of the New York art scene, and now Louis wanted her to sacrifice her sacrifice. No, that wasn't it. He wanted her to work with him. That was understandable. Hadn't she wanted other artists to work with her on *A Sculptor's Theater*? If only she could cry. At least the cold beer felt soothing.

What a little love can do for you. Billy Holiday's sad, haunting voice from a radio next to the cash register worked into her tension. When the melancholy sounds of the sax moved in the same slow, throbbing rhythms as the bubbles in the Miller Brewing Company display above the radio, she began to relax.

Two men smoking heavily were in animated conversation. They hardly took their eyes off each other, as if to do so would break concentration. The wiry one, his work boots clamped on the rungs of the stool, repeated the name Malcolm X. He wasn't saying "Malcolm's *ex*" but "Malcolm *X*." She couldn't hear the other man, partly hidden by the speaker, but he responded often and enthusiastically by slamming his fist on the counter. And every time the bartender heard a thump, he looked up as if he were being summoned. The fist banging of the one certainly fired up talk from the other, or was it the other way around?

"Watch Malcolm X," she heard the wiry man say. Then something about "broken from the nation." Was that from the song "May the Circle Be Unbroken"? The fist-banging man began shouting even louder, as if he wanted others to hear, "King and Malcolm. What a team!" To Lucina, they seemed like ecstatic boys celebrating the victory of their hometown baseball team.

Then she understood: they were talking about Martin Luther King. Malcolm X must be the guy she and Louis had seen on the TV talking about Blacks owning their power. His fierceness had fascinated her.

Hadn't Louis said it was the most important alliance to come out of the Civil Rights Movement since Kennedy gave support to King? The guys at the bar were talking about that same Malcolm X who supported Black militants. She wanted to shout out to them, but they would think she was drunk and playing with them. She wanted to say, "Maybe Malcolm X can help King piece together that dream ripped apart by Kennedy's death."

The wiry man was standing now. "The way I see it—" His eyes met Lucina's for an instant. "If you don't have a dream, what do you have?"

"A nightmare," his companion answered, slapping money on the counter.

As the two men strode out the door, Lucina noticed how pale the taller of the two was, and how tan his friend was.

Watching them through the window continue down Spring Street, their arms about each other's shoulders, still talking animatedly, she realized: *The wiry man was not tan! He was Afro-American. He was Black, like King and Malcolm.*

The bartender motioned to her. "Yes, the check," she called out.

Yes, she repeated to herself. *Yes, I'll tell Louis tonight. He'll be so happy!*

13
Lucina and Facts

Now that her evenings were spent reading manuscripts, proofing galleys, and doing layouts for Louis' magazine, it became harder for Lucina to stay alert during her day job at the *Socialist Review.* Her thoughts wandered with the mundane secretarial work given her. Her studio space, now given over to the business of the political arts journal, was being outfitted with all the proper equipment. The group would buy two used ping-pong tables for the collating work and a second-hand electric stapler on Canal Street. They'd already purchased the light tables and drawing boards for the graphic work.

Though her sculptures—lining the walls of the converted studio and covered in white sheets—pressed against her psyche at times like needy ghosts, Lucina resolved to give her best to the work of the still-unnamed journal. She must get over her unease with the others. After all, she was smart—her college grades had been admirable—and more than that, she was practical and clearheaded. Renata dispelled her feelings of inadequacy. An editor for several established leftist newspapers, she occasionally volunteered skills of all kinds to the fledgling journalists. "Believe me, honey, your commonsense will be a steadying force in this group. Nothing like a wise woman to keep egos rooted." Renata made her feel really needed.

Emboldened, Lucina spoke against the growing tendency for small journals to grab attention with crisis journalism. "We aren't a yellow newspaper. Our journal should chronicle artists and organizers who work for the long haul."

Louis and the editorial staff agreed but still wanted a gutsy name. Up for consideration was *Political Arts Liberation*, with the acronym *PAL*. Lucina put in her two cents: "A magazine that publishes translations of Vietnamese poetry, detailed reports by SDS researchers, and essays on liberation struggles all over the world, needs a name with more bite." She was right, they agreed. *PAL* was just too chummy.

"Let's take the time to think up a really evocative name," she suggested. "Revolution, like evolution, is a long process." The job at the *Review* gave her insight on how change could be manifested. There wasn't just one way. She was already feeling critical of the armchair radicals in the office who put down the clumsy street activists. *Were they exposing her own unease, she wondered, her frustrations at giving up her sculpture work and studio?*

She must pull herself up by the seat of her pants—her father's expression—and accept her decision to work with Louis. If young people like Chaney, Goodman, and Schwerner could give their lives for a more just America, surely she could give a year or two to the work Louis felt was so vital. He believed the magazine could serve as a persuasive tool for the Movement by softening the establishment's growing hawkish stance.

It was thrilling and humbling to witness firsthand the students like Roy, who had quit college to become community organizers. Though he seemed at times to be in love with his own long-winded analyses, she knew his longings for peace and justice were bone-deep and authentic. It seemed like some wonderful awareness was spreading through young adults, causing them to speak out with such force. They were crying out for mutual love, hungry to care for others as much as for themselves. They were struggling "for the good of all," in the words of the Guatemalan revolutionary Otto Rene Castillo. He was one of the poets they would be printing. His passionate exhortations for love began to inspire her own: *May my burning heart flame Love for all beings…*

*****

Early one Monday morning as she typed names and addresses on the labels for the monthly mailing of the *Review*, she felt an uncomfortable pang in the back of her head, just below her left ear. The discomfort grew into an ache that required more than the pressure of her fingers for relief. She headed to the women's room to take an aspirin, passing by the receptionist's desk.

Two fellows in their late twenties, with manuscripts in hand the size of New York City telephone books, were getting directions to the office of the chief editor, her boss. As she passed, one of them, a cap jauntily slanted on his head and a red goatee jutting from his chin, called out, "Good day, madam," not a greeting an American fellow would use. Even if he were flirting, she liked his intelligent look. Both of them wore the small wire glasses political intellectuals were into at the time. Even as she introduced herself and asked where they were from, she'd already sized up the situation: these two expected that their manuscripts, no doubt chronicling recent developments on the Left in France and Germany, would be welcomed here. She'd already seen it happen several times: intelligent, politically innovative, and usually young writers would come to this independent socialist publishing house—it enjoyed an excellent worldwide reputation—sometimes by invitation and sometimes by willful determination to request help in getting tracts edited and published.

The outcome was always the same: unknown writers were turned away. The *Review* had far more excellent articles than it could handle, they were told. No one bothered to explain that the editors wanted articles by established political analysts, not young radicals with fresh, unproven approaches.

When Lucina described her job to the two hopeful writer-activists as "helping to prop up armchair radicals," they laughed at her frankness and were eager to talk. Thinking she could negotiate an in with the editor, they gave their names and political affiliations in Berlin, outlining their intent to publish documents written by the German SDS. "Oh, you have the same initials as our student group!" she exclaimed. But then she clarified her role. "Sorry, Klaus and Heinrich. I'm a nobody subscription coordinator here." They would have to speak to her boss.

Mr. Handleman mustn't see her rubbing elbows with the writers coming to see him! His prestigious *Socialist Review* was rooted in decades of leftist analysis. He would see her journal project with SDS as willful; he would never mention the two journals in the same breath.

She felt for the men. Handleman would not be interested in their "off-the-cuff" manuscripts—just one of the phrases he used to denigrate the writings of young radicals. Her mind was churning. How could she meet up with the young Germans? How could they escape this prison together? She gestured them in the direction of Handleman's personal secretary with "Catch you later, don't worry," and a beguiling smile.

Moments later in the women's room, she composed a note for the receptionist to give the men, who would leave feeling rejected and disillusioned. Handleman would thumb through their manuscripts politely, congratulate them on their work, and then hand them a list of other publishing houses, already knowing those places would be as reluctant as he was to accept their work. He might even explain, "Our articles have to be backed by seasoned research. Of course you understand. We have a vision to uphold and a public that depends on us." Who could argue with that? His dismissal would be accompanied by cordial pats on the back.

At first, men like Handleman had seemed to Lucina like brave elder statesmen for the New Left. But recently she had begun to see him as a cynic and had allowed herself the same kinds of judgments of old leftists that her comrades from the magazine held.

The abrupt, questioning voices coming from Handleman's office wrenched her stomach. Heinrich and Klaus weren't taking this rejection politely. She quickly delivered her note to the receptionist:

Klaus and Heinrich—Meet me at the cafeteria across the street at one o'clock. I can put you in contact with an SDS political-arts journal for your manuscripts, with a good possibility of publication.

In comradeship,

Lucina Holzer
Subscription Coordinator

*****

The morning dragged on. Handleman was taking more time than usual with them. He must be feeling guilty about his rejection and doing his utmost to look like a good guy. In recent weeks, her excitement over the new magazine's progress had made her job bearable. The first issue would include accounts of Ché's relationship to Castro; Chile's military development under

Allende; and the imperialist tactics of American corporations like Nestle's, with their chemically saturated baby formula. She'd even xeroxed her collective's mailing list onto labels the day before. But today she could not contain her restlessness.

When the editor's door finally opened and the young Germans emerged, manuscripts under their arms, looking tired and disappointed, Handleman ushered them toward the receptionist with a "good luck." Funny, he usually managed a smile with his departing words. He'd once said to her, "No matter the little disagreements, leftists are brothers in spirit." But today he seemed strangely preoccupied.

And suddenly he was coming toward her with a huge pile of papers in hand. Had he guessed her intentions regarding the Germans and their manuscripts? Had he concluded that she was misusing her position to obtain material for a rival publication?

"Miss Holzer, step into my office, please." Only three hours before, she'd been "Lucina."

After shutting the door, he ordered none too gently, "Have a seat!"

He held up a large stack of subscriptions to the *Review*. She barely managed one-word responses to his barrage of questions. Yes, she'd filled out both top and bottom in preparation for sending them out with the first issue mailed to new subscribers. No, she hadn't checked her work twice.

"Don't you see what's at the bottom of each of these?" Handleman's voice was nasty and shrill. His intense black eyes—she'd once thought them attractive—drilled at her under thick, heavy brows.

She stared into his eyes, which were spinning like Tamborcini's circles.

"You stamped three hundred of these subscription requests 'paid,'" he accused. "See the red ink: PAID?" His finger hammered over page after page, as if he were stamping out the taboo word. "If I'd let these go through, the company would have lost exactly seven thousand five hundred dollars and seventy-five cents. And that amount, Miss Holzer, is what you would have owed me!" His mouth finally clamped shut, but his eyes continued to accuse.

Lucina felt like vomiting. The pain in the back of her head was shooting into her eyes. She felt a flush of tears; her lips quivered. Had she really done that?

Handleman wasn't through with her yet. "One more mistake like that, Miss Holzer, and you can look for another job. Do you have anything to say for yourself?"

Lucina put her hands on the arms of her chair and forced herself to her feet. She must remove herself from this man—as quickly as possible! "I think I see clearly now," she responded slowly, deliberately, "how essential it is for the workers to own their own company."

It was Mr. Handleman's turn to be overcome. He managed to mumble, "What the hell!" before Lucina continued.

"I'll be more careful in the future, Mr. Handleman. It's not only unbelievable that I marked those subscriptions paid— it's also downright revolutionary."

Handleman was still trying to make sense of her comments when she darted from his office, fled past the receptionist's desk, and caught the elevator just as the doors were closing. In the privacy of the elevator she barked out jubilant primal sounds.

Only when she was in the street, headed for the cafeteria and her SDS comrades, did she let herself shout out loudly, "Thank God Almighty. Free at last!"

Rune was somewhere deep inside her psyche winking one eye in kind and excited approval. As she continued yelping and yahooing down the street, an old woman with a cane who prodded by her said something like, "Keep it up, sweetie."

Yes, she would quit her job and sign up at Office Temps. She would try to find a placement where they taught typesetting skills. Then she could be even more useful to the Movement. Now, onward to discuss publication possibilities with Klaus and Heinrich.

14
Collating *PAN*

Klaus and Heinrich stayed at the Spring Street loft, enjoying instant notoriety in the protest community. Night after night, students and artists gathered around them to hear news of international uprisings. In exchange for the promise that some of their material would be published in a later issue, they'd offered to help with the second issue of *PAN*. Yes, a name had been found: *Political Arts Network*. The acronym, with its Greek root meaning "all," suggested the piping out of news and commentary worldwide. It had other meanings too: a steel drum; yield precious metal; the god Pan, who could cause terror or *panic*; and criticize severely. In their enthusiasm, the group was blind to the potential ridicule they'd set themselves up for. By their third issue, members of another political track were spreading the slogan "Let's pan *PAN*," which actually served to double the demand for the journal.

The dull work of collating was spiced up with talk of the emerging similarities of student coalitions growing across America and Europe. One evening, six workers were collating copies as Heinrich gave an account of his American cousin's participation in writing "The Port Huron Statement for the Students for a Democratic Society" in 1962.

"It's very cool." Klaus cut into Heinrich's account. "That motorcycle guy—kind of a James Dean philosopher—he was the head guru for your SDS, no?"

"Are you talking about a Hells Angel?" Johnny, an NYU student, puzzled.

"He means C. Wright Mills, Harvard professor." Roy, now a community organizer in Newark and a liaison to the New York City branch of SDS spoke up. "European activists memorize Mills' lectures." He was so eager to fill in the blanks in Klaus' remarks.

Thank God Marin's here today, Lucina thought. *She'll help me understand what they're talking about.* Lucina had written to her admitting how afraid she'd been to give up her sculpting work. But with Marin and Louis teaching her, she was coming around at last. The pressured job at the *Review* had also turned her around: being fired was the best thing that could have happened to her. *Like cold water or a slap on the face*, she'd confessed to Marin. *I must wake up. All the world is telling me I have to join with others and fight injustice.* How she'd worried that Marin had already given up on her. It had overwhelmed her—how much she'd missed her moody friend and needed her. And angel Marin had forgiven her. Calling her up like that: "Of course, sweetie. I'll help you and Louis put that journal together."

Her friend's openness had brought back a memory. When Lucina was seven, she'd told her mother, "A friend is the most beautiful thing in the world, Momma. I pray to God every night—that someday I'll know how to be a beautiful, faithful friend to someone."

Whenever Roy corrected the German students' comments, Marin eyed her knowingly. They agreed: Roy was acting like a pompous jerk! Yes, she and Marin felt the same way. They were both impressed by how much these German students did know about the beginnings of their SDS.

Louis kept them to the task. If spirited discussion slowed down the collating work, he barked out, "Keep going, guys. We're not stopping until we hit three hundred issues."

Lucina suggested changing their routine. From stacking just a few pages at a time, they could circle the ping-pong table and stack the entire issue at once. "We could save time," she offered.

Louis teased her. "Ever since you met Tamborcini you're crazy about circling."

Lucina set him straight. "Shh! They don't know that jerk, Louis."

"Okay," he shouted out. "Let's do circles, then." A new routine began.

By the time Louis had finished a lengthy explanation of Khrushchev and Kennedy's confrontation in the Cuban Missile Crisis—how it had forced student radicals to move out of their cliques and dialogue with liberals—Klaus was admitting to a certain dizziness.

Someone suggested they could reverse their collating direction to counterclockwise.

"Okay, about face," Louis commanded and Klaus revived immediately.

Heinrich, who was left-handed, now became confused about page order and asked for a turn operating the electric stapler at a separate table. This gave him time to collect his thoughts. "You here—you want true participatory democracy, yes? You keep a dialogue with your major parties, no?"

Roy took him on. "It's more like a tension," he explained. "We have to shout to be heard. Then we read our ideas in their commentaries!" Roy had no trouble moving and talking at the same time.

Klaus piped up, "For us in the Sozialistischer Deutscher Studentenbund, our SDS, we also have to develop procedural opposition to our major parties." He began listing all the factions currently vying for power in his country.

Why was his voice beginning to irritate her, Lucina wondered. Was it due to his clipped accent—though his curly brown hair and boyish smile certainly didn't fit the movie stereotype of Hitler Youth? Maybe it was his rote recitation of political parties and agendas.

When she could hear no more, she butted in, "Can I ask you something personal, Klaus? Who supports you?"

Heinrich and Klaus stayed silent as Roy shot her a smirk and tried to maneuver the conversation away from personal scrutiny. "She means, is your SDS supported by any of the parties you mentioned?"

"Not the Christian Democrats and not the Social Democrats. They're the two major parties," Heinrich offered quickly.

"Very conservative, the Christian Democrats," Klaus added in a somber tone. "We young people have no voice there."

Any hope Lucina had of turning the conversation to a more personal tone was smothered. She would've been very glad to admit how her parents had stopped sending money for her birthday, and how they were becoming increasingly disturbed by her political activities. By now jargon was flying back and forth between Louis, Roy, and the two Germans.

Marin was shuffling along and humming Kurt Weil tunes, keeping her eyes glued to each new stack of papers in front of her.

Suddenly Heinrich's face went solemn and angular, like a mask. "We think STASI has followed us here," he whispered, eyeing Lucina's sculptures, hidden by sheets.

Lucina's eyebrows shot up. "Here? To this loft?" These super-serious fellows with their German accents and ingenuous looks fascinated and disquieted her. But who was STASI? There were no shadowy figures in raincoats and low-brimmed hats among them. Behind Louis and Roy her sculptures, covered and lined up against the wall, seemed like ghosts. No way could these STASI agents hide under their white sheets!

Louis tried to catch Lucina's eye. He was aware of her unease; her face always revealed her feelings.

"You think the East German Secret Police have followed you here to New York City?" For once, Roy spoke slowly, haltingly.

"Maybe not yet," Heinrich admitted. He put pressure on the stapler, causing disturbing pops, as if to punctuate his remarks. "But soon it will be true."

"What is this STASI?" Marin demanded. "Stop stapling, please. I can't hear anybody!" Her discomfort echoed Lucina's.

"We'll deal with STASI," Klaus added obliquely, "when Rudi Dutschke heads Studentenbund. In a couple years we're going to be on the streets making the long marches like your Caesar Chavé."

These two think they're bugged wherever they go, Lucina decided. *Maybe that's why they showed up in New York, at her office. They were running from STASI. And that's why they couldn't talk personal!* "You mean Cesar Chavez," she said, flashing a quick smile at Roy, who still seemed preoccupied by Heinrich's revelation.

Heinrich was now all enthusiasm about Chavez. "He makes the long marches with his workers, and the fastenings."

Lucina took a deep breath and nodded toward Marin, who was humming again. The mysterious STASI had suddenly disappeared.

"Fasts," Louis corrected.

"He's politicizing his issues," Heinrich continued excitedly, "stopping the silence around the terrible working conditions."

"We call them marches to the sun," Louis interjected. "Migrant workers have to go where crops are being harvested."

"Now Chavez has lots of people marching with the workers in California so everybody knows the issues," Roy said.

"That's interesting, isn't it, Marin?" Lucina's hands were bone dry, as if the pages had sucked up her juices. She wished the work were over and she and Marin could go off somewhere for a cold beer and some jazz. She knew Marin was now dating their good friend, Al; she was dying to hear how they were getting along. You never could tell with two moody artist types!

"What pay do the pickers get?" Heinrich had stopped suddenly to spit on his hands and was rubbing them vigorously as if spittle were hand cream. The group behind him halted abruptly to prevent a collision.

"A buck fifty an hour." Roy had the exact figure on the tip of his tongue.

"How much are we making?" Marin's attempt at a joke silenced all of them.

Then Louis was all enthusiasm. "Spaghetti and meatballs when we get fifty more collated."

"Really, honey?" Lucina quickly clamped her lips shut. A show of affection for Louis seemed out of place here, as they were the only couple.

Klaus dropped his shoulders as if he'd been holding them at military attention for the past two hours. The others watched as he counted the stapled copies. "We've done seventy-five issues," he announced proudly.

Lucina looked sharply at Louis; her eyebrows raised. *Isn't that enough to deserve a break?* she was trying to say. A whiny sound suddenly sailed through the open window. It turned into a wailing siren torpedoing past the loft building. Lucina studied the reflections of her comrades, caught fast in the rippled window glass like in a watercolor. As they listened to the disturbing sound, they seemed frozen in time like her sculptures.

She sidled up to Louis, resisting an urge to grab at him, and demanded, "We deserve a break!"

"Okay," Louis nodded. "We'll do the rest, 225, after supper." With his okay, everyone relaxed. Sergeant Louis had said, "at ease."

Klaus and Heinrich lit up cigarettes. Marin whipped her arms up to the ceiling and stretched them hungrily. "Anything you say, Louis." She laughed good-naturedly, though she was bent out of shape by the factory-like regimen.

"Let's go to the living-it-up area." Lucina felt cheery now. "We've got lots of cold beer there."

As they trundled to the other end of the loft, Klaus asked what was under the white sheets. "Looks like the Klue Kux Kan. How do you say it?"

"Oh, just my sculptures," Lucina said, trying to sound casual. But Klaus, already talking animatedly with Roy, didn't hear her.

They jockeyed an assortment of worn chairs to an equally worn kitchen table, adorned with one empty Chianti bottle filled with wildflowers. In the space nearby, a modest sofa scrounged from the street, two small, unmatched tables, and several painted bookcases—overflowing with read and unread manuscripts for the journal—stood by patiently.

Lucina handed out beers while Roy answered Klaus' questions about the links between America's SDS and SNCC.

"They're both into voter registration and organizing the unemployed. You've heard of the ERAP projects in the poor urban ghettos, haven't you?"

"Yeah, where the proletariat show the bourgeois kids what they don't know," Klaus quipped. He licked the foam off his lips before taking another long drink.

Roy seemed to slip into reverie. Then he asked Lucina if she needed some help.

Maybe he's more sensitive than I thought, she considered. Suddenly he was jerking his shoulders up and down as if to get rid of tension. She set down a bowl of potato chips in the middle of the table to snack on—Louis was cooking up spaghetti and meatballs—and clasped Roy's shoulders. "Roy, Roy," she said, kneading the muscles on both sides of his neck.

"Feels good," he said.

Lucina felt herself relax as she worked at Roy's tension.

*****

A few feet away, Louis watched her for a few moments, smiling. *She's always reaching out,* he thought. *Always massaging someone. Maybe our bodies are replacing her sculptures. She needs to be touching. It's her way to feel a part of all this.*

15
Lucina's Journal

By trading her studio—where she'd slowly, painfully forged sculptures and some personal truths—for *PAN*, Lucina was giving up a home and entering a tempest. It had taken years to develop her art, establish a studio, and promote her shows. Now that once-vivid life was disappearing. Yet she still didn't see herself as a politico. At demonstrations, she heard a tentative, apologetic voice, her own, drowned out by a sea of words and rage. No wonder she questioned the wisdom of her life change. She was overwhelmed and exhausted.

What pushed her forward? Several elements joined forces and propelled her, she realized: Louis' sense of the rightness of their struggle; the collective energy focusing on fairness and justice for all, in particular the have-nots; and the growing awareness of her government's wrongs. Suddenly Vietnam wasn't such a strange, faraway country. McNamara and his generals wore the same arrogant faces as racists in Mississippi. She knew now: the decision to bomb North Vietnam was directly intertwined with the murder of the three civil rights students. Both acts assumed supremacy and the right, even duty, to subjugate others. Surely Malcolm and King's newly forged solidarity was a carefully worked-out strategy to fight back against imperialism and racism rampant in the schools, the cities, and the government offices of America. She had gained a moral clarity: regardless of her personal discomforts, she had a responsibility to herself and her country to work with others to make it better. Overnight.

She must embrace her politically savvy comrades and their homage to discourse, debate, and protest. Facts were weapons to expose and dispel the enemy. That she tended to move dates and battles around almost whimsically, as she arranged and rearranged her sculptures, would not do. Her left-brain would have to shape up!

For practice, she prepared a short speech about events leading directly to the bombing of North Vietnam.

"You don't have to fret about this, Lucina," Louis advised her. "Brilliant analysts like I. F. Stone will have a column in our journal. We need you for the graphic work. And that's fun for you."

Her cheeks flushed with his squelch. But she persisted. "I just had—an idea, Louis. We could have—well, you know, impressionistic interviews—with average Americans. You know, workers, housewives, artists—me. Get the average person's take on the war."

She could see how her awkward stuttering touched him. This was not the bold Lucina they both knew: the sculptor Lucina who made such mind-boggling images.

"Why not keep a journal of your own?" he offered. "Have discussions with yourself about events that are of concern to you. You can play with your facts there and not have to worry about anyone's opinions. That's what I do in my poems." Observing Lucina's silence, he added, "We have to be careful when we talk about the war. Both of us. I guess that's what I mean."

"That's just it," Lucina boiled. "You can put some of your poems in, but my sculpture, my work, will never make it into *PAN's* pages." There! Finally she'd spoken up. After all her sacrifices, couldn't he be more sensitive to her? He hadn't even agreed that maybe she could be one of the average Americans interviewed.

"You could write a song about people rising up all over the world, babe."

Tears brimmed her eyes. Maybe he was trying to be helpful, but it felt patronizing and controlling. Was war only men's business? Not when women and children were blown up by so many of their bombs! Why did she have so much trouble thinking about war, or finding the language to hold up a conversation about it? Louis could spout off about McNamara's speeches and point out every inconsistency. His poetry fit right in with *PAN's* philosophy: art that spoke out. He was articulate and political. He understood the endless maneuvers and counter-maneuvers that made a war. And his poems lashed out at the twisted justifications for slaughter in a way that thrilled her.

But her sculptures—her primitive, non-verbal beings inhabiting a silent landscape devoid of battles and politics—what use did they have in this turbulent world?

What if she and Louis joined their art forms? His words, her images. That's how she could fit in. Perhaps a street theater? She'd already joined the arts in her sculpture shows. She knew something about how to affect people emotionally. They had to bring the war home to the average American. Make each person feel the horror and want to rise up against it. She would bring up this idea when she felt stronger, clearer.

She began to make entries in the black bound journal he had given her. The first was a cartoon drawing of *Rune* saying, "If you can't speak out, then sing, damn it!"

The drawing confirmed the whimsical connection she could conjure up between herself and the inanimate object. Her imagination imbued life into the thing, even after it was made.

She was only half conscious of what lay behind her idiosyncratic inventiveness. Was she substituting a secret liaison with a sculpture for a need to be playful and dramatically expressive with other people? She remembered that Louis had suggested she write a song. *He honored her creativity, but he sure didn't think she could handle politics!*

Under the drawing she wrote, "I miss you," thinking not only of her wooden doppelganger *Rune* but also of her mother, father, and brother.

In another drawing, *Rune* implored, "Sing a little louder, Lucina. I'm listening." Her *Rune* was like a twin helping her keep her spirit alive.

Soon she was writing regularly in her book.

16
Finding a Way with Words

Journal Entry. January 13, 1965: Many artists, like Louis and myself, have banged the door shut on our private lives. Forget quiet studios! Being rich and famous by the time I'm thirty! My dreams have to be sent back to the welding shop, reworked with blowtorch and hammer into raised fists.

January 21, 1965: Last night I dreamt about a pocket watch that was going to explode, maybe because I'm conscious how every second that passes means another life is lost in Vietnam. I hope Louis and I don't explode with the demands we make on ourselves.

January 28, 1965: My sculptures (poor haunting things) are taking a back seat to this hideous war. But Louis is writing anti-war poems that devastate me. Why has this war disturbed so many young people to the point we're ready to put ourselves at risk to stop it? I think we feel it's America's last chance to show real humanity. I still don't understand how Kennedy and Khrushchev could have played out near-nuclear holocaust like it was a chess game to win over our annihilated bodies. It's pretty clear that our government's involvement in Vietnam is badly disguised racism.

February 21, 1965: We heard the terrible news about Malcolm X. Shot down by his enemies. Could they really have been some of his former Muslim "brothers," who became patsies for the CIA? Who knows? A group of us were at the Cedar Tavern, talking about our next issue of PAN, when some guy came in with the news. I can't believe this has happened just when millions of people are rallying to the team of Malcolm and King. It's a false hope, crippling to depend on one strong leader. What is this charisma obsession! The so-called charismatic leader is here today, gone tomorrow. He (hardly ever a she!) mobilizes people to act, then a counter-event like this assassination happens and everyone's left floundering like children without a parent. It's not smart to have just one leader. I really want to be my own leader.

February 23, 1965: The Black Panthers say there are two different tracks in America. For whites it's propel up, for Blacks propel down. Roy says Malcolm's death will hit inner city ghettoes like a bomb. How can those large estates (I'm talking about larger ones than my parents') owned by Dow and DuPont executives, even with their expensive burglar alarm systems and thick walls, be immune to Malcolm's murder? They aren't immune to hurricanes or radiation fallout.

I think of my parents on the outskirts of Chicago. They work so hard to keep the shrubs pruned and the crab grass contained. I feel sadness for them that doesn't go away.

March 3, 1965: I read today how the Gulf of Tonkin incident last August, I think it was on August 4—I better get my facts straight now—fired up SDS, the white student left, to attack America's imperialist policies. That translates into "radicals throw stones at McNamara." Next month, April 17, SDS will mobilize a huge March on Washington, protesting the escalating war in Vietnam and the continued racism here.

March 23, 1965: Louis doesn't like me to say this, but all the tedious work we put into the journal seems like an avoidance, a holding back. Even though we've gotten great response from our first two issues, we're all agitated. We're sitting on our asses, reading through manuscripts that have crusty food on them, by depressed people like us in their twenties and thirties. We talk more and more about wanting to do something more active, more confrontational. But what? It makes me feel really tired when I think about what we're not doing. I'm not ready yet to push my idea—street theater. I have to think it through more.

April 7, 1965: Louis says we should go out on street corners and talk about the war. We've started to go to Angry Arts Against the War meetings. Artists of all media are desperate to use their skills politically to stop the bloodshed. It's so great that Al and Marin go too. I don't feel so alone now that our two friends have hooked up. They both have dark secrets that they can probably share only with each other. How often do two people you love hit it off? And they met for the first time in our loft! Al, so wry, midwestern WASP, and my Marin, so mysterious New York Jewish. Louis has a sister in Marin, and me, a bro in Al. Not that we get on like peaches and cream all the time. If I come on too strong with an opinion, Al tightens up. And if I hug Marin too much, she sticks her rear end out like "That's enough." But somehow they're a perfect complement to me and Louis. We're demonstrative and easily fired up. They're cool, more contained. A balanced foursome.

And meeting Jenny and Hans at Angry Arts last week! I haven't seen Jenny since Berkeley; we tried to give each other the support we weren't getting from our parents, we were being super-serious about our creative selves. She was always so generous with her praises about my work. Hope she's still dancing; she moves so gracefully. It's like every action is a dance. She's been looking for a guy as long as I've known her. Someone offbeat and politically aware. Hope this guy Hans fills her needs. She sure has her eye on him—is she smitten or anxious? I love that Hans is Danish and younger than she. He's quirky and fiery in a different way from Klaus and Heinrich. I think he needs comrades to keep him from going off the deep end. Jenny showers him with kisses; they're so cute together.

I'm getting these fantasies! What would it be like to live with other couples, say Al and Marin, Jenny and Hans? Together we have so much energy and skills; what if we could make protest images that speak to people? MLK has a dream, and so do I. A new kind of family that creates together for love, peace, and fairness.

But talking about the war on street corners? How can someone like myself, so inarticulate and fuzzy about facts, get up in front of people and talk about military zones and strategic warfare? Just the vocabulary makes me sick. I can't even have decent conversations with my parents about the topic without screaming at them for reading Time *magazine. My mother locks herself in her bedroom; my father goes silent and turns on the baseball game. When I visit them, the house turns into a mental hospital. Maybe I shouldn't visit them until I learn some diplomacy. You need diplomacy to talk in public for sure, unless you want broken bones from sticks and stones.*

April 15, 1965: We all agree. We have to use pressure techniques. Demonstrate, write to our congressmen, refuse to file income tax returns, become draft resisters, conscientious objectors, disrupt induction centers, etc. I sometimes get scared for Louis and me. We do need to eat and have a roof over our heads. We're going to end up living in filthy movement offices. Oh god, how did this happen to me? Still, with the Vietnamese being massacred, our lives are up for question. Why them? Why not us? What can we do that makes sense to us? I've stopped sculpting completely and begun making a large painting of Vietnamese women holding their napalmed children. What a horror. With each brush stroke, my nausea increases. How can I think any more about form and color in the context of such atrocities? I'll be lucky if I finish two large paintings this year.

April 17, 1965: What a Happening! I'm still too overwhelmed to be able to say all I felt. We were in Washington, D.C., on Saturday with twenty-five thousand marchers, almost the number of US soldiers in Vietnam. I'm so proud of SDS for organizing this march on the Capitol to end the Vietnam War. The largest peace march so far. To see thousands of protest signs among the cherry blossoms made me weep for all the murder and destruction, when our Mother Earth offers us such beauty. To hear Joan Baez sing out so strong "We Shall Overcome," leading us all to do the same. And Bob Moses, the African American leader of the Mississippi Freedom Summer, made the connection: our government's refusal to enforce civil rights in the South is directly connected to its escalation of the war. Yes! Racism drives this country's brutality. We made a statement. First picketed the White House (it's dripping in blood), then marched to the Capitol. To be part of a massive force, wailing and sailing with our banners and placards down the Mall, an army for Peace, Freedom, Life, Love and Justice for all. A thrill I'd never experienced before. I'm ashamed of my fears.

Journal Entry. April 23, 1965: I'm pulled more and more toward collective work. It's going to take a lot of us to do something. Millions. I did like working with other artists on **A Sculptor's Theater** *shows. I wonder—could we do some kind of theater? Make use of Louis' poems? I'm good with images and making things—props, sets, and masks. Maybe it would be too much fun to do any good, and besides, Louis is married to his journal,* **PAN.**

I watched people become happy, like children, when they marched with my giant wooden figures in my shows. People get a thrill out of parades and drum beats. What if we made scenes where women, children, civilians, animals were massacred along with soldiers? The argument that America needs to save the Vietnamese from Communism would be exposed for all its hypocrisy. If life isn't honored in Vietnam, how can it be honored here? People need images and drama to understand what's going on, as well as facts.

May 4, 1965: I've lost my studio home, but maybe, just maybe I can find another kind of home with Louis. I'm feeling confused, like I'm trying to divide myself up in too many different ways. How could I even be thinking about marriage? Me married! I don't really believe that when you say "I do," presto you have the promise of a permanent home. I can't believe Louis and I are really thinking like this. He thinks that when he visits me at Camp Monroe, where I'm going to teach art to kids for two weeks end of June, that we should just go and do it. Get married at the Justice of the Peace. He's already investigating the whole procedure. "Why now?" I ask him. He says, "You've been bugging me about getting my divorce papers filed. So, I did it—we're free to have some bureaucratic asshole take charge of our lives." I told Louis it didn't sound like he really wanted to get married. "Besides," I asked him, "would being married change our relationship?" I don't think it would for him. Maybe for me; I might be less in awe of him. Of his power with words. Maybe I'd talk more, like my mother does. Or maybe I'd believe what women are supposed to believe: In the eyes of God, my behavior needs to be sanctified by marriage; only then will it be okay to have this guy sleeping next to me every night. At least my parents might feel more comfortable about visiting us. And maybe Louis would change toward me, too. Maybe he would never doubt that his wife could write an analysis of the war.

I can't believe it. Here I'm thinking about us doing theater together; wed his way with words to my way with images and scenes. And he's saying, "Let's do it." But he means, "Let's get married." Maybe getting married could be like our first play together. Isn't all the dress up, the rituals, the pomp and circumstance exactly like an elaborate drama, where mothers cry, brides beam, and grooms get drunk?

When I think of it like this, maybe I can do it. I have a good dress, and I can make my own veil, that would make it proper. And Louis will have to wear a white shirt and a tie. And maybe a suit coat. We'll have to act out our parts with presence and authenticity. We'll have to believe that we really are the bride and the groom.

17

Is This a Marriage?

They'd tried to do something normal by other people's standards. That was the point, the whole reason they'd gone through the humiliating process. But it wasn't a real process; and it wasn't helpful, just tawdry and finally sad.

Was it a mistake to try to fit in—just for once toe the line, follow the rules? Those goddamn rules! What a fantasy she'd concocted: her mother happily chirping, "I know, dearest Lucina, you did it for me. Your father and I will come to New York and see you now. You and Louis can meet us at our hotel for lunch. We'll go shopping. I'm sure you could both use a good pair of shoes."

They should never have humbled themselves like that! She'd taken a two-week job in June as an art teacher at that smug church camp in the Catskills to make some extra money for herself; and Louis had accepted the mop-man job on their janitorial staff just to be with her. Bad enough how they treated him like a dimwit, not understanding the profound, visionary poet he was—so what if he couldn't fix their broken chairs? If not for that camp they might never have done *it*, fallen into a rabbit hole run by wigged-out imposters.

The only saving grace was the veil. Buying the lace for a discount at the general store in Monroe had been a coup. And she enjoyed designing it to fit on her head, like a clever hat for one of her sculptures. Louis got a kick out of it too. His Lucina, sewing and measuring cloth like a gentleman's lady. But when it was finished and she'd modeled it for him, he'd asked, "Is that what it's supposed to look like, Lucina? You look like a beekeeper." Their laughter was so loud they had to close the door to their cramped room and muffle their ruckus with mildewed pillows. The only good part of the whole day? Ralph, Louis' old friend from his University of Wisconsin days, came to be their best man. Even he didn't know what to say about her veil.

So, why hadn't she known immediately upon arrival at that suspect house? Clues were everywhere: rose trellis falling down; car covered with mud in the driveway; rusty, dilapidated eaves and crab grass all over. They'd gotten caught in a mistake! After all, Lucina knew about well-kept and tidy; her parents might be rule-bound and narrow-minded, but they had self-respect and kept a manicured lawn and a cared-for home. How could this be the establishment of a purveyor of justice and peace, an appointed member of the legal community? Even upright Ralph was too busy trying to make them feel good: "Marge and I are delighted you guys will have an official paper like us!" Yes, even Ralph failed to put the kibosh on the proceedings.

When the front door opened, there stood a frowzy woman. Lucina never used that word. But there was Frowzy, staring at them as if aliens had come calling. *She can't be the Judge?* Lucina muttered to herself. She felt her body stiffen as she introduced Louis, herself, and Ralph—"our very best man"—to a woman of sixty who had daubed the wrinkles in her face with makeup to look forty, but had forgotten to smooth out the wrinkles in her taffeta house dress.

"Are you the couple that called yesterday?" the woman managed dryly, as a man's voice sounded behind her. Lucina prayed, *Please, let there be a dignified man wearing a gray suit waiting inside, smiling, ready to lead us to the chapel, and all will be well, forever after.* Her veil was in her bag; her cotton dress was ironed; hose clung to her legs. She'd even polished her shoes.

And then they were inside the house. A voice poured from a cluttered study, definitely not a chapel—President Johnson's, drawling righteous maxims at them from a small box with a rabbit-ears aerial. "I'll turn Lyndon down a bit," the woman murmured coquettishly. "Come into the dining room and have some coffee, dears. The judge will be down in a minute."

Eerie sounds rumbled above them. When a man's voice shouted words not allowed on TV, Louis and Lucina looked at Mrs. Oscar Scottini—she had to be the judge's wife!—for some reaction, if not explanation. Nothing was revealed in her stiffly smiling, made-up face.

As Lucina and Louis drank the bitter coffee Mrs. Scottini offered them but not Ralph!—together with her name, Lavinia, and some papers to sign, Lucina felt a terrible sadness. How could whatever she and Louis were doing here make her parents happy?

While Louis fidgeted with the papers, she stared longingly out the window at the rented car that promised to take them back to a real life, and Ralph sank into a sofa in the study.

Soon a humped figure stomped down the stairs, and Mrs. Lavinia Scottini rose to lower him into a dining room chair catercorner from his attendees. "Judge Scottini," she announced, "will take you through the gateway to blessed matrimonial bliss." Tears miraculously flooded her eyes.

As the judge fumbled for his glasses, Lavinia covered his awkwardness. "It's a pity none of your family could be here today, my dears," she said, obliterating the presence of their chosen family, Ralph. "You can think of me as an older sister," she continued mawkishly, making Lucina reach anxiously for Louis' hand under the table. When the judge was finally ready, papers in some kind of order, Ralph was called in as witness.

Ralph stood beside them—*our bodyguard*, Lucina felt—donning a proud, fatherly look and the dignified demeanor of a marketing manager for General Electric, which he was. She imagined he was recalling the respectable chapel service he and Marge had enjoyed just two years previous. Then, before the judge could say those words from movie weddings, Lucina snatched the homemade veil from her bag. Fitting it over her head and closing her eyes, she placed herself in a sacred tent, not the customary white but cobalt blue, her favorite color. It was her wedding, and wasn't she in charge?

Actually, she'd retreated, depending on Louis to handle the situation. Later she clearly remembered Ralph handing each of them a green jade ring and saying, "You know what to do with these," which made the three of them laugh and relax for the first time.

That's when Lucina became aware of the unmistakable stench of alcohol emanating from the judge's bulbous nose. Later, she was confounded to think that she could be so aware of this body part, yet so fogged out as to what was actually going on in that room. Had she said her vows correctly? Had Louis looked at her when he said his? Her uncertainty deepened even as "the judge" pushed papers toward them to sign. Had she encouraged Louis to divorce Miriam to ease his suffering—or for some other reason? And—embarrassing to admit—was she, Lucina, now going through with this disturbing ceremony not for her parents' sake, but because she needed to tie the knot with him? Then she remembered commanding him, "It's either her or me, Louis."

Years later she would confess to a friend: "Those words haunted me like church bells tolling Good Friday. And how could Louis and I have reasoned our dark clouds would vanish by undergoing a ritual we barely understood or believed in?" Her claim, "Now my parents will visit us, Louis," brought him no joy. He just saw more stiff-lipped relatives making judgments as they averted his dark Jewish eyes. But she knew why she needed that veil! "To hide behind. I wasn't following their rules, and my own weren't firmly in place yet."

*****

Ralph, like the gallant friend he was, knew just what could take the bad taste from that dour experience. Yet as they were on the highway leading to the racetrack, Lucina woke up from her twilight-zone marriage and anxiously pulled the sacred document, just purchased for seventy-five dollars, from her bag. Unsnarling its edges from the once-holy veil, now a costume-prop taking up too much space, Lucina followed the small, scripted print with her finger: "Lucina Altman married Louis Holzer on this sixth day of June, 1965."

Horrors—it's all wrong! she fumed silently as they hightailed it down Route 81. *My name has been Holzer for twenty-six years and today is the twenty-sixth of June, 1965, my birthday! Louis decided we should get married on my special day.*

She would wait until the next day to tell him their "sacred" ceremony was illegal. They must go back to that profane house, that soused judge and maudlin wife, and have the document rectified. Either that or immediately retrieve the seventy-five dollar fee.

Thanks to a hot tip, they'd each pocketed twenty-five bucks with Dolly's win, a welcome reward after the Dickensian—no, Beckettian—ceremony. But the aborted attempt at fitting in had not yet ended. After the horse races, Lucina called her parents' home.

"Mom and Dad, you'll be very pleased. Louis and I went to the justice of the peace of Monroe, New York, today."

Silence from the other end.

"The justice of the peace, to get married."

Silence.

"Mom, Dad, did you hear me? I want you to feel comfortable about visiting us."

Out of the terrible silence a voice croaked, "This is no marriage, Lucina. You can only be truly married in the church. And you know that!" In her mind's eye, the veil she had labored over so carefully, so hopefully, settled over her entire being like a shroud.

"But Mom, Louis is Jewish. We couldn't get married in the church anyway."

"That's your problem, Lucina. You've made your bed, now you have to sleep in it."

No one said goodbye. Lucina's sobs drowned out the click of the phone.

*****

Though their marriage certificate was rectified the next day, Louis and Lucina decided to keep their detour into the legal system to themselves for the time being. Ralph promised he and Marge would keep it secret too. Marge had been with them in a way: she'd pressed Ralph's blue jacket for Louis to wear and bought him a new silver-gray tie.

The next week, a large package arrived at the loft on Spring Street addressed to Lucina Holzer in her father's precise printing style. Inside were two separate boxes. One held twin bedsheets; the other, a scrub brush, scouring powder, naphtha soap, and cleaning cloths. She wept and downed three beers in a row, as her hope of finally gaining family approval disappeared into froth.

PART III
FIRE DRAGON STREET THEATER

18
Honeymoon for Six

Journal Entry. July 18, 1965: I know our life is going to keep changing during the summer. We're going to Vermont with four other artists: Marin, Al, Hans and Jenny. Will it be like my fantasy? I want us to do something vital and creative together. Our discussions are getting so intense, I hope we don't drive each other crazy. I am going to push for doing street theater. I'm convinced that's where it's at. At least we're taking a break from PAN. Roy is thrilled to be in charge of the summer issue.

July 28, 1965: Yesterday we arrived at this little cabin hidden in the woods near Sandstorm, Vermont. I was skeptical about going somewhere blind, but it's free to us and cute. It was so generous of Jenny's cousin to let us have it, though we will pay for gas and electricity. It's like some miracle that the six of us have hit it off so fast. And now we're going to be together for several weeks. I can always take walks by myself. And we're all feeling the same thing. We have to do something gutsy together to fight this war, make sanity. It's exciting and scary. Louis and I get the biggest bedroom because he's a good talker.

He and I are still in love. When we make love, we blend. And no one here knows we're married. Louis said it was good we did it—even if it was a nightmare—because now I would be more relaxed about his past, and think of us as really being together. The judge corrected all the documents, so it's legal.

The other day I wrote in my journal the words "my husband"; just those two words. Then I erased them. I can't bear to have any of these wild-eyed radicals (I love that expression) find out. It made me feel in control to write the words down and then to take them away. They'd think we were trying to be normal, and I don't want to be normal. I want to be me. And I sure don't know what that is.

Louis and I decided that we could never own each other, not even through words. But we are part of one another, and nothing can ever take that away from us. A depressing day for me has sunlight if Louis writes a poem. When I make a drawing, it delights us both. I guess we'll always be artists. I have to go now and help Jenny clean the kitchen. It stinks.

July 29, 1965: I have to learn how to fit into a group but not lose parts of myself in that gangly creature. Will my ego become vague? The shapes of my limbs unclear? "You have to surrender yourself to the group," Louis tells me, and that scares me. Will I have to weld myself together again, sometime in the future? If there is a future.

A lot of the time I am uneasy, unfocused. I'm very aware of everything that's flying around me: the birds; the swarms of insects hovering above my head in the field behind the cabin; the flies that seem to listen to the news reports with us, but just for a while. They can't take it either, so off they go, swirling round and round the ceiling, like crazy helicopters. P.S. to myself: I can't believe how much I've been writing since we got here. Maybe I'm becoming more comfortable with words since Louis and I got married. That's an odd thought. On the other hand, it could just be that hanging around with talking heads forces me to write my thoughts down since I don't talk that much.

19
Soul Searching in Vermont

Despite intentions to come up with an action plan in the first week of their Vermont retreat to Help Stop the War, other priorities took over. It was enough to adjust to a new setting, the group, and shared chores. Plus, each couple needed chill time: Hans and Jenny hashed out some problems in their bedroom; Al and Marin stayed strung out in the hammock under Norway pines; Louis and Lucina, imagining a kind of honeymoon, often disappeared into the woods.

Though the six buddies had a common desire to weave their various creative disciplines into political action, finding how to do that wasn't easy. First off, communication had to be improved: they had to listen better, speak more clearly, stick to the point, take turns, and not shout. They kept reminding themselves that their paths had crossed for a reason.

It wasn't until their eighth day at the cabin that they called a meeting. Over beers and snacks they recalled how they'd connected: Lucina and Jenny met in Berkeley before the Free Speech Movement was off the ground; Lucina met Marin at her improv group's performance at the Judson church; Louis and Al hooked up at a Lower East Side poetry reading; Marin and Al at the loft; Hans and Jenny at a Tompkins Square Park peace rally, and then they all came together at an Angry Artists Against the War meeting. But it was afterwards, over hamburgers and feisty talk until two in the morning, that the six discovered their affinity.

The attractions between them were palpable but not always understood. Why was outgoing and talky Louis so taken by tense and reserved Al, who carted Lucina's sculptures around New York City with his pick-up? Did Marin, melancholy and preoccupied, need Al's muscles and silence as her shield? Her sorrowing eyes and groping hands sure found a dedicated midwestern lover in Al. Hans, a nineteen-year-old Dane, was their youngest: small and sinewy, fragile and angry, he replayed every verbal bout with the others to measure how well he stood his ground. Jenny, a gentle presence, calmed her golden-haired and blue-eyed Dane. But when provoked by him or Louis, she could flare up like a forest fire fanned by a sudden gust.

This first informal meeting ended with a plan to meet regularly to share updates on the war and to brainstorm on the kinds of actions they were prepared to take against it as a group. At least they'd managed to affirm the desire to work as a unit. But soon the beautiful weather inspired this wily bunch to head to the nearby village and have some fun.

They found a cozy counter in the back of Sara's General Store, where banana splits were a specialty and Josie, a feisty teenager, worked the soda fountain.

"Why would guys like you want to stay in a nowhere place like Sandstorm even for a few days?" she asked bluntly.

Hans was in one of his smart-aleck moods: "We're going to collect maple syrup and market it. *Ja*, maybe start a pancake business in the city."

Spotting Josie's confusion, Lucina took over: "We needed to get out of the city to figure out what we're going to do for the rest of our lives. So it doesn't matter where we are as long as it's beautiful."

"Okay, so don't tell me!" Josie mocked a pout while adding nuts and pitted cherries to six banana splits. "And I'm going to star in a Broadway play next month."

Josie's spunk made them wake up. They really didn't have a good answer for her. Al asked her questions about fun places to visit nearby. She eagerly relayed detailed info about mountaintops for climbing and streams for skinny-dipping and showed them her sturdy boots from L.L. Bean. Lucina wondered what Josie thought about America's assault on Vietnam. She would ask her sometime when the others weren't around.

Back on Main Street, Hans started up about a pile of leaflets he was carrying. "I'm going to stick these on store windows. Ja." Al and Louis came down hard on him. "Oh man, not that anti-imperialist flyer," Al groaned. "We don't know what people's politics are in this town." "Al's right," Louis added. "Let's make some connections first, Hans. Build some trust." Hans backed away in anger. "I'm an aktivister! That's what this is about!"

"Look, Hans. You're not alone!" Louis barked. "You're here with five others and you have to remember—what you do affects all of us. Let's talk more in our meetings about the political tactics we think will work the best."

"That's the problem, Louis. You want to talk about it—I want to act."

"Make your own waves in the bathtub, kiddo. We'll talk later. See ya." Since it was Louis and Lucina's turn to make dinner for all of them, Louis pulled Lucina away from the others.

"Let's go home now. I don't want asshole vibes around me."

"It's a good thing I rented a car, Louis—and that I know how to drive it." Lucina waved to the others, "Have a good time at the Hilltop Market, you all. We're going back to make supper."

When the country road calmed her down, she commented, "I hope you and Al find a gentle way to handle Hans' enthusiasm."

"Enthusiasm is one thing; mindlessness another," Louis muttered.

*****

Back at the cabin, Lucina whispered tensely as if they were being followed by an unfriendly presence, "I hope you know what we're making for dinner, Mr. Louis."

"Just talk regular, Lucina. No one else is here, remember? Are you still upset about Hans?"

"I don't like tension in the group, that's all."

"Get used to it, babe. We're not robots. Hans has to learn organizing skills, that's all."

They were in the kitchen, where Al and Marin had set mouse traps under the sink to quell an unrelenting march of invaders, when Lucina let out a sudden shriek. As Louis reached for her, she whimpered, "Oh no," and pointed to a baby mouse squashed under a thick metal clamp. "I'm never going to be a warrior, Louis. I can't take any creature getting hurt."

"It's okay, Luie. We all have to learn how to be tougher. Okay, I'll put mousie in the garbage. Now, supper! I know what's good—something you and our comrades like."

Louis quickly lined up a variety of vegetables on the kitchen counter. "Which one tonight?"

"All of them," said Lucina. "A feast."

While he boiled a large pot of water for pasta and washed lettuce, radishes, tomatoes, and cucumbers for a salad, Lucina cut up broccoli, cauliflower, eggplant, mushrooms, garlic, and onions. The knife's sharpness was unnerving; Al had sharpened them the day before. *One moment a whole onion,* she thought. *Then all these thin round sections. That's happening to me. I'm being sliced up into parts of myself, too.*

"What you thinking, babe?" Louis poured her a glass of Chianti from the communal gallon and a glass of seltzer for himself. "You're so quiet." He offered the glass of wine to her. "Let's have a fun evening. We actually had a good first meeting this afternoon with everyone. We're all raring to figure out what we want to work on, don't you think?"

Not sensing his nearness, she swung to face him, knocking his arm. "Louis, be careful!" Too late, bright red liquid marred her white shorts. She rubbed quickly at the stain with some of his seltzer.

He waited patiently then pulled her again to him. "Don't tell anyone, babe. You are my wife," he whispered playfully into her ear.

"What does that mean, Louis?" She wanted to laugh, feel happy to be alone with him, but tears flooded her eyes.

"What, Lucina! What?"

She rested her head against his chest. "I'm very afraid, Louis," she whimpered.

"We're doing the right thing, Lucina, don't worry. Just keep drawing. That always makes you feel better." He went to the stove and stirred pasta into the boiling water. "You don't have cainotophobia, do you?"

Lucina sunk into a kitchen chair. "I don't know what that is."

"Fear of newness."

"You don't understand, Louis. I have entomophobia. I know this is going to sound silly, but I think a bug is going to fly into my ear and drive me nuts!"

"What kind of bug?" He tried to keep a straight face.

Lucina burst out in snorts and sobs and finally laughter. "A cainotophobia bug, you asshole!"

20
War News from General Electric

During a late morning in mid-August, the six comrades huddled over a small brown box, transfixed. Collapsed soda cans, dried orange peels, peach pits, and ashtrays overflowing with pulverized butts surrounded the object—not a sacramental but a GE radio.

"The bombing has escalated again," revered General Electric shouted. Compressed lips pulled at cigarettes with increasing agitation as the war news and smoke wrapped around them.

Al rubbed his hands, ready to fight. "Fuckin' hawks. Damn! Damn! Damn!" With each damnation his body jerked more upright.

Lucina tore herself away from the horror of melting bodies and settled on the couch. Its marred purple covering seemed like a large bruise. She must block out the reports or she'd vomit. Wait! She could soothe herself by drawing the others.

I can draw chairs. Weak legs, broken splats, extruding guts, missing rungs, splintered pegs, rusted nails. This I can put on paper. But us? How can I possibly capture our oddities? I know, I can just suggest them. And our cigarette smoke will camouflage our bodies and expressions.

Drawing would quiet her nerves. She reminded herself: she was no longer that anxious Berkeley student struggling with those first sculptures, certain they looked like the ambiguous shapes children presented to their parents. Nor that tense learner, her left hand cramping with the effort to capture every word in lectures. She remembered how slowly Dr. Strecker had spoken, each word a precious offering: "The Fauves intoxicated each other with bold strokes and colors. German Expressionists exploded emotions. Artists from the Parisian salons fed on each other for sustenance, pulling each other into the unknown." How he'd captivated her with those romantic tales!

What about the artists in this room with her? *We're artists who don't talk about art anymore. We're mesmerized by the news barking from that damn radio! We're captivated by other people's madness. What is Mister Hans haranguing about now?* "*What we do should* forstyrre—*disturb people.*" *Is he out to piss off Louis again?. He wants to turn ploughshares into swords, make art into weapons to fight the hawks. Louis is right. I'd better keep drawing to keep myself calm.*

She would make an entire book of line drawings: chairs holding ghost-like figures. On the back of each page she could make written entries. She flipped through yesterday's drawings. One page showed Jenny's long, nimble hands—good for dance movements or playing an instrument. Al's jaw line, like a clamp or a Dick Tracy jaw. Marin's eyes. They're fixated on something that's already happened, something sad. Whose hand clasps the beer can? Whose foot clings to the rung of a chair? Had she found their vulnerable or their strong parts?

In my way, I'm trying to understand them.

"What are you doing, Lucina?" Louis called out from across the room. "Wake up! We're talking about interesting things."

She shouted back, "I'm not sleeping, Louis. I'm inventing a composite person: the artist who will help stop the war."

Louis flashed her a tender smile.

Then Jenny was beside her. "What are you two talking about?" She looked down at her sketches. "Nice, Lucina. I wish I could do that. I can't even draw a straight line."

Lucina sighed. "Artists don't draw straight lines. And gorgeous dancers like you, Jenny, move in arcs and curves and spirals."

Next she would draw Louis' head resting on his leather chair. Head and chair together would look like a kind old person.

Louis lowered the radio and eyed those near him. "We have to make a plan." Did he know she was drawing him? Could he feel her energy?

Hans spit out some strange facts. "Five hundred tons of Agent Orange were sprayed on five hundred acres by five hundred planes this week."

"You made that up, Hans," Jenny snapped. "Why the same number?"

"See—that's how the imperialists think. Next week it will be a thousand."

Jenny groaned, "Oh, that's probably true."

Marin reported on an article she'd just read, detailing how napalm was made and exactly what it did to the flesh. Napalm was her obsession. She also had the latest number of casualties.

"They're all liars," Louis declared. "McNamara's comments at his press conference on Wednesday were inconsistent with the ones he made on Monday."

Jenny reported on the weekly cost of the war, then translated those figures into money lost for food, schools, and hospitals in the US.

Al described a photo in the *Times* the day before. "Vietnamese women stood by a charred hut where their children lay in a heap." He also spoke about an American soldier who'd started shooting at his own men.

"Why can't women stop this?" Jenny whined.

"Like how?" Hans challenged.

"Like stop fucking their men," Louis quipped.

"Don't give 'em ideas, Lou," Al said.

"I don't mean us," Louis said.

Lucina had a sudden image of Al falling off his chair and sobbing. She should add to the conversation, make an effort. "No peace, no piece," she mouthed in a singsong.

"That's a great slogan," Louis said.

Jenny giggled, then sank exhausted into the couch.

"Too subtle," Hans threw out.

"That's not so subtle," Al countered, squinting at Lucina as if she were an uncomfortably bright light.

"See—who knew what Lucina was trying to say in her sculpture show?" Hans grumbled.

She should ignore the comment—she hadn't known Hans when he'd come to her show. Her pencil was doing double time. *An androgynous look, with his long hair, narrow shoulders. Yes—tight pouty lips and two horns. It's Hans!* She had to respond. "I wasn't 'trying to say,' Hans." She glowered at him across the room, hunched over, eating potato chips. "For god's sake, I was trying to play!"

"Play? We have to teach."

"You don't like to experience things, Hans." *Maybe the horns should be longer, sharper.* "How can you change anybody without experiencing yourself change?"

"Who's going to change who?" Al let out a cloud of smoke that enveloped him.

Al's just shy. He has to hide.

"We have to change, Al," Marin said quietly. "That's what Lucina means."

"Hopefully, we can change hawks to doves," Jenny said. "Before they obliterate the whole country."

Lucina quickly covered what she'd drawn so Jenny couldn't see it. Then Jenny was glaring at Hans. "So Lucina didn't have Vietcong flags in her shows—so what!"

Hans deflected Jenny's looks, then aimed sharp words at her: "*Lort*! If we're talking how to stop murder—guerrilla art is it!"

He's upset because Jenny didn't stick up for him. She watched him grip a cigarette with his lips and bend toward Al's flaming lighter so his delicate profile was edged by an orange glow.

"We should be talking about a war crimes tribunal," Al said quietly.

"Are you kidding?" Louis snapped. "This country supported Hitler."

"I can't take hearing about this war twenty-four hours a day, Louis," Al charged back.

Lucina tried to catch Al's glance. "I thought it was only me." He stomped out his cigarette in slow motion, stone-faced. *Maybe he didn't hear her!*

"It's good to be hard on ourselves," Louis said. "Self-criticism is the beginning of forming moral objectives."

She turned her attention to Louis' face. *His features are so strong—a stylized mask. The formidable nose, the sensuous lips, the forehead like a mountain. Inspired when he talks, happy when we play volleyball after dinner. Lets off steam like a kid. Will we be able to make another dinner alone? I must ask him again: Does beauty or horror drive you more? Ever since the bombing began, his poems are tortured offerings.* She watched his hands churn the air, imploring the others to listen. *All those words. What is he saying? Something about Mills' interpretation of the publics. I should try to talk about that with him, too.*

"Could you repeat that, Louis?"

"I said, Lucina, I feel like words are inadequate to move this country into action. Americans suck on words like they were candy. Or their mother's tits!"

"You know who you sound like, Louis?" She made circles in the air with her finger as he grimaced in agreement. Their secret code for Tamborcini.

"The riots last week," Hans broke in. "How come no one talks about the assassination?"

"You should talk about it, Hans," Jenny said in real support. "You have a tongue."

Al offered Hans another cigarette. "What do you want to say, man? You know, whites didn't kill Malcolm."

Jenny moved rapidly to Hans and leaned into him, as if wanting to protect him from Al's question.

Lucina snapped her journal shut. "America can't deal with Malcolm, alive or dead." She forced a smile at Hans. *She really did like him! Just not when he got too pushy.*

Louis sighed, put his hands behind his head and leaned back in his chair, looking at her. *Does he want me to push for a plan today?* she wondered.

Al shot up from his chair and stretched. "Marin's making tuna sandwiches for lunch." He headed for the kitchen, shoulders hunched forward. "I'm working on my truck this afternoon. Fuck Vietnam! It's making me really sick."

She felt the departures of the others in her nerves and muscles. She was an onion, peeling away layer by layer. She flipped through the pages of her journal to find an entry from the day before:

August 14, 1965: I'm trying to get some words in edgewise on daily discussions about art, reality, politics and the war in Vietnam. Before supper, I like to take a long walk in the woods. I want to find out if trees talk to each other. And can I remember a route from markings such as stumps, large stones, and areas of moss and areas of pine needles? I'm trying to tread both softly and slowly, without falling over. I want to learn how to be invisible in the woods. Snapping twigs frighten away animals.

I've been taping crickets. One cricket starts up a rhythm to the south, while another adds a compatible, but different rhythm from the north, and so on until you have a veritable rhythm band.

Louis tries to focus on his poetry but is easily pulled back into one of the worn-out rocking chairs on the porch or the big leather chair in the cabin ready to pour his two cents into the next interminable discussion. He's more social than I. I'm too easily upset by our discussions.

Johnson is lying when he says we're winning this war. Dead Vietnamese, not to mention dead American soldiers, are an embarrassment for him, not a tragedy. America wants a base in Asia to push its markets and monitor its competitors. Simple as that.

I never thought before how a small group of people might work to stop a war. One thing I do know: I don't want the group to be privy to my bug obsession.

When everyone gets mad at everyone else, the couples go to their separate bedrooms and fuck. I cry a lot. Louis explains to me how the war in Vietnam started, and I describe to him how I feel in the woods, tranquil and terribly alive at the same time. He laughs at me about my bug fetish and tells me to reread Kafka.

The only time I relax with the group is when we break for beers or poker or play volleyball in the front yard. Then Louis gets a chance to do his wonder shots, always accompanied by a great shout. Soon all of us are whooping it up, before we—

"Lucina!" She was back in the room as figures departed through the doorways. *They're breaking out of frames, she thought.* Louis towered over her. "You've been hiding in your journal long enough. Come on, let's take a walk."

21
In the Woods

Two figures enter a dense wood near Sandstorm, Vermont. In this cathedral of green there are no stained glass windows pierced by light, no anchoring pews, and no lofty steeple. But the tops of trees make a lacy peace with the sky, and star moss and pine needles make inviting seats. He puts his cheek to the rough bark of a spruce and breathes in deeply. She snuggles into him like a trusting puppy, takes his delicate hand and moves it along the bark, teaching him to caress the tree. Something is sticky there; together they smell the pungent resin on his hand.

He spins away from her, an elf in a bear's body dancing on slippery needles; he tumbles and spreads himself flat on his back. She flings herself on him, nibbles his ears, and licks his cheeks.

The forest whirls as they make love, she on top, riding deep into his flesh within a cascade of light and shadow. Together they enter a visceral ecstasy.

In the shadows of a birch grove, he imagines beasts, larger than bears and fiercer than tigers, watching them; his passion grows.

She strokes his throbbing penis, marveling how such an organ could exist and be so accommodating to her. "You are the beast," she says.

In the emotional churning, his face awes her. Something in his eyes, his soft, exposed lips, his grand nose, his immense forehead. The undulating hair capping his large head. She promises herself: when the war is over, she will do it. She will paint him, a portrait larger than any of her sculptures.

She is lost in thought.

"Did I hurt you?"

"No, you didn't, Louis, but your face did."

Their sounds of coming shatter all caution. They roar with rapture.

They splash in a stream lapping over stones and leaves under boughs of oak, maple, and beech. The cold water startles them back to themselves and the preciousness of the moment.

Lucina sits on a large rock and watches water surging past. "I feel like I'm moving and not moving. Look, Louis! The stones shape the water and the water shapes the stones, all at the same time."

Louis sits on a grassy place nearby, examining Queen Anne's lace as if seeing the delicate umbrellas for the first time. When he spots the faint moon nestled against a patch of blue, he turns abruptly to her. "I wish the world was this beautiful, Lucina. I can't forget all the crushed dreams."

"Mine and yours?"

"All of America's crushed dreams reach up to the moon. I'm writing a poem about it."

"Oh, Louis, I love how you describe things."

"And they want to go and put our bloody flag up there. For what? We need to reclaim our dreams, feed each other here on earth. Not stick our goddamn prick in the moon or Vietnam."

She moves to sit by him and sees again that orange light flooding his eyes. "You're more than handsome, Louis. You're breathtaking. But you need exercise. You've got to get out of your books and your head. Let's do some exercises together now."

*****

In a field near their cabin, they worked with their bodies. As Louis stretched his arms and legs, his muscles rippled with energy. Then they jogged for a mile on their road. "Damn it, Lucina," he panted. "You're giving me back myself." They walked to the small pond behind the cabin to relax and watch the fork-tailed swallows dive and soar above the pond, playing tag. "If only I could move like that!" Louis laughed and pulled her to him.

"Stick with me and you will, honey." Lucina rubbed her sweat into his bare arms. *How long had it been since they were alone like this, just the two of them, for hours?*

Louis talked about the books he wanted her to read: *Tragic Sense of Life* by Unamuno, *Ulysses*, and *The Brothers Karamazov*. Away from the city, the relentless pressures of *PAN* and protesting the war lifted as nature offered rest and revival. With the carefree movements of the swallows, tensions eased. And suddenly he was pouring out his youthful promises to her, his commitments to Hart Crane, Walt Whitman, Garcia Lorca. "I commit myself to them again and in your presence, Lucina." He leaned into her, tears running down his cheeks. "Like them, I will always bear witness to man's injustices to man in my poems."

"That's what you do, honey." She rocked him in her arms, his strength and his fragility in delicate balance. "You're really blessed. You know what you think and feel and you can express it."

There was envy in her praise; he sat up and eyed her directly. "Don't worry, babe. You'll find your words, too. In time."

She cried out. "I've been mute so long!" She hadn't yet shared her journal entries with him. "But tell me, Louis. What moved you to write, before you made promises to all those guys?"

"New York City, what else? Every time a Staten Island ferry strikes the docks, it rattles me and wakes me up to possibility. You know what inspired my first thoughts on fairness and the American Dream? The Statue of Liberty."

"You're like a true American poet, Louis."

"I should read you my first poem—so optimistic. I imagine a time when all the communities of the world will converge like the cables of the Brooklyn Bridge—and make a new harmonious world—a world that joyously shares all its goods. I don't know where it's stashed."

"Were you always so serious?"

"Working to stop this evil war is a continuation of my promises. Yes, Lucina, I was born to remember."

"Tell me more about your relatives. That poem about your uncle and your twin nieces? That took my breath away."

"That's right, you saw the photos on my parents' bureau. All those people died in Hitler's death camps. Every night I saw their faces staring into mine, asking me to speak for them. I have to keep them alive somehow."

"Oh, Louis. This world is so unbearable!" She turned from him to the pond again. *Please, God. Don't let the tension back in.*

"But listen, Lucina," he grabbed her arm. "We have to remember the good stuff. Look at the seeds in this pinecone. They are bearers of life and they are beautiful!"

"That is so lovely, what you just said…"

"I want to know about you. What made you want to make sculpture? How come you didn't make small things, little clay pieces?"

She settled back to him again. "I did in my student days, but that was just practice. I knew I wanted to make larger-than-life figures in wood someday. We didn't have grand bridges and majestic statues in my hometown. But we had some awesome things, especially for kids. Giant stilt figures wearing incredible masks appeared on Main Street for our holiday parades. I'm sure *Rune* came right out of a July 4 celebration! But it wasn't just outward spectacles that affected me. My parents' quarrels, the secrets we were to keep under the rug, made me want to find another kind of world, one I could be happy in. And our landscape, the flat countryside stretching on and on, devoid of hills and valleys, made me invent things. I filled up the empty spaces with my longings. Also, all the churches haunted me, especially how their pointed steeples stabbed the sky. Churches were not homey and gentle for me. And I hated the cloying images of Jesus on the cross. It felt like I was supposed to worship death, not life. I could relate to the resurrection myths, that new life comes out of the ashes."

"Were you always uncomfortable with words?"

"In high school, I wrote a story about a woman who couldn't talk or cry. I got an A on it, but I ripped it up. It seemed so odd."

"But you wrote about her. You made a story with words, Lucina. See? Probably your mother didn't let you talk about your feelings. She seems to me to follow a pretty strict guidebook on rights and wrongs."

Lucina suddenly shut down. "You don't really know her!" She felt that old need…

Her refusal to talk anymore about that early writing or about her mother silenced him as well. They returned to the cabin feeling terribly close and terribly alone.

*****

151

The day after she and Louis had found deep closeness and awkward walls between them, Lucina wandered into an old barn on the property. On August 16, 1965, she wrote in her journal:

I heard myself call out in the darkness, "God, please show us what we ought to be doing to stop this bloody war!" The only response, a rustle in the hayloft. A mouse? Or a bat? I stayed squatting on a bale of rotting hay and let my mind wander, finding solace in the quiet darkness, the earthy smells, and the darting grace of a barn swallow. Then it happened. From the rafter, I thought I saw a man hanging from a rope. When I blinked my eyes, he was gone. What had I seen? A morbid image from my mind? A forewarning of tragedy? I've been reading about lynching done in the South to terrorize the freedom fighters. They're murdering real men. This must be stopped. Each lynching murders the humanity of every American.

And now, riots in Watts for past several days, near Los Angeles. Many dead or injured. Confrontations between the police and Blacks. The news made it sound like War!

I must look to nature for comfort—star moss is so soft, pine needles so comforting. Yet I'm stalked by anxiety. I have a crazy obsession. Sometime during the summer, I'm positive a bug will fly into my ear.

I must believe in Louis and me. Our goodness. We're not refugees, weighed down with suitcases and illusions about this country. Louis is first generation, one parent coming from Eastern Russia, the other from Southern Spain. It makes me sad, how he was hounded in grade school for his Yiddish accent. I think each new bloody nose taught him about hate and fear. Am I more "American" because I'm second and third generation, one grandmother from Alsace-Lorraine, another from England? We're the same now, not silent; challenging what words like **choice, freedom,** *and* **equality** *really mean in the face of intolerance and greed.*

Just as my mother found comfort in gardening, I found comfort in sculpting. I have to find other work now for my hands. Massage? Making things—but what? I think I'm somehow looking for that God I prayed to in church as a child to help us find the way.

22
Fire Dragon Street Theater

"Six Lifeless Bodies Found Near Radio in Vermont Shack." Lucina muttered an imagined news flash to her companions sprawled about the living room. "No more playful swallows, no delicate Queen Anne's lace. No star moss. No sunlight…Well, I need cricket sounds, not asphyxiation from Gauloises and Camels!" The nervous twitching around her affirmed her angst. Their retreat was coming to an end, and they'd been captive in this dark room for many days, still without a concrete plan.

Jenny had stopped eating, Louis snapped at everyone, and the day before, Al had scalded his hand badly attempting to entertain Marin. "A pot of hot coffee can't be a talking puppet, Al!" she'd scolded. Luckily a clinic nearby had taken him right in. As for Lucina, she wouldn't go outside without wrapping her head up.

Marin and Jenny plopped down on the tattered couch beside Lucina. "We're holding ourselves hostage, Lucina," moaned Marin. "Punishing ourselves for not being able to change a damn thing." Jenny, pawing at the couch, groaned, "We're going to be swallowed up by this monstrous sofa if we don't come up with a plan today."

Then Louis hollered from his comfortable leather armchair, "We have to focus on the war, damn it!"

"Which one?" Hans snapped from the far corner of the room. "I say we do something about Watts!"

"First things, first, kiddo!" Louis commanded.

Marin suddenly cut the air with karate chops. "I'm getting ready for the pigs, if anyone cares. No matter what we protest, we have to face their billy clubs." Her lips continued moving as her hands froze, making Lucina peer at her with a worried expression.

"Louis is right," Al barked out. "We have to do Vietnam first, then do Malcolm." He too sliced at the air with his bandaged right hand, echoing Marin's jabs.

"What are you guys talking about?" Lucina snarled. "Do this, do that? What is 'do'? We say the same things over and over. How are we going to 'do' anyone when we can't 'do' ourselves?"

"Lucina, that doesn't help." Louis glared at her from his leather throne, making Lucina clench her eyes shut with remorse.

"Let's put a time limit on this, then quit." Jenny stood, raised her arms, then flopped over like a rag doll. "I'm going to town, with you guys or without you." Louis watched her swinging her arms with an amused look.

Al went to the kitchen and brought back a bowl of apples. "This will hold us for thirty more minutes." Marin half-heartedly reached for one, trying to stay with her thought. "Just put those huge photos of the Vietnamese on a stage. Then project a map over them with the names of chemical companies that produce napalm circled in red and the words "Guilty of war crimes. They make napalm." What's the matter, Lucina? Don't like it?"

"I pray it's not DuPont, Marin. They and my dad did send me to college. But if it is, I will join the protests in my hometown. I can see my parents' faces now—I'm already their lost cause. Oh, god, if they'd seen me set my raggle-taggle Jesus on fire in my shows…Do you know who's going to make that horrible stuff, Marin?"

"I know of one company, Lucina. My friend's brother works at Dow Chemical Company. He's a civil engineer and an anti-war activist. Dow is trying to win a Pentagon contract to make napalm. He says it's made very easily, "washtub chemistry" he calls it. Gasoline, benzene, and polystyrene mixed together. It burns and melts the skin and deforms people immediately, if it doesn't kill them. A form of napalm was used in World War II on the Japanese. This will be an improved napalm. If Dow wins the bid, he will quit his job—and it was hard to come by. But this goddamned country is going to be burning up the Vietnamese people any day now with this stuff and we…"

Jenny broke in. "And if my Dad hadn't died of a heart attack at fifty-five, he'd have one now, hearing us criticize companies and put down this country. He was a sergeant in World War II. For him, America was always right, no matter what."

"My woman is keeping track of that shit," Al mumbled in Louis' direction. "We should probably let Hans talk now."

"I was talking, Al. Not Hans!" Jenny retreated to the couch, determined not to lose her cool again. "Men are impossible," she muttered.

Hans flashed Al a smile. "Tak, Al. We could do it in a grocery store. Guerrilla theater. There's a fight over some meat, and then fast—it becomes 'Nam."

"A grocery store?" Louis groaned. "What's wrong with a stage or the street?"

"You don't like anything I say." Hans' face went red.

"Not if it's odd!" Louis eyeballed him. "How do you get people to watch your play in a grocery store?"

"Are we really talking seriously about plays?" Lucina started up. "Is that what all the 'do' is about?"

"Where've you been, Lucina?" Louis was excited now. "Haven't you been thinking the same thing? Some kind of accessible theater?"

"I take it we're talking street theater," Al said. "I agree with Louis. We should stay out on the street, Hans. Bigger crowds."

"We can make a little parade," Lucina said.

"I don't see a pied piper here," Marin quipped.

"Does everything have to be dreary?" Jenny questioned.

"Nobody here plays a fife," Marin returned. "That's all I meant, Jenny."

"We could use a banner to attract people," Louis added, giving Marin a kind look.

"Fuck attract!" Hans barked. "I say stir up. Attack."

Marin shook a finger at him. "I'm tired of your ranting, Mr. Hans." She hesitated a second, then threw up her arms in excitement. "How about a dragon? You know, a giant dragon with fire coming out of—"

"A Fire Dragon!" Jenny cried out. "The avenger of napalm's devastation."

"It's an exciting image—or should I say inciting?" Al offered. "People are afraid of dragons."

"Not of good dragons," Marin returned. "Think Puff, the Magic Dragon."

"Our dragon should inspire fear and trembling in the hawks," Lucina interrupted, "and courage in us."

"Fire Dragon Street Theater," Louis enthused. "Jenny, I like that."

Jenny laughed. "Do I get a bonus?"

"I said 'dragon' first," Marin whined mockingly.

"Now, girls," Al chimed in. "We haven't decided anything yet."

"We're trying to, honey." Marin gave him a playful swat on his good hand and he relaxed.

"Street theater can help people change their minds—I just know it. Banners and parades to build anticipation." Lucina closed her eyes again, her face softening into a smile. Was she remembering her theater sculpture shows? Her *Tall Figures*, her *Rune* on wheels. The excitement of a play?

"At least make people wake up," Jenny added, nudging at Lucina, who looked exhausted.

"So, is this what we're going to do?" Al yawned loudly.

Jenny stood and stretched. "Haven't we had enough talk about it? Ten minutes, folks, and I'm out that door."

"Yes. Devastating photos of burnt Vietnamese," Lucina said, clenching her eyes shut. "I have to agree with you, Marin. They should be in our first play."

"Masks are good too," Al said. "Johnson and McNamara blowing smoke in people's faces."

"No more smoke!" Jenny swatted at the gray mass hanging in the air over them. "We should outlaw smoking."

"What about making a Fire Dragon? Al and Lucina, could you do that? Fire and smoke spewing out of its mouth?" Louis wiped an apple against his chest, then took a large bite of it, looking pleased.

"No to terrifying our audiences," Lucina said. "The Living Theater patented that act."

"Yeah, and what about fire laws, man?" Al said.

"How about a town-crier dragon who spews the news." Marin broke into laughter at her comment.

"Or *The Times* with rhymes." Lucina jostled Marin playfully. "These are good ideas, my friend."

"How can we compete with New York City sirens?" Jenny called out as she moved to the front door, throwing it open with a bang. Cricket chirping poured into the room.

Lucina jumped up excitedly. "Hooray for us! We've decided to make plays. Let's sign an agreement right now."

Hans, who had been quiet since Marin's reproach, moved to Jenny as she stood in the doorway. Turning toward the room, Jenny now sported a mustache made from a lock of her hair. "I'll play the macho guys," she riffed and began gyrating like a rock band guitarist, sending Marin into laughter again.

"You're crazy, Jenny," Marin finally managed. "We're all losing it."

Louis, standing for the first time in three hours, announced in a falsetto voice, "I'll play Lady Bird." He squeezed his legs together, pushing his privates back between his legs.

Lucina reached out to him. "Stop it. I like your little thing."

"It's not so little!" Louis' expression flickered from mock to real embarrassment. He eyed Lucina pointedly.

"It's so difficult to be a gentle man." Lucina started, trying to ignore Louis. "Guys are supposed to be understanding and hard at the same time."

"Oh, you want it hard?" Al shot back with a silly grin.

"Oh Al, you know what she means!" Marin chided. "It's not about the plumbing, it's about the testosterone. Men are the—the killers—in Vietnam." She spoke deliberately, trying for the right words.

"Louis is a loving man!" Jenny let out, bowing her head suddenly.

Hans' eyes darted back and forth between Louis and Jenny. "Black Panther women are faithful to their men," he uttered cryptically.

"I don't know what you're trying to say, Hans." Jenny, still focusing on Louis, started her gyrations again. "Like I said, I'll play the machos."

"Sometimes I'm ashamed to be a man." Louis' comment changed the mood immediately.

"Well, you people are too serious. But I ain't playing any woman." Al reached automatically for his shirt pocket and another cigarette. "Too fuckin' hard!" The pack was empty. He wadded up the wrapping and lobbed it into the straw basket filled with newspapers by the couch. "I just want to know—" He grabbed Marin's shoulders roughly. "Are we really going to do this shit?"

"You mean, do the street theater?" Louis, mirroring Al, began wadding a paper in his hands.

"He means, do the Fire Dragon Street Theater, honey." Lucina went to Louis and kissed his cheek.

"Fucking A, we're going to do it," Al said.

Louis' ball landed solidly in the basket. "Score," he said, grinning broadly.

"I can't believe it!" Lucina shot up from the couch, surveyed her companions, and headed for Jenny and Hans at the open doorway. "Okay, I'm going out there too…" She hesitated, feeling her head and mumbling, "Today might be the day."

"It's just a matter of figuring out how to do it, I guess," Louis said, still pitching wads of paper with Al.

"And where," Hans called back, pulling Jenny down the wooden steps into the sunlight.

*****

When they were alone in their bedroom, Lucina questioned Louis. "Are you really sure you can give up doing your magazine?"

"I'm not giving up *PAN*, Lucina. I'm letting Roy take over for a while."

In the darkness smelling of wet pine and stale smoke, she saw her beloved sculpture *Rune*, her masterpiece—no! She wasn't a *master* and *Rune* wasn't a *piece*. Her sculpture was a *womanwhole,* huddling in a corner of the loft. And she thought of Joel, Louis' son, present and not present in his life. Of course, there had to be many, many sacrifices made in this struggle to right the wrongs… "Don't forget, Louis, it's our baby you're giving over to that kid. I changed my whole life to work on that journal."

"We've got to let go of those babies, Lucina. We've got to let go!"

"Yes. We'll be out in the streets—really fighting the hawks!" She leaned into him, not knowing who needed comforting more.

His hands clamped her shoulders as he pulled her to the bed. She wriggled out of her shorts and T-shirt, looking out the small rippled-glass window showing the field where they'd done their morning stretches: *It could still happen tomorrow, she thought. My obsession. A bug could fly into my ear. It won't happen today because we've finally made a plan. We're going to do what I wanted to do all along. Make a street theater!*

23
Bugged

By the end of August, they had a plan: the Spring Street loft would be their rehearsal and workshop headquarters. Al and Marin already lived nearby on Elizabeth Street; while Jenny and Hans would relocate to the Lower East Side from a mixed neighborhood in the Bronx, where they'd been living. Louis would serve as a consultant for *PAN*, but the Fire Dragon Street Theater would be his main focus, as it would be for Lucina.

Though their four comrades were eager to head back to the city and prepare for their new focus on street theater, Louis and Lucina wanted to hold onto summer a little longer; they would return to the city in a few days.

"Jenny, tell your cousin we'll leave her cabin as clean as we found it," Lucina shouted at the rusty Dodge Dart inching away from the cabin, hands waving from every open window. As the car holding their first little theater family disappeared into a dust cloud, Louis hugged her hard. "Alone at last. What should we do to celebrate, Lucina?" He was more than happy to have them gone—especially Hans, who drove him crazy with his "guerrilla this" and "guerrilla that" bravado.

"Let's call Marge and Ralph to join us for the weekend. Bet they could use some country time."

"I need Lucina time," Louis countered. "Let's think about it. Maybe tomorrow."

"They're good for us, Louis. We're so serious about everything." She remembered the day Louis had introduced her to his old college buddy and Marge, his girlfriend. How anxious she'd been that they like her. Well, they'd had chemistry back then, and it remained in spite of increasing life-style differences. The Conrans were now properly married with secure jobs: Marge, a creative-writing professor at Boston University; and Ralph, a General Electric manager and part-time photographer. Though they owned a Volvo and Charles Eames furniture, they seemed almost apologetic about their middle-class life and couldn't stop heaping praise on Louis and Lucina for living the artist's life in a loft. They were also from the Midwest with family roots similar to her own, which helped make a bridge to her blood family. And they really loved Louis. His deep commitment to the anti-war movement seemed to awe them.

We're close because we're artists, she thought, following Louis back into the stuffy cabin. *They need to make meaning out of their experiences just like we do. If they weren't so comfortably settled, maybe they'd join our street theater gang.*

"Lucina, can't you just be with me for a few days?" They were in the kitchen and Louis was needy and hungry.

"They love Vermont, honey. Marge says it has a scraggy roughness that inspires her stories." Lucina had already imagined the four of them sharing their bedroom; it had two double beds and was the nicest bedroom. And since privacy was being challenged by the group, why not test it with a devoted couple that she really loved? "We can be at ease with them, honey. They already know what they're doing. Come on, loosen up, babe—we're supposed to be open. It's not 'Tea for Two' anymore."

She stopped her goading and watched him pull Marin's leftover dinner dish from the frig.

"No, it's not," he returned. "It's pasta and veggies for two, warmed up on the stove."

As he scooped the mix into two bowls and plunked them down on the small table in front of them, he eyed her sternly. "Listen, I'm not ready to share our bed with anyone, if that's in your mind."

"Not with the Conrans!" she scoffed. "They're like my family—though not judgmental. But you know, if we go on the road, we might have to sleep on cots next to our theater pals. Who knows? Maybe we'll end up in jail together, the guys in one cell and us women in another."

"Lucina, we're going to do street theater, not rob banks!" He pushed a fork toward her. "Eat your food, babe."

"I'm just saying we could expand ourselves first with Ralph and Marge. Just being open. Besides, they're 100 percent monogamous, substantial citizens, and they want kids. It could just be cozy—like a grown-ups' pajama party."

"Tomorrow. We'll talk about it tomorrow. I want to read some Neruda tonight. Have you caught up with your journal writing?"

*****

As Louis read late into the night, Lucina snuggled into him, her short breaths tickling the hairs on his chest. Maybe it was the eerie presence of moonlight in the room, or the cricket rhythms filling the space with a palpable energy—but something inspired her imagination. Still dwelling on Ralph and Marge, she was visited by a colorful dream:

Their two friends were cuddling in the bed next to them. Marge was talking in a dreamy voice about her childhood. "My brother and I used to make onion sandwiches around one o'clock at night. We'd stay up all night playing rummy and eating them."

Louis sat up suddenly, rubbing his eyes. "That's not a sandwich! That's getting ready for a sandwich."

Marge was not put off by his sarcasm. She seemed pleased by his attention. "Oh, how we loved our onion sandwiches. Four thin slices with mayonnaise and salt and pepper, between white bread."

"That's all?" Louis was incredulous.

Lucina hid under her pillow, trying to snuff out convulsive laughter. And Ralph, standing up on the bed, called out to her, "Come on, Lucina. I know you're laughing. What's so funny?"

"Marge's onion slices reminded me: my family allowed only one piece of anything in a sandwich."

Marge, Ralph, and Louis all looked at her with some kind of mock pity. Then Louis, wanting to impress everyone, described the contents of a hero sandwich for twelve from Mangenero's, until Ralph told him to stop because he hadn't eaten any supper.

The dream ended with her offer to make blueberry pancakes with sour cream, topped with bacon and sausages. Her offer made them all so happy they floated like balloons up to the ceiling where they listened to the wind howling with the crickets.

*****

Louis heard her scream. He found her slapping at her head in the bathroom—one ear over the washbowl.

"It's finally happened, Louis," she screamed. "Just like I said it would."

He implored her to wash her face in cold water. Maybe she'd had a terrible nightmare.

"Something flew in my ear while I was asleep. Something's in there."

Her anguish convinced him she was awake and absolutely positive that a bug had at last gone into her ear.

"It's going to lay hundreds of eggs, Louis! They're going to invade my gray matter. I won't be able to talk or move or think. Louis, you've got to stop this destruction."

"I'll pour some warm oil in there," Louis said after a futile attempt to locate the invader with a Q-tip.

"Yes, honey. Try anything."

"Warm oil will feel good," he assured her. "That will get *it* for sure."

"Oh, Louis, thank you so much." Tears flooded her eyes.

"Hey! You're my sweetie. I take care of you."

"I mean for calling the bug *it*, instead of *him*."

"For god's sake, Lucina…" *All the news of bombing Vietnam has made her crazy! When she starts making masks and props for us, she'll feel more herself again.* He fumbled through the chaotic contents of a drawer near the sink. "Who cares if it's an it or a zit?" He found what he was looking for, and went off to find a spoon and a match to warm the oil, muttering how he'd known all along that it wasn't the right time to have Marge and Ralph visit them.

*****

What Louis did not know: Along with her fear that a bug was going to invade her, Lucina had begun to worry about their lovemaking. This had come about after hearing a particular speech by Jerry Rubin in which he'd interpreted America's bombing of Vietnam as the patriarchal penis penetrating the Vietnamese vagina. Though making love with Louis gave her much pleasure, she wondered: What could it mean for her psyche, her self-development—to always be physically entered and not be able to enter in return? Was she merely a vessel to always be filled by his pestle?

167

Remembering that Marge and Ralph had visited them only in her dream, she felt some relief. *They would never have been able to sleep through all her shrieks.* Would they have asked her to describe in great detail what the fluttering feeling was like? Marge might even have seen her as exaggerating the situation, just to make an intriguing story.

Then Louis was back, instructing her to bend her good ear toward the sink as he gently poured the liquid into the bug-infested ear. She could just imagine Ralph commending Louis for his quick thinking.

The warm oil was comforting. The fluttering feeling disappeared. Then she was sobbing and Louis was shuffling her back into bed. She kept the bad ear, her left ear, turned down to the bed, hoping the bug and oil would soon pour out.

Between fitful periods of sleep, she chanted om. Maybe the sound would vibrate her eardrum and force the culprit out.

No dead insect appeared in the morning on the towel under her head.

Lucina stirred the oatmeal as Louis made them coffee. When she let out a whimpering sound, he offered, "When things are still long enough, Lucina, they're probably dead."

She pressed her vulnerable ear against his chest. "So, Louis, since a bug never came out, I have no measurable proof that a bug went in. Do you think I'm a bit nuts?" She saw herself going to the neighbors down the road and asking to use their phone. She would call Marge and Ralph and tell them about her bug obsession and what had happened that night. But would they believe her? Who could say? She loved them—their solid partnership and the way they grounded her and Louis. But Louis still needed time alone with her. They could cherish Marge and Ralph together; remember the wonderful times they'd shared—

and how Ralph's presence at their bizarre marriage rite had been a healing balm. She could make a plan for them to get together in the fall. Certainly by Thanksgiving Louis and she would need a break from their street theater comrades. For now she would force herself to stop thinking about the invisible bug.

PART IV
CHOICE

24

The First Play

Fall was in the air when the troupe of six began meeting in the loft three evenings a week, allowing time for their various day jobs. Their rehearsal sessions focused on theater exercises. Eventually, concrete ideas about the content of their first play would come up as they learned to move and act together. Their aim: alert audiences to the horrors of war through a short drama. Marin and Jenny, with their backgrounds in theater and dance, guided these first workshops, but each of them initiated exercises, inspired by their particular skills and interests, that increased group communication and awareness.

Marin focused on physical exercises done in a circle so each one could see how the others moved. Jenny worked with movements that expressed specific emotions which were imitated and passed around the circle. Lucina stressed mask-like facial expressions that interpretated a wide range of emotions. Hans introduced a stylized way of creating mini-scenes with two actors: one initiating a specific motion/emotion and related fixed facial expression, and the other inventing dialogue appropriate to that expression. Al brought out his guitar and led the group in singing anti-war songs. "Ain't Gonna Study War No More" was a favorite. Louis worked with him, focusing on clear and effective articulation. "If you go off-key a bit, don't worry," Louis suggested. "Just sing like you mean it and loud enough so someone across the street can hear you." They were learning expressive ways to communicate.

After several exercise rehearsals, they were ready to make a play. Lucina started them off with a theme: "Why those of us in our twenties oppose US aggression in Vietnam."

Marin spoke up excitedly. "Al wrote a dynamite short story called *Choice*, about a young man's moral struggle with the draft. I think Sam, the main character, speaks directly to our theme."

"Of course," Louis chimed in. "That's the issue all our brothers are wrestling with. Al and I are exempt now because we're over 25. And Hans—well, you're lucky not to be an American citizen. But think of all the guys being forced to kill—"

"I'm twenty-four and just thankful I'm not a guy," Jenny emoted.

Al, already more comfortable with the others from the singing work, agreed to read his story to them. "'The Star-Spangled Banner; Fourth of July; fire crackers; red, white and blue crepe paper on my bicycle wheels—I was always proud to be an American, just like my folks,' Sam says." From that first sentence to the last—"I don't want to kill the Vietnamese to prove I love my country!"—a heavy silence hung over Al's listeners.

Louis was ready to have them work with it immediately. "We just have to turn that powerful monologue of Sam's into a few dynamite scenes that flesh out his moral dilemma and the choices he's faced with."

"We can use mini-scenes like we've been doing in our exercises," Lucina added. "And add some masks, a song, make a stylized drama." The decision was soon unanimous. They had their character and plot. Now to build a play!

Al's excitement over using his story was palpable. "Guys, look. I've been working on this. I can put Sam's dilemma into scenes for you right now. Scene One: He wrestles with his family's argument, 'We have to combat Communism!' by asking, 'How can destruction of civilians and land have any humane motive?' Scene Two: His new friends' leftist analysis supports his feelings: 'US involvement in Vietnam is blatant exploitation of another country's civil war to occupy a power base in South East Asia.' Scene Three: Then his own realization: 'The US is employing McCarthy scare tactics to manipulate support for its aggression upon this small country.' Scene Four: Sam is devastated when he gets the notice from his draft board to report for a physical. Scene Five: What will Sam decide to do? Enlist and become fodder for an immoral war? Defy the draft and be put in prison? Go into hiding? So, scenes like that."

Excited clapping filled the rehearsal space. Their play would be based on Al's story. And he should guide the work—he'd already conceptualized dramatic scenes they could work with.

Before the next rehearsal, Lucina and Marin investigated techniques used by politically oriented theater companies to express complex emotional situations by physicalizing them. Lucina found photographs of the San Francisco Mime Troop reinterpreting family conflict through physical confrontations using boxing or ropes. "We could have Sam pulled by a rope one way by his dad and another way by his mom," she offered. Marin, familiar with the Living Theater, suggested using their techniques to show how the same object—say a knife, rope, or gun—could be used to harm or to help people. "We can work with this in our last scene when—" She choked up suddenly. "Guns are killing weapons. They should never have been invented!"

Jenny, Hans and Louis dug into their own backgrounds to root out their emotional reactions when they stood in opposition to power figures like their parents, their teachers, or an organization. They then developed group exercises for expressing those emotions.

At the next rehearsal, it was Marin who came up with a punchy, stylized technique for building scenes. "Using the scenes Al outlined to us last time, we can freeze the essential action in poses like Lucina did with dancers in her *A Sculptor's Theater* shows. Like this—watch me! This is Sam confronting his parents." Marin twisted her body grotesquely. "Sam's body first bends out of shape, but then—watch!" She sprang up, squaring her shoulders. "He stands tall and tells them his viewpoint. Whoever plays Sam uses body language to speak, and someone else says the dialogue. Okay? And this is how you show Sam refusing to be intimidated at the induction center." She took on an exaggerated pose, similar to a karate combatant warding off an attacker. For each scene outlined by Al, she demonstrated dramatic mime movements to tell Sam's story.

Lucina was impressed. "I love how you're incorporating mime in our work, Marin. In the street, our gestures have to be exaggerated. See, Hans—Marin understood what I was doing in my sculpture shows! Dancers miming and taking on freezes that made a conversation with my sculptures. We want clear, compelling images more than heady dogma."

Jenny spoke up loudly. "Let's not come down on Hans. It's his exercise—joining movement, freezes and dialogue—that's giving us a technique to work with. All of us have to let go of preconceived notions of what makes a play a play, damn it! We're not doing Shakespeare. I mean, let's keep true to what we said in Vermont: 'Collectively, we'll find the way to be artists-who-will-help-stop-the-war.' No head honcho here! So cool it, Lucina."

Others spoke up as well: "We're inventing our own style…We don't have a blue print…We're improvising together." At one rehearsal, when Lucina began an academic discourse on Duchamp's explorations of movement, the Futurists' wit, and how Dadaists had influenced Happenings, there was general dissent. They didn't need Professor Lucina to lecture them! Workshops were about building *Choice*!

Along with movement, acting, and projection exercises, the troupe with both Al and Marin's guidance began to construct a series of highly stylized friezes or frozen tableau, to be meshed with short narratives. In this way complex emotional material could be presented in a simplified manner. Jenny said it reminded her of her Sunday school's presentations of the nativity story. Al said it was like making a serious comic strip.

The actors learned to change tableaux with rapid-fire precision: they showed the father, grasping a rope tied to Sam and pulling him to serve; then Sam's mother, pressing for conscientious objector status, yanked at him with her rope. Marin wondered how the group would feel if they had the mother suggest, uncomfortably, that he claim to be homosexual. "Or mentally challenged?" Hans piped up. At the play's turning point, when Sam had to make a choice at his draft board, Louis showed how they could show him transforming into a new kind of hero—not the patriot Uncle Sam points his finger at, but Citizen Sam, who because he loves his country speaks out for nonviolence and each country's right for self-determination. "At this point," Louis observed, "he can tell his family and friends, 'Vietnam belongs to the Vietnamese.'"

One frieze showed a stone-faced army officer holding Sam's draft card, renamed "Sam's death portent." In the next, Sam clutched the two ripped halves of his draft notice. With Sam's idealistic and super-responsible refusal to serve in an unjust war, the actors decided that his character would not accept the inhumane punishment of possible imprisonment. So how would they end the play: He runs away to Canada? He contemplates suicide?

Lucina asked to direct the ending scene. "Sam will hold a gun to his temple as he stares at photographs of burnt children," she suggested. "Every muscle in him is tensed to foreshadow his possible death at his own hand. This terrifying image will start a debate: how can this senseless war be stopped, so responsible young men like Sam won't consider killing themselves? That's how powerful this final image must be!"

Both Marin and Jenny strongly disagreed with this ending.

"To even show Sam considering taking his own life is immoral and irresponsible," Marin commented. "How can we suggest such a thing to other young men caught in this dilemma?"

Jenny chimed in. "Buddhist monks are already immolating themselves in protest. We need to end murder, not promote it."

Marin continued, adamant. "We're making powerful images. Let's show Sam being a warrior for peace. I don't want anyone killing themself in a play I'm working on!" Clearly distraught, she stood up abruptly from her chair and headed to Al in tears. As he comforted her, the others seemed confused, not comprehending her strong reaction. Lucina's attempts to talk to her were repelled. Tension around the scene had bent everyone out of shape—they needed time-out.

*****

When they reconvened, Lucina defended herself with Marin and Jenny. "Look, I get what you're saying. Sam is not actually going to kill himself. It's just one solution that comes into his mind. Haven't we all thought of it?"

Her head shaking *no!* to this defense, Marin cried out sharply, "Some people have tried it! Or known someone else who actually did it," she added. As her face wrenched in uncontrollable spasms, she gave Lucina a desperate look. But Lucina, staring into space, was grasping for her owns thoughts.

*****

After much debate, the gun-to-the-head image would stay. The majority concluded that Sam's tragic assumption as embedded in the image—he has no choice—could be the driving irony of their play: young people, by refusing to kill others for their country, were feeling forced to kill themselves instead. But to dispel any possible confusion about the actors' intent in *Choice,* they would add an anti-war, anti-death song to this final image, with all five of them singing directly to Sam, "Listen, brother. Better to live for one's country than to die. Citizens all, we must stop these senseless deaths—we must rise. We must stop the war now!"

When they began to rehearse the scene, Marin was once again adamant. "Please, please, you guys. I need to sing the song alone, to Sam. And after all, Al is playing Sam."

Perplexed by Marin's moods, the group tried to reason with her. "Marin, try to understand," Jenny spoke. "We don't want it to look like one woman is sorrowing for her man."

"Look at it this way," Hans added. "A chorus is all the people—in solidarity."

"Yes," Lucina chimed in, glad that Hans had gradually become less edgy and was adding such good energy. "That's it. Sam's tragedy is not only personal—it's a whole country's dilemma!"

"I understand what everyone is saying," Louis enthused. "Change happens when groups of people work together. That's what we're all about here."

Al, at first watching these interactions from the posed, perplexed persona of his Sam character, suddenly became himself again, fiercely needing to protect his Marin. "Marin needs to do it!" he cried out vehemently. "It's you guys that don't understand! Just like Sam's clueless family! Damn it! She needs an audience to hear her pain. All kinds of people—gays, guys, parents. It's not about her ego!" Marin broke into uncontrollable sobs. Always so careful not to sit on the gritty cement of Lucina's studio, she suddenly sank to the floor in a mound, covering her head with her hands.

While the others stayed silent, Marin slowly pulled herself up and stood before them, tears still streaming down her face. "I'm sorry, I'm sorry for my—I haven't talked about this to anyone, only Al—not even you, Lucina—" As she spoke, she continued looking at Lucina as if timidly checking for her friend's reactions. "My brother Michael was younger—but we understood each other. Sometimes I felt he was my twin. My friends said we were so serious. Actually, we were both sensitive and that's why we were so melancholy. He was a drug user in high school. Just before he was to graduate, Michael shot himself in our garage. I found him—dead."

The sounds coming towards her—expressing empathy and shock—encouraged her to continue.

"He left us a note. Our parents were so devastated and puzzled. But I understood his message. He wrote: 'Cory will know why this was the only way.' That's all he wrote. Well, Cory was his friend all through grade school and junior high, who had moved away because his dad was in the navy. We hadn't seen Cory for years. But I knew, I just knew what he was trying to tell us. But you have to understand—I couldn't talk about this with our parents then." She stopped again, her eyes moving to meet those filling with tears. "Michael loved Cory— he never had a single girlfriend; I mean like dating a girl. He was gay—my brother was gay and he couldn't talk about it. Nobody talked about it. In fact, it wasn't supposed to exist—what did Oscar Wilde's lover call it, 'the love that dares not speak its name?' Well, it had awful names in our school—any time a kid hugged another kid of the same sex, someone snickered, 'faggot boy,' 'bull dyke.' It was sick, sick! They must have tormented Michael…"

Marin awkwardly scrubbed her face with her hands as if to wash away the grief. "That's it. Now you know what makes me not here. I'm just not here at times. In this world…No more! I can't say any more."

*****

Marin's abrupt exit left the group raw and hurting. Jenny was the first to speak to their shared unease. "It's clear to me, and I hope to all of you. If anyone has the right to the song, Marin does."

Lucina, stunned by Marin's account, struggled with an apology. "I wasn't sensitive—I didn't hear Marin's agony—Oh, I'm so sorry…I'll make it up to—" She broke off, leaving the space to find her friend. There was no more discussion. The song belonged to Marin!

At the next rehearsal, Marin's passionate alto voice filled them with awe, like a prayer. "Can't we live, not die for our country, for our loves! All life is precious. All love is sacred," she sang out. The song ended. "Not one more person should die in this war!"

Louis told her, "I'm so sorry for your loss of Michael. He must have been a beautiful, caring person, like you are. I feel I'm seeing you for the first time, Marin."

*****

The Fire Dragon Street Theater first performed *Choice* at the *Open Forum Newspaper* benefit in October. On a makeshift stage in front of enlarged photos of Vietnamese women and children burned by napalm, Sam's story was told through dramatic friezes, narration, and Brechtian songs. A review came out in the next issue of *Open Forum* filled with praise for the troupe's innovative style in denouncing the war. It ended with the comment, "The gung-ho news reels of American World War II inductees marching enthusiastically and patriotically to war have at last been given a face-lift with this 1960s morality drama exposing the tragedy young men face in all wars."

The stark style brought mixed reactions from the audience. In particular, the final scene and Sam's suggested suicide set off intense pushback. One young man in the front row, with political buttons all over his jacket, scoffed, "You guys should be giving us alternatives. Aren't you working with the Left? Don't you have a vision of change?"

Suggestions were shouted out to the actors: "Sam can escape to Canada, England, Europe…He can help build a global anti-war movement…He can enlist students from all over the world to demonstrate against the war…Why shouldn't he stay in this country, go underground and be a voice for the Movement, like the political prisoners do from their jail cells?"

The audience had taught them. Al took the criticisms to heart. "I knew it was a dumb ending," he grumbled. "I shouldn't have let you guys convince me and Marin otherwise."

Lucina addressed him, "Look, Al, I know I was the one who insisted on the suicide scene, but at least *Open Forum* saw my point. Shit, Man, we all have things to learn. The important thing is we sparked a lot of thinking."

Their critics had forced them to think deeper. Why hadn't they let Sam break out of his morally driven death stance and become an outrageous, courageous activist? But wait! There shouldn't be only one resolution; there should be dialogue with the audience spurred by the questions: What can Sam do? And what would you do if you were in Sam's shoes? With many requests to perform for anti-war coalitions in the city, at each performance they could explore different ways of resolving Sam's dilemma. The ending of the play would actually stir up new beginnings.

It was Al who inadvertently came up with a logo for their first flyer. Another of his coffee-pot-puppet spills, landing on Lucina's tablecloth, formed a shape very much like a leaping dragon. She developed the shape, adding teeth, flames, and a longer tail, making an eye-catching silhouette of a Fire Dragon. They now had a solid play and a gutsy logo.

25
A Hard Act to Follow

On November 2, 1965, performances of *Choice* were brought to a standstill. Yale pacifist Norman Morrison had just immolated himself outside the Pentagon to protest the wanton killing of children in a Vietnamese village. Movement groups stopped doing benefits; it was a time for mourning and introspection. That a professor from the privileged classes would ignite and kill himself under McNamara's office windows irrevocably changed the tenor of protest throughout the country. By sacrificing his life, the man had seared his image on the American soul.

Compared with Morrison's deeply conscientious and horrible death, the ideals, the scholarly research, and the artful morality plays born from the peace movement seemed the pandering of the privileged. All during December, members of the Fire Dragon Street Theater saw themselves as just another breed of political intellectual, not that different from the armchair radicals many in the group had come to scorn.

Then in January 1966, when movement leaders Tom Hayden, Staughton Lynd, and Herbert Aptheker returned from the Hanoi peace talks, the doves and the hawks broke out in undisguised hostility. Demonstrations became battlegrounds. Cops no longer showed restraint: they shot off canisters of mace, cracked down hard with clubs. The students retaliated by throwing rocks and sometimes molotov cocktails. Many street theater groups would not perform at these violent confrontations; a twenty-minute play needed a period of calm to be witnessed.

*****

But as spring approached, the theater group leapt into motion again. They would become a living newspaper and respond to each new event, using the techniques they'd developed for *Choice*. They would travel outside New York City and perform at colleges, inspiring anti-war rallies by students. They'd learned some lessons about nudging the Movement forward. They wouldn't use the popular "Turn on—drop out" chant, but slogans like "Mobilize against the war, mobilize for justice" and "Speak out—fight back." Along with performances of *Choice*, they could do workshops with the students, giving them techniques for building their own political theater groups while finishing their college work.

They had many pivotal events to dramatize. They would interpret Norman Morrison's immolation at the Pentagon, the shooting of Black citizens in Watts, the grape pickers' strike, La Huelga. They questioned themselves regularly: Shouldn't they have an ecology play and a play about the massacre at Wounded Knee as well? And what about having women protagonists for a change?

*****

Sometimes the actors dressed like guerrilla soldiers, sporting used army shirts and boots. At other times, gypsy-like, they tied on bandannas and donned bright casual clothes, letting their bodies breathe. Lucina wrote in her journal: *I carry my*

186

grandmother's guitar on my hip like a rifle and wail out like a banshee.

Louis wondered if Lucina's stepped-up political zeal was some kind of exaggerated reaction to her repressive Protestant upbringing. Not only was she strutting about with her guitar in a cocky manner, she was threatening to give all her sculptures and drawings away.

"Lucina, you warn me about being extreme—like how I sometimes rant on and on if I think someone has acted stupidly. Remember Tamborcini? And I know sometimes you can't take how I read my poems. Like I'm too much. Too forceful. Well, I'm not afraid to tell you you're going overboard. This idea of giving all your artwork away is insane. I know it's been hard to give up sculpting and have your studio taken over by our crew. But what are you up to?"

"Not just making things on my own—that's over with, Louis! I'm not alone anymore, fretting about not doing enough. There's all the work we've done together on *Choice*. Our group is sharing the burden to make a difference. And it's fun, thinking with all of us. It's giving me energy, hope. I want to be a radical. I want to give myself completely to stopping this war!"

"You've been getting too chummy with Hans! Listen, we're complex, you and I. We're political but we're artists as well. Keep your damn artwork. I love it. I love your work, Lucina. Someday you'll go back to it."

She couldn't believe it: Louis was crying real tears over her work. And then she was crying with him. Of course he was right. She'd wanted to escape how hard it all was. She'd wanted things to be simple but they weren't.

"You're right, honey. I'm sorry. There's a part of me when I get an idea in my head, I don't want to let go of it. Like my insistence that Sam put the gun to his head. Why can't I see clearly sometimes?"

"Maybe you let your emotions lead you?"

"Or maybe I don't let my deeper emotions instruct me, Louis."

No more was said about giving away artwork; *Rune* stayed safely wrapped in her sheet in the corner of the theater's rehearsal space along with the other pieces. Still, Lucina knew that eventually she might have to store them somewhere. The theater work was taking off; it was inevitable Fire Dragon would have to go where the action was.

Journal Entry. March 3, 1966: When we do go on tour, we'll probably have to get rid of the loft or sublet it, if that's allowed. Everyone is moving, it seems, like it's all one big Happening. But some people are running for their lives. I've got to plan a little ahead, if I can. I'll probably dissemble **Poet, Arrival,** *and* **Door.** *Maybe friends can each take a section. I hope the paintings of the Vietnamese, the drawings of Louis and my mother, and my other very best drawings can stay in the Spring Street loft. They can hide in the area between the storage closet and the ceiling. And if I sublet, that will be one of the conditions for whoever takes the place. The only sculpture I will keep will be* **Rune.** *Marin's friend Shauna Cozen has a big loft and Marin said she really likes* **Rune.** *Her jewelry business doesn't take up that much space. If she would take* **Rune** *I could even pay her. I need someone to take care of my womanwhole until we've ended this war. Simple as that.*

When I told my mother I had to let go of some of my sculptures, she got quiet. She really only likes some of my small student pieces anyway. She actually said to me last year, "You wanted to be an artist so you could be different." Before that it was, "Since you're different, Lucina, it follows that you would be an artist." Why does she have to figure me out? Now she probably thinks I'm nuts, one of those mindless rabble-rousers who make a lot of noise. I have faith that when she sees our plays, she will understand at last. I am her daughter, after all. You know what? I'm afraid to ask her what she really thinks of me now. She can't keep track of what I'm up to, and I can't keep track of what she thinks of me.

Of course, she thinks Louis is leading me around by the nose. How could I suddenly stop making art when I told her it was like life and death to me? Obviously, in her mind I'm under his influence now. She sees me as a chicken without a head, proselytizing for violence. She doesn't understand protest—pulling your head out of the sand and shouting for what's right. She always said she was a Mr. Milquetoast. Grin and bear it. Of course her hands are tied—that's what she told me once—because she never untied them. Well, we're untying our voices and speaking our truths! A lot of people think we're inciting unlawful behavior. When I told her Fire Dragon Street Theater might perform in Watts this winter, she said, "Are you going around starting fires?" That was so insulting! I left their house immediately, with no plans to return for some time.

Father keeps a safe distance from me, not commenting on my political activities at all. I guess he wants his wife to handle me. But when it comes to commenting on my sculptures, he doesn't hold back. When I told them our theater group would travel to wherever we were needed, and asked if they could store some of my pieces in their garage, they said they did not want my things on their property. As if my pieces might come alive and trash their house or something. That's when Father made the crack about five dollars and my work. "I'll give you five dollars to throw the whole lot of them in the river." How could my own father talk to me like that! I wanted to kill him. They're just like that gallery owner in Chicago. I wanted to punch that smug guy, telling me he couldn't sell my things because "they aren't dustable." On the other hand, he could have said, "Because they're ugly!" It isn't even true that art that can't be dusted doesn't sell. What about Tom Doyle's humungous wood sculptures? They're rough beams hacked out with a handmade ax. And Lee Bonticou's relief paintings look like the insides of drainage pipes. Even Noguchi's rough-stone monoliths are dust collectors. But does somebody go over them with a toothbrush? These guys sell big-time.

Actually, I should find that gallery guy and thank him. His thing about "dustable" drove me to make **A Sculptor's Theater** *shows and keep my pieces alive with music and dance. Forget about selling them. My sculptures have too much value for price tags. And look! If I hadn't done those sculpture shows, maybe I would never have thought about doing street theater.*

26
No More War

Lucina looked out the loft windows: the weather report was wrong! It was a beautiful day. May Day. They would perform *Choice* again, the ever-evolving *Choice*. Crowds of people would be in Central Park hungry for a play. With all those new green leaves making them feel good, they would breathe hope. On a day like this, the idea of Sam going into hiding and building an underground movement for peace might even strike a Republican onlooker as a possible way to go.

Once more she reviewed the ending they'd come up with, the ending that was always changing. Sam still held a gun in his hands to remind the audience that not only are soldiers expected to use guns in 'Nam, but American citizens are also allowed guns to protect themselves. *And of course the N.R.A. is a huge political force in this country. Our gun-obsessed, violent country!* Lucina's mind was racing. *Who told me that group claims to be America's longest-standing civil-rights organization? That it was founded by religious leaders who wanted to protect freed slaves from the Ku Klux Klan? That's baloney! Mainly the Right supports it and the Right doesn't fight for civil rights. Confusing.*

Now Marin and the chorus would make it clear that Sam would not use his gun to kill for his country. The song asked, "If Sam goes underground, will he carry a gun along? Or, will he put it down, and with his body and his voice be strong? Sam, be nonviolent. Sam, be strong!" Louis came up with a great ending to the play: "What choices does Sam have? What can each of us do to stop our government from waging war in Vietnam?" He transformed the play into a real-time dialogue with the audience.

By mid-morning Louis and Lucina, nervous sheep dogs, rounded up the others. "Time to get going! Several of us will have to carry the Fire Dragon."

Their dragon, a twenty-foot-long construction of papier mâché and cloth over wire, which could be disassembled into sections for easy transport, would be used for the first time. A definite crowd gatherer. "We have to be mindful," Louis counseled the new recruits, Hugh, Courtney, Jack, and Joan. "We want to attract people, not frighten them; frightened people are unpredictable." They would each carry a section of the dragon in a large canvas bag. And Al would carry the red drum, Louis and Lucina the musical instruments. Marin, Hans, and Jenny would take the large plastic boxes holding their props and flyers.

Lucina, remembering Hugh from Tamborcini's *Breaking Out* show, had given him a call to come to a workshop. "We're adding live music to our images," she'd told him. He'd come to an open workshop with his pal Courtney, both eager to join the troupe and do something creative and political. Friends since attending the High School of Music and Art, they'd each gone to college for a couple of years, Hugh to Goddard and Courtney to Bard, when they decided to drop out of academia and back into the New York art scene. Courtney acted in Off-Off-Broadway shows and Hugh played jazz gigs in the Village.

They were thrilled to be embraced without further tryouts and interviews.

"You guys have guts," Courtney enthused.

"We saw *Choice* a while back, at the Open Forum," Hugh added.

They went on. "We're with you—challenge a system built on racism and violence."

"Fight slavery, like in our Civil War."

"Those that fail to learn from history—"

"—are doomed to repeat it."

The troupe members clapped vigorously for their obviously rehearsed comments.

Jack, brought in by Marin, was another welcome newcomer with his background in yoga, meditation, and mime. Lucina felt his training in self-awareness would balance the more free-spirited members. Jack asked if his girlfriend, Joan, trained in acting and meditation, could help them out at times as backup.

While the others readied to leave, Hans, blond hair covering his shoulders like a shawl, leaned against the loft wall, smoking. He was observing the scene more like a visitor than a participant.

"Aren't you psyched up yet, Hans?" Louis couldn't hide a grimace. "We need you to carry props and flyers. And no, we will not shoot smoke out the dragon's nostrils. Too many crazies ready to accuse us of arson already. We got to be mindful."

Lucina tensed with Louis' mistrust of Hans. *Yet the guy did seem to be hovering, sniffing out an opportunity to what? Create tension?* She put a hand on Louis' arm and pulled him toward her. Their suspicion of Hans was no good. "How much money do you think we can pull in, honey?" She gave him a quick kiss.

"We have to do six performances to bring in the three hundred bucks we need," he answered quickly, still eyeing Hans who stood in the doorway looking glum.

"You know, I have a weird feeling about today," Jenny commented as she bent easily from the hips to pick up a prop box filled with small masks, crushed felt hats and flyers which she quickly handed over to Hans. "Maybe it's my cramps. I can't wait till we're back at the loft, drinking beer and counting our coins, just like greedy capitalists."

"Starvation wages, I'd say!" Hans snorted his comment and cigarette smoke at Louis before bolting out the door with his load.

Louis sputtered back, "Asshole."

*****

Out on Spring Street, they made last-minute decisions. Should they wear their colorful bandannas and caps on the subway? Yes! Draw attention. Let New Yorkers know the Fire Dragon Street Theater would perform that afternoon in Central Park. Marin had a few flyers to pass out on the train. They would be performing on the stone area by Tavern on the Green between one and five o'clock, in the hope of pulling in more upscale folk and bigger collections. They should tell people!

In the crowded subway car, Al's new ideas for the wrap-up were passed along. "When Sam contemplates the gun in his hands, and just as the chorus finishes singing, before Louis opens up the discussion, that's when we should work the audience. We can be chanting, 'Help us build a movement to stop the war.' Maybe if people chant with us, they'll be more generous with their handouts. What do you think? After that Louis can begin a dialogue with them."

*****

"Why are we there, killing Vietnamese?" Louis' shouted question reverberates like a trumpet call as the actors weave their way from the edge of Sheep Meadow onto the roadway leading to Tavern on the Green's patio. A large swarm of park revelers, pulled by the troupe's impromptu parade, their haunting question, gyrating dragon puppet, colorful banner, and snappy drum beats, now gather around the actors as they set up a stage area on the restaurant's flagstones.

When everything's in place—musical instruments, props, colorful plastic boxes for actors to stand on, Hugh whistles a tune on the fife. Al joins him with a rhythm on the wood block and tambourine, while Lucina keeps a slow, steady beat on the red drum. The five actors still inside the dragon's body circle their playing area and welcome the crowd as Louis addresses them directly: "Our play is called, Choice. As we take you into the life of Sam, a twenty-one-year-old American about to receive his draft notice, ask yourselves: 'Is it our war to fight? Does he have to go? Does he have a choice?"

But wait! Who's that young man dressed in a clown suit hovering by Louis? The clown whispers, "Watch out. There's a turf war in the park today. Cops are beating down on some hippies in Sheep Meadow right now!" Then the white-faced messenger, his bulbous red nose bobbing, flees into the crowd.

"Louis, what did that guy want?" Lucina cups her question guardedly, still beating on the drum.

"Okay, change of plans." Louis motions the others closer to him. "Don't engage the audience at all. The fuzz are getting antsy. Do the play exactly as we worked out. And don't react if the cops show up here. Just pass the hats then snap, we do the show again. Understand?"

A blast on the shofar; a ra-ta-ta-ta-tat of drumbeats. Hugh, Louis and Al chant in unison, "How many men? How many men, women, and children have been killed today?" The play has begun. As the chant continues, Marin and Jack start the first frieze. They pose as Sam's mom and dad, mimicking Grant Wood's *American Gothic* couple in front of a farmhouse. Instead of pitchfork and broom, they clutch an American flag, a rifle, and a giant photo of Sam, labeled "Our son."

Sam, played by newcomer Courtney, enters the frieze, a rope tied around his waist. His mother, played by Marin, holds one end, while a Vietnamese woman, played by Hans, holds the other. Mother shows the back of her son's photo, with the printed statement "We hate Commies. Go ahead, President Johnson, kill those monsters." The Vietnamese Woman holds up a sign: "Two of my babies were killed today." Sam, pulled in opposite directions by Mother and the Vietnamese Woman, freezes in a pose of tortured anguish.

Louis mounts his soap box and begins narrating: "As you know, American military forces are fighting a war today in South East Asia, in a small country called Vietnam. Most of us never heard of this country, never said its name, until the summer of 1964, when our forces..."

Lucina proudly watches Louis. His golden bandanna and silvery cape turn his skin dark. *My Sephardic troubadour is prince of the park today,* she thinks.

"Many of us have friends, brothers, sons in Vietnam," Louis continues. "We have serious questions about that war. Why are we there, killing Vietnamese? Think about this question as we take you into the life of Sam, a twenty-one-year-old American who is about to receive his draft notice. Think with Sam. Is it really our war to fight?"

Lucina surveys the faces pressing in on them. Curiosity, confusion, even contempt flood into her. *God*, she prays, *let them open up to us.*

After another blast from their shofar, Sam's story unfolds through a progression of friezes and Louis' narration, accompanied by a slow, pronounced drumbeat. By the final scene, the rhythm and loudness of the beat intensifies.

Gradually, the audience becomes attentive, some even simpatico. By the time Marin and the chorus sing the last song, some onlookers begin crying out, "No, no, he won't go!"

As Sam freezes into his final pose, that of the conscientious objector, Louis states again each progressive decision made by Sam. "He will not go to prison…He will not commit suicide… He will go underground and work with other resistors." But why the sudden silence from Louis and the drum? The dramatic rhythm of the play has broken! The crowd is alerted; something seems amiss. Sam breaks from his freeze; where is his prop? The actors are baffled, disturbed. Where's Hans with the gun? He's supposed to hand it to Sam with Louis' final comment, a question: Shouldn't resistors be able to protect themselves?

But there is no Hans. There is no gun. Courtney playing Sam improvises and mimes the weapon's shape and weight, caressing the stock, fingering the trigger. Louis also fills the sudden gap. "Is this really our war to fight? Think with Sam, what should he do? What is his choice? What is *our* choice?" Lucina follows up with a series of drumbeats, and then abruptly motions the actors to fan into the audience with hats to collect donations.

Spectators nearest the stage area back up suddenly as if to protect themselves. From what? The dragon! They don't know that it's Hans wearing the dragon mask, darting about frenetically without its body.

Louis whispers sharply at the dragon's head now coming toward him. "What the hell are you doing, Man? Get out of that mask! The gun, Hans! Give Sam the gun!" His voice rising to a shout can be heard by the onlookers.

The crowd, excited by the frenzied dragon mask, takes up the chant: "Hell no! He won't go. No, no, no, Sam won't go!"

Jarring shouts erupt again, this time coming from the spectators on the flagstones leading to the roadway. Momentarily, two policemen, anger tightening every muscle in their faces, slash their way through the aroused crowd to confront the actors.

One points at Louis. "That guy with the beard and cape!"

"Yeah, the big mouth. Let's get him," the other snarls.

Dragon-headed Hans darts pell-mell into the crowd. Jenny, clutching the Fire Dragon Street Theater banner, tracks him like a hawk, her face frozen in disbelief, anger, and fear. *He's gone crazy—he didn't listen to Louis!* She just knew something bad was going to happen in the park today.

*****

The uniformed men tear Louis from his soap box, rip the silver cape from his back, and hurl it in Lucina's direction. Grabbing him by the belt, they drag him through the jarred and baffled crowd across the rough flag stones to their waiting squad car, a silent accomplice. Not one spectator moves to stop the assault. Are they wondering: Is this part of their play? Like that crazy dragon?

Lucina rushes at the attackers, screaming, "Leave him alone, bastards!"

Al is behind her, grabbing at her arms, trying to pull her back. "Lucina, stop it! They'll get you, too!"

"Louis, Louis!" she shrieks. "They're going to kill him!" She claws for the cop jabbing his stick into Louis' ribs, as the other rams him into the back of the squad car.

"Don't you hurt him! I'll kill you monsters. I'll kill you!"

Al throws his arms about her, pulling her away from the moving car. Through the rear window, Lucina sees the cop coming down on Louis again. Now she knows what they're doing! They're going to take him to a secluded spot in the park, beat him mercilessly, and leave him there, unconscious.

*****

Lucina could not find the words to address the congregation gathered at the Tavern on the Green, bearing confused witness to the attack on Louis. She saw them as mourners at a funeral. The cops had murdered her Louis.

But Al came through. He mounted Louis' soap box and explained what had just taken place. "Right before your eyes, two New York City policemen dragged off Louis Altman, one of our actors, and probably right at this moment they are beating the hell out of him. Is this a real democracy? Is this a free country? I don't think so. Where is there justice for Sam? Where is there justice for Louis? We have to pack up now and go find our brother." He was off the soap box now, holding back sobs, holding himself together, imploring onlookers to serve as witnesses to the assault. Would they give him their names and phone numbers so that when this attack was brought up in court…? "Yes, the Fire Dragon Street Theater will take this to court! Justice for Louis will be carried out." He could not continue.

Several went to him with their cards and avowals to show up in court and bear witness. One, dressed better than most, still looking ironed and unruffled, handed his card to Lucina. He was a lawyer. "I was eating lunch inside. Heard all the shouting … I've been wanting to get a hook in with you people. That war is crazy. This stuff with the police is even crazier. We've got to stop it."

"Will you go with us—now—to look for Louis?" Lucina begged, clutching his arm.

He nodded, grim-faced. "I've got a few hours, let's go. They're probably booking him in the park's precinct right now."

Lucina, Al, and Joseph Solares, the lawyer, headed for the precinct, while the other actors gathered up the props and instruments. All this time, a small group of young people huddled together. Holding hands, they rocked and chanted softly, "Tell Sam, we won't go. No—No—No more war. We won't go. No!"

*****

It was seven in the evening when they were able to get Louis released from the Central Park Precinct. Mr. Solares, enraged by his unjust and cruel beating, acted as his lawyer. Louis had not been locked up but kept in a holding room; his supposed crime was resisting arrest. When Al and Lucina got him into a cab with them, Louis, in shock and pain, could only stammer out what he'd gone through.

"They hid their car—beside a stone bridge. 'My brother's fighting for scum—like you.' That's what he said—the one who beat me. It's because I'm a Jew—kept calling me 'Commie Jew boy'.

Lucina could see bloody welts on his scalp—his wrists raw from the handcuffs. He cringed and jerked when she tried to stroke him. "We'll get you to a doctor, sweetheart. We'll take them to court—those pigs. The lawyer got their names and badge numbers. Did they break anything? They'll pay for this!"

"Kept whacking my back with their clubs—then I said, 'you bastard,' and Petrocelli, he had a Brooklyn accent, threw me against their car and whacked me again. The other one kept saying, 'Take it ease Joe'—his name, I think, was Tommy." Louis looked down at his crotch—"Can you still see it, Lucina? I peed in my pants, couldn't help it."

Al, sitting in front, directed the driver. In the back seat, Lucina was holding him with her eyes, fists clamped shut, afraid her touch would feel like more blows. Louis, his head sinking into his chest, gritted his teeth, trying to hold back sobs. Lucina heard Al talking to himself and saw the driver's sharp glances in the cab's rearview mirror, as they sped down the West Side Highway toward West Houston Street. *Probably wants to get rid of us as fast as possible!*

"What, Louis? What are you trying to tell me?"

"Should have—fought the bastards—harder."

"No, sweetheart—it's me—I didn't protect you!" She knew right then: *this brutality on his soul and body will remain a terrible humiliation for both of us for a very long time.*

27

The Parks Belong to the System

Lucina stared out the window of the loft at the cobble stone street two floors below. The stones were as gray as the day. The shrouded shape to her left kept pulling at her, chilling her. It was her *Rune* sculpture, still wrapped in its white sheet for protection. Protection from what? Definitely not from blows from a billy club!

Louis was still sleeping in their loft bedroom. She'd tended to him all night—ice packs, compressors, Tylenol and keeping his back and head raised—all to ease his pain. She hardly slept, watching for any bleeding or increased discomfort. Al was on call with his truck, should they need to take Louis to an emergency ward.

She shuddered, suddenly feeling pelted by blows, like Louis had been. There was no protection here. The white sheeting around her sculptures seemed to be gags, silencers. Something essential in her life had been snuffed out—not only sculpting but innocence as well. And now the person that meant the most to her was in shock, covered with welts and bruises. She understood his brooding, accusing eyes: nothing, no one, could ever repair the humiliation brought upon him. Thank God they'd rescued him from that park precinct, booked on phony

201

charges: disturbing the peace, resisting arrest. And not any charges against the two police officers who attacked him!

Suddenly, Louis was calling out to her from the bed. She found him struggling to sit up right.

"You, my Lucina, took care all night! I felt your sweet love. Don't worry. My sores will heal. What's important—our play. It's really good. Damn it! Did you hear—everyone was shouting when those jerks were grabbing me."

Her beloved Louis! He was strong. His life force would always prevail. It was weak of her to be so despondent. She couldn't help it; her chest and back ached with him. That young liberal lawyer, Joseph Solares, would help them press charges.

"Just rest, honey. Are you comfortable? I'll make you some breakfast now. Today you must rest."

As she prepared coffee and oatmeal, her mind wandered back—before the street theater, before the work on *PAN*, before she knew about Vietnam and Mississippi, when she was still innocent, a sculptor showing off her work. Ignorant was more like it! *Remember how Louis said tinklow for tinkle and mellow— the sound Rune's xylophone made when he ran his finger nails up and down her keys? How it had touched her. That was before the war had forced them to follow its horrifying beat.*

But *Rune* had brought them together, and she was still there with them, through thick and thin, along with Lucina's other works, also wrapped. They were lined up against the wall by *Rune*. If they hadn't come first, there would be no *Rune*, she must remember that.

When Mr. Solares called to follow up about Louis, he needed Lucina to understand something. "No one in your group has the kind of money it would take to confront the police department, Mrs. Altman."

"But Mr. Solares! We can't let them get away with this. We have to fight them. If not in court, then in the streets."

"Listen to me, Lucina. In the court's view," Mr. Solares spoke gently, "it's you, the actors, who violated the law. You didn't have a permit to perform, did you?"

*****

The city's parks did not belong to the people at all; they were clearly the system's turf, guarded by armed police. And they were rapidly becoming off-limits to any group that challenged that system. She flashed on the clown who had warned them that day. He'd been on their side. He'd been trying to protect them, protect Louis. How could she find him again?

The cops were smart. Insidiously smart. They attacked Louis in places where no one would see his wounds and their brutality. Yet, even the dark glasses he began to wear couldn't hide his bruised pride.

Two weeks later, the troupe was invited to perform again as part of the Angry Arts Festival in Washington Square Park. Louis could be disguised with a mop of black hair and have no major roles! But reality had to be faced: their spirit had been depleted; Norman Morrison's immolation had saddened and overwhelmed them; the attack on Louis had terrified them. They would have to decline.

But how would they deal with Hans? He'd purposely trashed their play–didn't give the gun to Courtney. And Louis had clearly warned them about the cops. Had anyone confronted him yet! Shouldn't he be kicked out? They had to help Louis first. Al, Marin, Lucina, and Louis agreed: his actions had certainly led to the attack on him. Han's jutting into the crowd was like a challenge to the cops–smart alecks' showing off on their turf! But, Louis was their target: Jew boy who did all the talking. If Hans had carried the gun to Courtney, Louis' last speech would have ended well before the cops had reached him. He would have seen them coming and could have escaped, somehow. He would not have been harmed! Their spirit would not have been broken. And now, Louis had to heal; that was the first priority.

Whenever Lucina saw Hans now, she wanted to whack him, sit on him, and question him. But he was stronger and could hurt her! And she did not want Jenny to leave them—so responsible, so helpful. Besides, Jenny had begged, wept, and promised she would make sure he would never ever do anything like that again. So for Jenny's sake, they couldn't slam the door on Hans. But he definitely could not attend rehearsals or meetings, that was for sure—not until Louis had healed and they could all question Hans and make a collective decision: how to deal with his digression.

PART V
SALLY AND KAREN

28

Lucina Meets Sally at the Corner Bar

In the weeks following Louis' beating by the cops, Lucina had trouble sleeping. She tossed and turned, often waking him in the middle of the night. Her days were also filled with angst. She was snappy with the others in the group—even with Marin, whose presence had always calmed her.

Louis remained good-natured about his sleep interruptions, until one night, after a series of whacks from the half-asleep Lucina, he couldn't take it anymore. "Go sleep on the couch, babe. I've been kicked around enough."

Lucina dragged herself to the narrow couch nearby and worked herself into its uneven padding. She tried to calm herself by again remembering the sweetness of their first meeting at her show. How patiently Louis had worked with her to dismantle *Rune*, all of the sculptures in fact. Though he'd been carrying a tornado of emotions around the breakup with his wife and son, he'd slipped quite easily into her life. She finally fell into uneasy sleep, trying to recite one of his last poems for Joel.

In a pre-dawn dream state, she imagined moving her hands over the wooden surfaces of her last sculptures. She traced the arm thrusting through a church window; caressed the portraits of herself and Louis suspended in a doorway; and stroked the doweled, pointed hat of *Rune*. Her hands felt huge, yet sensitive, like primitive receptors, more alert than her eyes or ears.

When she awoke with the symphony of street noises, her hands were clasping her breasts; her vagina was moist. What was going on? She ached with need. Then she remembered her dream: how she'd been stroking her sculptures with longing. Could that small ritual she'd carried out with her sculptures a few days before—touching and blessing each one like a priest does his flock—have opened some center of intense physical pleasure in her? Why at this time when she was mourning the brutal treatment of Louis' body was she also tuning into her own sensuality so acutely?

There was something else: within the dream, a terrible sadness, like a dark weight, pulled on her. She sensed it had to do with her mother's accusations which hovered constantly in that vague area between conscious and unconscious thought. Her sculptures, Louis and now the street theater work, involvements she had chosen to pursue, all went against the grain of her parents' values. She was still in active struggle to leave home— that's what it was. She was struggling to be her own person! Her own parents.

Harsh images played out in her mind, newsreel clips on triple speed: women holding burnt children; soldiers aiming rifles at the foreheads of kneeling Vietcong; Norman Morrison's charred skin, his cheeks flaking off like the blackened skin of marshmallows held too long in campfire flames. She rubbed at her eyes. Wake up! Wake up! Get out of this mess, this impossible misery.

Louis' uneven breathing sounded on the other side of the screen wall. He desperately needed rest. Though his bruises were disappearing and he'd been carefully monitored by a doctor, her anxiety was preventing the very thing he needed.

In the afternoon, she headed for the Spring Street Bar to catch a few moments alone. She needed to think. How could she adjust, make sense of the violence that had careened into her private life? Maybe a beer would relax her.

"Can I buy you another?" A gritty voice shook her out of despondency. She'd been staring at the Miller's beer sign by the cash register for some time, desperately wanting the playful bubbles streaming in colored water to help her lighten up and be hopeful again. "You're almost empty."

Two large blue eyes, so far apart she couldn't look into them both at the same time, peered down at her. The woman's spiky brown hair framed a serious face. Her denim work clothes were covered with spots of paint. An artist. She was asking to join Lucina. The bar was crowded—she couldn't hog a whole table.

"Oh, sure. Sit."

"What do you like?"

"You don't have to buy me a—"

"I know I don't have to—I want to! How about a dark German beer this time?"

Lucina had no energy to resist. She relaxed her tense shoulders and sat back in the uncomfortable metal chair with a sigh. "Is it okay, you know, to mix beers?"

The woman, probably a few years older, given the gray hairs already showing at the temples, laughed easily, as if Lucina's comment was meant as a joke. "I'll get you Heineken dark."

"As long as it's made by the good Germans," Lucina let out.

The woman's mouth tightened, making Lucina suddenly self-conscious. *Well—there really were some good Germans. Klaus and Heinrich, for example.*

Lucina watched the woman talking in a friendly manner to a middle-aged man with a mustache at the bar. They seemed to know each other. Maybe she was a regular there.

"I don't know how you like it." The woman set a chilled mug on the table with the bottles of beer. Was that flirtation in her voice? Her gaze was so direct, so open.

Lucina ignored the mug and sucked thirstily at the cold bottle. "This is good," she said, smiling as her tablemate grasped her bottle with a nod.

"Do you like—" the woman began.

Lucina looked at the label to recall the name.

Her table partner was pointing at the wall to the right of the bar. "I mean, over there!" Three metal pieces hung side by side, forming a triptych.

Lucina had not noticed them before. "I really liked the paintings they had on display there for months. But these are kind of simple designs, no wrestling with image."

The woman's mouth curled into an expression halfway between a grin and a grimace. "Well," she said. "I've only been doing it for a year."

"Oh—" Lucina was speechless with embarrassment. "You—made them?"

"I appreciate a frank appraisal. But what do you like about them?"

Lucina took a deep breath to quell her apprehension; she'd already stuck her foot in her mouth with this stranger. "I'm sorry, I really spoke too soon. The textures are really interesting, and the splashes of color—and I like how you've broken up space. I can see the faces looking in all directions."

"I didn't make any faces there, as far as I know. It's abstract. Look, I don't want to put you on the spot. It's okay, I've gotten enough compliments and a review in the *Voice*."

"How to win friends—" Lucina stopped short. She should shut up. But she'd given a spontaneous reaction; she couldn't help what she felt. So, reviewed in the *Voice*, after only a year of sculpting. Good for her. It had taken Lucina a master's degree and more than two years to begin getting reviews, and never in the *Voice*.

The woman thrust her right hand toward Lucina. "Now that we've had an embarrassing moment, let me introduce myself. Sally Marsh, welder and typesetter."

"Hello, Sally. I'm Lucina Holzer." Lucina spoke in a warm tone, as if to push away the previous awkwardness between them. "I'm a former sculptor, present street-theater activist."

"Is that so?" Sally's enthusiasm was guarded. "Have I seen your group perform?"

Lucina fell silent. Here it was again: strangers' questions about her group always felt suspicious. All the insinuations, mainly from her family, that her theater work was part of a conspiracy to destroy hard-working, upright people's values, suddenly sobered her.

"Sorry, didn't mean to pry." Sally's voice softened.

Lucina breathed in deeply. She wanted to let go of her wariness. A sudden giddiness grabbed her. Was it the dark beer? It did seem stronger than the Bud she usually drank. She felt something loosening in her. And there were Sally's large blue eyes watching over her like angels. The image of kids jumping up and down on a trampoline, silly with happiness, came to her.

"We perform in the parks a lot. On weekends." Then the image of the police dragging Louis away made her avoid Sally's eyes. She shouldn't give out their name.

"Are you the wonderful group with a dragon and an incredible drum? I think it's red."

"That's us!" Lucina was incredulous. In all of New York City, that she should meet someone, a stranger, who knew them? It was the first time. "Yes, we're the Fire Dragon Street Theater." The pride in her voice amazed her. It was terrible how her family's criticism had squashed the deep pride she really did feel about her present work.

"I love that name," Sally said. She was fishing for a cigarette in her shirt pocket. "Do you mind?"

"Oh no, go ahead."

"My last one for today… So, you said you were a sculptor?"

"Well, I hope I can always carve out a life, one that makes sense. But you know how life lives us sometimes—"

"And you have to go where it takes you." Sally's face changed drastically, like a rubber mask being pulled on, creating a sad counterpart of the happy mask of seconds before. She suddenly looked worn, like someone who sucked on too much booze, too many cigarettes. Maybe a broken heart? It was amazing how a face could change in seconds.

When Sally looked into her eyes again, Lucina felt as though an immeasurable amount of time had passed, and that each had sifted through some valuable, wordless information about the other.

"I'm a dropout from upper-class Connecticut." Sally's clipped pronouncement jutted out of the silence. It had the weight of a headline. Paragraphs, chapters hung beneath that statement.

"That's so interesting—" Lucina hesitated. Here was yet another thread. Dropouts from privilege and also sister-artists. How much more did they have in common? She'd already sensed that some of the same heaviness and dissatisfaction that weighed on her was in Sally, too. And now a fumbling but explosive energy charged between them.

Their conversation continued for another hour. Sally described how she felt like an alien in her parents' house. She debunked the spirituality binges her friends went on, like believing people chose their parents to learn lessons not learned in a previous life. Yet, she definitely would have chosen farmers, she said, parents who could root her spacey self. Not a golfing, executive father or a consumer, socialite mother, who made her feel subhuman. She hungered for direct, real, physical exchanges that allowed life's oddness. All the social artifices her parents had constructed to keep life at arm's distance, to keep life pretty and on the surface, had literally driven her to drink. Though she was trying to keep it down to two beers a day.

Lucina told Sally why she'd become a sculptor; how she saw it as cutting a path for herself; how making images helped her discover who she was and what she might be someday. She talked about her last work, *Rune*. How the piece held a mystery that she was still trying to understand. That when she plunged into political work with the magazine *PAN*, then the street theater, she'd covered her sculpture with a white cloth, yet knowing it would always hold a sacred place in her heart. She was trying to explain why the covering wasn't merely to keep dust away, but was honoring her sculpture and herself, when Sally broke in.

"Why should we cut off parts of ourselves?" Sally barked out so sharply Lucina gasped.

"It's just for a while," Lucina countered firmly, wondering if she were consoling herself or Sally.

"Be careful of that…putting off, waiting for tomorrow." Sally was all seriousness. "Welding and my partner, Karen, have taught me that. All we really know is what's happening right now." Sally's emphatic hand swipe, meant to emphasize *right now*, sent the unused beer mug flopping off the table. With amazing dexterity, Lucina caught it before it hit the floor.

"God, you're fast!" The intensity of Sally's look and voice made Lucina blush.

"It's all the improv exercises we do," Lucina said. "I can't tell you how many blows from a cop's billy club I've learned to ward off the last two weeks in our workshops."

They were outside the bar, high from the beer and each other. Two dark German beers were like four Buds, Sally told her. They exchanged phone numbers, each writing her own with a red pen on the other's palm with an agreement: Whoever needed to talk over a beer could call the other. The corners of Lucina's mouth pulled up into a continuous smile. Sally's eyes were beams touching her all over. She did not want to separate from that warmth.

As Lucina turned quickly to head back to the loft, her right Ked caught in a crack in the sidewalk; she was falling. Slowly.

Arms were holding her, firm. Sally was enclosing her in an embrace. Then Sally's mouth was on hers. She felt her body lift upward—their two mouths pressing hungrily in a floating space, like two creatures determined to cling, if only briefly.

Something soft entered Lucina's mouth. It felt good. Very good.

That night, looking back on the afternoon, Lucina saw two streams of water side by side, shooting upwards into the sky. They were the geysers she'd seen in Yellowstone Park when she'd worked there for a summer between her junior and senior year of college. And when she recalled her cartoon image of two kids hopping ecstatically together on a trampoline, she knew: It was she and Sally, the kid parts of themselves exploding playfully in each other's presence.

29

Louis Meets Karen in a Bookstore

Thank God, he could break down and cry with Lucina. He would let himself be the fragile kid again who couldn't take teasing, yet had trouble fighting back. He was a connector, not a fighter. That was it. Lucina was a trusted part of him now. He could show his vulnerability with her.

Al talked tough to Louis. "Don't let that beating eat you up, guy!" But he stopped making comments meant to be playful when he saw how deeply Louis' spirit had been injured. "Hey man, they should have come after me. I would have kicked the shit out of them!" only made Louis moan. Al quickly added, "Anyone brutalized by the cops deserves hero status." And Louis knew Al wanted to be a true friend.

Still, Louis didn't want special attention. He didn't feel like a hero; he was a victim of bullies. Mainly, he felt impotent and quite alone. He saw that Lucina's caring was entangled with her own cloying guilt: she hadn't forced herself between the cop bastards and him; she should have made them cart her off with him. And Al's brotherly concern was tempered by his girlfriend, Marin's, unease. Louis heard her say to him, "Your Louis can do no wrong."

He needed his old friends, the poet muses who'd fed him for so many years. Once again, the poems of Lorca, Crane, Neruda, Whitman, Williams, and Roethke gave him comfort and direction. These men had transformed their suffering with fierce imagination, visionary language, and will power.

He promised himself: if he didn't mend soon, he would just quit this performing stuff that really wasn't his thing, anyway. It was Lucina's! Lucina and her theater-sculpture Happenings and her passion for drama. He would go back to his desk and stay put. Follow his dream—write great American poems. Someday people would compare him to Whitman, to Sandburg. No, he wasn't wedded to street theater!

When Lucina told him she was going to the little park on Thompson Street to write in her black journal, he did not question her. He knew she went to the corner bar instead. Didn't WASPs drink when they were upset? The beating had crippled them both, bruised their selfless, innocent optimism. Louis knew they each needed space to heal, to dream again.

He suddenly hated the plastic boxes stuffed with props. Lucina's once tidy studio looked like an unkempt second-hand store. How much Lucina had given up! No, he would not hound her about drinking too much.

He became addicted to his Village bookstores again. The Eighth Street Bookstore was his favorite; for hours at a time, he wrapped himself in slender publications of the newest poetry. He loved those works throbbing with duende and surreal journeys, rich in imagination and outrage. He had always been hounded by the tragic sense of life—not the fact of death, but the insidious ways men treated each other. Poetry was not a way to coat over harsh realities with pretty language. Poetry was the finely honed language of awareness, of connecting and inspiring people to own their better selves.

For his SDS buddies working now on *PAN*, each escalation of the war, each new civil-rights injustice in Amerika was further proof that a grassroots uprising had to be forged immediately. He watched in silence as Roy stripped the magazine of poetry and arts commentary declaring, "We have to focus on immediate analytical information, Louis." When Roy suggested he was indulging himself with his "bourgeois literary afternoons," Louis decided that the only way to survive the dark hole he was in was to distance himself both from the theater work and from *Pan.*

While Louis' absence from rehearsals was encouraged by the troupe, Hans' absence was forced. They needed time to figure out how to handle him. A less compassionate group would have booted him out immediately. But Jenny convinced the others that he was mixed-up, not malicious. Everyone knew behind her pleas was the fear of his deportation; his green card was outdated. "He fucked up, but he needs us," she pleaded as she continued rehearsing with the others, developing exercises that might inspire a new play to go with *Choice.*

As for Louis? He was trying to control his anger until he felt stronger. Thank God Lucina had dealt with the loose cannon. "You're a suspect politico, Hans," she'd told him. "Your actions at Tavern on the Green betrayed us. Louis could have been permanently injured. A true activist has compassion for his comrades. You should be kneeling at Louis' feet. Your brainless actions allowed the cops to vent their anger on him, alone. You can be sure when Louis is healed, we'll all meet to figure out how we can deal with you." Yes, she really told him off. But she hadn't chastised him in front of the others. Maybe this last act of kindness toward him would finally wake him up.

But Louis' anger with Hans matched his anger with the cops. *If Hans hadn't been such a fuckin' egomaniac, taunting the crowd, firing up the police! How could he deal with this anger? The terrible memories in his head...the insidious marks on his back.* His thoughts went again and again to his family, the photos his parents kept in their bedroom of relatives killed in the Nazi death camps. He was "Jew boy" to those cops. They were Nazi racists, anti-Semites. They were Jew haters!

He began jotting phrases down in a notepad in the bookstore. *Hatred can't destroy me—each heart beat is a plea—a raised fist, for Love...* A new poem was forming in his gut.

*****

Yes, they did have it! A new edition of Theodore Roethke's poems. His volume was falling apart. He would buy it. He would buy two and give one to Lucina.

"Do you always buy two books by an author?" A striking woman with a cloud of black hair was waiting behind him in the cashier's line. What a beautiful smile! It sent a ray of sunlight into his cramped heart. "Is it in case one wears out?"

The woman was as tall as him—tall for a woman—and that delighted him. Lucina was so small. "One is for me and one is for my—"

"Let me guess. Your honey?"

Louis laughed. "Yes, that's right."

"Roethke's work is fabulous," the woman enthused. "He's so clever. Who else writes about weather in a beard? I also love the gay poets, Ginsberg, Lorca—talk about intense."

"You love poetry, too?" The woman was wearing a wonderful scent, a cross between pineapples and was it honeysuckle? Lucina had made him smell the yellow honeysuckle flowers in Vermont.

"I couldn't live without poetry. I should buy that volume. Oh well, next time. Right now I'm studying the anarchists."

Louis looked at the volume the woman plunked down on the counter, the writings of Emma Goldman. He stayed rooted, halfway between the checkout counter and the exit door, waiting for her to follow him out. Maybe she would like to go for coffee?

After all, Lucina wouldn't be done with rehearsal until nine o'clock.

"I'd love to. There's a little coffee shop on Sixth Avenue that has great eggs."

"It's almost five o'clock," Louis said, pleased that the woman's stride matched his and that he didn't have to slow down. "That sounds like breakfast."

"Oh, I always eat breakfast for supper and vice-versa. I don't like doing what everybody else does. That way I keep my mind clear, so I can think."

"What do you need to think about?"

"How people mistreat each other, lie about it, get hooked on it. And make manifestoes to justify their sickness."

"You've got it figured out." Louis was aware of a sudden happy feeling in himself. He'd been so locked up, so heavy. Was it the woman's perfume, or the woman? Her ideas, or her voice? She seemed oblivious to the traffic bearing down on them at Sixth Avenue. As she continued to lament the human condition, he grabbed her elbow and steered them both across the street, barely dodging a taxi rushing the red light.

As they entered the greasy spoon, she said. "I guess you can tell I'm an anarchist."

"Never would have guessed," Louis said and led them to a booth in the back, away from the windows. "By the way, my name's Louis. What's yours?"

"Karen X, political sister of Malcolm. I loved that man. I should say it in the present. I love Malcolm X. His death made my love even stronger. Somehow for me, he embraces the essence of the anarchist's spirit. The right of the individual to address injustice in their own way, but mindfully, humanely. People didn't trust him because he was too human. King and Malcolm influenced each other. Their outlooks changed. Love should change people, or it isn't love. Don't you think? He was big enough to change—wise enough to see what people needed."

Louis felt buoyant, suddenly lifted from the horror of the past weeks. "I agree. All of us have to continually change to stay really alive. You know that verse by Lao Tzu? "We form clay…""

"Into a pot," Karen chirped up.

They continued together, "But it is the emptiness inside— that holds whatever we want."

"I love that," Karen enthused. "It's so simple and happy, somehow."

"How many people know that verse, Karen?" Louis felt touched; he lowered his eyes, so Karen couldn't see they were tearing up.

"Let's eat. I'm famished." Karen brushed aside the menu a waiter was offering her and ordered, "The same, John. Two over easy, home fries, rye toast, and a chocolate milk shake."

"The same," Louis nodded. "Except a coke instead of a shake. We'll both have breakfast, okay?"

*****

Then his plate was empty, revealing an American flag in the center with the words "We love our country." The time passed so quickly … he was already forgetting how his eggs tasted. Karen's plate was all white, and no flag. He looked about the diner, half expecting some kid looking like Hans would be grinning maliciously at him. Boy, did he need to lighten up!

She was a talker, yet it wasn't as if he felt uncomfortable about listening. He was hungrily taking her in: the twinkle in her brown eyes; the shine of her black hair; the calming, almost monotone run of her voice. Her hands, the long fingers. She wasn't Jewish; maybe Italian or Irish.

A beautiful handmade silver ring caught his eye—he and Lucina didn't wear rings, except for that bizarre day they'd gotten hitched. It was elegant against her white skin. When she threw back her head and laughed, he suddenly saw the bubbling stream at Sandstorm, Vermont, where he and Lucina had occasionally escaped from the others. Would she think he was prying if he asked about a boyfriend?

He grabbed the check over her protests—her hand was on his arm, lingering—and he was calling out to her, "leave the tip," just as he did with Lucina. He paid for them both at the cash register.

On the street, she turned to him. "Come up to my place. I want to show you my books."

He hesitated, feeling a tug in his stomach. It was his turn to bring back some groceries after the rehearsal. What time was it?

"It's only six if you're worried. Not late. I won't keep you long, Louis."

He followed her around the corner onto Greenwich Avenue to a brick apartment building that seemed vaguely familiar.

"Do you know someone who lives here?" Karen had her key out; she was unlocking the door and beckoning him in. "It's just a little hike up."

Louis smiled broadly. "It's just very similar to my old apartment building on Avenue C—you know Galway Kinnell's *Avenue Bearing the Initial of Christ*? Seems anarchists and poets always live on fifth-floor walk-ups." The last time he and Lucina had fucked at his place was when the cops had accused them of throwing bricks. *Don't bring that up to Karen. Sex and violence, too loaded. Stay with poetry.*

"Well, we only go to the fourth." Karen was huffing. "It's good enough for this anarchist and good exercise for the heart."

Their footsteps made a nice sound as they bounded up the last flight of narrow wooden steps.

On the door of Apartment 4A was a photo of Emma Goldman in a bathing suit, looking seductive and playful.

"Anarchists like to have fun," Karen quipped, blinking her eyes in a teasing way. The door was open and she was slipping into a long corridor that opened onto a cozy room walled with bookcases from floor to ceiling. It seemed to Louis like no object was out of place.

"Wow! This is great!" He'd had a room just like this when he was in college, a large apartment he'd shared with another student, who was never there. His precious books had been carefully filed alphabetically by the author's name. The collection had awed all his friends. Where were his old pals now?

Karen had him by the hand and was pointing at one shelf. It was labeled "The Rosenbergs." One whole shelf was dedicated to them—accounts of the trial, biographies, political analyses. "These are priceless," he whistled. She was showing him a series of small, green paperbacks, the complete transcripts from the trial. "I'm writing my own theory of what happened to them—and what they possibly could have done to save themselves."

"You really think they had a chance, Karen?"

"I need to think they had a chance. Otherwise, I couldn't stay in this country. They had a network of people ready to smuggle them out. They wouldn't take the risks involved. They were too innocent. I don't think they believed America would really execute them."

Louis sat down on the couch placed in the center of the room, facing the windows. Directly in front of the windows was a small desk. *She must sit there and look down on the street.* "That's where you write?"

"Yes, I like that the sounds from the street enter my thoughts. Keeps me from drifting into nonsense."

"Makes sense," Louis offered.

As Karen talked about her writing habits, she looked at Louis in a questioning way. "I don't know, but you really look familiar. Have we ever met?"

It seemed curious to Louis that she hadn't mentioned this before. Now, in her apartment, that possibility suddenly gave their encounter a special twist, like fate was playing with them. "I don't know. I used to read my poems quite a bit."

Karen's eyes opened wide. "That's it. I heard you at St. Marks. *The Poets Against the War* series. Now I remember. You came on last. And woke everybody up with your fierceness. You kept making a circle with your hand above the pulpit, I mean lectern, like you were hypnotizing us. I remember that."

"Really!" It was the first time in over a year that he'd thought about that reading. It had been one of his last, and best— before *PAN*, before Fire Dragon, before his assault.

"You inspired a whole roomful of people. You inspired me."

"I inspired you?" His voice sounded fragile to him. It was getting late. As her warmth flowed into him and his body relaxed deeper into the soft couch, he felt his fatigue. He had to go grocery shopping for Lucina.

Then Karen was next to him, her hips pressing against his, her hand on his leg pressing heat into him. Her fingers, flashing silver curves, were moving toward his crotch. Should he jump up? His penis was pushing against his jocks to reach her, be touched by her. When she did, he moaned softly in response.

The books, like somber presences, were watching over them—or were they watching lasciviously, he wondered, like guys at Forty-second Street peep shows stared at girls? As she stroked him harder and harder through the rough cloth of his jeans, he heard himself groan. How could this be? How could this be happening?

"You have such wonderful energy, Louis." Karen's voice was like another hand stroking at his forehead, his eyes. He could explode from so much tension, so much rubbing. "You're a beautiful man. Has your honey told you that lately?"

And then he relaxed. He had come, and she, this beautiful woman he'd just met, was talking about the camaraderie of souls, the arc of love between people who wanted good to win out over evil.

He stood. The late afternoon sun reflected on the windows across the street, into her windows, streaking a band of light over the books they'd looked at only minutes before, the Rosenberg books.

He saw a face on her desk; a photo of a woman in a silver frame was smiling out at him. It wasn't Karen.

"Is that your sister?" Louis asked softly.

"No. Well yes, my political sister. We work together on the newspaper *We Rise*. She's a brilliant sculptor and an anarchist like me. Sally is…" Karen halted, looked earnestly into Louis' eyes, then spoke. "Look, why should I hide anything from you, Louis? Sally is my honey!" She edged Louis out the door; her phone number on a scrap of paper was clutched in his hand. Her voice flew down the hall. "Call me some time."

By the time Louis was out on the street again, he'd made a decision. Karen X was an audacious flirt! Worse than that— he found her terribly attractive. He felt suddenly uncomfortable with his dampness. Why hadn't he wiped himself dry? Damn it! Now, where had he put it? The grocery list Lucina had given him wasn't in any of his pockets.

<h1 style="text-align:center">30
Secrets</h1>

Noticeable changes came over Hans during the weeks he was ostracized by the troupe. He was not the Hans Jenny knew. He seemed depressed, defeated. She couldn't always take his banter, his bravado—but she had accepted those aspects along with his devotion to her. No other boyfriend had treated her so gallantly. He took her needs seriously in bed and in their daytoday living. He was playful and easily pleased with her. What had made him do such an awful thing?

The theater work had wound him up, Jenny realized. It got him too excited and anxious. And Al and Louis, like older brothers, were always chiding his ideas, not really trusting his instincts or his politics. So he'd become what they believed he was, an impulsive, untrustworthy misfit.

Then overnight, after the police attack on Louis, he quieted down, became contrite, and was ready to do whatever Jenny suggested. "*Tror du på mig?* Jenny, do you believe me? I'm a changed Hans. What can I do? I want to talk. Jenny, Jenny, ask them to talk to me. I need them to understand and forgive."

When he saw himself in their eyes, he withered, he grieved. How could he make amends for what he'd done to

Louis? Jenny's ultimatums, along with Lucina's promise of a harsh reprimand, crushed him. How could he get out of the black hole he was in? He was ashamed and desperate. He needed them. He'd been thrown out of his college in Copenhagen for organizing with young environmentalists to stop the onslaught of cement and roadways that demolished people's homes; for challenging the rich landlords who destroyed any humane city planning. His parents had never understood what he was up to, just that he'd upended their dream of him becoming an architect. They'd wanted him to go beyond his meat-butcher dad and his work-at-home seamstress mom and become a prominent figure in their beloved Copenhagen. He'd wanted to do this, but in his own way. So he'd fled to New York, where other students had dropped out because they too were rebelling against greed and capitalism with its destruction and obliteration of human need. He was frustrated and hurt. He needed to be seen as a caretaker, someone who fought greed.

It came to him suddenly in a flash: he'd been expelled from college, from his parents' house, and from his city, and he was taking his anger out on this group, this little family that had taken him in. Why should they understand him? He'd never talked about himself; he'd never told them what had happened to him. He was afraid of them. They could have him deported any day—report him to the officials, send him away from Jenny who loved him. He'd acted out, used the dragon head to hide under and fuck up his part. And then another truth: he'd refused to give the gun to Courtney; was it because he'd wanted to play Sam? Be a man who could own himself and his beliefs? He had a lot to own up to, that was for sure.

Was it because he was a foreigner? He had to stop hiding, stop defending himself. He'd acted blindly, destructively. Some great guerrilla warrior he was! He'd caused courageous, articulate Louis to be badly beaten and broken. He'd caused

Lucina and all the others terrible grief; he'd betrayed their trust. He had to own the truth. He had to ask forgiveness, he had to believe they would all forgive him. He must talk real; lay down his armor, his banter that had become a wall to hide behind.

"Jenny, this is the first time since booted from Copenhagen, my homeland, that I can cry for real. I need to explain to them. Tell them—*Jeg er ked af det.* I'm sorry. I need to be forgiven, be loved, like a brother, a comrade brother, the brother I always dreamed to have. I can be a friend for them, Jenny. For Louis, Lucina, Al, Marin, and the new comrades, Courtney, Hugh, Jack and Joan. My chosen family."

*****

After a workshop, some weeks later, Hans faced the members of the Fire Dragon Street Theater and broke down in convulsive sobs, only speaking after a long shared silence. They listened solemnly, warily; only slowly could they let their guards down as he sputtered forth harsh self-criticisms and promises to make up to them for his unforgiveable behavior. He stuttered out a partial explanation of what had driven him to New York and the real source of his hurt and anger. And how he was blindly, destructively acting out because he hadn't been able to tell them the truth about himself, about his shame and his fears.

"That can never happen again, Hans." Louis, steely-eyed, made his point abruptly as Lucina nodded, jaws clenched.

"I know! I can learn. I want to be a true comrade. Tell me whatever you want, to teach me better." The exchange ended with the troupe agreeing to let him continue working with them; but if he messed up one more time, it was over.

*****

Hans' genuine remorse—his awareness that bravado was armor hiding his humiliating expulsion from the life he'd known; his admission that his real need was to be trusted by his new family—all helped considerably to restore the group's trust in him and renew enthusiasm about their mission.

Lucina watched Louis' body relax—his gloom lift. And certainly the time spent with his books had done him a lot of good. Louis welcomed her attention, glad she too had lightened up. Yet even as they joyed in a renewed closeness since the beating, each secreted their new encounters, glowing and dangerous, in their hearts.

Sally and Karen had dazzled them, not like gorgeous sunsets can, but as bright lights from an approaching car can startle one in the darkness of night. Those lights could not be confronted directly, only taken in carefully, sidewise. To comprehend such encounters head-on was far too risky and challenging; it could cause blindness.

The war, the police assault, and the day-to-day uncertainty of their lives had taken its toll on their spirits and libidos. Now their senses were aroused again, opening them to each other for the first time in months. When they made love on the couch one afternoon, each pondered separately that to have indulged in a little erotic pleasure with someone else, given that their own closeness was once more alive and well, was a good thing after all. Life was more than angst, horror, and death. There was beauty and excitement; there was passion and sex. And that they'd responded so eagerly to intimate acts their blood families would call "cheating" could only mean they'd needed new sparks.

Together they remembered Vermont; the fantasy animals watching them in the woods; their trysts without the others nearby to worry over. They cried and laughed as Lucina came four times and Louis' erection lasted an hour.

However, their initial acceptance of these marvelous and productive chance encounters did not mean they would be repeated. Affairs were not what they were about.

Lucina did not go to the Spring Street Bar looking for Sally. Louis did not go to the Eighth Street Bookstore hunting for Karen. They made no use of the proffered phone numbers; nor did they toss them. Yet even with the resolve to conceal from the other what had happened—though their natural bent was to confide—and not to stray again, they could escape neither their fantasies nor the accompanying guilt they both carried.

Especially at night, Karen and Sally sashayed through their thoughts. And though Louis knew Karen had a Sally—he'd seen her photo—no way could he know that the ghost had also savored Lucina's lips, those same lips that now kissed him so eagerly. And though Sally had mentioned Karen's name, it had not registered in Lucina's consciousness.

Somewhere in the middle of all this drama and revitalized lovemaking, the two began to talk about the summer and the possibility of the entire theater troupe, including their new recruits—Hugh, Courtney, Jack, and Joan—and perhaps a couple of faithful groupies, escaping the city to some beautiful country setting.

31
Lucina and Louis Meet Sally and Karen in a Sandwich Shop

Louis became restless at dusk, a mystical time when light married darkness. Sometimes Lucina wondered if his ancient primal self was called to witness the dying of the sun—if by performing some private ritual he was renewing his faith in its return. He seemed to enter an altered state in the twilight hours—she called it his "wonder mode"—where he began a search for things. He searched for his good gold pen, the sports section of the *Times*, his latest Neruda book. She watched him move tentatively about the loft, like a lost soul, until he stopped and looked out the window, upward to the sky, infused with mauves and violets, and then he or she would say, "It's that time again."

Even Manhattan birds knew that this was the time for prayer and silence. Starlings offered their final medleys to the passing light; country swallows knew it as the time for play; they took dips into ponds—ritual baths—perhaps giving homage to the leave-taking of their shadows before going home to barns and tree cavities. People, searching for inner peace, took time off from chores at this time; they sat at windows and reflected on their lives. Both Lucina and Louis agreed this was a holy time.

Lucina loved dusk; its muted light eased the harshness of the changes in her life. Though she missed the studio that had been her private workplace, at this time of day she was able to appreciate the creative work being done in the space, and by so many thespians! Wasn't there another word that rhymed with that word from ancient Greece, she mused? Yes. Lesbians. And didn't that word come from Ancient Greece as well? Someone called Sappho from the Isle of Lesbos had sung her own poems. But why was Lucina fastening on these words? They were just Greek to her.

On one Saturday night in late June, the space was filled with an assortment of masks in progress. Strips of papier maché layered over balloons had been left to dry and become the strong foundations for masks that could be worn over heads. Lucina and Al were directing the project for use in future plays.

The space was strewn with new props that might come in handy—who knew for what. Marin had found a large abacus—Al said it was the end of a baby's crib—with colored wooden beads that moved up and down on brass wires. Hans, who was now desperate to win favor, brought in cardboard tubes he'd collected from nearby streets, to be used for flag poles, megaphones, and table legs. There were plastic boxes filled with costumes, knights' armor, an ape's head, a fur coat, and giant shoes made out of cardboard.

Lucina sat by the large casement windows—iridescent sunset colors lit up the windows across the street—and let herself dwell briefly on some palpable resentment she still carried for having given up her own work space. Calmed by the diffuse light, she nudged herself out of grumpiness. "Life is change, and change is growth," she recited, wondering why she had trouble understanding her own words.

Spring Street had quieted down; horns honked less loudly at this special time between day and night, or so it seemed to Lucina. Artists called out more gently from their lofts to their friends waiting below on the street.

Louis was calling out to her. "Lucina, would you like to go for a walk? We could take the Staten Island Ferry and watch the end of the sunset from there, babe."

She'd planned to start putting noses, mouths, and ears on a couple of the dried balloons, but the thought of enjoying the last of the sunset excited her.

"Oh let's, Louis! We haven't done that for so long."

Too often she forgot that they were riders on a circling orb, and that the sun, their star, made this short ride possible. Suddenly, her misgivings rose up: the lingering nostalgia for her own studio; the annoyances of the theater work. There were constant petty disputes over who would direct what—they usually used the word *guide*—and play which role; who would say what and how. So important at the time, these disputes were really like so many tiny ripples on the ocean. If one could only see the earth from afar and get a true perspective!

They would do it right, buy salami sandwiches and sodas and eat on the boat. They could pretend they were immigrants seeing the Statue of Liberty for the first time. Louis knew of a sandwich shop on Canal Street that stayed open on Saturday nights; taxi drivers stopped there for pastrami heros and hot coffee. They should walk down Broadway, all the way to the ferry terminal even though it was noisier than West Broadway; they might make the seven o'clock ferry and see the sun's last rays.

The traffic was heavy, but the sidewalks were empty. "Someday, I bet there'll be a lot of stores here for suburbanites, and swarms of sightseers dying to see how the artists live," Lucina mused, grabbing ahold of Louis' arm. She wondered again how she'd ever ended up in a place so foreign to her childhood landscape. "God, Louis, it's all cement. Hard, unrelenting cement. Why do I live here?" She searched the buildings towering over them. "Wouldn't it be great to see angels looking down on us and know they were our protectors?"

"I see one!" Louis pointed to a large white-stone building across the street. "See! That's Gabriel tooting at you."

Lucina strained in vain to see some winged, golden-haired creature smiling back at her.

Louis took her head in his hands and aimed her sight to the corner of the building in front of them. "There!"

"Oh, Louis." She laughed giddily. A creature with a gaping mouth, bulging eyes, and lion's feet was protruding from a cement perch. "It's a gargoyle! Why did they put that up there where nobody can see it?"

"We saw it, Lucina."

He was as gleeful as she. She grabbed him tightly, so delighted with his childlike spirit. "I love it when we can see special things together, Louis."

Canal Street was filled with a stream of people headed east. Of course—it was Saturday night, a night out in Chinatown restaurants.

"You sure you want to see it get dark from a boat? All the cement buildings you're so in love with will be lit up like Christmas trees." They both laughed at his image. Louis looked longingly at a group of young people about their age, joking and jaunting past them. "We could go instead to the Dumpling House on Mott," he offered.

"Louis, we made a plan!"

"Okay. Just giving us options."

They turned right, as the sky opened to them with its breathtaking display of swirls and streaks of rose-pinks and violets. They headed to the tiny sandwich shop next to the hardware store where Lucina had bought casters for *Rune*.

The shop felt empty, only two customers hunched together at one of the small tables.

At the take-out counter, Lucina studied the sandwich menu even though Louis had already ordered two salamis on rye. "Really thin slices," he told a young man with bushy eyebrows and mustache.

"What's that one, Louis?" There was always a sandwich name she'd never heard of.

"Bratwurst. That's some kind of German sausage."

Suddenly a voice called out Louis' name. Were the sandwiches done already? But the voice was behind them. They turned to the tables by the wall, where two women customers were waving at them.

Lucina recognized Sally immediately. The short brown hair; a certain angular thrust in her gesture. She was waving and smiling broadly. The other woman—hadn't she mentioned someone at the bar, someone close to her?—waved self-consciously.

Then Louis was walking toward this woman, who was now standing, and reaching out to grasp her hand. "Lucina, this is Karen."

"Oh, hello, Lucina," Karen offered, smiling.

Sally's smile disappeared as she looked back and forth from Lucina to her Karen. "You've met before?" She seemed confused.

"No, no," Karen stuttered. "Just Louis."

They were all laughing nervously and Lucina was introducing Louis to Sally without looking at her. "We're going to the ferry to watch the sunset." She noticed a silver and turquoise ring on Karen's left hand.

Louis was clearly excited by the encounter. "Come with us!"

Lucina felt heady, her cheeks flushed. How did Louis know Sally's friend? It came back to her: yes, Sally had said her name, Karen, at the bar.

Now Louis was taking charge. "Our sandwiches are ready. Should I order more? Lucina, you get four Dr. Browns."

Sally and Karen protested. They had just eaten like pigs.

*****

The four of them were out on the street looking upwards. Black clouds streaked across the sky, covering bands of translucent purples, a reminder that the sun had almost set and rain might be coming. Lucina had the sensation of something sweet on her tongue: chocolate and lemon. She was aware of avoiding Sally's glance and of her own lips pressing tightly together.

A few drops spattered on the sidewalk and on their bare arms; the four drew closer to consider an alternate plan.

"There goes your sunset boat ride," Karen said. Her curly black hair and soulful eyes impressed Lucina. But where had Louis met her?

"Come to our loft," Louis suggested with urgency. "We can hang out and talk. Lucina and I don't socialize very often outside of our collective."

As rain pelted down, halting traffic and sending pedestrians to store entranceways, the four bolted into the subway.

*****

Lucina was wiping the scarred oak table of crumbs from the sandwiches. "It's like another time, isn't it, Louis?" she said. Karen and Sally sat on the couch smoking and drinking leftover wine from the troupe's last communal feast.

The two women were eager to talk about themselves. They lived in the West Village on Greenwich Avenue, but not together. Lucina had little experience with lesbians, but something about their comfort with lighting each other's cigarettes and sharing memories made her think they were lovers. Although Sally had not mentioned it, they were very active in politics, wrote essays about their beliefs, and were working on the political paper *We Rise*. They were focused on women's issues—obsessed was more to the point. They talked about the invisibility of women in management, in government, the military—"Just about everywhere," Karen said, "except for the nurturing roles. We're supposed to drown in mothering."

Lucina tried to recreate the Sally she'd met two weeks before at the bar: the artist, welder Sally, ingenuous about herself and her excitement about living in New York. But this Sally, nodding to every word from Karen, was different. Her Sally was tough, sharp, witty; this Sally, more contained, was obviously linked to Karen. Or was it just another aspect of the same Sally?

In the aura of Karen's grand gestures—she talked with her face, head, hair, hands; everything about Karen gestured—this Sally seemed tight and cautious. The other Sally had softness in her angles. This Sally hooked her arm around Karen's shoulders for a few seconds as if to plug into her friend's electricity. When Sally gave Karen a knowing glance, touching her hand, Lucina's adrenaline and agitation rose. Could she be jealous? She'd met the woman only once. Yet, a kiss joined them. A deep, sexual kiss! Had that Sally trifled with her? Did Karen know Sally did that—found women in bars to come onto? Maybe it was some kind of weirdo, turn-on thing between them? Suddenly Lucina felt exhausted.

And what was this about Louis knowing Karen? Strange how she kept smiling so brightly at him. Suddenly the two women seemed too loud, too showy, and yes—too sexual!

That was it. They both exuded sensuality. Louis kept bumming cigarettes from Karen—so he could take something from her hand, Lucina decided. It was horrible.

Lucina excused herself and went to the darkened end of the loft. She wanted to stretch and get out tension. When she returned, Louis and Karen were talking nonstop about SDS and the leftist groups visiting Hanoi. The latest escalation in the bombing was meant to send a message to anti-war groups: the government, not the people, ran America. *We Rise* was sending some of their people to the Hanoi meeting. Lucina wanted to put earmuffs on to escape the hurricane of words. She wanted to take refuge again in the other end of the loft—her former space—away from the torrent of words, the torrent of Louis and Karen.

She cried out, "Sally, I want to show you something."

Sally followed her at once, as if anticipating some private interaction between them. Some new boldness filled Lucina. It was a familiar and unfamiliar feeling. Was she being driven by that kiss? Yes—she knew for sure now—she was definitely attracted to Sally.

Sally sat down on the stool by the windows and looked around slowly, obviously fascinated by what she saw. "This is interesting—your workplace." Soft jazz floated up through the open window from the loft below. Lucina laughed: the papier maché heads looked like comic imitations of the mannequins in a hairstylist's shop. But when Sally's glance moved to the white mass against the wall by the workbench, she fell silent.

"What's that?" Sally pointed to the white shape. "What's under that sheet, Lucina?"

Lucina stood on one of the plastic boxes to unhook the sheet covering the top of the sculpture. It fell to the floor, showing a pointed hat made of thin dowels fixed to a carved head. She pulled a second sheet covering the frame, and then a third concealing the wooden trays that looked like breasts and the many slats that formed a skirt.

Sally laughed. "It's like unraveling a mummy."

"She's more like a Mommy," Lucina quipped.

When *Rune* was completely revealed, both women backed away and stared in silence. Lucina could hear Sally's heavy breathing, could feel it resonate in herself, in her chest. She felt heat in her hands, on her cheeks. She licked at her lips; they were dry, tender.

"Wow! This is incredible," Sally enthused. "I've never seen anything like it. It's like a priestess or an ancient empress. Haunting. A question and an answer at the same time."

"I call her my 'womanwhole,'" Lucina blurted out, excited by Sally's response. "Not 'masterpiece.'"

"I like that!" Sally nodded, then suddenly faced Lucina and clasped her shoulders. For a second Lucina thought she was going to kiss her again. She felt faint, like she was falling backwards.

"It's about a woman! A woman!" Sally shouted out as if to an entire crowd. Her voice seemed both angry and ecstatic. Fingers were digging into Lucina's flesh. "It's about loving a woman, Lucina. Really loving a woman. When are you going to learn about that?" Lucina heard pain driving the reproach.

She pulled away from Sally's grasp. She heard Karen laughing uproariously from the other end of the loft. Louis must be telling one of his stories. It couldn't be about the assault in the park. That wasn't funny. Maybe it was about the magazine—something about Klaus and Heinrich, how they'd thought that C. Wright Mills was a member of Hells Angels.

"Sally, let's go back to Louis and Karen. Louis tells great stories. To me he's like some kind of *Rune* all by himself."

<h1 style="text-align:center">32</h1>

<h2 style="text-align:center">Lucina Gets a Phone Call</h2>

"I'll get it, Lucina!" For the first time since moving into the loft, Louis was no longer complaining about the phone being at his end. The phone rang only once—Lucina told him he could smell a ring coming—and Louis was on it.

Sometimes she didn't want Louis to answer. Her friends—the few who were left outside the troupe—might assume that Louis was in charge of her and her loft, the street theater, the phone. He was a take-charge kind of guy; so she had to stay strong and independent, not like a kid again in her parents' house, where the phone was off-limits to children except in unusual circumstances.

"It's for you, Lucina. I'm not sure who it is—sounds like a businessperson."

Lucina grabbed the phone and shooed him away, back to his desk and his incredible paper-shuffling act.

"Hello—Lucina? Can you talk to me?" It was Sally.

She cupped the phone. "I'll be on for a while, Louis." He was smoking a cigarette and lost in his thoughts. She pulled the kitchen stool toward the back windows as far as the cord could reach. She would face the window and speak low, so Louis would think she didn't want to disturb him. "I was thinking about you, Sally." She wouldn't ask about Karen right off.

"I want to explain something to you, Lucina." Louis was right; Sally had a business voice sometimes. "You must wonder about my relationship to Karen, and how I could have—" There was a sudden intake of breath. Sally was smoking. Of course—Sally smoked when she was nervous.

"You seem very close." She felt her mouth go dry, tension in her neck. She hadn't wanted to talk about Karen. She'd wanted Sally to apologize for speaking so roughly to her.

"We're very close. She's an incredible person." *An incredible person.* The phrase echoed in the phone. "We have a very close connection."

"What is it? What do you want to say to me, Sally?"

"We have an open relationship, that's what I wanted to tell you. So you wouldn't think I was cheating, or whatever you do think."

Lucina hesitated. "I think…of you."

"I hope it's good." Sally's voice was suddenly warm and tender. "Karen and I were wondering if you and Louis would have dinner with us. At Karen's house—mine is smaller. We'll make spaghetti and meatballs. Do you like that? Karen likes Louis and well, you know—I like you, a lot!"

"I'll get back to you about that invitation." She slid off the stool and braced herself against the wall as she mumbled a polite thanks and goodbye. She felt giddy and frightened at the same time.

"Who was that, Lucina?" Louis called out from the bathroom. He'd been near her all this time! But with the door shut, he couldn't possibly have heard.

"Guess what, Louis? Sally and Karen want us to come for dinner on Friday." She paused. "But that's when the Eighth Street Players are coming here for a communal dinner with our group."

"So, what did you say?" He was suddenly next to her.

"I said yes, Louis."

"Good. We'll change the date with Eighth Street for two weeks. I like them, Karen and Sally. They're smart. There's something sad about them, too. Maybe it's just—they're serious like us. You seemed to hit it off with Sally." He grinned at her with some kind of private pride. Had he read her thoughts—sensed that something had happened between them?

"And what about Karen? I mean, I didn't know you went for tall women that much." Why hadn't she questioned him—asked how they'd met? But if she began prying, then…

"Let's not tell anyone in the group, Lucina. We need to have some secrets—don't you think?"

"You're right. We get to have a life of our own. You know what? Let's tell the others we're seeing an old friend of yours. And they can go ahead and have the communal dinner here without us."

"That'll be good for them," Louis agreed. "And for us."

For no other reason than a giggly sense of conspiracy and joy, they flew down to the other end of the loft. Amidst the huge papiér maché heads in various stages of completion and stacks of past issues of *PAN*, they started dancing. The only music they needed was in their heads, their bodies. They swirled and leapt; they did Russian leg struts and tango ochos, caressing the air with their feet and hands. When they tired of moving, they found drumsticks and beat rhythms on the workbench and the cement floor.

They couldn't hear Woody, the painter who lived below them, banging on the floor and shouting out his window. Finally he blasted TAPS from a beat-up trumpet he fooled around with on his painting breaks. Only then did they hear him.

"What the fuck are you two doing? The paint is falling from my ceiling!" Woody, craning out of his window, shouted at the two heads hanging out the window above him.

"Cut the shit, Woody," Louis shot back. "You've never complained when ten of us are rehearsing. So, how's it going?"

"Okay. I just couldn't take your energy, I guess. Myra broke up with me last night. You guys want to go to Kasts for some scrambled eggs? I could use some company."

As they hopped down the steps to meet Woody, Lucina concluded that she would call Sally the next day when Louis was at his job and say yes to dinner.

Louis was chanting in his thoughts: *Karen eats breakfast for dinner, too. Karen eats breakfast for dinner, too.* She sure brought the kid out in him. And he and Lucina? Heck, they were so close, no one could challenge that.

Oh, there was Woody at the curb, looking really down.

33

A Good Lie Can't Hurt

"I shouldn't have mentioned it."

"What, Louis?"

"I was talking to Karen about dinner tomorrow night, if we should bring anything. She starts telling me how burnt-out she and Sally are over the *We Rise* takeover."

"What takeover?" Lucina stopped washing dishes at the small kitchen sink—it looked more like a washbowl—to face Louis, standing up from his desk chair. He certainly wasn't wasting time getting chummy with Karen.

"The women there are about to kick the guys out. There's a lot of in-house fighting. I told her we were looking for a place to go in July and August—that you really needed to get out of the city—and she asked if she and Sally could come. I told her maybe. She sounded desperate."

"You know how the others feel. We have to be careful, Louis. We hardly know Jack, and his girlfriend will be there sometimes. Plus Marlene's coming for the summer. She already came to a couple workshops after Tavern on the Green, when you were healing. She was so horrified by what the cops did to you—and we need her teacher skills to keep us organized."

"You're talking like I was away from rehearsals for months. I had a great talk with Marlene. I wasn't that out of it. Her heart's in the right place."

"I'm just thinking how our troupe is growing. So, about Sally and Karen. We don't want to upset them—but they aren't working with us."

"I know, I know, Lucina. I couldn't come out and say no to Karen."

"Why couldn't you, honey? You know—you never told me how you met." She sidled up to him in a teasing manner, and then stopped abruptly. She didn't want him questioning her about Sally.

"They're going to want to talk about it over dinner, Lucina."

"We'll put them off tonight—tell them the group is going to figure out our summer plans next week."

*****

Louis and Lucina headed to Karen's apartment with a mix of emotions, like teenagers going on their first dates, or double-dating friends. Louis had flowers, Lucina a festively wrapped bottle of Chianti. Yet their excitement was injected with unease. It was as if Karen and Sally were sirens beckoning them to forbidden pleasures.

As they plodded up the narrow stairway, Louis stopped on the third floor. "It's 3A, right?"

"You told me 4A, on the fourth floor."

"Oh, okay. I wrote it down somewhere."

Lucina stared at the photo of a woman, posing coyly in a bathing suit, pinned on the door of Apartment 4A. "They're into pinups," she whispered. "Is that a younger Karen, honey?"

"I have no idea," Louis commented casually, pushing the doorbell.

Karen appeared immediately. "Welcome, you two! Oh—what lovely tulips." As she ushered them into the hallway, a sweet, woody smell enveloped them. "Come into the kitchen, I'll get them into a vase." Louis ambled off toward the right until Karen called out, "Straight ahead—you know! Oh, I forgot, you guys haven't been to my place before. Hope you two like incense. It's sandalwood." She was ushering them into a large, cheerful kitchen.

Is it the blouse—those short puffy sleeves? And not wearing a bra! Lucina hadn't realized how perky and feminine Karen was.

Sally welcomed them in the kitchen. Lucina stopped herself from moving toward her and called out, "Hey, Sally. Good to see you and Karen." Sally wore tan pants and a matching short-sleeve shirt of the kind you could buy in the Army and Navy Store on Fourteenth Street. *One dresses like a guy and the other a girl, maybe a butch-and-femme thing? They both look like women to me—though Sally is more angular and Karen more curvy.* Thinking of them touching each other down there turned her on; she'd never been close to a lesbian couple before.

"You hungry?" Sally was asking. She gestured for them to sit at the kitchen table, covered with a checkered tablecloth, napkins, and what Sally described as "good silver pilfered from my mom and pop's house."

Lucina giggled. "Wow, Sally! If we eat with them, will we be your accomplices?"

"That would be nice," Sally rejoined seductively, flicking her tongue between her lips, meant for Lucina's eyes only.

"Well, I for one can appreciate nice silverware without any bourgeois guilt," Lucina quickly announced, taking the seat next to Louis. *What if he'd seen Sally do that!*

"Guilt—schmilt. Let's eat—I'm famished," Louis said.

She could see the dark rectangles on Sally's chest where a soldier's name and stripes had once been sewn. *Women leftists often wear used military garb—gives them guy power or something. Why haven't I talked about Vietnam to Sally?*

"I'm making spaghetti and meatballs," Karen piped up. "But I like to cook the pasta at the last second. How about some appetizers first?" She offered a tray of crackers and cheese, celery and carrot sticks, hot peppers and small onions. "I forgot to ask what kind of wine you like," she apologized, setting down four wine glasses.

"Oh, I'm sorry—where's my head?" Lucina handed the wrapped bottle to Karen. "We brought you Chianti in a basket, so you'd have a pretty candle holder."

"Perfect, perfect," Karen said as Sally applied a corkscrew to the bottle.

In the cozy, colorful kitchen, as Karen puttered over the stove, they jumped into talking like old friends. Louis was upbeat. Unbeknownst to Lucina he'd brought a poem. "Can I read you something I'm working on," he asked them.

Karen's delight overshadowed Lucina's feeble apology for his taking center stage. When Louis finished reading, she stopped stirring to stare at him. "I love it. It's more playful than Roethke. Whoever wrote about a beard being a hiding place for sweet creatures. It's adorable."

Louis smiled appreciatively at Karen. "A beard can protect a man's sweetness as well…"

"Louis likes to grow a beard," Lucina offered proudly. "He looks very different—older, like a college professor." She was about to say he looked more Jewish in a beard, but stopped short. She was quite sure he was the only Jew in the room.

"I can imagine you looking more Jewish with a beard, Louis. But you have such a sensitive face—a beard would disguise that." Karen spoke with unabashed candor.

Why did Sally close her eyes just then, Lucina wondered. *And Louis' face light up with delight? He just accepts praise. No countering with some self-deprecation.* Why hadn't she noticed this so clearly before?

"I really want to hear about your theater group, Lucina," Sally broke in suddenly, filling the wine glasses as Karen served generous portions of pasta and sauce.

"Well, there isn't much to say—it's a lot of work," Lucina managed, then focused on her food. The two women both apologized for the simple meal and the lack of decorum, Sally emphasizing that she herself was definitely not a skilled hostess. Lucina was confused: Did they think she and Louis required special attention? Or was Sally suggesting a butch couldn't be a hostess? She tried not to think of them embracing each other, but the wine was making her high. *Do they just use their hands— Sally on top...?*

Every time Louis started talking about their theater work, Lucina tried to turn the conversation to some political news. When she nudged Louis under the table once, he just moved his chair. But when she started talking about the troupe's interest in making an ecology play, Louis scowled at her.

Karen made more apologetic comments about the meal. "It's not a gourmet meal—I've never learned how to use herbs." Lucina wondered if Sally had helped her—or maybe a butch didn't cook at all. Maybe she just took out the garbage like dads did.

Louis got them to talk about their work for the *We Rise* paper. They both wrote articles about women's issues. When Sally mentioned the growing lesbian-feminist stance, Lucina wanted to ask more questions. But it was clear they didn't want to talk about the political upheaval. *Probably because there isn't enough trust between us yet,* she decided. By the time Louis began telling funny stories about the crazy things that happened in their collective work, an hour had already passed. Karen suggested they move into the more comfortable sitting room, where there were small tables for glasses and plates.

Lucina was curious about the rest of the apartment. "There's one bedroom, Karen?"

"I'll show you another time. Didn't have time to clean it today. But the bathroom's good to use. It's to the right of the entranceway."

The sitting room had shelves of books, a desk, a couch, and folding chairs. "This is actually my work space," Karen announced. "I like the quiet, where I can think. You two make yourselves comfortable on the couch. Sally and I are used to folding chairs."

"It's hard working with a lot of people when you've been used to working alone," Lucina blurted out. *Be careful, wine makes you talk too much. We shouldn't be talking about our group any more to them—it'll get their hopes up for the summer.*

"It sure is," Louis added quickly. "You think you've worked out a really strong play, and then someone in the group messes it up." The comment seemed good-humored, but when he set his wine glass down Lucina noticed his hand was trembling. Sally and Karen stayed silent, as if they noticed it too. Then in a quiet, somber tone Louis began talking about the beating in the park. Lucina saw how he was drawn to look at Karen, much more than at Sally. Probably because she seemed softer, more emotional.

Both Karen and Sally were incredulous. Tears came to Karen's eyes and Sally's fists clenched.

"You guys are really brave to play in the park," Sally said. "The Movement has a lot of enemies."

"And to feel impotent—not be able to protect your— partner," Karen added, her voice breaking.

Suddenly, through their eyes, Lucina saw the terrible situation in a new light. "You know, Louis, we can't blame only

Hans for your being attacked. There could have been pro-war goons in the audience, wanting to start a brawl and egging the cops on."

"Lucina and I have been really depressed about this. I should have run; she should have screamed louder for help—"

"But the cops are trained to beat on us," Lucina burst in. "We're enemies of the state." Talking to Karen and Sally was good for them! These women could support the two of them when their group couldn't. They made no judgments; they had emotional distance. Both women were aware political artists and good listeners. Maybe that's why the four of them had found each other. Somehow she felt safer than she had since that awful day in Central Park. But not for the summer! Living with them… Just then she felt Sally's eyes on her, as if she'd heard Lucina's thoughts and was trying to touch her face, her lips.

Louis had been responding to Karen's questions and talking on and on about Hans. "…admitted how fucked up he was…got involved in environmental activism…thrown out of college, deserted by his parents…no green card…" Meanwhile, Sally had grown restless.

Lucina broke in. "I guess there's always some envy and competitive feelings in close-knit groups."

Sally was nodding. "It's terrible how friends can become enemies when politics are involved."

Karen stood suddenly. Patting Louis' shoulder, she asked, "Who needs something more to eat?"

"Or drink?" Sally added.

"Yes, great!" Lucina would have more Chianti and Louis more spaghetti and meat balls.

*****

After Louis and Lucina had helped Karen and Sally clear up, the group returned to the study/sitting room. Karen joked that she didn't need a living room, since they lived in all the

251

rooms. Then Sally reached out for Karen's hand and began talking very softly about her struggle with alcohol and drugs. "First, an escape route from my repressive family—then a dead end." She looked at each of them for reactions. "I'm still fighting my addictions," she added, pointing to her wine glass. "It's been grape juice all evening for me."

"Talk about being courageous, Sally. Good for you." Louis spoke with genuine admiration.

Lucina couldn't find words. *So why was she still going to bars*, she wondered. *Not just to check her wall hangings. She'd definitely had a beer that day!* Something didn't compute. Probably she didn't want Karen to know she still went to bars— and definitely not that she'd kissed her, Lucina, at one of them!

Now Karen was talking about her physical problems: one leg was shorter, which put her whole body out of kilter. Louis' face twisted with concern as she showed them her shoes—one had a much thicker sole. "See, I can look normal," she laughed. "But I couldn't do sports and my classmates called me Limpy. So I became political to make things better."

"You've been through so much, Karen. I could never do that." Lucina felt ashamed for having sized her up as a perky, pretty femme. The woman had suffered this deformity all her life, and had some humor about it.

*****

Lucina tried to keep her focus equally on both women. If Sally's gaze fell too long on her, she tensed. With these new emotions pulling on her, she had the urge to blurt out then and there: "No way can you two live with our theater group this summer. It would be the end of Louis and me." *Oh dear God—if he knew the extent of her longings! Louis was frowning at her. Was he reading her thoughts? Certainly Karen's deformity had upset him—he must really be into her, that's why. How could*

252

they concentrate on theater work with those two around! But, if Sally wanted to meet with her, alone…?

"I think I'd like some coffee now," Lucina said. "Is that possible?"

"You know—that's a good idea," Karen said. "Oh, I forgot. We have some chocolate chip cookies for dessert." Lucina smiled appreciatively when Karen asked if she would help her. She really needed some distance from Sally—and from Louis.

During a heartfelt departure, hugs all around, Karen asked Lucina pointedly, "Could you talk to your group soon about our joining you for the summer? We could really use a break from the upheaval at *We Rise*. We'd pay you something. Louis did tell you about our women's takeover plan for the newspaper?"

Lucina was miffed by her insistent tone, or was it the way she smiled at Louis and held onto his arm that bothered her?

On the subway ride to Spring Street, Lucina thought again how Karen was so open to them about her leg. How she'd wanted to console her somehow. "You must have wanted to kiss Karen goodbye, Louis?" she asked aloud.

"I didn't touch her, Lucina," Louis snapped.

"I didn't say you did! I asked if you wanted to."

Louis stayed silent. When the subway doors opened on their stop, he ushered Lucina out quickly. On the street, only a few people passed them. It was quite late.

"Listen, I can tell you like Sally—" Louis spoke carefully taking her arm. "But I guess since she's a woman, you really didn't want to kiss her in that way. Am I right?"

Lucina hoped her silence would stop Louis from continuing.

"Louis, I just didn't understand all the things Karen was saying about her health. What else is wrong with her besides her legs?"

"She has angina, Lucina. She told me that over the phone—an irregular heart beat and there's heart problems in her family."

"She wants you to worry about her—I can see that. You have to take care of yourself! We have to tell them they can't come away with us this summer, Louis. It would be a disaster!"

"We can't say it like that. I'll take care of it, don't worry. We need to keep our connection with them separate from the group. I'll call Karen this week and tell her the troupe has decided we aren't having any guests. We're just focusing on our work, making more plays, preparing for our paying gigs. They'll understand that."

"That's lying, Louis. But okay, say it how you want. Obviously you enjoy talking to her, right?"

"There are good lies and bad lies, Lucina. It's okay if you're not actually hurting anyone."

"I agree. They must have other places they can go to. Well, the sooner you call her…I just can't take worrying about this anymore!"

PART VI
THE YELLOW FARM

34
The Yellow Farm, July '66

Al and Louis had finally found a summer place large enough to accommodate the Fire Dragon Street Theater and their work for six weeks. On the way back to the city in the group's Chevy van, they relaxed and congratulated themselves.

"We did good, Al. Marin and Lucina are going to be ecstatic. Let the goddamn Beatles have India, Fire Dragon is going to the Yellow Farm."

"Whew, Lou. So, it took four trips to find Eden! This ole Chevy is holding up good. Smart of the group to chip in for it—my pickup was on her last legs anyway. Who would have believed we'd find a place in the Berkshires at this late date? You've got business smarts, Lou. I wouldn't have thought of going to a Vets Against the War storefront to ask around for places to rent."

"We get a farm house, plenty of bedrooms, a barn to rehearse in, chicken coops, sheds, an apple orchard, grassy fields. All rent free for just caretaking and repairs on what do you call it—the septic tank trench? You know how to do that, Al. Right?"

"Lucky the owners are movement folks. So, you handle them, Lou. I'll get the septic tank trench done. You know me, man—a dude who keeps his tools under the bed, ready for action. We should set up a Hare Krishna commune, charge rent, make some money. We haven't gotten paid for one damn performance. All those rich kids dropping out of the system and joining groups—they still have their hands on their dads' purses. Just saying—"

"Yeah, well—let's see how it goes with thirteen of us, never lived together before. Look, we'll find a way to make some money on our plays. I'm just glad to be walking on dirt and not cement for six weeks."

As they crossed the George Washington Bridge, headed for the West Side Highway, Karen and Sally came into Louis' thoughts. They could have stayed in the barn for a weekend—relaxed—watched a rehearsal. But no, they'd insisted on coming for the whole time. Good thing he'd lied to them! Imagine if he and Karen had wandered off in those hills? Holy shit, Lucina would have burned with rage if she'd found them fucking under the pine trees! That would have been the end of Karen—and then Lucina would have lost her new friend Sally, too.

*****

When the troupe saw the Yellow Farm's enormous barn glowing like a field of daffodils, they thought they'd found heaven. Skies had never seemed bluer, leaves so green. Gnarly apple trees, clouds pressing against hills—a feast for the senses. This was a magical nest, a resting place for a while. They could rehearse in the barn or outdoors! And what of the craggy sheds with rusty stoves, the raggle-taggle chicken coops, and those mysterious woods to explore—to say nothing of the wondrous grass for catnaps. It would take a few days to settle in before getting to work.

Away from the hot cement and city pressures, concerns narrowed down to the practical: Who wanted rooms in the house? Who wanted a shed or a coop? There were magical places to fix up and fit into—no one looking over anyone's shoulder to say how or why. Who'd seen a yurt before, with its conical roof like a weathered witch's hat? Lucina secretly called the yurt *Rune II*.

She breathed in the colors and textures, already imagining a landscape she would paint someday: sky made of thick cobalt and cerulean blues laid down in rhythmic strokes like waves, like Van Gogh had done. Apple trees that danced against the sky, their leaves a hundred different shades of green. And around each leaf, emanating warmth and joy, a fine outline in Naples yellow.

Marin was as ecstatic as Lucina about the place. "This is my best fantasy. I've been in a black-and-white film noir all year," she said. "I'll dream in Technicolor again."

*****

Private spaces blossomed into the personalities of their occupants. "A baker's dozen to be eggs-act," Louis joked. He and Lucina picked a corner bedroom on the second floor, seeking some of the privacy they'd given up to group life. Lucina assumed a wife's caretaker role—in spite of feeling her attempt at becoming a wife was a travesty—and decided that Louis should write his poems at the small oak desk in the corner by the window. "Thinking at a desk always rejuvenates you, honey," she insisted.

Though Hans had come through with a backstory and an apology, there were bound to be new tensions among them. She reasoned to herself: *Communal living, sharing tasks and space won't be easy. But our room, at least, must be a safe zone.*

She also claimed a secluded shed where she could vent her tension. By exercising her vocal cords, transforming hoots, hollers, and shrieks into shaped tones bearable to herself and sometimes to others, she felt considerably better. She wondered how many singers had once been screamers who'd found the same secret: unwanted emotions could be turned into the most magnificent sounds with correct breathing and manipulations of the vocal cords. Singing became a daily habit. Singing would keep her calm! Writing would do the same for Louis. And if she needed to, she would invite Marin for talks.

Jenny and Hans claimed the room next to Louis and Lucina. With an insatiable need to fuck loudly and often, they rolled and rocked the bed, unaware that the sound of a heavy metal bed frame knocking against a shared wall planted nightmares in their housemates of billy clubs smashing down on soft flesh.

Lucina wanted to kill them. But Louis pulled the covers over their heads and calmed her. "They're just doing guerrilla sex again," he said, hugging her tightly. He was trying out the peacemaker's stance, as she had suggested. "A hornet's nest demands utmost caution," he added slyly, but she was fast asleep.

Al and Marin liked a bedroom on the first floor with a view of the apple orchard. The room was large enough for Marin to do her physical exercises, and for Al to fashion puppets in papier mâché. Also, there was room under the four-poster bed for his tools.

Hugh and Courtney took two small upstairs bedrooms, content with a single bed, a chair, and a closet where they could cram their belongings. They complemented each other: Courtney was either bubbly or forlorn, depending on an emotional clock no one else could read, while Hugh stayed wry and contained at all times. Though each of them flirted with Marlene, the schoolteacher with them for the summer, they stayed closest to each other. What went on with them when they journeyed into those seductive woods, they didn't say and no one asked.

Marlene, a life-skills and sex-education teacher, fell in love with a downstairs room that must have been a sewing room, as threads and small pieces of cloth were visible everywhere in woodwork and molding. She said it made her feel peaceful to sleep in a room where a woman had spent time working on her craft. She also told Louis that she could keep track of them all from her first-floor lookout, since it was near the kitchen. Mainly she loved the large windows, letting in lots of light. Lucina was sure Marlene could help handle any group disputes in concrete ways.

Jack, a yoga teacher, who would help them deepen their breathing and relax their minds and bodies during the summer, wanted the yurt. But with Marlene's suggestion—"it ought to be kept free as a meditation space for whoever needs it"—he agreed to "bunker down" in the barn loft. "I hope you mean 'hunker down,' my friend," Marlene offered kindly. "I mean, we're not in a war zone yet."

Jack's girlfriend, Joan, a yoga fanatic, flitted in and out of the group like a willful butterfly. But when she was there, she followed through on her chores faithfully and engaged in her yoga practice, usually in the headstand position. Hugh joked that he recognized her feet but not her face. She shared the loft area with Jack, while the barn's main area was kept free for the troupe's rehearsals, unless the weather was nice and they wanted to work outside.

Woody and Trish, faithful groupies and sometimes prop carriers, were also invited to spend the summer. They both contributed to food expenses, and each had a car that could be used by group members. Woody, the painter who lived beneath the rehearsal space on Spring Street, claimed a shed near the main house. Trish, a writer and tie-dye artist who'd favorably reviewed the troupe several times, transformed the large chicken coop into a dazzle of sensual colors and aromas. She gathered rough boards and fashioned a desk and shelves; lined the chicken nesting boxes with maroon and orange cloths making drawers for her clothes. With the smell of chicken manure gone in four days through her ceremonial cleansings with sage, she was ready for guests both human and otherwise. It was a hideaway a child might want but wouldn't have the skill to make. Trish's Roma ancestry was born again in that coop. If someone felt lonely or at loose ends, they would be drawn to her nest for restoration. In the cozy quietness of her place, a beloved deceased aunt or a vanished former lover could be remembered.

A couple of small rooms were left empty on the first floor of the big house to serve as quiet studios for anyone who needed them. Yet even as the personal spaces took on aspects of their inhabitants, the buildings held odd creaks and smells and always the putrid odor coming from the back, where a flower garden covered the septic tank containing the wastewater from the house.

*****

In these rumbling, rambunctious times, many makeshift groups like the Fire Dragon Street Theater were questioning the nuclear family, with its typically dominant father, conciliatory mother, and rebellious, impatient children. But no one had taken a crash course on how to create a new kind of family overnight. As this group of thirteen struggled to do things differently, with awareness and sensitivity toward each other, it seemed everything was up for questioning.

Young people on the Left had already learned to speak out and speak up to politicians, professors, presidents, and police—even when being beaten. Lucina observed that the men in the troupe, especially Louis, were more adept than the women at this. As she and her sisters became increasingly aware of this imbalance, the articulate, outspoken guys began to seem aggressive and macho. The younger men, Courtney and Hugh, also felt challenged by Louis. And Hans, who'd grown up with a harsh father, became uncomfortable when any of the guys got worked up. It wasn't until the late 1960s, when the women's movement took off, that women spoke out easily on topics important to them in a mixed-group situation, the men being required to listen or leave the room.

There were lots of differences among the troupe members that could cause tensions and resentments. Newer members—Courtney, Hugh, Marlene, Jack, and Joan—listened and watched for a while before pressing their viewpoints. Yet it was necessary for the senior members—Lucina, Louis, Al, Marin, and Jenny, though not Hans, as he was still on probation—to encourage input from the newest recruits. Excess passion and verbosity intimidated and annoyed quieter types. Each one had to be sympathetic to the others' styles and needs. Self-reflection was imperative. Impatience caused hostility. One's own expectations could not be assumed to be shared by others until the group agreed.

How were these dynamics playing out at the Yellow Farm?

*****

Lucina was doing a lot of reflection. How would she and Louis be changed by the weeks ahead? Their attempt to find friends outside the group hadn't gone well. Sally and Karen were extremely upset with them—not answering calls. The crime didn't justify their punishment. What if Sally refused to see her again? Lucina must put Sally out of her mind, focus on those she was with! But how to be with them all and feel at ease? She was explaining, or was it defending, Louis too often—a self-appointed mediator trying to help opposing entities find peaceful coexistence. Was this role rooted in childhood—her praying that

Mom and Dad wouldn't argue so much? She should let Louis fight his own battles. He could take care of himself, except when cops with billy clubs attacked him.

Lucina felt tension when Courtney complained about supper chores while eyeing Louis petulantly. Louis told him to stop being annoying. He confronted the aggression head-on, then let it go. But she, Lucina, couldn't let go. She spoke to Courtney about it, in private, and reasoned with him. "You get to choose when you want to do each chore," she reminded him. "But obviously, we have to share the work; no one gets waited on here, brother." He thanked her, then said no more. Was she protecting Louis, she wondered? Or trying to stop Courtney's disturbing whining? She could request a group meeting to discuss complaints that needed addressing. But first, she'd better examine her own behavior more closely.

Why the need to remind the new recruits what Louis had done for them? "He organizes most of our gigs…He and Al got us this place for the summer…If it weren't for Louis…" She heard herself going on and on like an overprotective mother. Similarly, she needed the group to recognize her past accomplishments—a sculptor with an MFA degree. Of course, her attempt at giving lectures on art and theater history had crashed like a lead balloon. A group has its own whims and ways, she decided, like a person does; it just takes time to figure things out. And to do that, you have to be sensitive to each member. Take Jenny, for example: For all her beauty and grace, her coquettish gestures were more like pleas to be loved. That didn't mean Courtney and Hugh could accuse her of being sexually provocative. Courtney had to look at himself. To Lucina's mind, he disguised his adoration for Hugh by always trying to one-up him. There were so many sides to each of them. Marin, though obviously devoted to Al, sneered at his shyness with the impatience of a critical older sister. How could all of them own up to actions that hurt each other?

It fascinated her how Hans seemed to be working out his own way of reconnecting to the group. After dinner, he'd started telling stories, obviously exaggerated, where he was the hapless victim in confrontations with the police. In one he was the valiant flag carrier whom the police targeted. As he screamed for help, they handcuffed him and dumped him and his flag in the paddy wagon. But miraculously, he used the tip of his flag to wedge open the paddy wagon doors and make his escape. Always both victim and survivor, he was becoming a more and more comical figure.

Louis' actual brutalization by the cops made Hans' scenarios seem like comic-book fantasies of a want-to-be activist. Lucina decided the kid was indirectly countering his shame for his reckless acting out and betrayal of the group at Tavern on the Green. Well, whatever he was up to in his head, he was definitely obsessed with being treated unjustly, she decided. Better he acted out in his storytelling than in their performances! She would run some of her thoughts by Louis to hear his interpretation. It was tricky, though; she had to be more and more careful about what she shared with Louis. Sally alone—that was only for herself. Her thoughts about Sally and Karen together—those she could share: *They're so deeply involved with that group at* We Rise. *Why couldn't they understand our need to limit who could stay with us? Damn it! They sure didn't! Fuming mad like we betrayed them. Well, we better focus on our members, just like Louis said we needed to. We need good vibes so we can have focused rehearsals. That's our job. And we need to work on some new plays.*

She went to her private shed so she could vocalize, clear her mind, hear her own thoughts. She would talk out loud if she needed to! She sat on the log she'd hauled into her space. *In the past, I would have been figuring out how to begin carving this log. Today I'll call it my "talking truth seat."* She'd hung a small mirror on the shed wall and adjusted her position so she could look at her face as she spoke. It was like an acting exercise.

"First thing you have to figure out, Lucina Holzer…" She eyed herself seriously, then wrinkled her brow, realizing she was already talking out loud. Good thing no one was nearby. "Why is Louis a target for animosity—and what is my responsibility around that?" She decided to wear her baseball cap, like another character, and try to answer.

"He's the most out there, like a scout, plunging us into new and sometimes dangerous territory. Meaning he takes the most risk. His skill with words can run roughshod over the faltering articulations of the rest of us; his indomitable sureness seems like courage, but maybe it's armor, just like Hans' bravado hides his insecurities. Al, Marin, and I sometimes hang back when Louis makes a suggestion. Maybe we're shyer and more afraid than Louis. Or maybe our caution is our wisdom. Sure, Louis insisted someone should keep a beat on the red drum throughout our dramas, that there was hypnotic power in a drumbeat. But it's also been shown: an incessant drumbeat can build up frenzy and enrage people. Wasn't Hugh beating on the drum the whole time the cops were stalking Louis?"

Lucina, cap off now, gave herself an encouraging nod in the mirror. "How can we voice our complaints in a helpful way? Al, Marin, and I don't criticize Louis behind his back."

Cap on again: "Courtney and Hugh hide behind bushes and shoot arrows at him. Meaning they're not upfront with their feelings. I mean, these two guys could be projecting a power figure from their past onto Louis—getting revenge on a mean, insensitive father." Imagining what a mean father would look like, she growled at the mirror and shouted out, "Fuck you! Fuck you, Louis!" in a deep voice, imagining it coming from Courtney and Hugh. Pausing a moment to study her growling expression, she thought, *Damn, I'd be mad at a father who looked at me like that. But Louis doesn't browbeat those boys; they must feel impotent around him for some reason. Louis is not a mean person.*

"By being so outspoken, Louis actually puts himself out there," she was speaking aloud again, "and others can rip him apart. Maybe he's so scarred from being teased as a kid for his Yiddish accent and his awkward body that he's neurotically drawn toward emotional chaos? To being attacked? I'm no therapist, but if he changed his MO—you know, his modus operandi?—I think that's what it's called."

Cap off: "Okay. Next question. How can Louis avoid being attacked? No one goes after Al, except sometimes Marin, who wants him to speak up more."

Cap on and nodding to herself, Lucina answers: "I'll say to him, 'If Courtney, Hugh, or anyone else grumbles, you and I don't have to fix it. And above all don't be confrontational. I'll tell him about my experience with my parents: the less I argue with them about the government's aggressive policies in Vietnam, the more they want to know my viewpoint. Of course, in *Choice*, Sam's parents don't budge from their rigid 'America right or wrong' stance. They don't hear him at all so he feels he has to shout his anti-war feelings at them, but it's to deaf ears. No communication. No acknowledging the other's viewpoint. And definitely no thinking together."

Cap off again: "Is Louis feeling too responsible for what goes on in this group?"

Cap on: "Maybe it's a matter of trusting that other people are doing their share of the work. I don't think he realizes that mainly they need him to re—" She broke off. She saw a hand tapping on the window next to the mirror, then a face pressing on the glass, staring at her. She stood, confused and embarrassed.

Marin, now knocking on the door, called out to her: "Lucina, can I come in for a minute?"

Oh, Lord. It's Marin! Has she been watching me the whole time? Hearing me carry on about Louis...

Lucina opened the door, her face still tensing with all the facial gyrations she'd been trying out. "Marin, come in—I've been wanting us to talk together." She worked her face into a friendly look.

"I was just jogging by and I heard voices—and someone shouting, 'Fuck you, Louis' and 'Louis, we have to figure it out.' But is he even here? You're alone, aren't you? Are you okay?"

"You're going to think I'm crazy, Marin. I'm trying to figure out how we can tell each other things that are bugging us, before they get out of proportion. Do you know what I mean?"

Marin plunked down on the floor in front of Lucina and hugged her friend's knees. "Do I know what you mean?" She threw her head back and laughed hysterically.

"What is it, Marin? Honey? Did I say something?"

"Luie, if we had tuned into each other's needs months ago—it was so painful, when we were putting *Choice* together— and you and I were butting heads about the gun scene. I so much didn't want Al to put a gun to his head, even if he was playing a character. I already lost my brother to a gunshot! Watching Al hold a gun to his head—you just didn't understand! And it wasn't your fault. I hadn't told you or the group. I had to collapse in grief before I could tell you. And before you, Lucina Holzer, could hear me. Of course, I needed to sing out to my dead brother, to all of you, to all the haters of gay people."

Lucina sank to the floor beside Marin and put her arms around her tenderly, both of them in tears. "I was such a blind fool—I'll never, ever forget how insensitive I was. If I'd been able to hear you—feel you—listen to you. It took you a long time to warm up to me again."

"So you understand now? I do understand what you mean. We all have to be able to tell each other important stuff about ourselves, or about each other that has to be talked about before we hurt each other so badly. So, is that why you were calling out Louis' name? With a lot of 'fuck you.' You're angry with him! Is he having an affair with someone, Lucina? Oh my god. I thought you two were like completely dedicated to each other—like married in your hearts and souls."

"Marin, it's not about that—I mean, Louis and I love each other deeply. I'm just so sensitive to what people think of him. I'm like a possessive wife. I don't want him ever to be attacked by anyone, cops or people in the group."

"Who's going after Louis? I wasn't aware of anyone…"

"Some of the younger men seem irritated by him."

"You mean Hugh and Courtney. They're probably just jealous. Louis has such presence. He knows who he is."

"He fools people that way—he's really so vulnerable and he doesn't know how to protect himself. And now here at the Yellow Farm, other things are coming out as well."

"Tell me, Luie. You can trust me. Al and I love Louis."

"I know you never talk behind his back about him—and he loves you both, so much. It's about the other women."

"Oh, so he is into someone here? That's painful, baby."

"It's just that I'm seeing a whole other phenomenon happening around him. You and Al go to bed pretty early, so you probably haven't noticed this. But late at night, over poker games or moon-gazing, one of the women snuggles up to him and pours out some dark secret to him. You can't believe it, Marin. He transforms into a warm, furry teddy bear who listens and cares like a good daddy. Jenny, Marlene—and last night Joan, who barely knows him, put her head on his shoulder and let out some confidence. I watched for a while and then I couldn't take it. And in exchange for his attentions, they show weepy concern for his welfare. 'Oh, Louis, please read us your poems…You're so funny, Louis. I love your stories.'"

"Am I hearing envy in your voice? It's true, Louis loves women. He isn't afraid of us. Al says he has a lot of the woman in him. Meaning he's emotional and shows it. Of course, you know that."

"Okay, maybe you're right. That weepy concern I'm pinning on Marlene, Joan, and mainly Jenny is in me as well. Jenny is 'so sorry about Louis being beaten,' as she keeps saying, that she's offered to give him a massage to unlock his tension."

"That's not a bad thing, Luie. She's had training in massage, you know."

"But Louis knows I can do that for him. I do massage him, more than he does me. I'm good with my hands."

"I don't think you need to be worried about Jenny's intentions toward Louis. She's continually seduced by her Hans and the way he flaunts his virility. You told me that you hear them fucking, right? Thank God we're not next door to them."

"A few nights already, it's been 'Fuck me—harder, harder!' Jenny crying out along with the hoot owls. But Marin, I'm sure I've heard Hans weeping. Maybe he's crying out for one of the men to embrace him, so that finally he can stop trying to be so tough and just be, because—" She stopped talking and took a deep breath. *Be careful, don't say anything you'll regret. Marin wouldn't understand how you even thought that Louis maybe needed that too. Yes, he likes how women cuddle up to him—but maybe what my sweetheart needs is not women clinging to him in the group, but a strong, no-nonsense guy to hold him and let him weep.* She looked at Marin's strong face, her deep eyes, less troubled since she'd revealed her brother's tragedy. Marin's mouth was pursed as if she was thinking about something troubling. Then it was Sally's mouth that Lucina was seeing in her mind. Sally's mouth that had come down passionately on hers. If she needed this from a woman—why wouldn't Louis need…?

"I'm glad you trust me enough, Lucina, to talk to me like this. We've been really careful of each other the past few weeks. I'm just so glad I jogged this way—and I wasn't afraid to look in on you. Do you have more to tell me?"

"I'm just wondering if my own weepy concern for Louis could be disguised guilt for having some envy of him. This supercharged, supercapable man. Beside him, I feel inarticulate, inept with words."

"That's bullshit, Luie. We're talking now—and you're being very clear, believe me."

"Well, I want to be as articulate as he is—I've just got to work on this, that's all. I can't stand having this hang-up—that's probably why I'm supersensitive to anyone who seems to resent his smart way with words."

"Talk about finding ways to own our hang-ups! Have you been tuning into Hans lately? He sure is finding an outlet for his anxiety and tension. What's he doing—entertaining us with exaggerated tales of his dangerous confrontations with Danish, German, and English police after the dinner hour? We have to find a way to put it in a play—so it doesn't get to be too much. I see it as some kind of self-reflection in a dramatic way that he can share with others. Wouldn't it be great if we all could do that—make up improvisations about parts of ourselves that we would like to change?"

Lucina looked like Marin had just expressed the most brilliant epiphany. Her eyes opened wide and her mouth dropped in some kind of wonder. "Marin, Marin—you're like the goddess of wisdom, Athena, or whatever her name was. You've just given me the answer to what I've been asking myself for days now. And why I came here to my hideaway today—to do a kind of exercise—talking out loud to hear my own thoughts—and try to articulate some kind of way to help our group. And you just say it outright, like it was the most obvious solution all along."

"What? What did I say? I don't remember exactly."

"'Wouldn't it be great if we all could do that—make up improvisations about parts of ourselves that we would like to change?' Marin, Marin, my friend—I need you so much. You're so insightful, you're so sensitive. And you're really so very beautiful." Lucina blushed with her outburst of love. If only she could tell Marin about the secret parts of herself—the parts yearning to touch and be touched by another woman.

35
Theater as Therapy?

Lucina, with Marin's input, set up a Reflection Workshop at the end of the first week to give everyone a chance to air any gripes they had about the summer's setup and to consider changes they could make in themselves to help the group function better. Though this kind of personal sharing would be a new experience for all of them, linking consciousness-raising groups with vital political action was becoming essential to movement work throughout the country.

Louis and Al supported the workshop idea and felt they should start out meeting in the barn, since they were used to working in a large indoor space. "It's an exercise in self- and group-awareness," Marin told them. "We share one aspect of ourself that we want to improve, in order to be a more valuable group player both day-to-day and in the theater work."

"All of us can't spill our guts in one meeting!" Al laughed.

"Al's right," Louis spoke up. "It's got to be an ongoing thing; we'll do it before our rehearsals. No big deal. I don't want to spend all summer analyzing ourselves. But doing it as an acting exercise, so we'll also be developing improvisation skills at the same time—that makes me feel better."

"I think we should ask someone to help us act out our self-awareness shit," Al suggested.

"Well, I hope it doesn't turn into a pile of shit," Louis quipped. "We already have to deal with the septic tank work, Al."

"Come on, Louis. You said you were open to new ideas," Lucina scolded.

*****

Saturday early evening found the members of the Fire Dragon Street Theater gathering in the spacious barn for a meeting. They each had a fair idea of what it would entail, as Lucina and Marin had talked up the plan for a group-awareness session to kick off their work together. They would explain their idea further when everyone was together.

The two women began by attempting to describe how a session on self-reflection to improve the group should work. But it wasn't going well. "I don't get it," Jenny whined. "I'm supposed to put myself down to you all? It's like a game high school kids play—taking turns dissing each other, or goading each other to take off their clothes, piece by piece."

In response to Jenny's complaint, Lucina spoke up. "Look, I'll be the first one. It's just another way of talking real with a friend." She'd already worked out how she might do this.

She would share experiences of how her family's ingrained rules didn't work for her. And by reading Betty Friedan and Simone de Beauvoir, she'd seen she wasn't alone. Their books affirmed how women have been manipulated by men's rules and needs for centuries. *The Feminine Mystique* challenged assumptions that woman's fulfillment depended on being a housewife and mother. *The Second Sex* implored women to take back possession of their destiny. She could add: "We want Vietnam to belong to the Vietnamese, don't we? Well, we women need to belong to us." She sure didn't want to simulate the overprotective mother or wife. And if she talked about this, she'd be implying that Louis also got caught in a role, that of the domineering father. She hoped that bringing this up would make them all think more deeply about how they reacted to each other. Would they feel she was lecturing them? Probably. There had to be a simple way to show—not talk—about this? She'd have to wing it; it was supposed to be a kind of improvisation.

When she stood before the others to model a self-reflection exercise, she felt self-conscious and at a loss. "Okay, I know this was my idea, but now that I'm up here, I'm blanking. What am I supposed to do—own up to something about myself that I want to change? What was that you said, Marlene? 'That I *need* to change for the group's sake.' Right. You're a teacher—would you come up here, be my support person, and help me do this?"

Marlene, looking surprised at being chosen, sashayed up to Lucina and did a curtsy. "At your service, madam," making others laugh. When she added, "You know it's hard to talk about yourself when you don't know everyone that well," many expressed agreement.

"That's so true, Marlene. And we haven't done this before. I'll be the guinea pig. Will you help me focus on one thing I need to change—I know, I know, there's a hundred things you all would like me to improve on…But geez, I have to start someplace." As Marlene took deep breaths, eyes closed, hugging herself, Lucina did the same.

Marlene: "Okay, Ready? So the time is now."

Lucina: "I don't want to play any role this summer that feels to me or the rest of you like it's coming from the nuclear family model."

Marlene: "So, what you're saying is you want a New Clear Model to follow?"

Lucina: "Teachers are so clever, aren't they?"

Marlene: "Yes, we are—but to your point. What is one thing branded in you from your family's model that you want to change?" In an aside, she whispered to her audience, "I should charge her for therapy!"

Lucina: "Now that I'm in the hot seat, I see how complex this is. I should have picked something easier to talk about, like table manners. Example: I shouldn't use my own spoon to serve myself from the group's platter."

Courtney yelled out: "Yeah! I saw you do it yesterday, Lucina—with the mashed potatoes."

Marlene: "I think we're avoiding the topic Lucina needs to talk about. What don't women want?"

Lucina: "Exactly, Marlene. I don't want to lock myself in some repressive role; I want to find new parts of myself. Sometimes I act like the protective wife who really gets upset when someone rejects one of Louis' suggestions."

Marlene: "He does have a lot of them, mainly good ones."

Lucina: "On the other hand, I get jealous—I admit it— when he gets all kinds of attention from everyone."

Marlene: "Wow, you're being brave, sister."

Lucina: "So, that's what I need to work on—seeing Louis as a member of my group, not someone I have to overly protect or, conversely, someone I worry is going to find a woman here who's just too attractive to resist and so…"

Marlene: "Okay, Lucina. You did it! You've got your work cut out for you."

As the two women sat down quickly, looking relieved to be done, many reactions filled the barn. Marin stood up to speak. "Can I just add to your gutsy reflection, Lucina? And you were wonderful, Marlene. You're funny! I want to say, it could have been me saying all that about Al. Living in a group is different from coupledom. This is great—I can see where I have to change, too. And Marlene—I wish you'd been my teacher."

When Louis volunteered to be next in the spotlight, questioning faces watched as he prepared himself to speak. Would he support or contest Lucina's feelings? "My brethren and sistren—just trying to include everyone here—I need to clarify what I want my image and role in this group to be. Forget that I'm the oldest male—I've been told I'm the most outspoken, articulate member and even the unnamed leader of this troupe. Speaking about the nuclear family model—what about the patriarchal-leader model? That's what we have to turn on its head. Males are assumed to be the leaders. Father—head of family. President, always a man—head of country. Doctors—PhDs or medical—assumed to be men. On and on. An articulate, smart, passionate, and hopefully somewhat caring man is always sought to take the leader's role. We grew up assuming that power figures are men, led by their Father, God." He paused to let his point sink in. "And we all know this is bullshit. How many of us had mothers that wore the pants in the family, but still deferred to our bumbling dads?"

His comments were met with appreciative clapping. Then Al called out, "When all of us, women and men, can articulate clearly what we're thinking, like you just did, Louis, we'll have shoved the nuclear family into the cellar." His comment turned clapping into cheers and foot stomping.

Then Marin shouted out excitedly, "Al guided us in building *Choice*, and then we all contributed. Let's stop stereotyping Louis as the leader. It's fucked up. Sure, he does a lot for us, but we all have to step up to the plate. Give credit where credit is due. Turn the old power figures on their heads." Several comments rose up in agreement. "Each of us has to become a power figure…The group is only as strong as its members…The meek shall inherit the earth."

Louis broke into these insights. "This is going to be an enlightening summer, comrades. I'm scared, but I'm excited about the changes we'll go through. But the fact is, I haven't admitted something about me I need to change. So, I call up brother Jack to be my co-conspirator, sorry, I mean my support person to keep me on task. Is that right, Lucina? Oops, I'm not supposed to rely on my—my sister-comrade, Lucina, as a crutch. Jack, get up here quick. I need you!" *Jack will be good at this,* Louis told himself. *He's always talking about knowing your true self.*

Jack, smiling broadly, hopped up to stand beside Louis, obviously pleased to be doing an improv with him.

"Yeah, Jack— I have to learn how to become more tolerant—maybe the word here is 'patient.' Lucina would say 'flexible.' Oops, there I go again."

Jack: "As Marlene would say—get to the point and stay there, Louis."

Louis: "Okay. So, in a nutshell. The only fucking sounds I can tolerate are my own and my partner's. If I wanted to get off on eavesdropping—peepholes—that kind of thing—I'd go to a brothel. Who needs off-the-wall sex happening in the next room? And you know who I'm talking about."

Jack: "Don't look at me, gang. I'm shacked up there in the hayloft with the mice and the crickets, and sometimes Joan."

Louis: "I guess if I can hear you, you can hear me. I don't know where I can go with this—maybe we need more schedules here. You do it in the daytime. And I'll do it at night. Or maybe what I have to learn is tolerance, like I said. What do you think, Jack?"

Jack: "I think the moral is: 'Don't let fucking sounds come between us.' Okay, that's enough. I think you all agree."

*****

There was general agreement that Lucina, Marlene, Louis, and Jack managed to make the reflection workshop less

278

formidable than many had feared. There was time for one more reflection. As they waited for a volunteer, Lucina spoke to the group. "If you all feel this way of looking at ourselves is helpful, do you want to continue tomorrow?" A show of hands confirmed yes. If the sun was shining, they would work outside in the afternoon. Louis' suggestion, that they incorporate the new exercise into the others that always preceded play rehearsals, was also agreed upon.

Hans volunteered to take a turn at the self-critique improv. His eagerness was obvious. He'd already been entertaining the others with his comedic confrontations with authority; he was improving his connection to the group, at least. In his fantasies he was turning into a comedic Danish superhero, somewhat like Batman but with long blond curls that were always putting his enemy off guard, so that they thought he was a girl.

"So, my fellow actors…" He folded his arms, trying to look calm.

Jenny called out, "Are you going to tell us why you're into your hero stories?"

Hans let his arms fall to his sides and ignored her.

Marin then questioned, "What about us? Your sistren, sister actors, aren't—"

Al interrupted, "I'll be your support, Hans. Let him do his thing, guys and gals," he spoke gently, then stood by Hans.

"Tak, Al, for your support. As a Dane among Americans, I feel invisible, the odd one out. Not easily one of the group. Most of you know I'm kind of a *løb vaek*, what do you say, 'runaway?'—like a lot of kids in the counterculture movement here. *Ja*, I tend to want actions to shake people up. See, I act fearless, but I'm shaking in my boots. So what I found helps me, is turning myself into a kind of comic-strip character who wants to do good but gets things mixed up. Like—that guy fighting windmills instead of real enemy soldiers?"

Al: "You're thinking of *Don Quixote* by Cervantes. A brilliant tragicomedy. Now to the point, guy."

Hans: "Aye, aye, Captain." At this point, Hans began slowly stripping down to his jock shorts, as if the discarding of his clothes was painful. Then he mimed comic karate chops aimed at Al, who in turn took on the pose of a martial arts expert, eyeing his opponent like a hawk while warding off each mock blow with ease. Hans, dancing like a crazy person around the sure-footed Al, was encouraged by the laughter in the barn to continue his circling several times, shouting out: "I'm Super Dane…avenging all evil done to man…and woman…my enemy is everywhere…just call on me…and I'll be there." Then Al, jutting his foot in the path of the frantic Hans, caused him to trip. Hans' fall turned into a somersault and their interaction ended in a freeze.

With the improv finished, Hans jumped up beside Al and shook his hand. Was this a preplanned or a true improvisation? Whatever it was, the appreciative onlookers received it with comments like "neat," "skillful," and "Hans and Al are natural comics."

Al summed up their presentation. "The moral of this story is: 'False heroes are bound to fall. So, keep an even keel— and make life real, make it matter for us all.'"

Lucina appreciated how Hans was trying to take himself less seriously and simultaneously win the group's trust. As he paraded about, still almost naked, she fastened on his white, baby-smooth flesh. Did he realize that from the back, with his long blond hair, narrow shoulders, wide hips, and delicate bones, he looked like a muscular young woman? She wanted to let her wariness toward him go, but she still saw him as a potential loose cannon. Why, she didn't know.

Hans had another comment. "I'm not going to act like a tough hero, when I'm still a flailing, frightened young man. And by the way, since this is truth-telling time, I own that mine and Jenny's fucking sounds are pretty damn loud. But as I said, I'm not going to be a braggart anymore. So, maybe we fuck under the bed from now on."

*****

It made Lucina happy that a second session of Growing with the Group—how many names did she have for this new exercise?—might take place the next day outdoors. As the group headed to the farmhouse to make supper, she commented to Marlene and Marin, "My loft's cold cement floor and all those screeches and sirens don't exactly make for a comfortable place to work. But here, Mother Nature is a wonderful masseuse." As she spoke, her attention was drawn to Jenny, slipping out of the barn with Louis. *I bet she's offering him her massage skills again!*

*****

Journal Entry. July 15, 1966: We were trying to decide who would lead our first outdoor workshop, it wasn't a rehearsal, in the field by the apple trees. Marin announced that three people were needed again to volunteer to do the self-reflection improvisation. And Al suggested afterwards that we would do physical exercises, deep breathing, and a meditation. Louis then said that our next time together should be a rehearsal because: "We have to get on with our play work!" And that's when Jenny jumped up shrieking. Louis' jaw and his notebook dropped. He's so affected by her—I guess he thought she was screaming at him.

And I thought Jenny had cut herself. She had a paring knife and a bowl of apples. Jenny is always doing something with her hands during rehearsal, as if the theater work can't capture her full attention. Jack told me later he thought she was having a primal reaction to the self-reflection thing.

I'm surprised he didn't say, "Let the spirit speak, sister," or something like that. He's been to India and has been a follower of Swami Satchidananda for a year. I hope he doesn't push us too much on the spiritual stuff. I like Al's approach to the sacred. He keeps his observations about God in his stories, which he mainly shares with Marin. I don't have to be privy to these observations if I don't want to be. I just wish Al could stop being uptight with me. Or is it the reverse? I can't help it if I find Marin attractive. Sally would be jealous—if she cares about me anymore.

I must be upset, I can't focus. Back to Jenny. We didn't know why she was jumping up and down, shrieking as if her clothes were on fire. Then Al let out a holler that made her noises seem like whimpers. This was followed by Hugh's wail, which went up and down the scale because Hugh can't make any sound that isn't musical. When I roared, we had a quartet. Actually, all I said was "Ouch!"

We were sitting in a bed of very large red ants, ones that knew how to bite hard. Everyone was brushing furiously at their rear ends and legs. Louis kicked at the now-very-noticeable mounds of earth swarming with red bodies.

"We'll have to ignite them out," Hans said in his quirky English.

Jenny goes helpless at times like this. She clutched his arm. I, ever practical, suggested, "Let's get some shovels and dig them out now." "Where will you put them?" Al, even more practical, asked. "In the driveway, and we'll drive the cars over them," I say. "They will have their revenge," Jack says. (I should have known!) "Every living thing is part of a chain," he preaches, "and has its reason to be. Destroy one part of that chain and the whole chain is in danger." Courtney moans. "Not now, Swam-ee, pleas-ee."

Louis came up with the best solution. "Let's just move to where there aren't any ants."

We picked up our belongings—notebooks, thermos jugs of water, mosquito spray—and followed Jenny, waving us on with her large straw hat to a cool-looking place under a big apple tree. We had forgotten to follow Courtney's suggestion– sit on the brightly colored cloth that Al and Marin want us to use for their new play idea, Dream Catcher. If we had, those ants wouldn't have chased us away. When we spread it out full size at our new location, it was large enough for all of us.

The group decided to skip the individual self-reflections this time—what we needed were whole-group exercises. So we did physical exercises led by Hans. Then Marin led us in deep breathing exercises, and finally Jack led us in a long meditation where we all turned into colorful balloons sailing over the lush Berkshire Mountains. After that we took turns sharing what we liked about the first week at the Yellow Farm.

Maybe not everyone is ready to put themselves out there like I did, and Louis and Hans. I'm going to let it go for now. At least I tried to be upfront about some of my mishegoss. I love how Yiddish words sound out what they mean, if that makes any sense? I'll have to ask Louis how he would express it.

36
Do We Need a Giant?

The next day they were under the apple trees again doing exercises. No one was prepared to try the self-reflection exercise, so they haggled about what to rehearse. Hugh thought they needed a separate meeting to decide. "There's so many factors to consider."

Lucina moaned. "That makes me crazy, Hugh. We're meeting now to start work on a new play. We don't need another meeting! We have a sketch already for our *DreamCatcher* play and for *Eco-Drama*. Let's work on them!"

"What sketches? Do you mean drawings or like a written outline?"

"We brainstormed ideas already, Hugh."

"Where was I? I don't remember what…"

"Come on! You're the one who said, 'Why *DreamCatcher*? We should call it *Catching the Dreamer*.'"

"That was Courtney, not me."

"I know the difference between you and your buddy, for god's sake!"

"Why are you two arguing!" Jenny barked. "Do it in private." Holding on to her bowl of half-peeled apples, she edged away from the others. "Let me know when you've decided what we're going to work on."

"We gotta be more patient here," Marin spoke up. "That's why we all have to do a self-reflection. I'll do one sometime, promise. Oh, please don't leave, Jenny."

But Jenny had already disappeared.

"I should go get my journal." Lucina jumped up. "I wrote down notes on *DreamCatcher*, what we came up with at our last rehearsal in the loft." Her glance aimed at Hugh. "It'll help us all remember."

Louis was impatient. "Hurry up, Lucina. We've got to get some work done. Jenny probably has to calm herself alone in the yurt. She'll be back in a minute."

"Then let's get going with our *Eco-Drama*," Al insisted. "I'll take notes. First of all, I see the earth as a giant, a force. Like Louis maybe."

"How about a giant of *both* sexes?" Lucina added, wondering if she should get her journal after they talked about *Eco-Drama*.

"Go get your notes now," Louis interjected. "We'll tell you our ideas…"

Lucina felt her body stiffen. She didn't want the others to think Louis could just order her around. Not after she'd exposed so much of her feelings in her self-reflection. And Al's comment stung. Why can't he see *her* as a force, too?

When Jack, taking off on both Al's and Lucina's comment, called out, "How about a giant ritual figure with the works, breasts, prick and balls," Lucina flashed on *Rune,* stoically wrapped up tightly in the loft for the summer. No one was there to even wonder what was under the sheet. *Maybe she and Louis should have found someone to sublet to for the six weeks?* Though she liked to say that *Rune* was a female power figure, in her heart she knew: she and *Rune* were androgynous, male and female. If the sculpture were with them, it could be the giant on stage. But what stage? Stage for them meant a park, a street, a field, a demo. *Rune* would not last long being shoved around on those stages. At least the sculpture was safe and sound back in New York, and no one was around to boss her.

"Let all the organs hang out." Hugh giggled so hard he farted.

"Go get your journal!" Louis was barking orders again.

"You sound like her father, man." Courtney always reacted when Louis was on her case.

"Okay, okay, Dad," Lucina pandered. She made her exit with a final comment, "This is just too nuclear-familial for me, and I don't fuckin' like it!"

As she made her way carefully towards the house, her old friends Ralph and Marge came to mind. They would get a kick out of her comrades' interactions in rehearsals! She missed them. If only they could've visited the group in Vermont. When she and Louis were with them, she felt more regular, more like she imagined she should feel, not always dangling in the unknown, wondering what was going on. Marge would have found a story in it all. Her short story "Beauty and the Bug" had come out recently. Nobody would ever know that she, Lucina, had been the inspiration. Marge should have dedicated the story to her, Lucina had thought as she read it. But actually, her friend's cute story didn't even try to express her own horrifying experience with a bug. It was Marge's story now.

It was good to get away from them all for a while. And Louis and she acting out! What were they doing? Especially after all their grand pronouncements about working together as comrades, without that possessive-couple crap. They had to learn how to act like group members; they certainly didn't want to be like Mom and Dad. There was no exact way to describe their relationship, no clear image to grab. So confusing. Except they loved each other and were struggling to be close to others in a real way.

*****

While Lucina was searching for her journal—why wasn't it by their bed?—the others were searching for the best way to dramatize saving their planet. "We should be doing a play about the corporation giants, ja?" Hans offered, hoping Jenny wouldn't feel he was dismissing her main concern, the little guys. He sat with the others on their huge white cloth decorated with colorful shapes. "Exxon and Texaco are the giants destroying the earth."

Marin nodded emphatically. "And let's not forget about the biggest polluters of all—the military giants."

Louis carried forth in his usual no-nonsense manner. "Wait a minute. I thought our earth was the giant. We want to protect Mother Earth."

"Right," Courtney agreed. "Can't have it both ways."

"Our Giant can be whatever we want," Hugh insisted, chewing on a piece of grass with a glint in his eyes. "It's *our* Giant."

Louis closed his eyes. Patience!

"Okay, let's keep going," Al broke in. "Our audiences will have a jumble of thoughts about giants as well." He took up his note pad and pen. "So, Hugh—what do you think when you hear the word '*giant*'?"

"Beanstalks, a guy named Jack, and an oversized goof."

Courtney guffawed. "And Jack slew the big bad giant, who lived in the palace at the tippy top of the beanstalk."

Marlene jumped in. "I always wondered how a beanstalk could support a palace and a giant. So, my friends, isn't it time to throw out the fairy tales, like the one that says 'We should protect 'Nam from the Commies?'"

"You're right, Marlene! We should eliminate all the bullshit," Louis added quickly, sending her an appreciative smile. *Lucina said he should generously praise the others.*

"Say you're stranded on a beanstalk with your lover and your best friend, and both of them are falling. Who do you save?" Hugh asked, suppressing a smile.

Louis fumed. Hugh's non-serious question was meant to poke fun at him—after all, Louis was a pro at challenging others with painful hypothetical situations just like that.

"You know what Joseph Campbell would say?" Jack spoke up calmly. "'Myths are visionary and fairy tales are cathartic.' If anybody cares—what we need is a Myth-Fairy, a visionary and cathartic hero. Throw out all giants."

"That reminds me," Courtney cut in. "Is there a game on tonight? I can't be a Myth- Fairy, but I'll be a merry fifth for poker."

"Can we try to stay with one topic for at least fifteen minutes?" Marlene groaned. "We're trying to find ways to dramatize how humans and greed and ignorance are fucking up our planet. And we can't goof around anymore. This is our time to work! Ah, here comes Jenny. Everybody, take a five-minute break. I'll catch her up on our ideas, both the good ones and the silly ones."

*****

Jenny smiled encouragingly at her cohorts. "This is really important—how to make a parable. Is that the right word? About what we need to do to protect our earth."

"Yes, protecting our earth," Hugh echoed. "We have to focus." Then he whispered to Jenny, "Where'd you go off to, babe?"

"I calmed myself down in the I-zone," she whispered back, referring to the yurt. "I really needed to center myself. My body's tensing up again. Guess I soak up other people's vibes too easily."

Hans watched Louis eyeing his girl as she sought a comfortable position on their cloth stage. "What are we making, another Paul Bunyan?" he barked. "I say we tell it like it is!"

"I also need to know exactly what we're trying to accomplish here," Jenny chimed in, paring her apples again.

"We're exploring images, Jenny, for our *Eco-Drama*," Louis responded, "like you just said. How do we dramatize saving the earth?" He felt Hans' eyes on him, so he directed his comment to the bright red triangle next to Jenny.

Jenny looked past Louis' right shoulder. "I'm not very much into this Giant image," she said softly. "All this country can talk about is the giants, the moguls of industry. What about the little guy, the average Joe?"

Louis sensed Hans' agitation with him growing. *And now Jenny's voice so sweet about a topic she usually hollers about! Crap! What a distraction. Gotta stop getting between those two. Hans is too perceptive to keep this up.*

Al was still writing.

Courtney was talking animatedly. "Jenny's right. Have a midget play our earth. Justice for the little people."

Marlene groaned at Courtney. "That's inappropriate, young man."

Hugh countered, "Does it matter if a giant or a midget saves the planet? Aren't we trying to show that all people have to care about the environment?"

"And do something about it. Now you're talking, Hugh." In spite of himself, Louis' glance moved from the red triangle right into Jenny's eyes. "So let's decide. Do we even need a Giant at all?"

Jenny held his look for a second then glanced away to the hill behind them. She said to no one in particular, "I really care about all of us, about us being here in this exquisite place. Just look! How beautiful it is here. So peaceful."

37

Rednecks

Like one multiheaded creature, the actors turned with Jenny to look at the orchard running upward to the top of the hill; the wooden buildings nestled here and there among the trees; the stone fence which made its way in a zigzag fashion to the right behind Woody's shed, dividing their property from the neighboring farm. Their eyes sucked in the same beauty that had touched Jenny and made her cry out to the silence: "How beautiful it is here. So peaceful."

No one heard the first shout. But after several cries shattered their reverie like rifle shots, they all jumped up. Lucina's piercing sounds were coming from the direction of the house.

The late-afternoon sun streamed through the branches of the white cedars clustered to the side of the house, causing patches of light and shadow in the grass and flower garden, like a surreal stage set meant to portend strange happenings. Through the ribbing of the trellis in the garden, making a patchwork of her body, they saw her tiny arms flailing near the back door.

Louis was off and running first. Then Al behind him, followed by the others, arms and legs working double-time, thrusting toward her.

Louis, in front of her now, saw his lover's hair, wet, stringy, hanging down her face: *she slipped in the shower; she cut herself.* But there was no blood. His arms clamped around the shaking woman.

"I was in the bathroom—I heard them shouting all kinds of things. I thought it was one of you playing a game with me. To scare me."

"Sit down here, Lucina. Sit down." He pulled her to a solitary bench by the rose trellis, badly in need of scraping and repainting. The others squatted about them.

"At first I shouted back. Then I realized—it wasn't any of you. I went to the windows upstairs. There were these guys, redneck types, hanging out of their car, a station wagon. Maybe they're still there. They were shouting, 'hippie freaks,' like that. 'Go back to Russia.' Or maybe it was 'Go back where you came from.' That jerky stuff."

"Did they come to the house?"

"I don't know. But they said they were going to come back with shotguns. That's what I heard: if we didn't leave, they were coming back. I think they're still out there." Lucina bent her head to her chest as if to hide. She started to cry.

Al put his hand on her head. "It's okay now. Louis, we should go look!" His voice was tight.

"Wait, Al. Just wait." Marin sat beside Lucina and took her hand.

"Somebody should go look. I was so scared."

Louis took over. "Go inside. Everyone go inside. Don't look out the windows. Al, come with me to the pantry. We can see the road from there."

"They're going to shoot us!" Lucina was sobbing openly now.

Marin and Jenny, on each side of her, helped her up. The three women clung as they made their way inside to the living room. Lucina and Marin sat stone-faced on the couch and Jenny retrieved a glass of water that she put to Lucina's mouth. As Lucina gulped at the water, Marlene could be seen scurrying down the back hallway headed to her room past the pantry.

Jack, Hugh, and Courtney had followed Louis and Al to the pantry but stayed a few feet behind, glad that their older comrades seemed so fearless. The pantry had small windows which looked out on the roadway. Al and Louis edged up to the windows until they could see a station wagon moving slowly back and forth, maybe fifty yards away. Louis ducked suddenly. "One guy has binoculars, Al. I think they've spotted us."

"Well, I sure don't feel safe in this closet. Could you tell if they're white guys or—"

"Shit! They're yelling something at us."

*****

When Lucina had finished drinking her water, Hans pulled Jenny from the couch, and the two tiptoed upstairs.

Marin's eyes widened in disbelief. "They aren't going to fuck now, arc thcy?"

Lucina laughed grimly. "They feel safer in their room, and you know Hans is in constant terror of any run-in with the cops. Oh my god, Marin! That's what happened—in the park with the cops! Hans was running from them. That's why he put the dragon head on and moved into the crowd—he was so scared for himself; he didn't think about protecting Louis."

Marin scowled. "Well, why didn't he just admit to that! He sure has no thought of protecting us now. We're sitting ducks, or as he would say, 'shittin' docks.'" She moved closer to Lucina and began to rub her back gently.

"Marin, they won't leave us alone. They hunt us down, even here."

"Do you think they're cops?"

"Whoever they are—there goes our idyllic Yellow Farm." Lucina shuddered and snuggled into Marin. "They've been watching us. No one has been living here for the last year, but now they know we're here. I bet they've been driving up and down the road since we got here."

Marin had her arm around her. "My god, I wonder if they can see in our windows at night. We walk around naked sometimes. At least, Al and I do. We should call the police."

"We don't want to make it worse than it is, Marin. Maybe the cops hired them to harass us."

"We have the right to be protected, don't we? I'm not going to wait until one of us is dead."

"Marin, let's stay calm. The boys will know what to do."

Marin's shoulders stiffened as she pulled her hands from Lucina's back. "The boys? Let me tell you, Lucina, the boys can't stop bullets. We'll never get any work done."

"Don't worry," Lucina comforted. "We'll handle it." Marin's tragic loss of her brother was so much harder to bear than some punk bullies. "It'll be okay. We have to be strong. We'll work it out—" Lucina faltered. The men were filing into the room like grim pallbearers without the coffin.

"What did you see?" Lucina's voice was as thin as paper.

"They said they're coming back!" Louis couldn't hide the trembling in his voice.

Marin shot a look at Lucina. "That's what you heard them say, too."

"They spotted us in the pantry—nailed me with their binoculars."

Al grimaced. "They could've had a gun. It was hard to get a good luck at them—the sun was glaring on their windows. They shouted and then took off down the road."

Louis groaned. "Damn! If I'd had a camera, I could've gotten a shot of them."

"You mean a photograph of them," Lucina whispered as if intruders might be in the next room. "We don't want anyone getting shot. Maybe we should call the police."

"I'm going to call Jeff," Al said. "After all, he rented to us. Too bad he's in San Francisco. But he should know how to handle them. Probably knows them." He dropped to the couch beside Marin and took her hand.

"Now I know what terrorists are," Lucina said. "People who make you terrified. I feel really terrified." Her face had turned ash white again.

Fixated on her, Louis summoned his confidence. "Look, the world is filled with people like that! They're just trying to scare us. The worst thing we can do is start something with them. We have to be smarter, keep to our business—it'll be okay."

Lucina eyed him warily. "You don't look like you believe that, Louis."

"No, he's right," Jack spoke up. "Don't energize them."

Hugh suddenly jumped up from the floor, where moments before he'd slumped right in front of Lucina. "So, let's get back to our rehearsal," he challenged.

Courtney shook his head from side to side, as if nothing made sense. "Now you want a rehearsal? You're crazy, Hugh."

Jack, still standing solemnly and alert as if on watch, let out a loud, "Fuck this shit!" followed by, "I need a beer."

"I do too," Lucina piped up. "I sure don't feel like talking about giants or saving trees any more today. I think we're all freaked."

Jack shook his head in agreement. "We should meet at nine tomorrow morning."

Sighs of relief rippled about the room as the group made a plan. "Can we meet in the house—in the rec room?" Marin questioned, looking at Al for some direction since he'd offered to run workshops that week.

"Okay, okay," Al responded reluctantly, rubbing his hands for some kind of comfort. "Everybody, bring a list of ideas about an image for our earth. Here, tomorrow morning at nine sharp. Something about its birth and how it's being systematically destroyed. We don't have time to quibble about this. Our earth has to be the power image—her destroyers are greedy, fucked-up bastards."

Louis could not relax. He paced back and forth, barely listening to Al, jerking his head to look out first one and then another of the small curtained living room windows.

Then Jack went on a pep-talk jag. They should just keep doing what they did best, making plays, and not let the little stuff get to them. They would never be a force as a street theater if fear won out.

And that's when Hugh gasped as if he'd seen a ghost. "Oh, my god—it's Marlene. Why is she out there?" And he was out the front door shouting, "Marlene, you dumb girl," making Lucina hide her head in her hands, mumbling, "I can't take this, Louis. Did Marlene put herself in danger by going out there to yell at those creeps? I'm going to get a beer and go to bed. Everybody fend for themselves for supper."

Jack slipped away quickly, saying he would tell Hans and Jenny about the rehearsal for the morning.

"Yes, in the morning," Marin repeated, her eyes fixed on Al who hadn't stopped kneading his hands. "Our work will save us," she uttered grimly.

Louis watched Lucina pull herself doggedly to the stairway and then turn slowly to look at him. Maybe he should call the local police? No, he would wait until Al called the owners, Jeff and Marsha, first.

38
The I-Zone

A few evenings later, Marlene tore through thick, wet grass towards the I-zone—the yurt, where she could find herself and no one was to interrupt you. She hoped Jack wouldn't be there. She really needed to meditate right away. Never had she been so pulled this way and that; but then, she'd never lived with a group of people before. Ever since those horrible men, local hate mongers or whoever they were, had frightened Lucina, Jack had practically moved into the yurt, disobeying the agreement that it be kept a free space for everyone's use. They'd all been "shook up" after all! What had given her the courage to get her Nikon, sneak out to the front yard, hide behind the clump of cedar trees and get photos—the license plate and the men's faces? If there was more trouble, there'd be some evidence to show the police. Funny! When she'd taken the room by the kitchen, she'd felt she would be some kind of watch dog. And she was right. Yes, Louis' beating had shocked her deeply.

She stopped for a second to look at the new moon cutting a thin arc in the sky—like someone just took a kitchen knife and carved open the black sky to let in a sliver of light, she thought. A sliver of light as fragile as life here on this farm. No guarantees at all. Would this group be together in two years? Probably not. Anything could happen, just like that car of roughnecks threatening them. So unsettling. And Jenny and Hans talking about having a baby. Could they really settle down like an old married couple? What about Lucina and Louis? That was another story. They didn't seem the type to have children together. Lucina was too into herself for that! Well, soon enough she'd be back teaching her rambunctious teenagers conflict management. A toss up, which group was more exhausting.

The yurt loomed ahead, a gray teepee shape, surrounded by pine and birch. A few late July crickets sounded from low-lying bushes near the door. Just wait until August when they'll be sounding like a full orchestra.

Good. Dark inside the building. Jack must not be there. Some time for herself, to think, meditate, feel safe.

She thumbed down hard on the latch and pulled. Jack said the door had swelled up and was hard to open. It didn't budge. She tried again, pulling with her whole body.

"It's locked," she said out loud. "But there's no lock on the door, unless it's been hooked from the inside."

Just then, scraping sounds came from inside, the kind a raccoon might make if it were dragging a corncob across the floor, or scurrying to hide.

She thought to call out, but the distinct sound of muffled laughter made her freeze. A woman's voice. In fact, it was Jenny's voice, she was sure of that. No one else had that kind of high, tense laugh, like fingernails running down a blackboard. So, Jenny and Hans, the "fuckers," as Al called them, were at it again. They were in the yurt fucking their brains out, not finding themselves at all!

She was really irritated: the communal meditation space was being used for animal lust. Of course, who knew what Jack did here by himself? Boys did tend to get horny. But those two? They had their own room in the big house to do that stuff.

Maybe she should go back to the house, meditate in her room or hang out with whoever was in the kitchen also needing company. She really needed something tonight, to help her forget about the day. No one had seemed focused at rehearsals all week, except for Al—and here she'd been told Louis was the big organizer. It was weird being with these couples. Thank God that Woody and Trish were here, too. She should hang out with them more. She just didn't feel like being alone in her room. Courtney, Hugh, and Al were probably playing poker or gin rummy in the dining area. At least the kitchen was a no-smoking space.

By the time she got to the house, her sandals were soaking and her feet cold. Yet it felt good, the cold on her feet, like she was awakening into some stronger, tougher part of herself. Maybe someone had left an interesting magazine in the rec room. It would be cozy to curl up there for a while, hear the fellows having fun playing cards nearby.

Two people were in the rec room: Lucina and—was it Hans? Yes, Hans and Lucina had their heads together, talking. They never hung out together. But wait a minute! Hans was in the yurt with Jenny. She'd heard them. Actually, she had not heard Hans. She'd heard Jenny. Then who was Jenny with? How strange.

Before she could say anything Lucina looked up. "Hi, Marlene. Come join us. Hans and I are shooting the breeze. Talking about our *Eco-Drama*. We're thinking about projections, making slides. Make it a Happening, with mixed media. Louis should be back any moment now. He took a walk by the yurt. Said he wanted to count stars for a while and chill out."

Marlene had a strong urge to put her hand on Lucina's head and tell her to go get her man, promptly. That the "flirt"— she did think of Jenny like that sometimes—had him trapped in the I-zone. She really wanted to warn Lucina. Was it her place to do that? Hans would be enraged, probably slap Jenny up good. He shouldn't know that Jenny was there, either.

"What's up, Marlene?" Hans got up from the easy chair. "You look really tired. Sit."

"It's been a hard day." Marlene sank into the chair and closed her eyes. She should be friendly. "At least the weather is nice."

"We never talk together, Marlene," Hans said, pulling a cigarette from his pocket.

"Please don't smoke now, Hans," Marlene said. "I'm sorry, I don't want to be unfriendly, but I really get sick from smoke."

"Have you seen Louis, Marlene?" Lucina spoke with some agitation. "Now that I know creepy rednecks are around, I don't want to let him out of my sight. Maybe I'll go look for him."

Marlene felt her chest cramp. "Oh, stay, Lucina. Can't the three of us talk about *Eco-Drama*? I'm really excited about it. Hans, it's okay—I can take your smoke. I'll open the window. I'm so glad I found you guys. I was feeling so lonely."

39

The Earth Needs Our Help

They would keep rehearsing in the rec room, where they hoped they would be safe from stalkers. Workshops scheduled through August would have rotating "coaches," a word they preferred to "directors." Al, still on as coach, read back his notes from the previous day's work, followed by warm-up exercises and then scene and dialogue development. Some of the warm-up time was used for massages; there were plenty of tight muscles and strained emotions. For the time being, self-reflection improvs had been put on hold; since their common scare, the group was naturally trying to be more sensitive to each other. As Lucina had commented, an assault by possible hostile neighbors felt like a group rape.

Al, not as comfortable taking charge as Louis or Lucina, hoped his wry, self-effacing manner and midwestern charm would put people at ease. He looked a bit like James Dean with his lanky, hands-in-pockets stance and rugged good looks.

"Okay, let's see if I can read what I wrote," he apologized inaudibly, making Lucina shout out, "Please, Al. Louder." She was so used to the charged voice of Louis that everybody else sounded like Mr. Milquetoast.

Al squinted at her under thick eyebrows. "So, I'm trying to talk about how we can image our earth," he barked out. "The first exercise was How Can We Personify the Earth? Jenny mimed a kind of Frankenstein character, gentle and misunderstood. That was good, Jen." A broad smile from Jenny gave Al more assurance and he upped his volume even further. "Marin did a golem creature with our incantations—really original. Jack and Courtney did a comical take on Jack, Giant, and beanstalk. Well, basically we agreed that our earth could be anything we want it to be, as long as we make sense. We're the shapers, so it can keep changing like the earth does."

As an assortment of responses darted around the room, Al's face fell apologetically. "Am I doing okay, guys—reading back my notes? Or should we have a meeting to decide how Al is doing?" He threw a sly grin at Lucina, who suddenly saw her father right there in Al's wry manner.

She tried a conciliatory tone. "What great exercises do you have planned for us today, Al?"

Al sank clumsily into a folding chair nearby, his notes falling to the wooden floor. "Jesus," he groaned. "I mean, does anybody but me really care about this shit?"

Jenny raised her hand, as if in a classroom. Seeing her gesture unnecessary, she spoke up. "Maybe we should do a play about us. This save-the-earth stuff is abstract. Here we are, a group of thirteen people living communally for the first time, trying to do theater and maybe find a way to make a living together. Why are we doing this? Why now? That's a play I could relate to."

"Thirteen of us squatting on this land," Louis called out. "We're a lucky number."

Lucina wondered at Louis' buoyant disposition this morning. Where was his worry about intruders—they still hadn't gotten hold of the owners. She was glad he was sprouting his beard again for the summer. It hid his vulnerability, made him look older, more reserved. Maybe after they'd healed from the assault they could spend more quiet time together, not just sleeping and consoling—but making love. When was the last time—after they'd had dinner with Karen and Sally? Try not to think about them!

"What's more important than caretaking nature, Jenny?" Al finally responded.

"You're right, Al," Jenny acquiesced. "But after *Eco-Drama*, it would be fun to make a musical comedy about us, right?"

Courtney interjected that they'd already decided to focus on the ecology theme, so why were they wasting time and everyone should please let Al do his job.

Al broke in. "Tak, Bro, as Hans would say. So okay, if there are no more interruptions, we're going to continue working on images for the earth's birth, followed by the earth's destruction. So far we've tried having a giant puppet emerge slowly through a slit in a large sheet with the sounds of a cymbal crashing and sparklers going off. I mean, this isn't exactly the big bang but it's effective. This giant puppet would be a Frankenstein, a golem, and a fairy-tale giant all in one. The idea is to make the earth's birth be fantastic, okay? We have to work on the fantastic part. Then we work on a follow-up scene, maybe coming out of that birth. Say, the giant earth puppet opens up and out comes an old man, or maybe a young man with a lot of sores all over him, oozing pus and flies. He's walking along a road with background projections of beautiful lakes and rivers being polluted by masked figures pouring chemicals into them. The walker's sores get worse and the polluters have names— Exxon Mobil, NRG Energy, Dow Chemical—and we watch the man die, maybe he's a Vietnamese. We're trying to bring a lot of things together here. That kind of sums up as far as we've gotten. Let's do some brainstorming on what we can work on today. Before we do our warm-ups and—"

Jack charged in abruptly. "Look, we have to make the birth scene sacred, take our time with it, not just have some puppet emerge through a slit. Maybe we could start out in darkness, or in silence if we do it outdoors. We can use the Native American creation chant 'Light was not, the day was not, and there was no sun, no moon.' And then we plant seeds in the darkness."

"Sounds poetic, Jack, but it's not visceral," Marlene countered. Not a full-time member of the group, she usually stayed in the background at rehearsals. But now her interest was piqued. "I personally need to have something real and physical to relate to. An image we can show with our bodies." *Definitely as the group's watch dog, I should speak up,* she reasoned.

"I got you," Jack answered. "Here's one way to do that. Say each of us personifies one aspect of creation. We can do exercises around this. For example, say you're the sky, Marlene. So you do reaching out gestures with your arms and you're wearing a bright blue T-shirt. And either somebody narrates, or you have a sign on your back saying "Sky." Then say, Courtney comes out smiling with a bright yellow hat on. He's the sun. It can be playful."

"I love it!" Lucina already saw herself as an apple tree. "Maybe it's a bit corny, but you know what? It's both palpable and poetic—like kids playing."

"The problem with poetry…" Hans fretted. "People might not take us seriously. All the deniers. There's no acid rain. No climate change. Never was a Holocaust. That kind of shit."

Courtney jumped up from his prone position in the back and went to stand by Al. "We can just turn that negative stuff around. The forests are not. Why? Acid rain got them. Fish are not—they were killed by pesticides and radiation and bomb testing. Rivers are not—PCBs got them. See my drift? We can say: 'You want to talk about whether we should support the war? Talk to the vets coming back from 'Nam half-dead from the Agent Orange they've ingested.' That's how we handle bullshitters."

Al was excited by the output from his comrades. "You guys are great. The point we have to make is how mankind is destroying natural cycles. In fact, man is not kind. I see us making beautiful plants, trees, flowers, animals, a whole beautiful earth emerge out of the darkness, maybe in silence. Then a big boom, and we'd have film clips of the atom bomb exploding; all the beautiful things would be covered with disgusting white dust. We could use gauze... Fuck! We don't want to make it pretty. Our big bang theory is that exploding nukes are destroying the earth! Our earth!"

"That's a brilliant leap, Al." Hugh stood up and clapped, inspiring clapping from others.

Louis, noticeably quiet so far, spoke up. "So, we've got a lot of ideas to work from. Now we have to set some scenes. Al, after warm-ups should we break up into groups of three, and maybe using our sound and motion exercises, come up with how we would impersonate a beautiful world before the destruction sets in?"

"Great idea, man," Al replied. Eyeing Lucina, he questioned, "Anything else to add?" His testiness had lessened.

"You could tell each threesome what image to work on," Lucina chirped out, glad she and Al were at peace again. "And then we can regroup and show what we've come up with."

Marlene stretched forward from her chair. "This is a great discussion. Just a few words or sounds can invoke incredible images, especially coming out of dark silence. Right now, I'm seeing so many pictures in my mind." She was speaking so softly with hands over her eyes that those not near her were confused. "Both beautiful and like a haunting nightmare, or something so disturbing, so disgusting you wish it didn't..." The group, stilled by her anxious pondering, was hunched toward her, trying to hear, when suddenly an unsettling ruckus of cries and shrieks shot through the room, smothering her musings.

Louis was at the windows in a shot, looking toward the road. Al grabbed a broom resting in the corner, turning it into a rifle. Lucina was on her hands and knees edging toward Courtney and Jack for protection. Then Marlene, erupting from her inward place, was laughing hysterically. "Oh, my god! We're so fucked up. Those aren't rednecks! Can't you tell crows when you hear them?" It took a few minutes and more nervous laughter before the others were ready to accept Marlene's confident assessment.

Marlene, usually shy with the group, had opened up, if only briefly. How could they know she was actually mulling over her disturbing visit to the I-zone the night before—certain that Louis and Jenny had been fucking in there? And if Lucina knew, for all her pluckiness, she would be crushed. If she and Louis broke up, the street theater would be blown to smithereens. Talk about the big bang! The redneck thing—nothing compared to that horror.

40

All Kinds of Happenings, Political and Personal

Al finally reached Jeff and Marsha, the owners of the Yellow Farm, now working as grassroots organizers in San Francisco. He asked them how to handle threats from possible pro-war locals. Their advice: "Ignore them. Work on connecting to people in the area who are against the war." They gave Al a long list of names, plus churches and organizations who would help them organize performances and workshops.

Louis decided not to call the police unless there was a second incident; likely, one of the guys in that station wagon had a relative in the local police force or in Vietnam. Who knew the repercussions of such a call? As Jeff and Marsha said, it was necessary to build up community support and find peaceniks in the area. Meanwhile, precautions must be taken: no nudity outdoors or even indoors, and no outlandish behavior in town to avoid causing unwanted notice of their presence.

The last week of July the actors gathered each morning to work on *Eco-Drama* and to scythe the field next to the apple orchard for a simple outdoor stage. In August they would do performances there, open to the townspeople. Maybe they could pull the rug out from under the bullies.

Only Al was privy to Marin's sporadic threats to head back to the city, where a police station was nearby. "We're so isolated out here. What if they come at us with guns?" she asked him. It helped that he pampered her with breakfast in bed every morning. Plus, work on the *DreamCatcher* play was serving to dissipate her fears. But when she insisted on taking long treks alone to meditate with Mother Nature, he threw himself into building the outdoor stage, swearing the whole time.

Group expenses and chores were shared by all thirteen at the farm: shopping for groceries and household goods, preparing meals, washing dishes, and taking care of the house and yard. Though Al stayed in charge of caretaking the group's Chevy van, now called Isadora, the cost of repairs and gas was also shared.

The actors learned to straddle two modes: one watchful and wary, the other relaxed and creative. As they tuned into their own rhythms, soon there were many sounds—guitar plucking, voice exercises, drum beats, fragile flute melodies, a trumpet struggling with a familiar love song—coming from the barn or one of the small sheds. Louis said he could always tell when Hugh and Courtney were high: there was either more silence than usual, or an onslaught of musical sounds as repetitious as the mourning dove's haunting coos in the late afternoon and early morning. Lucina's childhood in Belmont, Illinois, had been filled with the same haunting sounds, and now those birdcalls brought sadness over her parents' rejection of her supposedly unkempt life with Louis.

Still prone to playing a mediator's role, though with more restraint and awareness since her self-reflection improv, Lucina defended Hugh and Courtney's music. "Repetition is the essence of chant, Louis. Your grandfather was a cantor, so you should understand how chanting flushes out essence by plumbing depths." When she realized that words like *flushes* and *plumbing* were more related to waste disposal and septic tanks than chanting, she became alarmed: *My god! The summer is racing by and we agreed to dig a long trench as preparation for a more up-too-date filtering process using stones and chemicals. When are we going to get to that work!*

Until the septic tank work was finally organized, afternoons and evenings were free for other projects and pleasures: Al and Marin worked on *DreamCatcher* by holding a series of workshops to develop improvisation techniques. Jenny and Hans disappeared into the hills each afternoon, not always to make love as everyone assumed. Often they found separate secluded spots to catch up on sleep missed from frequent nights of bickering. To Jenny's chagrin, Hans' itch for guerrilla action had started up again. "This is no time to rattle warmongers in the area," she scolded. Of course, something else was going on there; Hans had almost sniffed out her secret tryst with Louis. No, he wasn't the only one suspecting hanky-panky between those two.

*****

One hot July afternoon, Louis begged Marlene to sit down with him on the bench by the flower garden and asked her straight out, "Why are you so mad at me, Marlene?" Silence and an angry, questioning look met him. "Are you upset with me for praising you at rehearsal today—how you're really watching out for us? I'm so glad you'll work with us, at least part-time. I know you have a demanding job with your junior high kids."

"You think taking photos of our stalkers took courage, Louis Altman? Nothing compared to the guts it takes to tell you why I'm angry with you!"

"Please, give me the respect I deserve as a human being and tell me what I did to you."

"Not to me! It's what you did to Lucina and the group. I believed in you—all your talk about our moral duty to fight injustice. What empty words if you don't live your own life morally!" Silence and a confused look came back at her.

"What are you talking about!"

"You—you—how do I put it? I'll just come out and say it! You and Jenny, in our sacred meditation space. You and Jenny were fucking in our I-zone yurt. You denigrated our group's meditation temple. If you don't tell Lucina, I will!"

*****

Late that evening, Louis was sitting at his desk. It felt good to be there, with Lucina falling asleep near him in their bed. He just needed a little caffein to sharpen his mind up, enough to finish his train of thought—how to tell Lucina about Jenny and him in the yurt so she wouldn't get all riled up. If she heard about it from Marlene, then she'd be really hurt and confused, because it wasn't at all how Marlene thought it was.

He went downstairs to see if any coffee was left in the pot from supper. Good! Just enough for a cup with some milk. Where was everybody? Usually there was a game going on in the large dining area. Maybe there was a full moon and the night gang was out howling with the wolves. Good—now he could stay with his thoughts.

Marlene wasn't going to say anything to me! Just keep it to herself and throw darts at me from her eyes. So upset—as if I would do that to my adoring Lucina. Thank God I straightened her out! Fuck with Jenny? When Lucina was still shaking from those terrible men scaring her to death? Jesus, I'm not some macho fucking machine. It seems Marlene needs Lucina and me—like we're some kind of perfect couple for her. She really cares about us. My beating by the cops—that's what decided her on our group. She felt protective of me, the way she is with her kids—her students. She's always been afraid to go to anti-war demos—wants to know how protestors and cops became enemies in battle. "Aren't cops supposed to protect people's democratic rights? The right of protest is inherent in a democracy," she says. I put her straight. Cops are bodyguards of the warmongers, the rich and powerful. No way are they protectors of the working class. No, Marlene! America's "democracy" is not the kind you want. She's some tough woman, though—grabbing her camera and pegging those stalkers. She put her body on the line—she could have been attacked by them! Jesus, no wonder she kept looking at me as if I'd wounded her. I knew something was eating her.

Louis washed his coffee cup and put it away. He needed to get back upstairs in case Lucina woke up and wondered where he was. His mind was getting clearer. Marlene was right, even if it felt like she was holding a knife to his throat—he had to tell Lucina what had happened with Jenny in the yurt. Lucina had almost come looking for him that night—but Marlene had convinced her to stay in the house and talk with her and Hans. *Geez! Marlene sure is guarding us. It's her training—stop trouble in its tracks. She doesn't have to tell me not to hurt my Lucina. My vulnerable, tender woman.*

Karen came into his mind, and a shudder went through him. He pushed her out of his thoughts. *She and Sally don't belong here—I was feeling so humiliated, so impotent.*

As he entered the room, he heard Lucina's voice. "Louis, where were you? I thought you were writing at your desk. What time is it? I guess I was dreaming…you wanted to do another self-revelation improv. We have to get back to including that in our exercises, don't you think?"

"It'll happen—when people are ready for it. Yeah, I was in the kitchen having some coffee. Nice and quiet there tonight. No one playing cards or hanging out."

"Sounds peaceful. So, come to bed—it's around midnight, right?"

"How'd you know?"

"The clock on your desk, honey. Remember?"

"Listen, I need to talk to you about something."

"You and Al have worked out a schedule to get going on the trench, I hope."

"No, it's something personal."

"You miss us making love, like I do? When I said I want to see you as my brother troubadour, I didn't mean I don't want to make love with you, silly. I miss us in that way."

"I do too—that's why I need to talk to you."

"I'm still sexy for you, aren't I, honey? We have so much on our minds, but our bodies have needs too."

"Lucina, I had a talk with Marlene."

"I hope so—she's fond of you—and so protective of us. Did she have some thoughts about our unwelcome visitors? That was so smart and gutsy of her to take those photos. I mean, we'll have a better idea what they look like—one has a beard, the other a long chin."

"Yep—she's super-aware. Nothing gets by her! But that's not what's on my mind. You remember a few nights ago—I was feeling really tense. And I said maybe I'd go to the yurt and try some meditating?"

"Of course! I'm sorry—I should have gone with you."

"The thing is, I went there and Jenny was there."

"She goes there a lot. So, she wanted to be alone to do her mantras?"

"No. She asked me to come in."

"And?"

"She saw I was very tense—"

"And she said, 'Let me give you a massage.' Oh, Louis, Louis. She caught you in her web, didn't she?"

"It wasn't like that. She was very caring and I was needy. Worried about you, about us. So, I let her massage my shoulders."

"Yes, and what else?"

"My head and face and…"

"What else?"

"She started hugging me and it just happened. We started kissing—and I was crying and so was she, and then we were laughing nervously. And then somebody was trying to get in the yurt. I'd latched it from the inside, by mistake. It was Marlene, trying to open the door. She called out, 'Who's there?'"

"But Marlene was with Hans and I."

"That was after she was at the yurt. Let me talk, Lucina! For some reason it seemed funny to Jenny and me—it was like the marshal was checking on us. You know, sometimes Marlene is like a tough marshal. I mean, she watches out for all of us. Anyway, we started laughing and when I opened the door, Marlene was gone."

"So, then what happened?"

"Jenny and I got out of there. We didn't want to be doing anything sexy with each other—not really. We walked in the orchard and I told her how much I love you and she told me how much she loved Hans. And we said goodnight like close friends. I swear, Lucina, that's what happened."

"I don't know what to say."

"I swear, that's all. In case someone tries to convince you otherwise—we did not fuck in the yurt!"

"Louis, Louis. Don't cry, my love. I believe you—we have to believe what we tell each other. Come to bed now. You're my heart. Let me show you how much I love you, baby."

Finally! Marlene believed me. And now Lucina hears me. It really makes her happy to know the truth! I'm so lucky to be loved.

*****

313

Other kinds of personal needs were being addressed and met by the occupants of the Yellow Farm that August. Woody's goal: ten new paintings, with each showing a different view of the landscape from his studio. Trish's: explore Ashland State Park and reservoir, as she had her own car and was free to come and go as she pleased. And she welcomed company on her buying excursions at the local yard sales.

When Joan visited Jack, they would stand on their heads for long periods in front of the barn. The purpose was to increase circulation. These strange upside-down animals inspired an occasional moo from a neighbor's cow.

Impelled by the offensive stench coming from the septic tank—an eyesore beneath the window where he sat at his desk—Louis was working on a long ode about human shit. Lucina watched his gold pen gliding briskly above the red lines of a new ledger, amazed at his ability to concentrate even in uncomfortable situations.

"Why shit, Louis?" His preoccupation both touched and disturbed her.

"Why not shit, Lucina? It's about being human."

No longer beset by a bug obsession, she took long walks with her guitar into the fields and woods, away from the house—with its odors and tensions—to think. Obviously, Louis' present preoccupation was a metaphor for all kinds of tensions circling them. Some of the others continued to chide him or demand extra attention. And he often got caught up in others' confusions. Like the time Jack expressed some understanding of the people who'd ratted on their actor friends in Hollywood during McCarthy's red-baiting and blacklisting purge. "They were probably threatened by their interrogators," Jack had said. "I don't really know what I would do if my family was put in danger like that." To Louis, there was no debating the issue: he looked at Jack as if he were the Gestapo. "What about the good

314

people who were ratted on, man," Louis screamed. Their lives were ruined by supposed friends!"

Getting Louis to lighten up about others' contradictions didn't always work when he was digging up his truth. *Maybe he's building a protective wall around his own shit,* Lucina decided. *At least he can talk real to me! I no longer need to suspect him and Jenny. He's told me what happened that night in the I-zone, and I believe him. We're all living so close to each other; I'm glad Louis and I have real feelings for the others here. At least we're not suffering too much over our breakup with Sally and Karen. Maybe they'll understand us better by the time we get back to the city.*

41
Louis' Ode

Inspired by Jenny's apple cobbler, Lucina decided to bake pies from scratch, using crab apples from the farm. Though raw crab apples were too sour to eat, in pies they would be out-of-sight. When she remembered the delicate tartness of the crab apple jelly her mother made, her mouth watered.

The orchards hadn't been pruned or sprayed for a few years and healthy crab apples were scarce. She assiduously gathered the small fruits blemished by warts and brown spots, like old people, she thought. They also looked a bit like kids' first lumpy attempts at snowballs. She must have once made such formless things. She stayed determined.

Jenny seemed glad they both liked to cook. She teased Lucina about her "little shmoos." Lucina had stopped throwing her funny looks whenever she said Louis' name. Now she dismissed Jenny's teasing with a hug and the comment, "In case you don't know it, Jen, I'm glad you and Louis are friends." A cloud between them lifted. She left Jenny in the kitchen, happily singing a song about friends, and went to find Louis.

There he was at the desk, all concentration, still writing his "Ode to Shit." She interrupted his efforts with kisses. How dear he looked in his undershirt and shorts. Her own dear hairy beast.

"I'll never understand you, Louis. I was done talking about my excrement when I was four. I remember when it was a big thing to tell my mother if I'd done number one or number two."

"See, that's just it, Lucina. You never talked about shit. You talked *around* shit. Number one, number two! What's that? You were deprived the language of scatology."

"Your obscene concerns have definitely rubbed off on me now, Louis. I'm no longer deprived."

"Good, so let me have my shit meditation. I don't bug you about your crab apple fetish."

"Touché. So, why can't I read what you're writing?" She plunked down on the bed with a try-me look; Louis swiveled his chair to face her.

"What interests me is how everyone has a different relationship to their shit." As Lucina blinked away her knee-jerk discomfort with the topic, he went on. "For example, when you, Lucina, take a shit, you don't look at the toilet paper every time you wipe yourself. I've watched you."

"That's disgusting, Louis! I don't want my toilet habits analyzed, thank you."

"Are you aware of how you wipe yourself?"

"I've been doing it for almost twenty-five years, haven't I?"

"How much toilet paper do you use every time you wipe?"

"I don't want to talk about this. Admit what you're really talking about."

"You crumple your paper up, wipe yourself once, and then throw it away."

"Don't you?" Lucina wanted to laugh and cry simultaneously.

"I wipe myself, then fold the same paper, and use a clean side."

"Such a good little boy, honey. Did your mother teach you that?" Hearing her own sarcasm, she leapt up and went to him, throwing her arms around his head. "Oh, what are we talking about? I wanted to make you crap apple—oh, damn it! You've got me talking like you."

Louis shut his journal with a slap. "Okay, I'm not talking about shit, Lucina. I'm talking about humiliation. I'm talking about a man on Avenue C going into an alley with a bit of newspaper, ripping the newspaper in half, taking a crap on one half and wiping himself with the other. I'm talking about how a man suffers and overcomes humiliation. I'm talking about the endless humiliations Jews have had to suffer and how they stayed human. I want to learn how to defecate on Broadway in broad daylight and keep my dignity. Understand?"

She didn't. She held up her pot of crab apple bits to him as offering, as diversion. The man was painfully serious. He didn't even blink.

"Not everybody likes crab apple pie, Lucina," he said. "In fact, I've never heard of it before."

"Well, you and Jenny have a surprise in store—she's been teasing me, too. You'll both be begging me to make more."

Louis lightened. "I don't want to tease you. I'm just saying something very complicated, that's all."

"Are you feeling all alone with your heavy thoughts, Louis?"

"I can't be analyzed." Louis gave her an enigmatic smile. "Actually, I was thinking about my discussions with Jack. We've been reading some Native American philosophy together."

"Really? So how come you got into that fuss with him about being a commie-baiter? That was disturbing."

"We were having a discussion, that's all."

"That's how people talk? Shouting and slamming doors?"

"We were just showing how strongly we felt. I've had discussions about politics with him before. We go at it tooth and nail."

Lucina put her pot of apple bits, which she'd been clutching all this time, on the floor and looked out the window, searching for the two maple tree with embracing trunks.

"Jack's a good guy," he said. "You like him."

"Sure, I do. And I don't slam doors on him. I'm very glad you two are connecting."

Louis looked down at his writing. He had revealed something deeply personal about himself and she had only partially understood. It was about dignity and humiliation, not about excrement at all. "Do you know what happened at Wounded Knee, for example?" His tone turned professorial.

"I don't know what happened at Wounded Knee, and I don't know what Wounded Knee is."

"People die from ignorance, Lucina."

She should grab her crab apples and run out of the room!

"The Lakota Sioux were all wearing their Ghost Dance shirts, thinking they were impervious to bullets. They were singing their chants, doing their old rituals, trying to gather all their dead ancestors."

Lucina sat back on the bed; if this lecturing continued, she might as well get comfortable. "So, what book have you been reading, professor?"

"Jack was telling me: for days and days they kept dancing to bring the ancestors back to the present. The reports on the Wounded Knee Massacre say the Indians were wearing their Ghost Dance shirts when hundreds of government soldiers surrounded them. The US military had come to take them into custody."

"Just because they were dancing?"

"It wasn't just dancing! They were gathering power through their dance. They did not want to fight. But the government agents say a medicine man incited his people to shoot first, and that some of the men had guns hidden under their blankets."

"Wait a minute. Why did this happen? Didn't it have to do with Sitting Bull's murder or something? His tribe was resisting the takeover of their land with guns."

"I thought you didn't know about Wounded Knee?"

"I didn't remember that was the name of the place. You know how I mangle facts, Louis."

"I know your memory is better than you pretend it is. You pretend it's not good so you can amaze yourself when you do remember. Is that it? Anyway, they were coming for Big Foot. Yes, Sitting Bull had already been murdered. The government's reports say the first shot came from a warrior. Big Foot's people say, 'No, these were peaceful people. They had built no signal fires, shown no intentions of war.'"

"Louis! We should make a play about this. People have to know. I feel it right now, in my bones."

"Just listen to me." Louis moved from his desk chair to the bed, making it bounce from his weight. "The US soldiers rounded them up like cattle. The government's reports admitted that the women and children who were murdered were some distance away from the first shots. Their bodies were spread-eagle on the ground."

"Sounds like they were running away."

"Yes. They had the aspect of birds shot down in flight. The ghost shirts didn't help them. They fell dead like any of us would if we were shot in the back and the chest. Men, women, and children murdered. For what? For the land they lived on? For the oil in that land? Those poor people really believed they would be safe in those shirts."

Lucina took his hand. "Why do I think you've got more advice for me? You're really telling me not to make crab apple pies—like it's an indulgence. Is that what this is all about, Louis?"

"No! I'm talking about how Wounded Knee is like Vietnam and Poland. See, I know about the genocide of Native

Americans. America was built on the backs and bodies of the Indigenous."

When Lucina stroked his head, an apologetic look filled his eyes. "I didn't know crab apples meant so much to you," he said. "I'm sorry."

"Every living thing means something to me!"

They'd worn each other out. When they lay down on the spacious bed, the room changed with their embrace. No longer sparring space or classroom, it was nest. It was home.

42

A Homey Feeling

After waking from a lovers' sleep—his arms were her arms, her legs were his—Louis launched into the shit topic again without agitation or pomp.

"Where do you like to shit best, Lucina?"

During their lovemaking, an old feather pillow had let loose a flurry of feathers. One rested in Louis' beard as he sat in his desk chair again, facing her. Lucina saw a tiny bird hiding in a thicket. His vulnerability. His naked body so unique in its build. Large belly. Thin, delicate legs. Short neck. Large penetrating eyes. Enormous head. Sensuous lips. How could people so vulnerable survive that long? Her thoughts brought pressure to her head. She must be patient with him. "I love to shit in the woods."

"What do you do with it?"

"You are so nosy, sweetheart." She smiled. "I dig a hole and push it in."

"What do you feel when you are poking at it?"

"It's not disgusting to me. It's like, wow! I made that stuff with my own little body."

"Then what do you do?

"I put sticks over it."

"Do you see what you're doing?"

"Covering my shit?"

"No. You're making a little house over your shit. A little shit-house."

"You might be doing that, Louis, but I'm burying it."

"Do you just throw the sticks on your shit pile?"

"No. I kind of crisscross them."

"A teepee for your shit. You've put part of yourself in the ground, and now you need a mini burial. So you build a monument to your shit."

"Doo-doo, you mean. I don't want anyone stepping in my doo-doo, or me stepping in it. You know, Louis, I don't think I can talk about this anymore."

He went to her and pulled her up into his arms, forcing her into a funny dance step. "Let's do the Ghost Dance, the Ghost Dance," he crooned. She resisted; she wouldn't play.

He pulled her back to the bed, where they sat back against the eerie wallpaper that reminded her of small green butterflies frozen in flight.

"I understand now. Those guys stalking us—it's all about shit." He stroked at his beard and the little feather freed itself and fluttered to the floor.

She rested against his shoulder, put her hand on his belly. "I'm listening."

"Working-class whites—self-appointed guardians of the community—stalk us. It's very primal, tribal. They spew shit from their mouths, to put themselves up by putting us down. They have to mark us with their defecation." He acknowledged Lucina's hand caressing his belly by stroking the top of her hand as well. "Hey, they see us getting dumped on in the media: peacenik hippies, outside agitators, destroyers of America. And they're jumping on the bandwagon. They're shitting on us. Now, if we were Black, Latino, Latina, Chinese…"

Lucina pulled her hand away and sat upright to think better. "Sure, then half the town would be riding by shouting racist jokes and pointing their fingers. So, what can we do about it?" She wanted him to cut to the chase. Then maybe he would talk about himself, how it hurt when people in the group put him down.

"If the town accepts us, those guys remain at the bottom of the totem pole. Are you aware of this pecking order?"

"God, Louis. I didn't grow up in an ivory tower, you know. My mother's biggest sense of failure? She didn't get invited to Mrs. DuPont's wedding. We were never high enough up there on the ladder. Am I aware of this shit? Do you think I'm stupid?"

"It all comes down to intimidation, humiliation. And it all has to do with how we take care of—"

"Don't tell me. Our shit?"

"Don't mock me, Lucina."

"Shit is shit, Louis and ours is out in the backyard waiting to be covered up by somebody who knows what they're doing. That open septic tank is not healthy."

"That's the answer! We've got to fix it, right away. Take care of our shit and gain respect from our neighbors."

"Not only that, honey. Jenny and Hans were out in the apple orchard yesterday naked. That's not going to get us community votes."

"Fools. Hans can't stop provoking. I thought he was getting ahold of himself with his comic self-portraits?"

"What about Jenny?"

"She's a different matter." Louis' voice trailed off.

"Yes, she likes to massage my man."

"I told you! Don't be jealous of her."

"I'm just kidding. I'll remind them—this isn't a nudist colony. Okay? But—you didn't tell me, Louis…How do you shit in the woods?"

"I don't. I don't want to mess up the ground."

"Talk about being careful. That's what you were saying—about keeping your dignity."

"That was about being forced to shit where I didn't want to."

Out the window Lucina could see sunlight spangling the leaves of the maple. It was getting late. She'd meant to spend only a few minutes with Louis, to get support for her pies. She quickly bent for her clothes, eagerly tossed off only a short while before.

Louis reached for his shorts and pants. "Let me know when your pies are done, Lucina. Then let's take the van to town, just the two of us. Good thing you have a license."

"You mean, sneak away?"

"I miss you, Lucina." Moisture came into his eyes.

"Louis, don't be so sad. The group needs you. I need you."

Louis turned to the task of dressing, keeping his back to her, as if suddenly shy. She saw his distancing as his need for privacy. Even people who loved each other very much needed privacy. Maybe his meditations about shitting and the rednecks were a way to center himself, not be continuously pulled by others' needs. He used his mind to quell his emotions. Thinking, always thinking.

"Oh, Louis," her voice quavered. "How did our lives end up like this? So different from our parents."

Louis spoke to the window in front of him. "We'll be okay as long as we remember how much we're like everyone else."

Not wanting him to see her tears, she bent down quickly to fasten her sandals. "There's a lot I don't understand these days about how I'm feeling."

"You get prickly a lot," he said.

Lucina felt her shoulders tense. "When I talk with the other women, things come up."

"Like what?"

"Like, how I'm not really that independent from you."

"I hate that! Only an independent thinker could have come up with the self-reflection exercise. You made yourself really vulnerable and open, babe. You're working to see me as a brother comrade, as well as your partner."

"How about you! My god, you told them—us—to stop seeing you as the head honcho! That really helped clear the air. But we don't change overnight. Lots of times when I'm thinking, it feels like I'm thinking what you would think. And when you're upset, I'm upset, too."

"So, what's wrong with it?"

"To be that connected? It's symbiotic. If we weren't lovers, I probably wouldn't be so affected by you. I think I can let go of my ideas more easily than you. You get so upset if the group doesn't want to do your image."

"Image, blimage. That's a lie! I hardly talk anymore at rehearsals. You told me not to."

"Louis, you'd better admit to your sensitivities. The whole point of a group is to come up with collective group ideas."

"You think I don't know that? But sometimes, Lucina, only one person can propel a whole group forward. I can see more clearly than others. You told me that."

"I know, sweetheart, but we have to give them a chance to find their ideas."

"Whose ideas haven't I listened to?"

At that moment, Lucina couldn't think of one example. Maybe she exaggerated Louis' behavior. Maybe it was more about her sensitivity to him. She would give him a massage later, after supper. Now she had work to do. She must make her pie!

He heard her sandals clicking rhythmically on the steps down to the first floor along with throaty, chuckling sounds. Probably she was laughing about their conversation about shit and the septic tank. Where she came from, the Midwest, you just fixed things, you didn't talk about what you were doing that much. Then he heard her voice in his head explaining, "It gives me a homey feeling to be baking a crab apple pie."

43
The Spider Web

Louis stared at the corner of his desk for some time. He was thinking about Jenny, about what had happened with her in the yurt, Marlene's I-zone. He'd told Lucina one truth—but there was another he hadn't told her. He'd wanted to make love! His cock had wanted to—while his mind and heart had said, "No!" With Lucina, his cock, mind, heart worked together, amazingly well.

He'd been able to keep Karen a secret, but how would he have kept Jenny a secret—a woman he worked with, ate with, saw every day? Face his truth! He loved Lucina wholly—and he was attracted to other women! No wonder he didn't make good husband material.

He was brother, comrade, friend, lover—dedicated to Lucina, but not husband. Not like Ralph. That guy would be faithful to Marge until death. But his truth? Since Lucina, two other women had attracted him. Who would be next?

Ever since Vermont, there'd been a spark with Jenny. Something just grew—curiosity maybe? Well, what about Lucina and Marin taking that long hike together? And Hans? He and Al went to town alone? No, don't make it a big deal.

It was a moment, that's all. Jenny adored her Hans, she made that very clear, and he, Louis, adored Lucina. But it was kind of sweet, how Jenny wanted to massage him, make him feel better. Their short sweet kiss had been so natural. Human beings needed each other.

Jenny wouldn't talk about it, even at one of those women's get-togethers. Because it wasn't a big deal. They'd gone through a test—come out the other side. Case closed. But Karen? Unresolved.

*****

How long had he been looking without seeing? Fine threads, an intricate, almost invisible construction, now imprinted his consciousness. He felt wonder. A large spider was weaving a bridge between the edge of his desk and the window ledge.

She was some kind of high-wire walker, moving delicately back and forth on her own threads while emitting the fine stuff to make more pathways in her web. But wasn't she also constructing a trap? Some innocent male would be forced into mating with her. And what about the other insects she might entrap? The ants, hornets, and flies that would become tasty food? Without thinking about it, without fussing, she worked.

All the time he and Lucina had been talking about shit, rednecks, ghost dancers, crab apple pie, and themselves, this industrious arachnid had been going about his, no *her* construction business, not even aware of the fragility of her location. She must be in a hurry to settle down. Was the desk now tree trunk; the window ledge, her branch? All the while he and Lucina were making love, that tiny black creature was shitting or spitting out one long thread for her survival.

"You're making a home," he said out loud to the tiny black ball sidling on the ledge near his chair. "And home can be wherever you are. When someone you love is making crab apple pies, that's definitely home."

Sudden warmth filled his chest. He relaxed. Yes! He would defer to the creature sharing his desk, retrieve his writing and go to the bed to continue writing notes on the shit the human race was capable of. Ode to shit. Ode to horror.

44

The Honey Man

Crab apples alone would not work. But mixed with peaches! Lucina put the soft yellow fruit into a large pan filled with water. She would simmer them for a few minutes to loosen their skins. That made them easier to peel. Then cut them up and stir them in with the apples, adding cinnamon, brown sugar, a little rum, and lemon juice. This mixture could marinate while she baked the piecrusts, until well done.

But how to light the oven? She tried to remember–who'd used it before? Looked clean enough.

Nothing happened when she turned the oven knob. So, where was the opening for a match? Of course, inside.

That's right–Al had used long, wooden matches a few days before, for the chicken barbecue. Were they on the cupboard over the sink? In the drawer by the silverware? No, right there on the kitchen table because Hans and Al had smoked during the poker game last night.

This was the hard part—on hands and knees, poking your head in a dark cave. Okay, put the lit match into that small black hole. Now, turn the knob up just a little bit—until the flame starts. Good—bring it up. A little higher. Higher.

*****

Later, Lucina described those next few seconds to Louis: how she heard the boom first, then smelled burnt hair, heard sizzling sounds, and saw sparks fall from her head onto her shirt collar. Sharp pain scorched her cheeks, her upper lip.

She screamed, shocked, helpless, and then he was there.

He led her to the sink and carefully patted her head with a wet towel. "Don't worry. You're okay, babe. You're okay. I thought those jackasses had come back again."

But when he realized what had actually happened, he panicked: she'd been burnt—her face, her hair! "Oh, my god, are you all right?" he asked again and again.

Lucina put her hand to his cheek, feeling that she must comfort him. "I was being careful." She heard a child afraid of being scolded. She searched his eyes; had she done something stupid? "The oven exploded."

Then searing pain, as if someone were dragging a sharp knife back and forth across her cheeks, and she cried out again.

"Don't worry, sweetheart. I'll take you to the hospital. We'll be fine—we'll be fine."

"It hurts so much, Louis. Will I be scarred?"

"Your cheeks are very red, but I don't see blisters. Should we ice it? Then I'll take you."

"I don't know, Louis. I don't know what to do."

"We need help!" Louis shouted out again, then felt relief as the back door opened. Whoever it was could run for Al; he'd take them in the troupe's van to the hospital.

A gray-haired stranger, clean-shaven and ruddy, stood a few feet away. "I'm the Honey Man from down the road," he announced. He wore work clothes, and a basket hung on his arm. "I heard somebody shouting for help. What happened to your face, ma'am?"

Louis' mind was racing: maybe the guy, whoever he

was, could drive them. "Listen, the oven exploded. Where is the closest hospital?"

The man—he was around fifty, Louis decided—walked directly to the oven. "Your knob is on wrong. I can still smell gas."

"She's burnt! We need a hospital."

The Honey Man pulled a jar from his basket. Lucina watched his huge, vice-like hands unscrew the lid. Then he was next to her, dipping large fingers into the mixture.

She must not move. With deft, careful strokes he applied a thick salve to her face: honey. *This man had come to help her. She knew it!*

Louis stared at the man, uncertain. He must act. His Lucina was hurt.

"This is the best stuff for burns." The voice was kind. "Don't you two worry. I've had medical training. The burns are surface, not even second degree. No blistering. In two days you will be like usual, except I hope more careful. Every house should have a jar of the Honey Man's ointment."

Louis got a chair from the dining area and helped Lucina into it. She was considerably calmer by now. Maybe the guy was right: there was no blistering under the shiny salve. The redness was fading as well.

"You don't have to go to any hospital," the man said. "Believe me—sixty-five years teaches you things."

Louis felt sluggish, drugged. Exhaustion pulled at him. The man's cheerful voice droned on. "Just keep this honey on your face for a few hours, and all you'll have is a sunburn for a couple of days."

Lucina was surprised how cool the honey felt. There was no uncomfortable sticky sensation. Was this stuff really the same honey she had trouble wiping off of counters?

"God brought you just in time," she said timidly.

The man went to the sink and carefully washed both

hands, then returned to the table. She couldn't believe that a sixty-five-year-old man could look so vigorous.

"Better get that oven fixed right away. Don't want to be doing that again."

"I wanted to make some pies for supper."

Louis assured her, "We'll get it fixed, Lucina. You'll be able to bake the apple pies."

The man stood near them, a benign presence. "That sounds nice," he offered. "Well, you're in luck that I happened by. My name's Fred Tompkins. I live in the big white house at the corner of Apple Tree Road and Woodland Corners."

Lucina moved her head for the first time since receiving the balm. "Is it that beautiful farmhouse with the fruit stand, about a half mile down the road?" She saw crow's feet framing his eyes. The lines were so striking—she would like to draw them.

"That's the one." He smiled appreciatively. "By the way, my honey tastes good in fruit pies—blends right into the juices. Natural sugar. You get your oven fixed up, then use some and think of me."

"You're our neighbor!" Louis blurted out as if some terrible weight had suddenly lifted. "Our Honey Man neighbor!"

"Yes, that's right."

Louis put his hand out. "I'm Louis and this is Lucina. Did you know we're from New York City? We're a repertory theater company here for the summer."

"See, Louis? We didn't have to fix the septic tank before anyone would visit us." Lucina's voice had calmed.

Fred Tompkins picked up his basket and headed for the door. "If people had to have everything fixed before a visit, we'd always be strangers. Jeff told me you'd be taking the place. I thought he said you were an anti-war, street-theater commune?"

Louis blushed. Fred had exposed his lack of trust.

"It's like a miracle," Lucina broke in, seeing Louis'

embarrassment. "I don't know how to thank you." She felt energy enter her from Fred's eyes.

"Thank the Lord," Fred said, easing out the back door. "She works in devious ways."

After the door closed, Louis noticed a small jar on the stove. Sunlight from the back window illuminated the golden salve with its small label: Honey is Healing Sweetness.

Louis kissed the top of Lucina's head, careful not to brush his lips against her still-red, still-sticky face. "You might not always get what you need, honey," he said. "But you sure did get the honey you needed." He wanted to tell her about watching a spider that very afternoon slowly weave a web bridging his desk to the windowsill. But she looked too inward and tired.

45
How Do People Change?

The Honey Man's appearance and rescue at the Yellow Farm sparked work on the septic tank. A hundred-foot trench had to be dug, going from the tank at the back of the house to the start of the first apple orchard. This trench would then be used for the filtering process to keep house waste from polluting the ground water. "One good deed deserves another," Al said and called a meeting to organize the work. "We're talking about hard labor here," he counseled, challenging his comrades to wrestle with a "real blue-collar job."

That week Al clocked in thirty hours of shoveling; Jack twenty; Hans fifteen; Marin, Marlene, and Lucina ten each; and Jenny, Hugh, Courtney, Woody, Trish, and Joan six each.

"When are you going to get blisters on your hands, Louis?" Should Lucina tell him Hugh and Courtney were calling him a slacker?

"Listen, Lucina," he countered, in no mood for her reproach. "I do more than my share around shit!" His preoccupation with the dynamics of humiliation had taken him far away from the concerns of the Yellow Farm to the death camps in Germany and the unconceivable torture. "What kinds of depraved minds would invent hideous ways to exterminate other human beings? Forcing starving helpless people at gunpoint into sealed compartments and then pumping in poisonous fumes, so you would die in twenty minutes! Hitler's monsters created efficient ways of murdering masses of people so their soldiers wouldn't have to suffer discomfort from shooting them. Some kind of deranged sense of caring! And I'll tell you something else about shit you don't know about. The Nazi death camps didn't have latrines. Jews slept and wept in their own shit. If they didn't die in the gas chambers, they died from cholera. And that's not all—my people were guinea pigs in medical experiments where slow, excruciating death was certain."

"No more, Louis! Why didn't my family tell me about this horror!?" Lucina slumped in a chair next to him.

"Just so you understand—Jews being forced to sleep in their own excrement was the least of their suffering. I still can't face the horrors my people endured—can't even grasp it—that's why I'm saying this aloud to you. Listen, you don't have to worry, babe. I'll do my share of digging here. That I can do!"

She tossed aside "slacker" and stayed silent. Louis had to follow his own drummer, that was it. Besides, she had other worries.

Although the so-called rednecks had not returned to terrify the actors at the farm, strange, unexplainable stuff was happening. A trench shovel disappeared only to show up days later in the barn loft. Twice, a ladder Marin had propped up against the largest Jonathan apple tree materialized the next day on Woody's roof. No fierce winds could be to blame, and everyone swore on their mothers' graves that they'd had nothing to do with transporting shovel or ladder or knew anyone who had. So who were the culprits? Maybe the damn rednecks who'd threatened them.

After picking up the developed photos of the two guys poking their heads out the windows of the station wagon, Marlene decided to research the word "redneck" in the local library; what did it really mean? She discovered the term once referred to laborers who worked outside and got sunburnt. And since the troupe saw themselves as cultural workers, they certainly didn't want to alienate the working class! After a debate, she convinced the group to say "stalkers" instead.

It seemed these stalkers were again making odd appearances. Jenny had seen a man with a scruffy beard and a tattoo on his left upper arm staring at her in the drug store, while pointing to the American Flag on his sweatshirt: he must have been one of them! And more alarming, Lucina was sure she'd seen the driver of the stalkers' station wagon in the Ashland grocery store, ducking behind a stand of local apples, the very morning before they were to perform for the August Peace Coalition Day in the Unitarian churchyard. When Marlene showed her photos to Jenny and Lucina, their suspicions were confirmed—the stalkers were following them around! Should they warn the others? The three women decided to wait until their performance was over; being included in a community program was a big deal for the troupe and this first performance in the area would need full concentration.

*****

After performing an abbreviated version of *Choice*, they encouraged comments from the audience. They were shocked at the number of students in the crowd who didn't know what to think about the war. Louis, never one to shy away from confrontation, unabashedly but calmly told them their eastern schools were not teaching them critical thinking. And in return, they had plenty of criticisms ready to throw at the actors: "Too generalized…Too one-sided…Not enough research to back up

341

your viewpoint." Lucina's gnawing headache grew: *For heaven's sake?* They were presenting a twenty-minute drama, not a PhD thesis! How often it seemed that those invested in supporting the war fell back on glib condemnations.

"How many of you have signed up to fight in 'Nam?" she questioned. Measured faces stared back at her. *They already have the confident attitudes their families must have to fight their way up the capitalist ladder,* she thought, too upset to continue the Q&A. Marlene's photos and a guy hiding behind an apple cart were front and center in her thoughts.

While Al, Louis, and Marin took over—they were more patient—she remembered Sally's take on her parents' adamant Republicanism. "My folks defend their wealth because they worked hard for it. They say capitalism creates the haves who propel the economy and lift up the have-nots. Welfare for the poor only encourages laziness and more poverty. Their justification for their indifference: 'You get what you deserve.'"

And what about her own parents? Even with less money, they were the same. The poor and minorities remained on the outskirts of their minds and their town as unacceptable. They had little compassion for those who worked like dogs yet remained poor, as if it were the poor's own fault.

Now Louis was almost pleading with this crowd. "Our brothers, husbands, sons, friends are being slaughtered in a war that's not ours to fight." Louis' intensity was so like Sally's earnest manner. How in God's name could she have handled her attraction if Sally had been at the farm—especially with the strong presence of Louis there the whole time? What a tug-of-war! The sudden feel of Sally's lips pressing on her own, her tongue exploring her mouth like a hungry animal, confirmed her decision.

"Hello, you're Lucina?" A short, solidly built woman in a denim jacket, her blonde hair striped with bright blue dye, approached animatedly. At her side was a tall Black woman, whose ornate earrings of concentric silver rings shone through her afro. Lucina, abruptly back in the hot summer afternoon, wasn't sure she could be the Lucina they were looking for, but their friendly manner pleased her.

"My sister's boyfriend is in 'Nam," the tall woman blurted out. "She worries about him all the time. I wish he'd seen your *Choice*. Maybe he would have become a conscientious objector."

"We're also interested in plays about women's lives," the shorter woman announced. "We're friends of Marsha and Jeff. She told us that a street theater group would be staying at their Yellow Farm."

"Oh, great. What are your names?"

"I'm Keisha," the shorter woman responded. "And I'm Aretha," her friend added.

"Good to meet you. Yes, the women in our group are going to be working on a play about moments in our lives that changed us drastically."

"Oh, that's so good to hear," Aretha enthused. "We need plays with strong women, Black and white. Keisha and I are researching contemporary women playwrights that really speak our truths. If only Lorraine Hansberry were still alive."

Keisha took Aretha's hand with a shy smile. "We're so hungry for plays about us—we're both drama majors at Grandmore College," she explained. "You know, the women's college not far from here. Can't wait to see what you're doing. Where will you be performing it?"

"We're going to perform a scene from our women's play later in August at the Yellow Farm. It'd be wonderful if you could come. How can I get in touch with you both? Are you in one of the dorms?"

"Dickenson House. Write to us. Oh, damn! I'm sorry, our ride is leaving," Keisha added, as Aretha pulled at her arm. "Can we stop by sometime at the Yellow Farm and watch rehearsals?" Signaling to a woman nearby, the two excused themselves hurriedly. As Lucina quickly jotted down the little information she'd gotten from them, Aretha called out to her, "It's Aretha Davis. Write to us!"

Two older couples—women in garden sun hats, husbands sporting golf caps—from the local chapter of the Christian Council of Churches, who had sponsored the event, extended their hands with a welcoming shake, adding, "Thank you for the interesting play" and an invitation to a sunrise Peace and Pancake Breakfast at their Methodist church nearby. Lucina didn't feel *Choice* had gotten the reception from them it deserved. Had it mainly poked at people's mindsets? Did leftists mainly live in the big cities? She couldn't wait to get back to the farm and be alone with Louis to analyze the couples' lukewarm reception and the complacent students. It wasn't going to be a piece of cake to build anti-war sentiment in small-town America.

After some delicious bulgur and vegetables made by women from the Unitarian Church, Lucina's headache eased. Who cared if this crowd saw her as a downwardly mobile street-theater hippie, with an inconsequential attitude and no clout? She wished she'd tried to grab their attention with clever points, as Louis had done. But even Louis, the silver-tongued orator, had pulled back from trying to enlighten the stodgy audience and had simply appealed to their humanity. Maybe he was onto a new tactic: don't try to change people's minds overnight. Thank God he was into his research and his writing; it was giving him people-wisdom.

By the second glass of apple cider, she was feeling relaxed. The sun was already behind the trees, and a cool breeze gave some relief. For the first time, she realized they were next to a small park in the center of Ashland. Beyond the dispersing crowd and the pruned hedges of the churchyard, she saw the bleachers of a stadium—a ballpark? And so close to the farm. They should all go to a local team's game and simply get to know people that way. And maybe there was something to learn from today's performance, after all. Maybe their play could incorporate a student who spouted McNamara's point of view to Sam. Then Sam would have to work harder to express his point of view. The play had to reach Sally's parents, Lucina's mom and dad, and the students who hadn't been taught yet to think for themselves.

The glaring question was in front of her again: *How do we get people to change their point of view, if it's more comfortable not to?* There were at least two, maybe three or four Americas hardly talking to each other. The whole country was polarized over the war. Moreover, the unspeakable horrors in the South wouldn't just go away! There were still the exclusive old-boys clubs. And Grandmore College close by—was it still into producing establishment wives…Wait! Keisha and Aretha didn't fit that mold. She'd better learn to be more flexible in her own thinking!

She wished she'd said something more dramatic to those two: "We carry our Fire Dragon Street Theater banner as proudly as Joan of Arc carried her sword." Something like that could have led to more dialogue about needing plays focused on women. Surely they had heroines who'd fought for some cause. But what were the issues that affected them directly? Were they studying the suffragettes and the struggle for women to get the vote and equal rights? Did they know about Harriet Tubman and the Underground Railroad carrying slaves from the South to freedom in the North, in Massachusetts, in this very area where the Peace Coalition Day had taken place? Of course, the Black woman would know all this; it was condescending to think she wouldn't. So local history could segue into a discussion on civil rights. If you had your facts right and you spoke in a sensitive manner, a conversation could open minds.

She had so much to say to Keisha and Aretha: "Our fiery dragon is a metaphor for transformative power. Don't you agree? We have to change this country's attitude!" Amazing how the brief encounter had gotten her mind going. No wonder they want plays about women! *Patriotism means supporting your boyfriend as he goes to die for a war that isn't ours to fight?* If they didn't come by, she would call Marsha and get their addresses. What dorm did they say?

The crowd had cleared away. It hadn't really been a peace day after all. It had been a don't-rock-the-boat day. They were the token anti-war act, followed by some local politicians raising money for a new disabled-veterans' wing in the hospital; a women's church auxiliary raising money for activities at the local nursing home; and discussions about other well-meaning projects and services for the community. But as for criticizing the government, connecting the dots, saying no to American invasion of a little country on the other side of the globe? People were lukewarm. So how could they connect the dots between their own concerns and the concerns of this community? That was the challenge.

While carrying the props to the van with the others, she stopped short. A half-moon hung in the darkening sky like a reminder of something she'd seen before. What was it? Something disturbing. A face. A man's face, with long chin and high forehead—like the drawings of half-moon faces she made in cards for her friends. The driver of the station wagon, who'd stuck his head out the window and seemed to zap her with rage.

Then she remembered a face bleeding through the crowd, like a face slowly appearing in a photographer's developing solution. She'd been too preoccupied with the cranky reception of their play to notice what in fact she'd been seeing during the performance—that strange man with a long chin and a high forehead, glaring at them! She spotted again the two birch trees where he'd stood off by himself, chain-smoking. He'd kept disappearing for a few minutes, and then suddenly he'd be there again, staring at them and lighting another cigarette. Definitely. He was the stalker she'd seen in the grocery story, the same guy who drove the station wagon. Damn!

*****

Journal Entry. August 10, 1966: I saw the long-chin man today, the man who terrorized me. He watched us all afternoon at the Peace Day. I don't know what to do. We're working so well on the drainage for the septic tank and new plays, and Louis is writing. I'm afraid everything will fall apart if I bring up that man to the group. And then, what's really incredible? The women in the group have begun to express their uneasy feelings about many things. Like feelings of being invisible. Jenny put it into words first: "How come we don't have any women heroes in our plays? Sure, maybe our Earth Giant will be pan-sexed, but I mean a real heroine like Amelia Earhart, Jane Adams, or Sojourner Truth? Someone to sink our teeth into?" So, just like I told Aretha and Keisha—we're doing exercises separate from the guys and telling each other stories about our moments of change. It's like we're doing self-reflection improvs as a form of consciousness raising. For now, the guys that didn't do a self-reflection—Al, Jack, Hugh, Courtney—they'll have to figure that out. Let Louis and Hans help their brothers with that. I'm focusing on my sisters and our explorations! When I was making sculptures, I wasn't all that aware of what I was about. Now, with Jenny, Marin,

Marlene, and sometimes Joan, I'm learning how to grope out loud in front of them. I'm careful when I bring up Louis—I don't want to energize bad feelings toward him. The fear of men's power is in us. We can't be a bunch of scared rabbits. We have to focus on liberating ourselves. God! He's just trying to figure himself out, like I am.

46
Confrontation

Marlene looked through one of the wavy glass windows in the rec room on the hot afternoon of Saturday, August 22, 1966, and saw a line of cars extending from the driveway as far as she could see down Apple Tree Road. Why did it look like a funeral procession? She'd fallen asleep on the couch and woken up disoriented. Then she remembered: it was Play and Picnic Day at the Yellow Farm, their farm. They'd been organizing the event for the past three weeks, and she was in charge of props.

Through the kitchen windows, she saw a number of cars already parked in the field to the right of the apple orchard, and to the left of the almost-completed drainage trench for the septic tank. Her watch said one o'clock. Did people in the country arrive early? The play was not supposed to begin until three. She wondered: Was it safe to have cars parked so near the newly dug trench? Could their weight cause a cave-in?

They'd worked so hard on it; every day it was "get to the trenches and dig!" In fact, work on the trench had gotten more attention than the ecology play. She'd heard that Louis, finally into the trench work, had been up half the night digging.

Where was Al? He would know if all those cars would cause havoc on their trench. Marlene raced out of the house to find him, but he was not in the yard. Maybe he was in the barn, helping to set up their information and display tables.

When she got to the barn, Marlene saw posters, buttons, and pamphlets advising the ordinary citizen on how to help put a halt to the Vietnam War, along with racks of the tie-dyed T-shirts Trish had made. The exploding circular shapes framing the peace symbol looked like fiery flowers, or like what you saw when something hit you in the eye. Exploding-pain shirts, she said to herself and thought of Louis. He would like that—seeing and feeling melded together. But no, Al wasn't in the barn either. Then she remembered: Al had to go to the gas station and bring back ice. He was in charge of the drinks.

She sat down on a bale of hay—seats for the spectators— to catch her breath. Trish's fiery designs caught her eye again. Already people were wearing her shirts. She loved the garish colors; they made exciting currents run up and down her limbs. She'd talked to Louis about it—how her mind mixed senses together. When tree limbs scraped in the wind, she smelled burning wood. When she saw a certain kind of blue in the sky, she heard the most delicate bell sound. Maybe some of her wires were crossed. But it was fascinating, how that happened. And Louis understood.

Why wouldn't Jenny want to be close with him, too? He wasn't always flexing his ego like Hans was—like so many men were. And he wasn't reserved and aloof like Al. If she told him how the world was rushing into her through every pore, that her mind was tumbling with the flood, Louis understood. But Louis and Lucina belonged together; their union had to be honored. Jenny must have understood that, finally.

"Trish, they're gorgeous!" she called out, checking the barn again for Louis. Trish waved back, looking so pleased with the attention her shirts were getting, and how they were drawing people to the info table as well.

Stop worrying about the cars and Louis. It was time to carry the props from the house to the outdoor stage where they would perform. And there were always some last-minute repairs needed on a mask or instrument. Playtime was three o'clock, then the picnic at five.

Her head was clearing—good! Hugh and Courtney were setting up folding tables, borrowed from the Unitarian Church, under the grape arbor; Jenny and Marin were busy doing setups: paper cups, plates, and silverware. But no food yet. Potato salad would spoil in the heat. And the hot dogs and burgers were going to be cooked in the kitchen and brought out just at picnic time. They'd all agreed not to have fires with young kids jumping around like jackrabbits. Woody was going to do the cooking; that was nice of him to volunteer for that. Everyone was helping out.

Then she saw him: Louis with sunglasses and a visor directing the parking beyond the arbor. He would be charming the visitors and giving them instructions at the same time, plus keeping watch. He had a sixth sense about troublemakers! There was that anxious feeling again in her chest, or was it her throat? No, she would never act upon her feelings for him! She cared too much for Lucina.

What was it about this day? Folks from nearby, strangers with children and blankets in hand, heading for the apple trees, excited to be at the Yellow Farm for a play and a picnic. Incredible. It made her think of another time, or was she remembering something from a movie? She'd never actually experienced anything like this before. It was their dream come true: people from the neighboring community coming together at the farm for a happy event. The thought of separating soon from the troupe and returning to her junior high kids brought more angst into her chest, along with reflection:

This was the way to make inroads with the American people: invite them to your house and entertain them. But why weren't they filming it? Apparently, they would never chronicle anything they did. They would just do and do. History books would have no mention of the Fire Dragon Street Theater—she was sure of that. What a shame! The afternoon would contribute to the country's cultural-political history by building a compassionate community not based on one religious doctrine. Oh well, as they said, 'Live the present. It's a gift!' And right now, she had work to do!

Marlene lugged two boxes of props from the barn to the stage area. Ridiculous how many things they were using for *Eco-Drama*. A contradiction, cluttering a stage with junk to put across the idea that people ought to conserve and recycle. They hadn't considered that yet. And she would have to ask for help with the *DreamCatcher* hammock. She'd been too shy to take part in Al and Marin's rehearsals for it, but she'd eagerly watched them. Maybe they'd let her be a part-time actor in the fall.

Where was it? Oh, right—under a tarp in the nearby shed. Someone had to help her pull the hammock to the stage area. That frame was really heavy. Maybe Marin? That's right—Marin was fixing the hem on Jenny's interview dress, but she would help Marlene when she was finished.

*****

Louis' arms were exhausted. He'd been waving them like a traffic cop for over twenty minutes. Some woman was approaching him, smiling. "I'm Mrs. Fred from down the road, the Honey Man's wife." She was dressed in a long blue cotton dress and a straw hat.

"Thanks for coming, neighbor. I'm Louis."

"What a wonderful event you all planned. Backyard theater—I love it. My cherry cobblers are in the kitchen behind the potato salad—made with my husband's honey. Oh, I won't keep you from your work, Louis."

Louis' attention had fixated on two men heading for the barn—definitely the same pair he and Al had seen ducking behind a gas pump at Casey's garage the day before. Jenny had seen the bearded guy in town, and just that morning Lucina had informed him that Long Face had been stalking them on Peace Day. Yes, definitely the same jerks he'd glimpsed from the pantry window back in July. Marlene's photos had confirmed the driver's long face and his cohort's full beard. He must handle Long Face and Beard immediately—Lucina's names helped bring them down to size!—before they spewed hate on the performance.

Catching Lucina's attention, he gestured toward the barn. She nodded back, affirming that she would take over directing the parking.

Louis eased himself through the large group of people mulling over the anti-war paraphernalia and T-shirts. There they were, the troublemakers, wedged in the corner where the pitchforks and scythes were kept. Two big guys trying to make themselves invisible. He moved toward them, speaking out as he approached, "What do you guys want! You've been stalking us for weeks." They stayed silent, looking apologetic and confused. Louis was not put off guard by their innocent demeanor. "I can have you arrested for trespassing!"

Long Face took a step forward. "We come just like everybody else. Ain't you having an event here?"

"Yeah," Beard chimed in. "We seen the poster at Casey's Drug Store last week." A rose tattoo bobbed on his upper left arm as he gestured with an open hand. "You doin' a play or something, right?"

"Don't play dumb with me!" Louis barked, instinctively widening his stance and shifting his glance back and forth from one to the other. They were bigger than him, well over six feet. "That's your Oldsmobile station wagon parked out in our field, isn't it?" Ignoring the still-extended hand, he felt his hands close into fists.

"That field yusta be a field for winter corn," Long Face offered softly.

"What?" Was that a put-down? Once cornfield, now drainfield? The guy was trying to put him off guard.

"Yup," agreed the bearded one, whose rolled-up T-shirt sleeves showed muscular biceps, one with a name etched underneath a single rose tattoo. "Joe knows more about this place than any of youse 'ul ever know. There waren't no septic tank in back of the house neither. Didn't do it like that back when Joe's grandpa was here."

"Wait a minute." Louis put his hands in his pockets, thumbs showing; he must stay tough. "Who are you guys, anyway?"

Long Face reached out his hand again. "Joe Tompkins is my name," clamping Louis' like a vice. His companion offered, "Bud here," lifting a hand shyly toward Louis.

"My name is Louis." Rosebud! That's how he could remember that one's name.

"You're on my grandpa's old farm, Louis." Joe broke into a grin which showed large teeth and made his chin look even longer. "I come here every weekend when I was a kid. I planted that corn with my granddad. And right in this barn he kept twenty cows. First place I learned how to pull teats. That's how come I first got strength in my hands." He opened his hands proudly, palms up for Louis to see, as if they were his hard-earned trophies.

"Let me get this straight. This Yellow Farm used to be owned by your grandparents?" Louis kept his body taut. "Does that give you the right to harass us? I need an answer."

Joe nodded. "You've a right to that, Louis. I'm working up to it…My Grandma and Grandpa Tompkins owned this farm."

"Are you related to Fred Tompkins, the Honey Man?"

"You know, Fred? My uncle?"

"He didn't tell me this farm was in his family."

"Never does. Didn't get along with Grandpa. My mom and dad took it over."

Louis looked at Bud. "Are you a Tompkins, too?"

"Hell no," Bud grinned. "I got a normal-looking face, don't I? What you can see of it," he pulled at his beard and cuffed Joe on the arm good-naturedly. "No, the Tompkins took over Apple Tree Road way back. My family comes from the next county. We're the Gardeners. We own the Gardener Trucking Company in Ashland."

"Ah—" Louis hardly heard Bud's last words. The crowd hovering at Trish's table was breaking up in laughter. One very plump woman, holding a brightly colored shirt to her chest, was swaying with very sexual gestures. *He better stay focused on the two stalkers, surprisingly coming across as almost pleasant guys.*

"But I work with the sanitation department," Bud interjected with emphasis, as if Louis needed to know this. "Here in this county. Good wages now. I don't know about Joe's Grandpa Tompkins' cornfields, but I believe most of what he says." He winked at his pal. "He sure talks about this place a lot. Don't you, guy? John Tompkins, that's Joe's grandpa, he didn't have no septic tank. Nobody did back then, just outhouses and bags of lime." Bud gestured offhandedly in the direction of the farmhouse. "After he died, Joe's dad ran it for a while, then he sold it. A nice couple from Boston, Jeff and Marsha, bought it, fixed it right up with a makeshift septic. What a mess, and that was last summer. We had to come and drain that son of a gun on a Sunday morning. Wouldn't believe the stench. See you're doin' a good job to fix it up right and proper. About time somebody did. We'll be coming here soon and helping to lay down the pipes. Jeff and Marsha already set it up."

"Look, you guys." Louis shook his head in disbelief as if nothing the two men were saying quite computed. He had to make them own what they'd done. Ask them point blank why the hell they'd come to scare them with that obscene bullshit: "commie bastards"; "we'll be back." That kind of crap.

"You didn't ask us yet," Bud spoke up.

"What?" Louis cocked his head. "Didn't ask what?"

"About Joe and me. We're second cousins. Wouldn't think it—nothin' alike. But we git along. We're curious fellows."

Louis couldn't take anymore. "Look, you curious fellows. You know what you did. You guys terrorized my wife in July! You rode by in your station wagon and shouted obscenities at her—at us. I almost called the cops."

Joe's eyebrows shot up. "We was checking up on you, Louis, that's all. Country boys 'ul do that. We didn't know it was you—thought a bunch of hippies just moved in, squatters. They've been coming here from Boston and doing that—breaking into empty houses and squatting. I have to protect Grandpa's place. I even told Marsha I'd keep an eye on the place for them."

Louis' jaw clenched.

"Hey, I got a right to know what's goin' on with Grandpa's farm, don't I, Louis?" Joe's grin faded into solemnity. "Listen, I called up Jeff after that. He said he rented to New York City actors for six weeks. Sorry about that little bit of antics. Thought you were squatters, like I said. So, we've been checking you out, that's all."

"Why didn't you apologize when you knew who we were? You were both in that station wagon, weren't you?"

"Okay—okay," Joe had taken on a hangdog look. "We was wrong. I was still mad when I found out you got it rent-free from Jeff. I didn't want any freeloaders in my grandaddy's house. I guess we were having a little fun. Maybe too much beer. We was looking in on you, you might say. After that, we investigated you and decided you was okay—and also you was digging the trench."

"You didn't look in on us. You terrorized us!"

"Didn't think you'd be friendly to us, that's why. You know, us 'dumb country hicks.'" Joe pulled himself up to his natural height again. "Look, Louis," he stepped carefully toward his accuser. "That's why we came here, direct today. Now we know why you're here. Would an apology work okay now? We was wrong. And hearing you talk, I see how wrong we was. We thought you smart city people weren't afraid of anything, or anybody. Hell, the way you talked, real smart at the Peace Day, you probably talk to all them elected officials like you got an oiled tongue."

"Is that really fun for you? Terrorizing people? Red-baiting? Shouting obscenities isn't my idea—"

"I swear, Louis," Bud broke in. "That was Roger Dunham yelling. He was drunk. He can't help it. He's a loudmouth, but he'd do anything for you 'iffin you was in trouble. Except he's not here. He got shipped to 'Nam last week. Scared shitless. He was acting out with you guys."

"I thought there was only two of you."

"Rog was hiding in the back seat, yelling at the top of his lungs."

"I hope you guys aren't passing the buck on this Roger. An apology can only work if you two talk to the whole theater group, especially Lucina. That might do it. There's a lot we need to learn about each other. We'll talk more after the show, okay? I gotta get back to work."

Joe and Bud shook their heads in agreement, quite taken by Louis' take-charge manner.

"There's cold drinks by the open stage under the apple trees," Louis went on. "You know, where your grandpa's cornfields used to be. I've got work to do now." He gave the two men a dismissive wave and headed out the barn for the house. It was almost time to start the performance. Hadn't he promised to help Marlene arrange the props?

47
Performance at the Yellow Farm

The stage for the afternoon's performance was a flat, grassy field mowed ankle high. Pots of mums and zinnias marked the performance space with a frame of color. Several logs and hay bales were set in rows for benches, and behind that a scattering of tree stumps, boxes, and large stones served as seats. The troupe had hired several teens through the Ashland Community Center to help with the physical labor involved. This country stage demanded ingenuity to work. Most spectators had wisely brought blankets and pillows to soften hard surfaces.

A sound from the shofar—Hugh blew the ram's horn—quieted the gusty chatter. The play was about to begin. Children, and there were plenty of them, claimed their seats. The more agile ones settled on limbs of the closest apple trees. Four actors poised motionless within the Fire Dragon until Courtney started a slow syncopated beat on the red drum; then the papier maché animal, now a live thing, undulated slowly around the stage, winning silence and awe from the crowd.

Al announced the first presentation. "Scene One—Polluting the Earth, from *Eco-Drama: A Work in Progress*." He then introduced Lucina, who gave a short talk about the waste problem. Dressed in a casual summer dress—to show neighbors she dressed as they did—she relayed how America had never learned to clean up after itself, "like a badly educated school child given paints and brushes to use, but not instructed how to clean them. Americans produce and produce," she said, "without concern for the waste we create." *Of course, Louis' arduous scatology monologues had inspired her brief lecture.* Describing three different garbage dumps they'd found on the Yellow Farm's land alone, then naming the companies that had dumped waste in the nearby rivers for decades, she concluded with a general exposé of America's wanton use of natural resources and the extensive industrial waste and pollution produced—"a sure-fire route to ecological disaster!"

Then she brought up Vietnam. "It's not enough that the waste from atomic and nuclear bomb sites in America, especially the Southwest, have destroyed Native American lands. Now our military forces are in Southeast Asia, devastating that land and people as well. To put it bluntly, we are at this moment dumping our toxic shit on the Vietnamese. I'm sure you've all heard of napalm, which causes painful death by burns and asphyxiation, but do you know about Agent Orange? Since 1961 the US has been spraying endless liters of chemical agents on the country to strip away vegetation providing cover for Vietcong troops. That includes millions of liters of Agent Orange, which contains dioxin, a toxic compound that poisons soil, river systems, lakes, and rice paddies. Imagine the land you live on here being destroyed like that! It will cause serious birth defects in the next generation. Agent Orange is already causing deadly illnesses in American soldiers. You've seen Agent Orange eating away at young men in military uniforms on Main Street in Ashland. Limping and dying, they are victims of our imperialist destruction, along with the Vietnamese people."

With the end of her sobering speech, Lucina felt a terrible sadness come over her. The kids peering at her from their makeshift perches in the apple trees needed magic and joy—not war and disease. But the fierce hand-clapping that followed and the show of victory signs punctuating the air revived her. Somehow, miraculously, their audience today was simpatico.

Louis gave her a thumbs-up as he took the mike to continue the narration. Lucina felt an adrenaline rush: she'd improvised the last part of her talk and brought the war home when she spoke of the ravaged soldiers on Main Street. She could find words when she needed them. She wasn't inarticulate!

Louis was explaining that the five characters who were taking the stage were all named Bill. Each wore a mask and a costume caricaturing a different aspect of capitalist society, and each had a large one-million-dollar bill pinned to their shirt. After being introduced, the actors mimed actions symbolizing greed, not need. Bill Industrialist threw nuclear waste on a puppet representing a Native American child. Bill CEO presented a new car—"hot off the assembly line," he claimed—which immediately collapsed in a heap. Bill Entrepreneur captured a wild Brazilian bird and locked it in a small cage marked with a "For sale—$50,000" sign. Bill Financier dumped PCBs in the Hudson River with one hand and counted the money he saved with the other. Bill Military Commander-in-Chief, his enormous pants stuffed with hand grenades—converted pine cones—shat them out through a slot in his crotch until the stage was covered with his bombs, making a deadly minefield.

As the various Bills repeated these caricatured destructions in increasingly frenetic and robotic actions, a chorus took over Louis' narrative, chanting, "The Bills worship money and profit over people. To make more and more, they compete, kill, and destroy," accompanied by a funereal beat on the red drum by Courtney.

The jarring fifteen-minute scene caused a highly emotional response from the audience; even the kids, caught up in the crazy antics of the Bills, were clapping and booing. Nervous laughter escalated into angry shouts: "Stop profit over people!…Stop the bombing!…Stop American aggression!" The outcries inspired the actors to march into the audience chanting, "Stop the wars—save our planet." The chanting only quieted down when one excited child shook her fists so hard she tumbled off her tree-limb seat into her father's arms.

In spite of the audience's enthusiasm, Lucina moaned to Louis, "I'm waiting for somebody to start throwing rotten apples."

"Believe, Lucina. Believe," he enthused, hugging her. "Obviously, we've touched an empathic nerve today."

"But chances are some one here works for GE," she returned.

"I think it's about land, Lucina," he mused. "They really do want to caretake the land. See it as shared land. And here we are on John Tompkins' farmland. He was one of theirs. They knew him, they know his family. And we're showing we want to be caretakers of this land too."

"It's nothing like that Peace Day crowd."

"Yeah, but we can't make any quick judgments. Just be open to any positive responses. Listen, Lucina, I've got something to tell you, baby. But later. It's going to amaze you. We better be quiet, there's Jenny starting her scene."

Jenny, donned in a dress, heels, and a purse, did a little self-mocking curtsy. "I package myself for the man, the man," she chanted in singsong before pretending to trip over garbage bits left over from the previous scene. Marin introduced this second presentation, "Interview," an excerpt from the new women's play, *Moments of Loss/Moments of Gain.* "You are watching Jenny," Marin narrated. "She's on her way to an interview for a job teaching dance in an elementary school on New York's

Upper East Side, where the Mad. Ave. executives live and own all the property."

At center stage, Jenny was approached by Mr. Director and his fall guy, Mr. Ass Kisser. They shouted out question after question at Jenny, not waiting for any of her responses. When she managed to say a few words about the wonderful creativity of children, they smirked and tossed winks back and forth. As the two bullies continued to mime aggressive behavior, Jenny turned to the audience. "This story is true," she said. "I knew I would be a very good dance teacher because I care about children. I care about them having the environment to express themselves freely and responsibly. Obeying teachers, getting into straight lines, shouldn't take up all their time. Before this interview, I didn't know that many people directing schools could be so against providing truly supportive environments for kids. Or that so many school directors were into manipulating test scores so that they could receive more and more funding and perks that benefit them, not the students."

The Director edged Jenny to the door, bragging to Mr. Ass Kisser, "We'll bring her down a peg or two." His final words to her, "Don't call us, and we won't call you. You just won't do—you just won't do," were drowned out by boos coming from the kids perched in the trees. When the audience quieted down, Jenny ended the scene by stating simply, "Need I tell you: I was not hired. They said they didn't think I could discipline the children. I think tuning in to what kids need is the way to create loving, stress-free, and useful procedures, don't you?"

Jenny had barely finished her summing-up remarks when a group of women from the audience ran up to her, clapping and gushing praises. "Oh, thank you so much," Jenny responded, "We were afraid people might be offended by our style. Portraying the heads of children's schools as misogynist bully buffoons isn't likely to win friends—but let me talk to our audience first—they're still clapping—and I need to introduce our third act for today. Just stand near me, I really want to talk with you."

The four women stood aside, still beaming in some kind of awe, as Jenny calmed the crowd with, "Thank you so much! What a responsive audience today. Okay, folks—and by the way, you kids out there are making my day! If any of you want to take a dance class with me, see me later by the hot dogs, and sign up. Okay?" With some squeals coming from the nearby tree, Jenny announced, "Our third act for today, from a third play in process, will be *DreamCatcher*—or, as some of us like to call it, *Catching the Dreamer*. It's an improvisation needing the audience to make it happen."

As the six actors for the experimental *DreamCatcher* arranged themselves on the grass stage beside a large colorful hammock placed near the spectators, Jenny explained, "This is the dreamer-catcher, the nest in which an audience member will be invited to sit and tell their dream. The dream-teller will be asked to then repeat the dream slowly as we, the actors, interpret all the dream's elements: objects, moods, actions, characters. Hopefully, your responses will give us clues on how best to act out the dream. So, we're depending on you to let us know how we're doing, if you get my drift? So now, we need a dream-teller from the audience."

As Jenny coaxed the onlookers for a volunteer, Lucina felt tension leave her body: *Good! Two down and one to go.* She was already imagining the taste of a hot dog smothered with mustard when an elderly woman sprinted to the dream hammock. Unfortunately, the hammock was set too low to the ground. It took a few minutes to adjust it before the volunteer could settle comfortable to tell her dream. She also needed to be introduced to her audience. While this was going on, Jenny rejoined her four admirers.

"We're roommates of Aretha and Keisha," a small feisty woman offered. "They talked with Lucina at the Peace Day. They couldn't come, so they sent us—we're so glad they did. I'm Tish, and this is Sally, Joan, and Dot."

"Oh, sure. Lucina told us about them. We really want to hook up with you women!"

Tish put her hand on Jenny's shoulder. "You don't know how important what you're doing is...or do you? We're dying to get a women's theater group together. Could you come to Grandmore College and talk to us? Keisha and Aretha wanted us to ask you that."

Now Sally took over. "You Fire Dragon women could help us so much. Using theater like you do—to tell people what they don't want to hear, or can't, is where it's at!"

Joan and Dot, speaking excitedly at the same time, gushed out, "We'll be seniors next year, looking for jobs...We don't want to be secretaries...We want to use our creative skills, and we don't want to be bullied by male bosses." Joan took over: "Like the disgusting Director was abusing you." Then Dot: "What do you do for a living now, Jenny?"

"I work in a grocery store, but I'm starting to knit beautiful caps—so I know what you mean about needing to be creative. Oh—listen, they've got the hammock fixed. I have to watch this. Give me your contact info. We must continue this conversation."

"You'll be seeing Aretha and Keisha soon," Tish affirmed. "They'll come by here. We all need you desperately."

"Okay. Thank you so much, Grandmore College women. You're great. We'll be in touch very soon."

*****

The small wiry dream-teller, obviously well-known in the community, as suggested by the laughter and greetings being tossed out to her, began rocking gently in the Dreamer's Nest. As Anna Kirkland spoke into an amplified mike, her voice, with its mellow textures and lilting rhythms, invited rapt attention.

"I dreamt I got together with three of my friends one night. We had to decide what we could do about this terrible war. We wanted something awful to happen to President Johnson. But we thought—what goes around comes around, and we didn't need any more grief. We changed our thinking. We prayed that Lyndon and Lady Bird would come to the wise decision to take a long rest. They'd already worked very hard on juggling support for the war and organizing the War on Poverty, so they deserved a break. We imagined them getting very tired, slowly crawling into their four-poster bed in the White House, and going to sleep like Rip Van Winkle did, for years and years. When they woke up, or I should say, if they ever woke up, we knew the war would be over—because well, that was just it, they would finally wake up to the fact that the war was unjust, not about helping the Vietnamese, but about pushing America's agenda, and that it could only lead to destruction, not only to Vietnam but to America as well."

As clapping rose from the crowd, she waved at friends then continued, "What a dream that was! The reality? This country spends too much of our time and our money playing Russian roulette—I should say American roulette—with small countries. Why the hell are we in Vietnam? Let's get out now!" With this proclamation, Al did an adjustment of the hammock so Anna sat upright. She was asked to repeat the dream, slowly and clearly into the mike, as the actors dramatized it.

Watching the actors mime hypnotizing "the Johnsons" into sleep was both funny and strange. As the zombie-like Johnsons slept, the quartet locked hands and circled them chanting, "We don't want this killing anymore; money for jobs, not for war." When Lyndon and Lady Bird were forced out of their drugged-like sleep, back to reality, all six actors spread out the "wake-up cloth" with its brightly colored shapes. They lifted Anna from her dreamer's seat, chanting, "It's up to us, yes all of us, to stop this war that's so unjust," and circle-danced with her on their colorful cloth, holding hands and inviting audience members to join them.

Lucina looked at Louis, and both of them broke out in relieved clapping. How these six comrades came up with a simple but stark encapsulation of Anna's dream was amazing. Six people, thinking in collaboration, had been able to portray the dream's essence, with the support of their audience's oohs and right-ons. Lucina acknowledged to herself: *Al and Marin were certain all along—dreams told by our audiences can help build a common language of commitment and struggle. When Americans delve into their deepest, wisest selves, and dreams are one place to mine this richness, who can condone burning Vietnamese with napalm and destroying their countryside with Agent Orange? Anna, Hugh, Courtney, Jenny, Hans, Al, and Marin have just created hope for all of us!*

"Watcha thinking, Lucina?" It was Louis next to her, hugging her hard with excitement at their success.

Courtney had a bullhorn on the crowd. "Food's ready, folks! White buckets are for garbage—keep the Yellow Farm clean. Black buckets are for donations—keep the Fire Dragon Street Theater alive. We're a collective bent on shaking-up America. You heard Anna say it, "Why the hell are we in Vietnam? Let's stop the war now."

Several actors wove into the crowd holding black pails to collect contributions, while others carried large platters of hot dogs and hamburgers from the house to the picnic area. Soon bowls of salad followed, then cakes, cookies, and Mrs. Fred's cherry cobblers, all filling the card tables set up by the grape arbor.

Louis and Lucina found a quiet place to eat, away from the others. "This is like a dream, Louis. Did you shoo all potential hecklers away or something? It's just amazing."

"Lucina, Lucina, you're not going to believe what happened before the show."

"Oh, you mean when you went to the barn and I took over the parking. What was that all about, anyway?"

As Louis tried to describe his confrontation with Long Face and Beard, Lucina muttered, "I knew it was too good to be true. Something had to ruin our show."

"You're not listening to me—they aren't who we thought they were."

"Louis, I was there. I heard them!"

Louis put his plate down and rubbed Lucina's shoulders, knowing massage and silence would calm her. Soon he was explaining what the two men had told him. How nervous they were about meeting him—how Rose Bud was going to be working on the septic tank—how Long Face Joe's grandfather had built the Yellow Farm and the Honey Man was Joe's uncle. How badly they wanted to explain themselves and apologize to her, to all of them. They'd made a big mistake: they were sure poachers had broken into the farmhouse. "Let's say their excuses were 85 percent convincing. But they did apologize a few times."

Lucina felt dizzy, confused. How could reality change so drastically? In just a short time? Life was so odd.

"Do you want to meet the two of them briefly, honey? They're waiting for us by the shovels at our shit-ditch."

"I guess. But let's be clear. We were assaulted, Louis!"

48
Joe and Bud

Though Louis had told her their names were Joe and Bud, when Lucina saw the two men stuffing themselves with hot dogs and joking with an elderly couple by the open trench, to her they were the stalkers, Long Face and Beard.

Bud, gulping down soda, smiled shyly at her. "We'll be here soon to finish up this drainage trench. You guys did good work so far."

She felt nauseous watching a rose ripple on his fleshy bicep.

Joe turned from Louis and stepped cautiously toward her. "Look, let me explain to you what's going on here. I'm Joe and this is Bud, and you're Louis' wife?"

"I'm Lucina Holzer and yes, explain why you're here."

Bud addressed her gently. "See, it's what I do for a living, septic tanks. Look, if you hadden' been fixin' this—I would've been here every Sunday mornin' digging this trench myself. The county health commissioner has his eye on the Yellow Farm. You gotta understand, Lucina. We're sorry we scared you. It was a misunderstanding. We thought you all was someone else, squatting in Joe's grandpa's house. We should've called Jeff and

Marcia first to check it out. Louis told us, they wanted you to stay here."

Now Joe held his two large hands, palms up, in a pleading manner. "My grandpa salutes you from his grave. You guys did a great job on this trench. Cow dung has its place, pig manure too. But human shit and all the garbage people make has to be broken down. As you guys say, we gotta take care of our waste. I sure do love this place. Practically lived here when I was a kid. That thing that happened in July? Like I told Louis, we thought you was them hippy freeloaders from Boston."

Lucina drew her shoulders back and eyeballed Joe with a steady gaze. "Look, whoever you are. I don't know what your grandfather has to do with it, but you and your buddies have been following us for weeks, not only heckling us from your station wagon! Almost ruined our summer. We live in the city, but we're here to do important work." Her mind was racing to get a handle on the two men: *Could these two hulks really have climbed that skimpy ladder and put the shovel on Woody's roof!* "You're correct. Jeff and Marsha did invite us to be here. They respect the work we're doing."

Joe's hands relaxed into his jean's pockets. "I'm sorry, real sorry we scared you. We was having some kicks, I'll admit that. We didn't know who we was talking to. My grandfather built this farm and then it belonged to my mom, though she didn't want to live on it. I hated that she made us live in town. I'm tied to the place—wish I could've bought it. I've lived in this area all my life. I useta come to Grandpa's every summer, help him with the planting, the haying, milking, everything."

"How come you've been following us all around Ashland, the grocery store, the gas station, even the Peace Day event? And you haven't explained or apologized before!"

Bud put his hand on Joe's shoulder; he would try to explain things to her. "Look, we're not as smart as you city guys. I mean, our buddies are still reading comic books. Jeff and Marsha set us straight. Told us you weren't who we thought you was. Making up plays—talking to folks in the area—telling us about what's going on in 'Nam. What it's really about—that's cool. Real good talkers. Every time we open our mouths, we're stuttering. But Joe and I dig what you guys are doing. That's what I'm trying to say. We hate the war. Joe here has a way out. You see the way he slouches—his head hangs? He got polio during that fifties epidemic. He can't do much physical work. But I'm scared they're going to draft me soon. I don't have the guts to do what your Sam does—'Say no. Don't go. Go to Canada. Go underground.' That stuff."

Louis interrupted. "But we didn't perform *Choice* today—"

"You did it at the Peace Day." Joe stepped forward, lifting his head up straighter, and eyed Lucina shyly. "Bud and I watched the whole thing. Wasn't stalking you guys—really digging everything you was saying. Some of the guys we hang with, they don't think the same. They don't think. They would die for this country. Their whole thing is America right or wrong. You guys went to college, I bet all of youse. Not us—we're basically farm boys. Work with our hands. You can sit in offices, wear suits, and tell others what to do. Most of our buddies are in the military, on leave, or waiting to get in. They think you're all a bunch of spoiled cowards."

Still trying to figure them out, Lucina spoke flatly. "Maybe you need different buddies? Ones that can understand what we're about here!"

Joe shrugged with frustration: she didn't understand what they were telling her! "I was telling Louis this—Roger shipped out to 'Nam last week. We told Mike and Scott they couldn't come here today. They don't think things through so good. I told them Granddaddy wouldn't want no trouble on his land. I mean he's dead and buried, but he would know if anything bad happened here. You understand what I'm saying?"

What is this? The stalkers are now our protectors! Her glance fell again on Bud's tattoo and the word clearly inked beneath it: Sister. Sudden warmth filled her, similar to the feeling that came into her toward the Honey Man, she realized. Why was she always surprised when a stranger, a man, could cause some kind of tender feelings in her?

"Okay—I think I do see what you're telling us, Joe and Bud. I really do. If we respect you, you'll respect us. Like that."

Louis, who had stayed quiet so Lucina would have a chance to ask questions, couldn't hold back any longer. "I know, we're the new kids on the block. We're the strangers in the area, and we're on somebody else's land. But we want to make some inroads here. And you guys want to make some inroads with us. Let's start again—with more information—and give each other respect."

Lucina turned to Bud. "Listen, I'm really glad we cleared up who you are and who we are. If you have friends who are questioning this war, concerned about the caretaking of our earth, and support civil rights of all kinds, connect us to them—that would show us good faith."

Joe and Bud looked at each other and sighed: *these actors are no pushovers!* But it was going to be all right now.

"So, have you known Jeff and Marsha long?" Joe asked.

"I've talked to them on the phone several times." Lucina felt impatient.

"I mean, do you know them—about their life, I mean?" Joe rubbed his big hands together slowly, taking time to find his words.

Lucina started to edge away from the men. "A little bit." She really wanted to greet the people who were connecting to them and their work. "Why do you ask? Movement people don't usually talk about personal stuff that much. What are you referring to?"

"Yeah, well," Bud interrupted, "Ain't going to be any showers for these two."

What were they trying to tell her?

The two men looked at each other and shrugged. Bud flipped his empty coke can in the air, caught it and crushed it with one hand. Joe scuffed at the grass.

"You know thems breaking up, don't yah?" Joe's eyes widened. "How come they ain't here—how come you're here?"

Lucina felt cold sweat on her hands.

"Ain't all," Bud interjected. "Jeff's going to stay in San Francisco. Leaving his land and all that. That's the part I can't understand. Leavin' the town you growed up in, the way of feelin' and being. That's really harder for me to understand than the other."

In actuality, she'd had only one conversation with the couple over the phone. But she'd wanted to meet them, know them better. They were movement people in a complex relationship, like her and Louis. Marsha had told her they were learning new techniques to build community. Sometimes they lived only with each other, sometimes with a group. All summer she'd thought of them as a gutsy, together pair doing organizing work. "What are you saying about Jeff and Marsha?" She didn't want to hear gossip, and she was really hungry. One hot dog hadn't satisfied her.

"So, guess you didn't hear it?" Joe reached for one of the shovels by the trench, secured upright in the ground. Grabbing its handle, he used it like a crutch to keep himself stable. "So, Jeff, he's different. My uncle, the Honey Man, adopted him. You met Uncle, I take it. So, Jeff's my step-cousin. When he hooked up with Marsha, they said they would make this farm work again. That's how come they got it, them married and all, and older than me. But he ain't going to give back what his step-grandpa—my grandpa—wanted for the Yellow Farm. I don't expect gay guys ever do have babies with each other." Joe seemed to be holding back a chuckle, or was it an embarrassed smirk?

"I ain't seen no two guys make a baby yet," Bud spoke up. "But then—I didn't think they let guys like that in the Lefty Movement. Whad' I know?"

Lucina felt a chill run through her. "Are you sure that's true?" When both men looked at her straight on, she knew they were speaking facts, facts that disturbed and confused them. What about Marsha, his wife? Why weren't they saying anything about her?

*****

Louis and Lucina didn't get to bed until well past midnight. There were so many people to talk to—kind, curious and knowledgeable people; people who'd lived in the area for ages, and others who were trying to find a simpler life in the country; people who had enough ideas for plays to keep them busy for years; and a group of women hungry for plays dealing with their needs. She and Louis had wanted to talk to as many of them as they could.

As they lay in bed, crickets and tree frogs sawed rubber-band rhythms in full stereo through their windows. What a startling day it had been! First, that the performances had been such a success. Then the appearance of Joe and Bud and the news about Marsha and Jeff, about his being gay. No one was who you thought they were. This truth silenced them, and for several minutes they gave up their concerns to the music pulsating around them.

Then Louis had something to say. "You know, babe—I've been thinking. The Movement could use some gay men in it." He continued to muse, pulling at his beard. "It's pretty heavy on the straight macho stuff, don't you think so?" Lucina kissed him hard on the cheek and cuddled against him.

He brought up Joe and Bud, reminding her how genuine their apologies had been for scaring her. "Like they said, they assumed we were negligent freeloaders." She shook her head in perplexed amusement. "Can I give up my scary stalkers for two innocent farm guys, Joe and Bud?" Louis, too exhausted to answer any more of her questions about them, begged her to let him sleep.

"Okay, okay," she said, curling her legs over his. "I'll accept that it's 'Joe' from now on. "But, the other one has to be *Sister RoseBud*. That's the only way I'm going to feel okay about them." As Louis uttered, "Let it go, Babe," and she heard his breathing deepen, she resolved: *I'm not going to let every little thing that happens drive me nuts. I need to keep humor and lightness in my life. We learned this afternoon how comedy is a good communicator. If all our plays are as dead serious as Choice? Forget it. When people laugh they let defenses go and open up to the serious messages in our dramas, and the questions we raise.*

She thought about Anna Kirkland's giddy joy at being rocked about in the Dreamer's hammock. She was like a kid in a swing, allowing her delight to show itself, even in the midst of her terribly serious message: "Why the hell are we in Victnam anyway?" And the urgent need of the Grandmore College students to do what the Fire Dragon women were doing: help build a women's movement by dramatizing their needs.

The last things she thought of before sleep quieted her? The ladder and the shovel—how they disappeared and re-appeared. Since Joe seemed to be keeping track of what was going on at the Yellow Farm, maybe he knew. Or maybe there were some kids on Apple Tree Road who liked playing pranks on them. And hadn't Trish brought some town kids over for an afternoon to teach them how to do tie-dyeing? And what about all the teenagers from the community center who helped prepare the outdoor theater? Maybe one or two of them came back in the night to smoke grass, be with each other. Young people did need their own places to hang out, where they could just be and love each other. Maybe the most important thing she'd learned that day? Life held hard truths as well as amazing surprises.

49
Circling with a Full Moon

The Unitarian Church reception had taught them to be more receptive to people with different mindsets—their job was to inspire discussion, not suppress it. They would have to learn how to embrace the needs of many different groups. And the enthusiastic support shown at their Play and Picnic Performance inspired ideas on how to do this. Workshops with different age groups could inform the troupe as to what was important to inhabitants of a specific area.

Though Aretha and Keisha couldn't be at the Saturday performance, they called to beg the Fire Dragon women to stay in touch with them, and give them guidance around building their own women's theater at Grandmore College. Aretha was especially emphatic. "Please, I have a million questions to ask you. Ever since I was a kid I've wanted to act out with my girlfriends. You know, make a play to show the world we don't take shit."

The Fire Dragon women were thrilled with this urgent need to connect to them; they planned to meet with Aretha and Keisha in the fall, when they were settled back in New York City. They would talk about doing workshops with them. Lucina was already brainstorming how *Moments of Loss/Moments of Gain* could fire up women college students all over the country.

Before the troupe could reach out again to the community, it was time to leave their Yellow Farm. Jenny had to see a dentist; Al had a job interview; Marlene had meetings with her staff to discuss new curriculums; and Jack had to visit a sick brother.

The last three days were spent finishing the trench, dismantling the makeshift stage, cleaning the house, and returning the various spaces back to their original states. But they would continue their work as soon as everyone had settled themselves back in the city. Their new insights already led to dreams of a spring tour into the "melting pot" of their country, where they could put them to work.

*****

On their last night with a full moon shining above the farm, Jack felt inspired. He asked the others to come to the barn at nine o'clock to do a full moon ritual. Dressed in white shorts and T-shirt and with a peace symbol hanging on his chest, he looked like a spiritual guide to a hopeful future. "I want us to show gratitude for our incredible time together," he said simply. His wish was enthusiastically shared as they all followed him to the field near the apple trees; only days before, it had served as their performance day stage.

Directing his "tribe" to stand in a large circle, holding hands, he spoke out calmly and thoughtfully. "This ritual is meant to honor each of us as individuals as well as our presence within this group. To use a cliché, 'a group is only as strong as all of its members.' Now with the blessing of this circle of light, our moon, let's show love and gratitude for us all. What we'll do is simple and magical. Starting with Joan, each one of us will take our turn, slowly walking to the center of our circle, as we chant that one's name in rhythm together. When that person is in the

378

center, they will hold out their arms wide as if embracing us, and we'll then chant, 'We embrace you in our circle of light—you are with us whole and bright.' Does anyone else have something they want to chant?"

Louis spoke out. "After we've gone around the circle let's do the Arapahoe chant from the *Ghost Dance Play:* 'We circle around the boundaries of the earth, wearing our long wing feathers as we fly.'"

"Great idea, Lou," Jack enthused. "Connect to our root people tonight within our earth home."

By the time they'd enacted the ritual thirteen times under the full moon's glow, each one felt a mystical unity. After the Arapahoe chant, Lucina was inspired to lead them in singing "May the Circle Be Unbroken."

*****

Louis had some details to go over with Al, so Lucina asked Marin to sit with her for a while to moon-gaze a little longer. They sat on one of the logs used for seating at their performance, knees touching and holding hands. "I'm feeling both happy and sad, Marin."

"Why so moody, my friend?"

"With all our focus on reaching out to the community, I've missed just hanging with you."

"Me too. Dealing with performing and that ridiculous assault by Joe and Bud. I've had a hard time believing what you and Louis told us last week about them. Something about protecting their connection to the Yellow Farm...? Really? I despise bullying for any reason. What my brother suffered. Those bullies murdered him! That's how I'll always see it."

Lucina tightened her grip on Marin's hand, her eyes closing as she remembered the day Marin had broken down and told them about Michael. "I'm so sorry about your brother,

Marin," she whispered. "I wish I'd known him." She knew for sure, there in the full moon's light with the love and depth of feeling that Jack's ritual had given them all, how much Marin's presence in her life meant to her. It was Marin who helped her understand the necessity to have deep empathy with others' struggles; who'd forgiven her when she'd been unable to hear her needs deeply; Marin who could love both her and Louis, and not take sides when they needed a mediator. If only—if only—she and Marin could embrace and hold each other closely, woman to woman.

"We better get going, Luie. Tomorrow is going to be another exhausting day, packing up everything in all our vehicles. I'll call you when we're back and let's make a date to have lunch together, okay? Friends need to nurture each other, you know, as much as partners and lovers and verifiable married couples, like you and Louis—even though you don't talk about it."

Falling into their own thoughts, their hands unclasped. But the moonlight made a conjoined shadow of their two bodies as they walked slowly back to the house before heading to their separate rooms. Lucina saddened with the thought: *the next night they would be separated, once again, by many city blocks.*

PART VII
GROWING

50
What Moves You to Rise Up Fierce?

By mid-September they were ready to work again. With their stay in Massachusetts opening them up to performing in different types of venues, Louis, Lucina, Al, and Marin decided to put a tour in place for the spring. They believed their plays could speak to peace groups, college students, and concerned citizens of all ages and ethnic backgrounds. But which plays would work on the street, and which ones needed performance spaces? They definitely weren't geared to ruling-class white folk dedicated to keeping their privileges.

Their target audiences wanted information that exposed their country's empire-building motivations in Vietnam; uncovered the brutal treatment of indigenous people, the original settlers of their country; chronicled the pollution of land, water, and air in the greedy pillaging of our earth's resources; and laid bare the disparity between women and men in a patriarchal system. Their plays had not yet directly dealt with systemic and endemic racism in the US.

Marin and Lucina met for lunch to nurture their friendship and exchange thoughts on their tour plans. They had worked so well together—especially on introducing the self-reflection exercises, now key to constructing the women's play—that it gave them confidence in their instincts. As they enjoyed beers and hamburgers, they began penning a kind of mission statement to help in plotting the tour.

"We have made a choice. Our work is not meant solely to entertain, but to engage, educate, and create discussion, hopefully leading to action. We will research where our plays are most needed. The following considerations can guide us as we go about setting up a tour: Content and style of each of our plays must speak to our projected audiences. College women struggling to be treated professionally and financially equal to their male counterparts don't need a comedy of manners; they need our real stories, scenes directly depicting the challenges women face in the struggle for equality."

At one point Marin put her pen down and took a long drink from her mug. "Let's let Al and Louis write out their thoughts on the mission for our other plays, Lu. I'm beat. We'll be meeting in a few days with the whole troupe to get a handle on what our plans are for the months ahead."

"Agreed! Enough strategizing for today, Marin. Whew! I can't wait to do our movement exercises—my body aches to be stretched. By the way—I'm glad Al got the carpentry job he wanted. But what about you—are you job hunting?"

"I still have my part-time job at the library. And I'm going to take some courses in psychology at City College—I want to learn about child psychology. That'll come in handy in my future with Al."

Lucina wasn't sure what Marin was implying, but she was afraid to pry. *Would this future take her beloved friend away from her?*

*****

At the troupe's first fall meeting to discuss ongoing plans and procedures, early arrivals Jack and Jenny were soon engaged in a heated discussion. Jack, who hadn't questioned the women's work before, voiced intense concern. "Why can't we play the men in your plays? I mean, doesn't that make more sense? Here you've got six great guys to choose from. So—use us!"

The sharpness of his tone confused Jenny. She expected animosity from Hans or one of the older guys, but Jack? Their very own spiritual guru was rarely confrontational. She fretted: *We need good vibes at the first meeting together in the loft since our summer sojourn.* She wondered if Marlene, sitting nearby in the loft kitchen also waiting for the four o'clock meeting to begin, would support her. Always so mindful with her comments, Marlene was probably sensitive about not being a full-time member yet. Okay—so she would have to handle Jack's challenge alone. And right now his look was burning a hole in her. "In case you're not aware, brother, except for our women's play, our repertoire mainly focuses on men's issues. By playing all the roles, it helps us understand how we're being suppressed in many different situations. We need to just work with each other now to analyze what needs to change."

"Jenny, if we played your jerks, then you could put us in our place."

"How can I say it clearer? We need to hear ourselves think! The unjust distribution of power, pay, and credit in our patriarchal system has to be exposed."

"Please don't throw out pat political jargon, Jenny. It doesn't do your intelligence justice." Obviously pleased with his response, Jack reached out to put an arm around her.

When she shrugged his arm away, she heard him murmur, "sorry," and reach for his mug of coffee instead. *Well, he should be*, she thought. *I'm Hans' girl, after all. In fact, I'm my own girl, mister!* She must persist. "Hasn't Joan talked about this with you? Our work is going to help us all, someday. Right now it's uncomfortable because we're challenging the status quo."

Neither Jenny, Jack, or Marlene had expected this flare up. But it had to happen: tension between the men and women actors had been increasing ever since the scene from *Moments of Loss/Moments of Gain* had been met with such enthusiasm at their August performance. The guys witnessed several women students in their audience begging the women actors to do workshops and perform at their colleges. Jenny's story, "Interview"—soon to be renamed "Wink," (for the enigmatic and treacherous gesture which signaled abuse of power throughout the scene) "really turned those women on," they said. And when the Fire Dragon Women realized they were one of maybe four women's street theater groups in the country addressing women's needs, they began to own their relevance to the emerging women's movement, asking themselves hard questions: why were politically aware women still playing second-class citizens' roles, serving coffee, cooking the meals, deferring opinions to their supposedly more articulate boyfriends, and typing up their speeches instead of giving their own? No more staying invisible, silent—not making themselves fully present in their lives. Yes! Women's theaters of all kinds were definitely needed for consciousness-raising.

"Listen, Jack." Jenny broke into his resistance again. "By playing the parts of our oppressors—and I'm sorry if my political jargon offends you!—we're able to see exactly how we're being manipulated. Then we can do something to stop it. And when our sisters watch us owning our anger, they will too. Did you see our review in the September *Berkshire Activist News*? 'Fire Dragon Women's *Moments of Loss/Moments of Gain*, spiced with bizarre and bawdy actions, churned the audience's guts during their Yellow Farm performance.'"

She watched him nod his head and check his watch anxiously. *Has he decided not to challenge me anymore, or is he just anxious for our meeting to start?* she wondered.

Marlene, who had been following every word closely, finally chimed in. "Working with the women has changed my life, man." She looked pointedly at Jack, a smile on her lips for adding "man" to her pronouncement. Jenny had inspired her to own her wake-up call, right then and there. "I haven't told anyone else, but I'm letting you guys and gals know—I've applied for a January sabbatical so I can work full-time with the women and part-time with the mixed group. As Jenny says, 'the women's play is going to fire up the Left.' You guys are going to either be really proud of us or very jealous!"

As Jenny and Marlene hugged, Jack stood up quickly to greet Al, who had just ambled into the kitchen area. "How've ya been, my man?"

"Any more coffee, Jack? I need a shot of caffein."

"You're in luck." After pouring Al a mug, he turned to address the two women. "Okay. I hear you, Marlene and Jenny. This is a time that people are claiming their right of self-determination, correct? All our plays are meant to help that process. So kudos to women libbers. But hey! I'm a guy and I'm not sure exactly how I fit into your struggle. I do know I'm really glad the guys are dedicated to our Ghost Dance work. Talk about injustice! Call it what it was—genocide. So, yes! Rise up, resist, fight back. Sorry, ladies, if I don't always know what you want."

Al nodded emphatically. "Jesus, everyone's becoming an orator here. That's good, Jack. We all got a lot of work to do. And speaking of work—I was supposed to tell you they're about to start the meeting, you guys. Oops—I should say, 'guys and gals.'"

Marlene was moved to put her arm around Jack's waist, though his use of the word "ladies" was annoying. But, she trusted him; he always tried to act with heart. "Just support us, Jack, That's what we need. It's our turn to be heard. You know, I was wondering why Shakespeare had men play women's parts and women play men who were playing women or whatever. I think we need a lot more gender experimentation, don't you?"

*****

The meeting began with updating each other on how re-entry into the big city had gone. Who'd gotten a job, and who needed ideas on where to find one? Couldn't expect the theater work to support them for some time. Then Al, Louis, Marin, and Lucina briefed everyone about the plans for a spring tour. They read mission-statements-in-process which they were using to map out suitable venues for performances. Volunteers were needed to work with them on the research, letter writing, and phone calls necessary to set up this ambitious project. Obviously, it would take a lot of work during the coming months. With four committees set up to divide tasks and all ten members committed to the work, a tour would happen!

As the meeting progressed, rehearsal work was then discussed. The women needed to focus on their work; Lucina's real-life story, "Markings," was up next for conceptualizing into a play. And the mixed group needed to develop the *Ghost Dance Play*, dramatizing the uprising of Native Americans—or should they say "the Indigenous"?—against the theft of their land and imprisonment on reservations where their language and spiritual traditions were stripped away and abuse of all kinds was allowed.

Hans had an opportunity to suggest a technical innovation that many movement artists were employing. "See. I think I found a way to show the truth of those reservations. A lot of activists are working with filmstrips. Think of them as newsreels you carry in your pocket. We'll just need a projector, and wow! As we're performing Ghost Dance rituals and chants, we can project images behind us of those reservations, more like internment camps, like how Japanese Americans were imprisoned during World War II. The filmstrip can be evidence of why the Lakota Sioux needed to rally their ancestors in the struggle to stop the US military from massacring them. And comrades, I just want to say right now, Jenny is explaining to me why we can't put down women for being pissing mad. That's why we're doing the Ghost Dance—about the massacre at Wounded Knee. We support the Indigenous. We have to support our women rising up too."

Hugh and Courtney got off on Hans' remarks. Courtney thanked him for making the connection between the women's play, *Moments of Loss/Moments of Gain*, and their *Massacre at Wounded Knee*. "If you deny people their rights, suppress them—they must rise up, fight back, each in their own way." Hugh added, "This helps me figure out how to play Wovoka. My Wovoka is not a macho; he knows the strength of his sisters." Lucina clapped with the others after these remarks thinking, *Let's see how you guys will react when we women decide Wovoka has to be played by one of us.*

Hans was talking again. "After I messed up at Tavern on the Green—I know, I deserved that painful probation—it took a long time to regain your trust. And when I had the courage to do a self-reflection improv with Al, I faced my true, scared self. You've been kind and patient with me. Tak. I have to find the best way to get my fear and anger out, so I don't hurt anyone again."

Jenny was clearly moved by how persuasively Hans spoke, from the heart and with less of his nervous banter. Not the accusing outsider, he was feeling connected to them all. But would it last?

As Hans continued to rally support for a filmstrip project, Lucina felt the energy around her become palpable and uplifting.

She closed her eyes and saw lightning zigzagging in her head. Was it the memory of lightning bugs from the farm? Or the full moon ritual and sitting afterward with Marin? Whatever was causing such energy, she felt proud of her present family. She still had to work through her sadness over Karen and Sally. But at least that afternoon, their haunting shadows were chased away by excited talk and belief in the value of the theater work. Her former studio had been transformed into a vital work space for the Fire Dragon Street Theater.

51
The Cost of Attraction

When Louis called Karen to say he was back in town and could the two of them meet for coffee, he felt ice in her voice. Hoping it was protective distancing, since they hadn't seen each other for several weeks, he implored her to meet with him at "their" coffee shop on Sixth Avenue. His attempt at bridging the gap—"I've really missed you"—was met with a vapid "oh?" Her agreement to meet was followed by, "There are disturbing things to talk about," as she hung up quickly.

He felt her stiffness as she ordered a fruit salad and black coffee, even as her musky cologne brought back their exciting afternoon together—was that in July? "You look great," he offered carefully. "How's Sally?"

Karen shook her head as if to ward off any pleasantries between them. Then blinking rapidly, she seemed on the verge of tears. "You didn't hear about…"

"Hear about what?" His voice rose with tension.

"You didn't hear about all the lesbians getting evicted from the Twelfth Street building!" She spoke accusingly into his confusion, "Sally was evicted—didn't want you to know. All the 'undesirables,'—student politicos, lesbians, gays—were thrown out, accused of not paying rent on time, damaging property, using drugs. All lies by the landlord. She always paid her rent and never, ever used drugs in that apartment. He wouldn't give her a lease so she had no legal leg to stand on."

"That's really tough, Karen. I'm sorry." At least she was talking to him, opening up like she used to.

"Now he's leasing to hetero couples with steady jobs. Just think, Louis. If you shaved your beard and worked full-time, you and Lucina could live there."

"So, where is she living now?" He would ignore her jabs, try to coax out her old warmth toward him.

"Let me explain some things to you, Louis. Sally is overqualified for the temp jobs she gets, and the pay is low. She had to move in with me. And you saw my apartment—good for me, but too small for the two of us. We get along beautifully when we have some space between us. She had the whole summer before she had to move out—she wanted to rent her place to a tourist, make a pile of cash during those six weeks we asked to stay with you. We needed that money! But no thanks to you, we're scrounging. And fuck it, Louis, we're doing something really difficult, something brave politically. We're not making up clever plays about things needing to change. We're actually changing things. We're taking over the paper. Sally and I are visionaries—we hoped you and Lucina were, too. How wrong we were."

Suddenly she looked angular and hard. Soft, sexy Karen lived only in his mind. She was taut and sharp, just like Sally. That was it—Sally had turned her against him. Karen must have talked about their tryst, and her girlfriend had gotten into a rage about it. "Try to hear me, Karen. I really care about you. Lucina and I felt very close to you and Sally. You only wanted to be with us this summer if you could be there for the full six weeks. We had to focus on the theater work and how to connect to different groups—figure out what direction we should take." The woman who had once lifted his spirit, who had joyed in talking with him, was looking past him, not listening at all. His words sounded hollow. "Besides, I couldn't lie to Lucina about what was going on between me and you."

"But why would you lie? You could have told her the truth. Didn't you think of that?"

Louis felt his chest tighten. How could he tell Lucina? Look at what she'd gone through around Jenny—and they hadn't really been sexual. He had to protect her as she'd protected him. Because of her, he'd been able to write some—even see his humiliation by the cops as a way to help him begin to comprehend the endless degradation of his people. Shit! Didn't Karen and Sally see that he and Lucina and their comrades were fighting for justice, the same as they were?

"Listen, Louis. We were really depending on you both to help us figure out our situation: how to convince the guys at *We Rise* to move over—and be civil about it, so we wouldn't have to use force. Last spring you told me the women in your group were speaking up more. Now I wonder—you and she can't even be truthful with each other. Lucina seems to be mainly focused on you—how you were brutalized by the pigs—how members of your group wrangle with you. She's so tuned into men's competitive bullshit. Does she take the time to understand who she is and what she needs? Look how she gave up sculpture for your work."

"Jesus, Karen. You don't get Lucina at all. I thought you understood us. What we're doing. I thought you loved my poems. You love Roethke, Neruda, Lorca—and they're men."

"You and your poet persona. What is that about? Getting suckers like me to fall in love with you? Louis, you played with my heart. I'm embarrassed that I fell for your game. Ashamed that I jerked you off. Let's just say I offed a jerk! I'll never do that again. I'll never touch another man. We were desperate for your friendships. You could have helped us—and learned something by doing that. But you didn't because basically you're cowards. You and Lucina hide behind your couple fortress."

As Karen continued to berate him and Lucina, his glance fell on her gesturing right hand. The hand that had touched him, the long supple fingers, sensitive fingers that had skillfully aroused him. His desire had responded like a needy child hungry to be held by her, to be lifted up and shout for joy in her grasp. That hand now wore a silver ring with the symbol of Venus soldered on it, the female symbol now flooding T-shirts and jewelry. He wanted to seize that hand, clinch it until she cried. Then he would hold her and tell her he was sorry how things had happened. That he still loved her.

"We're really trying to make a difference, Louis. Sally and I have told each other everything about our feelings for you two. The once feelings. The extent of our intimacies. Everything about you and your girlfriend."

"She's my wife, damn it!"

"So, that's your new angle? Hide behind a wife?"

Her reprimands had finally beaten him down; he felt himself an imposter. Thank God he hadn't told her about the bizarre ceremony in Monroe, New York. How could that travesty justify him using the word "wife"? Karen was right; he couldn't claim to be a husband, just like he'd never been a dad. That's why he hadn't told her about the son he wasn't allowed to see. And what about the roles he'd chosen: poet, activist, friend, lover? Well, he wasn't writing that much; he'd been beaten up for being an activist; and he'd failed as a friend to Karen. And what about Lucina, his deep love? Was he really good for her? She was getting more and more into the women's work—and into women.

"You look like you're not sure what you're about, Louis Altman. You and your wifey sidekick don't know what real struggle is. You two sure don't know what it's like to be lesbian feminists!"

"You're right, Karen. We should have done better by you."

"Too late, buster. Justice will find its way. It's time for women to lead. And that's what Sally and I are doing. We're taking over the newspaper. 'By any means necessary,' to quote the Marxist philosopher Frantz Fanon."

"Can't you hear me, Karen? I was so taken by you. I couldn't have concentrated on my work this summer. I had to get ahold of myself. I usually tell Lucina everything, but this was just too hard."

"Let's cut to the chase," she said abruptly. "I have to leave soon."

"You have something else to say to me, Karen?" *Why was he being so tolerant of her, when he felt so disturbed? Her face had paled—had her physical problems worsened?*

"I know the truth, Louis. I know you had other people stay with you at the Yellow Farm. People know what's going on. I have a friend, Renée, and she knows Trish Gold. Trish told her about being there for six weeks—how great it was. And there was another guy and some woman who came and went as she pleased. Is that 'only the theater troupe'? You lied to us, Louis. Plain and simple!"

"Oh, you're talking about Trish and Woody and, and Joan—they're in the group! They help us with props, reviews, and promotion." For the first time with her, Louis felt fear. There was something in the fierceness of her voice, the coldness in her eyes that terrified him. Her love-energy had definitely turned to hate, and it was very scary.

"We thought you and Lucina were our comrades, ones we could really talk to. It appears you were embarrassed to have two dykes in your little drama clique. Is your heterosexual persona too hard to give up, Louis?"

"Stop making us your enemies. It's like you're not seeing who we are anymore. My people have been the world's scapegoats for centuries, Karen. I don't need you to do that to me."

"The most treacherous thing about you two? Your excuses."

"We did not lie to you! Lucina and I didn't know the pressures you and Sally were under. You could've been more up-front with us before this…this festering happened!"

"No more of your cover-up, mister. I think we're just about through here." Hesitating to take another bite of her salad, she slashed out again. "You couldn't accept your feelings for me. Well, I don't need cowards or liars in my life. Our woman-run paper will document all the crimes against women that men have committed ever since the big lie about Eve being born out of Adam's rib!" Her voice became harsher. "What's your Fire Dragon Street Theater, anyway? A playground for bourgeois artistes? Posturing activists? You and your 'accomplice,' Lucina—it should be 'Bitch-cina.'"

The grating voice had finally plunged into his heart. "You've gone too far, sister! That's really destructive and mean."

"You used me, Louis. Isn't Lucina enough for you, mister? You were trying to challenge my love for Sally. Well, I've told Sally everything. *Every thing!* You two don't even have the guts to be honest with each other."

For once, Louis, the articulate one, the one who helped others put their mysterious, unspeakable feelings into words, the poet of heart and longing, was speechless. Where had all of this blame come from? Like she had to grind him down. Like she was giving him too much power. Power over her. She didn't want to understand him or the situation with the Yellow Farm. Something else was working at her. Was it Sally? Sally felt threatened by Karen's feelings for him. Karen must be afraid of Sally's hurt, and so to pacify her, Karen had to kick him. How could he sort this out? He couldn't even tell Lucina about it. Then she would know how much he'd been into Karen.

"And the saddest part of all this, Louis. You don't know who Lucina is. Just as you weren't honest with her, she hasn't been honest with you. She and Sally had a thing going. Ask your wife, or whatever, what it's like to kiss a dyke. A real woman. I swear to God, Louis. If you and your pseudo-wife don't come clean with each other, you're going to lose her to some beautiful, brave, truthful lesbian."

"Why are you so jealous of Lucina? You're really fucked up, Karen!" He should shake her—slap her.

But when she slammed the book of Roethke's poems he'd mailed her during the summer down on his hands and stomped out of the restaurant without paying her share of the bill, he felt the same helplessness he'd felt handcuffed in the back of the cops' car, knowing they were taking him to a secluded spot to beat him.

How could he tell Lucina about this showdown with Karen? Then he would have to admit to...Oh, Jesus! Whatever it was they'd done. And she would have to talk about Sally's "dyke kiss." Whatever that meant. Damn! What a price they were paying for falling for those two.

*****

The searing meeting with Karen continued to eat at him. His shame at letting her touch him like that increased his empathy for others who regretted their actions. Women who flirted with men, then were forced unwillingly...Yes, now he too felt assaulted. Karen had come on to him—she'd made the move. But admit it! He'd let her. And now he was ashamed. Ashamed that he'd liked it, wanted it. And why? Because he'd

been beaten by the cops and needed to feel like a man again—
and she was a beautiful woman.

When the time was right, he'd tell Lucina the whole
truth—about Jenny as well. He hadn't made love with Karen—
he'd let her make him come. He hadn't made love with Jenny—
but he'd wanted to. Like that. Timing was everything. This was
not the time. The group was working well, Lucina was into her
women's plays, and they were planning a tour. The right time
would come and he would tell her, and never, ever keep anything
secret from her again. She was true love, deep love. Forever.

52

Again: The Cost of Attraction

Why had she come here? Suddenly she felt queasy, lightheaded. Bars didn't usually do this to her. She shouldn't have come to the Spring Street Bar alone. It wasn't safe with all the increased political unrest. There had been a demonstration earlier in Washington Square Park, supporting CORE—Congress of Racial Equality—and their march in a Chicago suburb, which brought out twenty-seven hundred troops of the Illinois National Guard. The increased police presence in her own neighborhood didn't make her feel safer, just more frightened.

Lucina heard a woman arguing with the bartender; why was the person so upset? Just find a seat somewhere and have a beer; space out for fifteen minutes. Maybe the woman didn't have any money. She should go over there and offer to help her out. Didn't look like a street person. That big O on the back of her T-shirt with a lowercase *t* under it? Like a person with a big head? Oh, yes—the symbol for female, or Venus? The woman was gesturing toward the wall where Sally's welded sculptures had once hung—but it was bare. Here today, gone tomorrow. Actually, here yesterday, gone today. Sculptures, peace, girlfriends. What lasted?

Edging herself into a bar stool she called out, "Heineken dark, please," then realized with shock: the woman talking loudly by the cash register was Sally, her once Sally! She looked so different. Tough, like a guy. And exhausted, like she was holding herself up. Her brown hair was cut as short as a soldier's. Her arms, jutting out from short sleeves, showed toned, well-formed biceps. Sally's arms. She must have seen her by now—the place was almost empty.

The argument escalated. Angry shouts resounded through the bar. Was Sally pretending to not see her? She must have told Karen about their kiss. "A mistake," she'd probably said. Maybe they'd moved in together, melding their connection. Of course, that was why Sally hadn't returned her phone calls. Lucina had been erased.

Well, she and Louis lived together and they hadn't cut the women off. It wasn't right—to be treated like this. They just couldn't live with Sally and Karen all summer. The troupe had to focus, and their theater work couldn't have taken any more distractions, what with that stalker crap and digging the septic tank. Why hadn't the four of them worked it out better before they'd left for the Yellow Farm? They'd all fucked up!

So, go over to her! What did she have to lose?

Sally was still haggling with the man behind the counter. "You said you'd pay me to hang my welding for six months! That's why I let you put it up here." Her fist was punching the counter.

"Look, Sally, nothing was said about paying you." The man's tone was flat. Was he trying to calm her? "I said we were donating wall space to artists because we support art. You already got your sculpture back, and I have a hundred artists waiting for that space. Your turn is up, so be reasonable. Okay?!"

Sally turned away abruptly with a "fuck you" and angled toward the door, her focus straight ahead.

"Wait, Sally! It's me, Lucina." The woman charged by her, unresponsive. "Please. I just want to talk to you. I heard what that guy said. Awful."

Sally halted, her hand already reaching out for the street door several feet away. "What are you doing here! Where's your boyfriend? What jackasses." She flicked her hand toward the cash register, but the man had disappeared into the kitchen. "Liars—all of you—say one thing one day, another the next. You don't know anything about real need!"

"Are you talking about me and Louis?"

"Coming on to me and living with a man. What is that? I want nothing to do with sneaky, bourgeois fakes! Betrayers! And your Louis? He's a cheat. A sneaking little cheat. He came on to my woman, and I bet you don't know a thing about it, do you?"

Lucina's mouth dropped. She hardly understood what Sally was saying. Had she been drinking? Was that why her eyes bulged and blazed! Definitely she was pale and thinner.

"You and your pals lie around all summer at the country club and think you're some big goddamn radicals. The establishment just loves you hippie-zippy types, with your home plays and puppets, distracting people from the real issues. Millionaire landlords are throwing good people like me into the streets. Don't even try to get a hold of me or Karen again."

"Sally, I can't believe this. Who are you talking to? You and I—we liked each other. The four of us meant something… we were just getting to know each other. You and I talked about our sculpture work—what it meant to us. I'm so sorry it didn't work out for the summer." Tears came to her eyes—she was going to cry right then and there. *What was it she said about Louis? A cheat?*

Sally was nearly out the door when she turned back, her eyes like flares. "That sculpture of yours—your precious *Rune*. The one hiding under a white sheet, just like you. Her name should be 'ruin.' R-U-I-N. That's right—*RUIN*! You, Holzer, ruined something that was happening between us!"

Lucina saw a pigeon on the street so startled by Sally's departure that it careened into a parked car, then steadied itself on the sidewalk before flying swiftly upward to disappear. *That bird couldn't get away fast enough*, Lucina thought. *And neither could Sally.* She trudged slowly back to her stool, her head spinning, her chest aching. *Who can I talk to? Louis? Marin? No. Keep it to myself. Have a cold beer and try to figure myself out for once!*

53
Phone Call From Aretha

In October the women resumed their separate rehearsals at the loft. After a routine of movement and vocal exercises they rehashed responses to the performance of Jenny's story, *Wink*, at the Yellow Farm, the audience's and their own. Both exaggerated and subtle gestures had been effective. "We're developing our own style here," Marin said. "The Fire Dragon Women Style. Probably each of our stories will need its own style to fit its unique mood, right? We've only just begun dealing with how to present our stuff."

Lucina was anxious to get to her own story: "When we start to work on my story, *Markings*, I hope we can find a style that fits with suppressed maternal rage. It's about a really vulnerable time with my mother—when I was trying very hard to connect with her. I thought it was working, but wham! She pulled the rug out from under my feet."

"We'll do our best when it's your rehearsal time, Lucina," Jenny responded. "I'm sorry, I didn't mean to be bossy—it's just that we still have to go over what didn't work in my piece, so we can fix it before we leave on tour."

"It's okay, Jen. You're right. I'm anxious about working on *Markings*. But one story at a time. I just think there's a lot of pain in what we're doing—digging up our wounds and then showing them off to strangers, some supportive, some not. I mean, do styles protect us? How can we get strength from exposing our hurts? We're not masochists!"

"Look!" Marlene spoke up. "We're part of a growing movement of women telling it like it is. What we need to do is give each other massages along the way and keep healing ourselves as we expose our traumas."

"Oh, Marlene, you're so wise." Lucina brushed Marlene's arm affectionately, adding, "Your kids must love you."

"Sometimes," Marlene laughed. "But let's get back to Jenny's play now."

*****

That night while Louis and Lucina sat at the table in the make-shift kitchen at the back of the loft, finishing up bagels with lox and scallion cream cheese, Louis gave Lucina his full attention: "How did your rehearsal go today, Luie—I really want to know how it's going with you women. Have you gotten to your story about your Mother yet?"

"Which one, Louis?"

"Where she locked her bedroom door and wouldn't talk to you."

"We will get to it—but we had to go over some rough spots in Jenny's play."

"I sure hope you don't take the spontaneous, crazy feel out of it. Don't over work it!"

"Louis! We know what we're doing. We don't need your directions." She stood up quickly, relieved that the phone in their sleeping area was ringing. Answer it and avoid another tension-

404

filled discussion with Louis about the women's work and how he was always pushing her to tell him more than she wanted to.

"Hello—Lucina speaking."

"Oh good. I hoped you'd answer."

"I'm sorry, who is this?"

"Aretha--Aretha Davis. We met at Peace Day this—"

"Oh, Aretha. Yes, yes—so glad you called. We missed seeing you and Keisha at our performance." She lowered her voice so Louis couldn't hear.

"Tish told us all about it—they really enjoyed what you Fire Dragon Women did. Something about how women are intimidated in job interviews?"

"Yes, we call it *Wink*. The audience's reaction gave us a boost. We really feel that women's theater, dramatizing hard stuff in our lives is where it's at."

"I agree. Listen, Lucina, let me get to the point of my call. We had talked about your coming to Grandmore College."

"We're so excited to be part of building a women's theater group at Grandmore. Do you have some dates in mind, so we can..."

"That's what I have to talk to you about, Lucina."

Lucina picked up a pen and note pad from the phone table and sat down. "Go ahead, I'm listening."

"Many things have become clearer in my life since August, Lucina. I'm overwhelmed by the work needing to be done."

"I know just how you feel. We have a spring tour in the works."

"I'm involved with extremely urgent work here at Grandmore. The administration is resisting the needs of us Black women students. It's our responsibility to fight the white administrators, and you know, change takes endless work. We're demanding a Black studies curriculum and a Black women's theater group be put in place by next fall."

"That's so important—we want to support that effort, Aretha."

"That's what I have to talk to you about—oh, how to say this? We need Black women actresses to talk to us now … how did, do they make it … in an industry that's so racist, it has to keep Black actors locked up in the image of the white man's stereo-typed minstrel shows. I think you know what I'm talking about…"

"I hear you—that's so terrible."

"We're trying to get Cicely Tyson to come here. You've heard of her—yes? We need a Black actress who's smashed the color barrier. She's getting awards for her acting in off Broadway shows; she was in Genet's, The Blacks and she's one of the few Black actresses to be a regular in a TV show!"

"I know. It's so fabulous!"

"This is our focus now, Lucina. A Black woman actress who's making it big. So, we'll be inviting her to talk to the whole student body, the professors and administrators—emphasizing why a prestigious college like Grandmore needs a Black Studies Curriculum, and a Black women's theater group. We need a stage to tell our stories and our hope is that she'll do some workshops with us."

"How can we fit into that?"

"I'm sorry, Lucina. The Fire Dragon Street Theater is doing great stuff, but you don't have any Black actors. It wouldn't be appropriate for our needs now. You need to integrate."

"So—you're saying—you don't want us to do workshops?" Lucina's throat and chest tightened.

"Another time, down the pike. Maybe when you are inclusive."

*****

Lucina couldn't remember how the call ended—did she say she would keep Aretha and Keisha posted on the results of their tour? She should have mentioned their performance at Jones College—part of a women's lib weekend. When she put the phone down, she felt so rejected, disappointed; the thought that Fire Dragon Women would do workshops at Grandmore Women's College had made her feel so proud, so useful. Adding Black women to the troupe was a challenge they had to take on urgently.

"Who was that, honey?" Louis found her huddled by the phone. "Did something happen to—?"

"Something happened to me, Louis! I'll tell you later—I have to call Marin right away."

*****

The women gathered for an emergency meeting the next day. Lucina reported the conversation as calmly and as accurately as she could. Then silence.

Marin spoke first. "I know, we've been thinking all this time—how great it will be—to go to Grandmore College and do workshops with women students really excited about making some kind of theater together. We could share our experiences and exercises with them, like older sisters. But that was our dream, not Aretha's. We didn't really know her needs..." She looked at Lucina for the right words.

"She couldn't tell us in August, I guess," Lucina added. "But let's give ourselves a little credit here. We are trying to come up with exercises that we think would be appropriate for all women, from different backgrounds. She seemed to like what we were doing—right, Marlene?"

"Yes! She was really affected by *Choice*—she said her sister's boyfriend was in 'Nam, didn't she? And Keisha was so excited that we were doing our own stories."

"We want to wake people up," Jenny said meekly. "I just wish she'd come here and told us face to face."

Marlene shook her head sideways: "Would you have? It's not easy to tell someone they aren't the right color. She liked us but we can't help them if they have to convince a resistant administration. What did she say about Cicely Tyson again, Lucina?"

"She said they need a Black actress who's made it despite our racist culture, someone who can teach them how to do it. Let's face it! We have privilege in this white-run country—even though we're not trying to get on Broadway. My god! Imagine how Black women feel. They're trying to be visible, respected, honored and…"

"I wish she'd kept our hopes up," Jenny butt in. "Couldn't she have just said, 'When you have an integrated group, we'd love to have you come maybe next spring.' Something more concrete."

Lucina stood, stretching her arms upward, and sighed deeply. "It's not her job to help us figure out how to make that happen. We haven't tried hard enough. She's right and courageous to tell us we aren't the ones to help them now."

Jenny stood up, teary-eyed. "She was so warm to us on Peace Day."

Lucina lightly stroked Jenny's back: "She still is warm, Jenny. We just have to learn from her. It's awful and so disappointing, we aren't what they need right now, but let's figure out what we have to do. Obviously, we need Black brothers and sisters! How do we do that?"

"Why would anyone want to join the likes of us?" Jenny fretted. "Just go find Black actors and invite them? God—what if they all say no—they're doing their own thing?"

"It's gonna be hard," Lucina said. "White people are clueless at what it means to be a Black person in this fucking country."

Marin forced herself up from the cement to stand with Jenny and Lucina. "We have to find a way—with open hearts and empathy. Right, Lucina?"

"Right. Do what Aretha says, break barriers, expand, grow."

"I talked to a Black actress, in my psychology class," Marin added. "She sure doesn't want to be directed by white people. I don't think she believed me when I said, 'We don't have directors, we take turns guiding.' She said she needs to do her own thing … 'our worlds are too different.'" She reached down for Marlene's hands. "Stand with us, Marlene. What do you think?"

Marin pulled Marlene upright and the four women faced each other. "Let's admit it," Marlene whispered. "We haven't tried hard enough."

54

The Blue Hat

On a Friday night in mid-November, Jenny and Hans failed to show up for a communal dinner at the loft. No one had any clues where they could be.

Lucina fretted: *Something happened! They wouldn't go for fish and then just disappear. They'd call.* But what could be done? Hans' visa had expired and he had no green card; that meant you don't call the police.

Not another loss! Sally had vanished from her life for weeks now. *That woman treated me like a criminal before she even knew me. I'll never understand what that terrible tirade was all about: "Bourgeois fakes! Betrayers!" No! Sally betrayed our trust, our connection, our attraction. Did she say she told Karen about our kiss? And more than that—she put down Rune as well. I was so open to her, telling her things about my sculpture I'd not told anyone, not even Louis. About carving out meaning for myself. Needing to shape my experiences. Being open to change. Everything Rune has taught me.*

Their kiss had been a love pact—a promise to always be true to themselves as artists, as women. How they'd both laughed when she'd used the word "womanwhole" instead of "masterpiece." Sally understood *Rune*, a regal female figure, standing proud and timeless, a model to follow. So why had she spit such ugly things in her face and belittled her beloved sculpture?

Every time she wanted to bring up this crazy, hurtful meeting to Louis, something intervened: a rehearsal, an unexpected performance, temporary work to pay the rent. The street theater didn't even pay their food bills. And now all the work of planning a tour. That very morning, she'd almost told Louis about the kiss. A week before, he'd looked her in the eye and said, "I did not fuck Karen!" If he could tell her the truth— couldn't she do the same?

*****

By eight o'clock the troupe had cancelled the communal meal. They'd have an amazing buffet dinner another time, promise, when no one had to go out at the last minute for fish. The invited friends agreed to a rain date and headed off to a restaurant in the Village. The actors, needing to comfort each other over Jenny and Hans' disappearance, made do with the bread, cheese, fruit, and salad Lucina put out on the small kitchen table. She broke the somber silence. "Who saw Hans and Jenny last?"

"They left the loft at five o'clock," Marin offered. "I ran into them coming down the stairs, excited to be going to the Fulton Market to buy fish for everyone."

"I saw them at the corner of Spring and Broadway, sipping on hot coffee," Hugh added. "They weren't high, Lou, if that's what you're wondering. Just cold. Said they were off to buy fish."

And that's all anyone knew.

Our group is like a family, Lucina thought. *A chosen family. Even though Jenny and Hans keep to themselves a lot—*

412

Louis says it's because of Hans 'wounded ego and Jenny's need to protect it—still, it's like a brother and a sister have disappeared. "And when you're like brothers and sisters in a group," she reminded the troupe members, huddled around her, "you don't purposely fuck up. We can't call their place—no phone. They wouldn't go missing unless..." As she heard her own words, she knew she was talking about Karen and Sally as well, still agonizing over them. Then her gut wrenched with the pain that had started with Sally's ugly words. She was gone from her life. Now what if Jenny and Hans never came back?

Hans could go haywire. But he'd changed since he'd apologized to everyone, and since his comic self-reflections. He'd made several thoughtful comments at their meetings lately. The poor kid—kicked out of college—completely rejected by parents. At least hers still talked to her. And he and Jenny seemed very close. She protected him if anyone came down too hard. But if the two of them were in trouble, what would they do then? Wouldn't they call us! Would Hans be strong like he wanted to be? Would Jenny cry?

*****

As Jenny and Hans made their way through Mott Street in Chinatown, about five forty-five, Jenny began whining, "I really don't want to walk any more, Hans!" She hadn't gotten her period and was scared she was pregnant. Plus, they'd smoked bad grass the night before, lots of it. Her head hurt and she felt nauseous. She wanted to tell Hans how she felt, but he was obsessing about Tavern on the Green again. *Must be the grass. He's flipped into paranoia and dragging up that old nightmare!*

"Jenny! I got to tell you what really happened. No one knows. Everyone was so against me, and I was scared Louis was going to throw me out. It would have been over for us, Jenny.

I decided to shut up—I caused enough trouble. Just say 'sorry' and 'I messed up.'"

"Hans, Hans! That's over with. You explained." She pulled him into a small ice cream store where they could sit at a table away from the street noises.

"The cops were going for Louis—I saw 'em. I had to think fast. Put on the dragon's head. Shout, 'The pigs are coming.' I shouted at people. 'Don't let them through.' You see what I was doing, honey? But nobody listened. They backed away—opened up the circle around us—let the cops get to Louis. I tried to protect him—you have to believe me. I told the group I went crazy because I was afraid of the cops. But the truth? I wanted them to come to me, not Lou."

Jenny hunched toward him, eyes wide in disbelief. "You wanted the cops to arrest you! Were you crazy? You'd have been deported for sure." She stared into his pained expression. *How could this insecure guy, fretting over and over what happened with Louis, come through for me? I can't be pregnant—I just can't have it!*

"I'm trying to tell you—my first thing was to protect Louis. *Tror du på mig!* Then I realized if they came for me, I'd be done for. No visa, no green card, no more us—so then I just acted nuts. I knew no one would believe me. I wanted to save Louis. He's a good man." Hans' head slumped; his shoulders shook as he sobbed.

Suddenly she remembered: the day after she'd massaged Louis in the yurt, Hans asked her to go to the apple orchard with him. He had something to talk to her about. "It's about Louis," he said. She was scared that he'd found out about her massaging Louis, the tender feelings between them—how they'd almost made love, even though they'd stopped because of Hans and Lucina. So she told Hans she was horny and suggested they just go to their room and fuck. Since then, she'd avoided talking with him about Louis.

Now as she wiped at his tears, she began laughing uncontrollably. "Oh Hans, I love you. I always believed you—I believe you now. I do, I do. You care about Louis—I'm glad."

"Jenny, I knew you would believe me." He stood up and wiped at his eyes. "I'm okay now. Better get the fish. Come on. We'll take the subway at City Hall to Fulton Street and then walk a few blocks."

*****

When they were out of the subway and on the street again, Hans was still fretting. "Why he doesn't understand me? We never agree."

Jenny could hardly follow what he was saying. The darkening sky bore down on them, threatening rain and sleet. "Oh, you're talking about yesterday's rehearsal of the Ghost Dance, with just the men? You and Louis disagreed on…"

"Ja. Louis and I argued about a gun. I think we need it in the scene. US Army troops slaughtered almost three hundred Lakota Indians. But Louis said, 'No gun, Hans!' like I was a kid. It was like we were back at that terrible day with the cops—and he was punishing me for not giving the gun to Courtney. Like he still doesn't believe I saw the cops coming after him."

"You know Louis has a thing about guns, Hans. Accept that! So now he doesn't want them—big deal. Have you stopped to consider all the issues the troupe disagrees on? You guys have to talk to each other better." Her patience was gone. All day she'd been worried, but she hadn't had a chance to talk to him. Now they had to get fish!

She would just die if she were pregnant! Why had she listened to his nonsense about the rhythm method? Sure, he pulled out, then ejaculated. Some of his sperm must have made

415

it inside her after he exploded. He couldn't hear her now—so focused on Louis. And damned guns.

Her boots were too tight, one heel rubbing. "Honey, would you mind? I'm really cold. Should have worn a heavier jacket. Can I wait here for you?" They'd come upon a triangle of pavement and benches. She could sit here. "You know where you're planning to buy the fish? I don't know why we didn't go to the fish store on Bleecker."

"Aw, Jen, come on—we always like exploring together! Why are you so tired? We're almost there. Besides, I can't carry thirteen pounds of fish by myself."

"Thirteen? You don't need that much."

"Louis said a pound for every two people, and there could be twenty-six of us for dinner."

"Louis, Louis! Enough. You're too obsessed with him. Hans, I want to sit here. I've got things to think about. You go get the fish. I do plenty for you. Who did the laundry? You said you would, but then you went off with your buddy." She plunked down on the bench and huddled into herself. Hans was too much. Arguing with Louis—now with her. He could get the fuckin' fish himself.

"Just give me the money, Jenny."

"I don't have the money, Hans. I thought you had it."

"No, Louis gave it to you."

"He did not."

She went through her pockets several times. No bills— just a few coins. "I can't believe it! What are we going to do?" She hugged herself as winds off the East River swirled around her.

"I'll use my head—that's what," Hans said. "I'm not going to go back and beg Louis for the money. I'll just talk them into giving me the fish at the market."

"Oh, sure," Jenny scoffed. "Some guy's just waiting there with a basket of fish to give away." If only she didn't feel so exhausted, so spacey. "Bad, bad grass," she said. "I hate New York! Everything is so fuckin' hard."

"I'll be back within an hour. It's only a few more blocks to the Fulton Fish Market." He pulled a Gauloise from the pocket of his jacket.

"An hour? I'll be frozen!"

"Go in that diner, over there. Get a coffee. I'll be back soon."

She watched him trot away, leaving smoke swirling behind him. She should have kissed him, said something kind. Well, the diner was a good idea. Should she call the loft, tell them about the money? No. It would embarrass Hans. They could be back by seven o'clock, in time to make dinner for the crowd.

Except for a dour-looking guy behind the counter and a young woman smoking nonstop by the windows, seemingly looking for someone, the place was empty. Nobody stayed around here on a Friday night! She sat as far away from the smoker as possible. It was bad enough in the loft at rehearsals. At least they'd made a rule that Hans could not smoke in their apartment. And if she were—oh god, she better not be—but if she were! After four weeks, would there already be lungs, a little heart? Can't take any chances.

Her thoughts held her so completely that she barely noticed the cup of steaming coffee in front of her, nor how it tasted as she put it to her lips and sipped. She wouldn't tell Hans tonight—not with the feast, assuming he could get the fish somehow. She would tell him in the morning, after they'd had a good sleep.

"Pardon for me asking," The chain-smoking woman was standing over her. "Where'd you buy that cap?"

Jenny was wearing one of her own creations, a bright blue, beret-style knit cap. It was the favorite of three she'd made recently. She and Hans had been making do with their odd jobs—housecleaning, stocking grocery shelves. But now she'd found another way, with her hats.

"I didn't," Jenny said, trying to be polite despite the annoying woman and her smoke. She should say she wasn't feeling well. But why had the woman hooked onto her?

"Sorry for bothering you, but that color—I just love it. You didn't make it, did you?"

Jenny stared without focusing—as if the bad grass had taken over again. Somehow she overlooked the drooping eyelids and unkempt fingernails, as the woman's neediness pulled on her.

"I knit my own hats, and I sell them occasionally," Jenny said, trying to play the coy entrepreneur.

"Wow—handmade! So, how much?" The woman was ecstatic. "Twenty-five, thirty-five dollars?"

Jenny struggled to focus on her admirer. Her gray eyes had flecks in them like pepper. "Takes me five hours each hat. I need more than minimum wage. Forty dollars is what I usually get."

"Oh, great," the woman said, extending her hand. "I'm Susan. It's worth that much, at least. I'm psyched!"

Jenny looked closer and saw a blonde woman somewhere in her thirties, hugging a crumpled black coat against herself and wearing too much makeup, as if in hiding. She had a pleasant smile—but what were those small circular marks making their way down the woman's arms?

"Tell you what." The woman spoke again. "I'll pay you fifty dollars for that hat right on your head! Unless you only want the thirty-five dollars you usually get?"

"I said forty!" Then Jenny laughed outright. "Maybe you'd like my whole collection."

"I knew you were the artist type." The woman parked herself at the table and stamped out her cigarette butt, smeared with bright red lipstick.

"Actress," Jenny said.

"Ah yes. Such an expressive face."

"Thank you." Jenny smiled self-consciously.

Her mind flashed on Hans at the market, trying to get free fish. Nobody gave away fish. Maybe half rotten vegetables, but fish? No. Fifty dollars could easily buy fish for twenty-six people. Who needed Louis' money! She could always make herself another blue hat.

"I might sell this one for fifty dollars," Jenny said. "It's one of a kind."

"Good girl," the woman said, as if rooting for her. "Don't ever undersell yourself."

Jenny bit at her lip. So, the woman was a little crazy— but nice-crazy. She had a warm smile and this sudden thing for the blue hat. *No, she isn't into her like that! She's just lonely and she digs my hat.*

"I'll get the money from the bank. Oh, don't worry; it's just around the corner. Take a second."

Oh-oh! She'd heard this line before. *Banks aren't open at this hour!*

The woman was standing, all business, next to her. "You'll have the fifty dollars in ten. Trust me! Come on."

In a moment Jenny was out on the street following a complete stranger. And she hadn't even paid for her coffee! What was she doing? The drama had pulled her—she was hooked on the scene and the money, that's it. *Oh my god!*

In front of them, a candy store offered to cash checks. "I can't believe it," the woman said, scouring through her limp woven bag. "I left my paycheck at home. Would you take a personal check? No," she added, before Jenny could respond. "No, you'd rather have cash. Everybody needs cash, right, honey?"

She should stop this—this following a wheedling woman. What was her game? *Just give me your address, Lady. We'll do business another time.* And she hated being called honey. Sweetie would have been worse. And Hans would be looking for her soon at the diner, definitely without any fish.

"Take a second," the woman was saying. "That's my building over there." She was pointing to a nice building on the corner. "I have cash at home. We won't have to come back here."

"Well, I do!" Hans would be amazed at her sale.

"You can trust me. Look, I'm shorter than you."

Maybe it was the long black coat, now covering the woman and almost dragging on the ground, which had made the stranger seem tall at first.

Jenny stayed beside her—she didn't want the woman to think she was afraid. What did she say her name was? Well, Jenny wouldn't give out hers.

In the lobby, Jenny protested, "I'll wait here." But the woman somehow pulled her along without even touching her. *Later, she would tell Hans she'd been unwillingly hypnotized.*

They were in the elevator, the woman again extolling her hat. "That extraordinary blue, the smart design, soon to be all mine."

The hallway was nicely carpeted. *She must have money to live here!* The woman opened the apartment door and turned to Jenny. "Excuse the mess; I'm not much of a housekeeper."

"I'm not either," Jenny said in a friendly way, trying to cover her discomfort.

The apartment entranceway had a series of posters: Dylan, Donavan, and The Supremes.

A small grand piano took up two thirds of what appeared to be the main room. "Oh, are you a musician?" Jenny asked.

"Susan tries," the woman answered.

Yes, that's her name—Susan. Jenny scanned her surroundings, immediately rejecting what she saw as impossible. *The grass again?* The entire room was shifting before her eyes.

What she'd thought was a couch, white and furry, was now lifting itself in the air. A black rug near it was inching its way toward a plush easy chair. And the chair was in motion too: it was heading for the piano.

"Dogs," Susan said with a lilt. "These are my big, funny babies."

As if on cue, the "babies"—six giant woolly dogs of various whites, blacks, grays, and tans—closed in on them. In their eager pawing and lapping, they would have pulled Jenny down if Susan hadn't intervened. "Now Elvis, Aretha, Janice," she began naming them. "Too bad they can't sing or clean the apartment," she said.

Then Jenny found herself on the real couch, crinkly and leathery, staring into the enormous moist eyes of the dog Donovan. *He has Dean Martin bedroom eyes,* she thought.

Susan was opening and closing every drawer in the room. "Looking for my hash, honey," she said. "I mean, my cash."

An alarm went off in Jenny's head. *What's wrong with this picture? Why had she let herself get pulled into this weird scene! Was it Susan's loneliness? Her own curiosity? Getting money for actual fish and not the throwaways that Hans would end up with?* A strong, stale odor of dope rose up from the real rug under her feet. "Susan, I have to get back to the diner. I was waiting for someone," she said abruptly. "My boyfriend, in fact."

"Why didn't you tell me, honey? I would've gotten the money and brought it to you."

Why hadn't she done that? Here she was in a strange house, with a weirdo woman.

"Oh, here it is," Susan said, momentarily pulling out a wad of bills from under a telephone book. "I knew it was here."

She sat down next to Jenny, holding not only a wad of tens and twenties, but a small handsome briar pipe as well.

She proceeded to light and puff at it eagerly, as if she were an asthmatic needing a pull on her inhaler.

"Let's finish the business deal with a toke. Like hash?"

"Ah," Jenny said, simultaneously drawn and repelled by the offer. Did she need this on top of bad grass? The woman's fistful of money encouraged her: she'd just been handed five ten-dollar bills. Maybe hash would be just the thing to take away her heavy feelings…

Jenny planted her lips far back on the stem to avoid the woman's saliva, then inhaled and handed back the pipe.

"Now, where's my hat?" The woman took the pipe and sucked so deeply that Jenny imagined her exploding like a balloon.

Removing her hat, Jenny looked at it fondly, memorizing its blueness. It did seem incredible—especially in a room filled with furry non-colors. Walls, rugs—everything matched the tones of the dogs now resting around them. Which came first, she mused, the room or the dogs? She sucked again at the pipe.

"Happy hash, huh?" the woman said. "So, how do I look, honey? Now I'm an actress too."

55
Catfish Heads

Hans had never seen so many people buying fish. Nothing would be left by the time they got to him. This was all Jenny's idea—to please Lucina. And why hadn't Louis made sure to give him the cash?

Twenty minutes later, a chubby man wearing a filthy apron half listened to his invented story. "I work for a church on Bowery—we plan a large dinner free—for homeless people. Do you have free fish please, to donate?"

When a condescending smirk spread over the seller's face, Hans felt like a kid caught with his hand in his pants.

"We don't give fish away," the man said flatly.

"How about leftovers—heads and tails?"

The man smirked again and disappeared. In five minutes he was back with a cardboard box tied with a string.

"Catfish heads," the man said. "Good for fish chowder— if you know how to make it." Before Hans could ask for flounder or bass heads instead, the man was off serving a customer. What if they came from the Hudson River—polluted with PCBs? The guy didn't give a damn about the poor!

There were carrots, onions, celery, and potatoes at the loft—he'd seen them in the frig. He knew how to make a good vegetable soup. Adding a little meat from the heads, not the eyes, would probably be okay. At least they'd tried.

As he wove his way through the dark corridors of Fulton Street, he imagined presences stalking him. He hurried his step. His watch said a quarter of seven; when he reached Jenny they should call the loft. Did they have enough money for the subway? Just keep walking to the diner—only a few blocks away. He felt hungry and tired—still hungover from the night before, that was it.

By the time he reached the diner, a half dozen "stalkers" had materialized from alleys and vacant lots in the gray wintry night. The stench had drawn large rats or skinny street cats, he couldn't tell. The box of fish heads was leaking, his wool gloves were clammy.

When he entered the diner, he saw two men seated in the back, but no Jenny. One of the men stood up quickly. "Leave the garbage outside!" he barked loudly, as if Hans were some mindless drunk.

Hans withdrew to the street, scouring the area for a garbage can. He found one at the corner. Place the box inside, that's good, now cover it. Those monsters can't lift off covers that fast. Have to ask about Jenny!

"Yeah, I saw her," nodded the seated man with a cook's apron. "I thought she was with that drug-head who comes in here. Dave, what's her name? Yeah, that's it—Susan. Thought she was Susan's friend. They was acting friendly, sitting at the same table together, right over there. Went out together. Must've been about an hour ago—right, Dave?"

The man with the mustache, who'd spoken so harshly to Hans, shrugged his shoulders as if he couldn't care less. "Who knows with that one," he grumbled. "Doesn't know a pickle from a pecker. Hangs out here with some musician group. I think they have a place nearby, and then something on the Upper East. Hard to know whose place is whose, right?"

"Where is the place nearby?" Hans turned to one man, then the other, desperate for any information they could offer.

The man wearing the apron was now behind the counter, making coffee at a big silver urn. He turned to Hans. "Her place is over there on the corner—693." He pointed northeast. "With the red awning. Can't miss it."

"Yeah, probably Susan took her there to see them big dogs," the seated man said. "Never seen the likes of them dogs. Have to walk 'em three times a day."

"Thanks." Hans was already out the door. He dug his box of fish heads from the garbage bin with disgust. *Probably should leave it for those cats and rats—they're hungry too.* He could feel their beady eyes. But he'd promised to bring fish back to the loft. He headed across the street with his foul-smelling parcel.

The apartment building he wanted was near a streetlight. A bright red awning was clearly marked 693. He climbed the cement entrance steps. Now what should he do?

Luck was with him; a young man was behind him: one of the musicians? The leather jacket and dark glasses made it seem possible. Hans stepped aside as the fellow pulled a key from his jacket pocket and addressed him.

"Hey, man! Do you know Susan? I got a letter for her from her Mom."

"Ya. Susan and my girl are hanging out." *Geez, what's happening here? Jenny must still be spaced from that bad weed. But she seemed to be okay. And she really heard me. Damn! Everything I said about Louis is true.*

The guy was in the hallway, hesitating. "The question is, does Susan know you?"

Hans let his shoulders sink an inch. "I'm really looking for my girlfriend, okay? And the guys working in the diner across the street said she and Susan came to this building."

The young man smiled. "Got it, dude. Check out 8A, that's where Susan and her musicians hang out. If no one's there, could you shove this letter under the door?"

Hans followed him to a small elevator at the end of the hall. In the elevator the man spoke again. "Hope you find your girl. Susan likes to pick up people—do hash or heroin with them. I think she deals up there, too. Sorry, man. Everybody's got to have their thing, okay? If you don't find Susan here, try uptown, 610 East Seventy-second Street. She hangs out there, too. With the druggies. Guess I shouldn't have said that. You look scared."

When the fellow exited at the third floor, Hans noticed his leather briefcase. He must be a manager or a producer, not a musician. Had the guy smelled the fish heads and wondered about him?

Hans repeated the uptown address over and over as the elevator lifted slowly to the eighth floor. He could remember 610; he was born on June 10. Seventy-two, seventy-two he repeated as he rang the buzzer for 8A.

He could hear the buzzer sounding inside, loud and annoying. By the tenth ring he'd decided even if somebody was in there, they weren't going to answer. *Where is my Jenny!* Feeling nauseous, he pushed the letter under the door.

Back down in the lobby, he felt a scary silence. Not like East Seventh Street. People on his block were up all night, coming and going.

On the street, the rank odor from his box hit him again; he felt like puking. Fish oil had leaked through the cardboard and onto his jacket. It must be on his shirt, too. Why lug the mess around anymore? Leave it for the beasties, but where?

Setting the box near steps leading to a side basement apartment of the same building, he took off his gloves and, without thinking, wiped his hands on his jeans. Should he toss the gloves? Had to keep his jacket—too cold. Should he call the loft? Go to the Upper East address?

A van pulled up in front of 693. Four guys got out and began unloading large black cases—they looked like instruments. Could be the uptown musicians, Susan's friends. Gotta talk to them.

Hans approached them casually. "Hey, guys." Only one of them stopped.

"What's up, man?"

"I'm looking for my girl. I think she's with Susan. Do you guys know Susan?"

The man gave Hans a knowing look as he reached for another black case. "You need a hit, guy?"

"No, no, I'm not into that," Hans said. "I left my girlfriend, Jenny, over an hour ago at the Downtown Diner over there. We're due at a party and I can't find her."

"Wha'd she do? Split on you? Hey, grab the tall drum. Help me out and we'll talk about it."

Back on the eight floor, the man unlocked a door next to 8A, where Hans had just been. The door had no number, he noticed. Maybe there were two doors for the same place?

In the apartment, several large furry dogs jumped up and licked the men. They seemed to enjoy it. There was a smell of hash in the room, but no Susan and no Jenny.

"She's been here, Jake," a slim guy with a long red ponytail said to one of the others. "Smell her?"

The other men collapsed into the chairs, still petting the dogs and talking to them.

"College gigs—oh, man," a guy with slick hair and a goatee sighed. "It's a lot of time on the road."

"Sorry to bother you guys, but I need to find Jenny."

"'Jeannie with the light brown hair,'" the guy with a goatee laughed.

"Just Jenny," Hans said. He pushed the white-haired dog away and moved toward the door, feeling faint.

"You lost your woman, huh?" The man who had shoved the drum on Hans earlier stopped slapping at the black dog. "Hey, maybe you're okay without her, bro."

Hans grimaced.

"Take it easy, dude. Just saying."

"You want a ride uptown?" the man with the red ponytail asked. "They might have gone to our place on Seventy-second. You can ride. But I got a few stops on the way. Name's Rick."

Hans was feeling worried and exhausted; maybe he'd be better off riding with this guy—than what, the subway? He had no money!

By the time Rick had used the bathroom, gulped some orange juice, and made rehearsal plans with the other men in the group—they told Hans they were a hot jazz combo, the Flashers—it was almost eight o'clock.

Hans edged to the door again. Why was he sitting here when Jenny might be in real trouble? But no way could he call the loft—they'd get hysterical and he would be blamed again for being a fuckup.

"Hey, if she's with Susan, relax," Rick said, finally tuning into his anxiety. "Susan's a good kid. Just likes her highs. And needs company—can't be alone. That's really all that's wrong with her, okay? You'll find your girl."

Hans let his shoulders relax. "Okay, Rick, thanks. I'm Hans. Can I make a call first?" He better tell the others what was going on. They must be so worried. No answer. Did they go to China Town or Little Italy to eat? No fish—no dinner at the loft. He could just hear Louis: "The kid can't even bring back some fish. Asshole." Okay, so keep his focus on Jenny. Find her and he can handle anything. But how could he call her when he'd told her they couldn't afford a phone! Ja—he was an asshole, all right.

Hans asked Rick if they could stop by the diner on the way—just in case. What? Locked up?

"She's not there, Hans—no one is."

*****

The ride uptown was slow-motion torture. Every time Hans told himself they'd be there soon, Rick had another stop to make. First the drugstore, so he could get Quell: "Damn those bitchy crabs! Shouldn't have one-night flings on tour—never know what a babe might be carrying in her purse!" Then coffee-to-go so he could stay awake. Then a stop at Fifty-ninth Street to return someone's drum. When they finally reached 610 East Seventy-second Street, Hans was stiff with tension. Like a miracle, a car pulled away from the curb and they swung into the space. Hans checked his watch—ten o'clock.

Rick wanted to go up with him—he had something to tell Susan. They stood outside of Apartment 4C for ten minutes, knocking softly at first, then loudly. A man in a bathrobe was on them. "Shut the fuck up, jerks," he screamed. "I'm sick and tired of the noise coming out of this place."

Rick quieted the guy and asked if he'd heard any noise there earlier. The guy fumed, "When isn't the place blasting with sound!" Then he admitted he hadn't heard any noise that evening. Just the two of them knocking.

Back downstairs in the van, Rick said, "Sorry, Hans. Don't know what to tell you. You're solid with your girl, right? If I was you, I'd go home. Just go home, man. She'll show up eventually."

Hans nodded heavily. Losing hope, his heart began to throb. "Yeah, I'd trust her with my life." Rick was giving him a kind look; maybe he could ask him for help. "Brother, do you think you could spare a couple bucks?" Hans hated his timid voice. He clenched his jaw and talked louder. "I don't have any money on me. I forgot my billfold tonight. Give me your address, I'll send it back—really. I work in a street theater. We make money playing around the city."

"No kidding," Rick pulled a ten out of his billfold. "Should've told me earlier. You guys anti-war?"

"Yes," Hans said. "We're anti everything establishment—at least I am."

"Know what you mean, bro," Rick said. After the two exchanged phone numbers and addresses, he told Hans where to get the subway.

At a corner phone, Hans called the loft again. Then the neighbor's phone. No answer. Jenny could be there, asleep. Where the fuck was everybody?

He remembered: Jenny had the only key to their apartment. Hans had given his to Ron, who'd wanted to take a girl there the week before and never returned the key. Now Ron had gone to Long Island for the weekend to see his parents. If Jenny wasn't there, Hans couldn't get in. But she had to be there. Even if she and that weirdo Susan had smoked a little…Yes, the diner closed, she went home and crashed. He would get a coffee at the deli, then head for the Lexington Avenue subway.

The walk through the East Village was comforting after the unfamiliar neighborhoods. A few bars for the locals were still open. A bakery shop was lit up; odors of fresh bread woke up his hunger. He hadn't had a meal for over twelve hours.

He climbed up to the fifth floor, his heart pounding. Jenny, Jenny, be there! Be there! He had his fist up ready to pound, then saw the open door. She must be there. She'd left it open—for him.

He charged into each of the rooms in the railroad flat, like a minesweeper. Not there!

Oh god! She was not there! Who had opened the door? Had he and Jenny forgotten to lock it when they left that morning?

Hans sat down on the unmade bed. Then he collapsed in fetal position and wept. If he called the police, they'd arrest him! So what? He must find Jenny. Find Jenny!

In the depths of troubled sleep, he heard a voice. "Hans, Hans open up!" He sprung up like a jack-in-the-box and raced to the door. "Jenny!"

He had her in his arms. "Where? Where you been? *Gud—Gud*! I thought you got killed."

They fell onto the bed. "Oh, I can't believe what happened to me." Jenny was sobbing.

"With Susan?"

"How'd you know?"

"Tell me—what happened?"

"She hypnotized me—then drugged me with hash. I got myself into it—she promised me fifty bucks for my hat."

"But where is your hat?"

"She's got my hat, and I've got her fifty bucks. Stupid me, I fell asleep on her couch."

"At Seventy-second Street?"

"No, at her place—near the diner where you left me."

"I was there, Jenny. And you weren't there!"

"Yes I was, Hans! I followed her there to get the money for my hat, so we could buy the fish. I was sure you wouldn't get any free, honey. I even looked for a fish place near the diner— nothing. Went back to the diner—closed. Didn't know how to reach you. I wasn't thinking clear—I just came back here. I'm sorry. Used Mary's phone to call the loft—no answer. I guess they went out to eat. But baby, what took you so long?"

"I got a ride. And the guy had a bunch of stops."

"Hans—this has been the worst night of my life. How come you never came back?"

"We must have just missed each other. Crazy how that happened—like a time warp. But where were you just now?"

"Next door, at Mary's, waiting for you to come home."

"I called you there."

"I don't understand. She got home just before me. I didn't feel like being here alone, not after my night with Susan. And no Hans. Mary gave me hot tea, and I just fell asleep. She must have too. Now I remember. I had this dream."

"Jenny, I can't hear a dream now. Tomorrow. I been up all night for you."

"But Hans…I dreamt...I had it."

"Yeah, me too. Had it with losing you!" He held her on the bed in the vice of his legs.

"I dreamt I had our baby. It was just beautiful."

Hans had no words. She was stoned. That was it.

"But it was a funny baby. It had big bedroom eyes, like Louis—you know what I mean?"

Hans pulled the covers over them.

"Big eyes, and oh my god! Now I remember. My baby had fur on its face like a puppy..."

"So now that you had *our* baby, Jenny," Hans whispered, already falling into sleep, "maybe you'll stop having a thing for Louis, okay?"

56
Before the Tour

When Jenny's period came miraculously the next day, the two vowed never to make love again without a condom and a diaphragm. Though she wasn't pregnant, the image of a little fuzzy puppy continued to haunt her.

Louis began to see Hans in a new light. Dragging fish heads around all night, hoping to bring back food for all of them, was really responsible. The poor guy had tried! And Louis was delighted that he and Jenny had remained buddies after their complex time together in the yurt. Their connecting had done some good; it had fired up her passion for her man again!

*****

By March, the group of ten still had found no Black actors willing to join.

One afternoon Al and Marin were hanging out at a table tennis club and started talking to a young Black mother and her nephew. They told her about the work the street theater was doing to help stop the war. Cheryl asked the inevitable: "Are there any Black actors in your troupe?"

Marin responded earnestly: "We're desperately looking for Black women to join us so we can honestly and accurately address racism in this country." Cheryl smiled. "Maybe I can start fulfilling that quest!"

Over hamburgers and French fries at the diner across the street, Cheryl deftly kept her nephew, Marcel, occupied with a drawing pad and pencils and enough tune-in to keep him happy, as they talked more about the street theater work. Cheryl, a social worker, had performed in her college's drama productions, with dreams of becoming an actress, but felt pressure from her family to hold a steady job. "Working to help the poor obtain health care and jobs has politicized me," she told them. Hearing Marin and Al talk about their goal to creatively educate and politicize audiences through drama excited her deeply. She could never forget how thrilling it was to speak gutsy, truthful, articulate lines on a stage. "Do I have to audition for your group?" she laughed, remembering her nervousness in college tryouts. "No way," Marin said. "We need politically savvy women, like you!" Cheryl would be at their next open meeting.

*****

"God, you heard our prayers! Cheryl will put us to the task!" When Lucina got off the phone with Marin, she thought: *Maybe Louis could find some small comfort in connecting to her young nephew. Cheryl's obviously very close to the boy.*

As for the other newcomers, Lucina wondered: Would Jim and Donna, thirty-year-old puppeteers from Detroit who were used to touting their own agendas, force changes in the balance of power, especially among the Big Four—Louis, Lucina, Al, and Marin? And would nineteen-year-old Dawn, a moody drama-school dropout from the University of California and instant buddy with Hans, want them to try some gutsy guerrilla actions like the new Yippie Movement was pushing?

As Louis and Lucina worked to build a rich and varied repertoire, Karen and Sally faded into bittersweet memories. Louis decided to suppress his questions about a "dyke's kiss" until he could tell all to Lucina. For the time being he could not own how he'd been sexual with Karen.

Though his appreciation and enjoyment of other women were parts of who he was, Lucina stayed essential to his very being. He loved men as well, but stayed focused on women to explore his sexuality. Marlene, tough-minded and super-responsible to the group, slowly transformed into someone quite fascinating. After he mollified her suspicions around his behavior with Jenny, they became friends. So he was thrilled when her sabbatical came through, allowing her to work with the women's and mixed groups. He saw hunger in her silver blue eyes, desire in her lean, taut muscles, and passion in her obsession with lists and record keeping. Her chart of *Troupe Members' Ideas Utilized or Trashed* intrigued him. He found her breakdown of *Who Volunteers to Carry the Props vs. Who Has to Be Asked* to be informative. And her list of *Who Collects the Most Money by Passing the Hat and Why* delighted him. Was she seducing him with her mind, he wondered, and in a circuitous way teaching him the importance of keeping track of all types of behaviors?

The subjects of Marlene's preoccupation may not have been ones he would have chosen, but her tendency to obsess felt familiar and necessary. He'd already decided that whoever kept a record, whether of money or faces, humiliations or victories, was not only delving into the soul of mankind but also keeping present in history even after death.

Furthermore, he was charmed by her idiosyncratic sensations. He'd never known anyone who experienced moonlight as a certain taste, or felt an ecstatic chill in the blue color found in certain shadows. Lucina had these curious fine tunings around colors too, a deep sensitivity to visual phenomenon. But with Marlene, the fascination almost seemed haunted.

Lucina couldn't own that her fantasies about Sally were as sexual as you could get, even though they'd only shared a kiss. The shape of her relationship with Louis was a work-in-progress, to be determined. And her openness to being with a woman, both discovered and silenced in the encounter with Sally, had posed a new question: Could she possibly share more than a comrade's kiss with one of the women in her troupe? Time would reveal all, she decided.

*****

By April, when bitter winds and icy streets gave way to earth and sea smells, the newest Fire Dragon family prepared to embark on a cross-country tour. Lucina was concerned that the old and new members should feel an organic cohesiveness, be excited about going off into new territory together. Though the new members had attended rehearsals of their plays and been easily incorporated into them, particularly within group actions, appearing to accept the repertoire with the assurance that their plays were always in progress, evolving through the performance experience and audience feedback, she questioned the strength of their allegiance without having a chance to give their own critical input. Though they didn't have time to do a major overhaul on a play, they could tweak it a bit, the goal being to increase group creativity and enthusiasm.

Besides, silence could hide deep resentments and invaluable criticisms. And what did Marin's cryptic comment mean? "Cheryl might jolt us awake like a thunder bolt." *Well, we better address this now, before we're on the road,* she decided. *Learning a part already worked out by others is one thing; enhancing/changing that role with one's own ideas, or creating a new role and concept to add to the mix, yet another.*

The upending conversation with Aretha playing over and over in her mind, she felt the urgency of knowing what was really going on in the newcomers' minds, especially Cheryl's. She could put it like this: "The tour we are about to take must have personal, political, creative relevance to you. Is there anything bugging you about our work? We older members invite you to tell us. We'll be facing a lot of unknowns on the road. We sure don't want suppressed resentments on our first tour. Take one of our plays and tell us how something about that play as presently conceived troubles you—then as a group we can brainstorm, all fourteen of us, on how to handle your criticism or concern in a short time. We'll all be thinking together." She scheduled a meeting.

*****

The troupe sat on folding chairs arranged in a large circle and listened to Lucina's request for input. They understood her motive was to make all members feel excited about the upcoming tour; but they needed more explanation.

"So, you're not asking all of us to rumble-grumble," Hugh riffed playfully. "Just the newbies."

"The rest of us have already put our babies together," Lucina said impatiently. "We need to hear from Cheryl, Donna, Jim, Dawn… So, we're fourteen young adults traveling in a caravan across the country with a mission, portrayed in our plays. Our offerings are meant to inspire dialogue and action on many different issues. I want all of us to feel a vital part of this 'Journey of Enlightenment' as some might express it. So to that end, I think it's necessary that our newest members pick one of our mixed-group plays or our first women's play, and critique some aspect about it that troubles you. Tell us how you think it can be improved or changed in a few rehearsals, allowing input from the rest of us as well. Let's see if this can work. I hope I'm being clear."

"Clear as mud," Marin joked good-humoredly. "Seriously, our new recruits definitely need to add their brilliant insights to our ambitious repertoire."

After drawing straws, Cheryl would go first, Jim second, Donna third, and Dawn last. "Okay, let's hear it from our creative, political, vastly experienced, and so needed new members," Lucina enthused.

Cheryl stood up quickly: "Yes, definitely! Though I'm the only Black person here—God dressed me in my beautiful brown tones—I believe we all have the potential to be multiracial in our awareness, as well as empathic and understanding. But it takes work. We are all subjected to how our family, community, state, government treats us. Which brings me to my deep concern. The Fire Dragon Street Theater doesn't want to be color-blind or deniers of racism. But, the troupe doesn't have a play about this issue, as yet." Cheryl looked around the circle with open, questioning eyes. "Well, I'm certain I'll be a force in making that happen. I'm pulled by your themes of fighting for civil rights and justice and telling the truth of how the country was built on the dead bodies of the Indigenous. Yet, hopefully in the future, we'll have one on how my people, slaves, were forced to come here and do the labor that white people exploited to build this America." Cheryl sat down still keeping an alert, open posture.

"So, enough about that unspeakable evil," she continued calmly. "My concern for this exercise has to do with your play *Choice*. Though I haven't a role in it yet, I expect to be instrumental in making it a more authentic depiction for all of us in this country. We have to incorporate the treatment of Blacks in the US Military. Let me give you an example. I, like the rest of us, watch the news every night: soldiers in 'Nam fighting other soldiers. And I ask myself: Why are human beings, who all look pretty much like each other, gunning each other down?" She paused. "Also, America's soldiers could be any race in the heat of battle, with sweat and mud on their faces. But when it comes to TV, only white G.I. Joes are interviewed. Blacks are at the bottom of the pecking order in war, just as Blacks are at the bottom of the social structure in America, this land of the 'unfree.'"

After this biting offering, Cheryl softened her pose: "Fire Dragon Street Theater, let me say this as well—I'm looking forward to learning about drama and acting and all this good stuff. It's lucky for me that Al and Marin like to play ping-pong, like me and Marcel. And I'm really grateful. Please don't get too bent out of shape over my very deep concern. We're all learning. You've embraced me in your group—that already shows our audiences that we're inclusive, and embracing of all the rainbow colors." Struggling to keep her center, she breathed in deeply and closed her eyes.

Silence. Lucina looked at each face—it was as if each one was looking inward, groping for any words that might pay justice to Cheryl's truth: they had not approached, not even been concerned with, she realized uncomfortably, what it would mean for Sam to be performed by a Black man. Actually, Cheryl's concern could transform their whole repertoire. Many issues in their plays were from white viewpoints and experience!

She watched as Hans rose and walked over to Cheryl: "My sister, Cheryl, has spoken the obvious. We need to accept our limitations and vow to each other that we can change and grow. I had to. I did a terrible injustice to you all, when I acted out in a disruptive manner at Tavern on the Green. You have to understand, my first concern was for Louis—I saw the cops go for him—I was desperate to stop them. And I was afraid for myself. My illegal status here. But my actions gave them clear passage to grab him and cart him off to a terrible beating. It's been very painful, but I have learned from my stupidity, my blindness. And that's why I feel I can stand here beside Cheryl and say to her and you—we have to forgive ourselves for our ignorance—but we can learn. And I will do everything I can to make our plays show awareness of what it's like to live in a country that considers only some of its inhabitants as whole human beings. I'm a white Dane, so even though I am an illegal immigrant, I can avoid being singled out. As long as they don't catch me, I can fit into the white man's rules and pecking order and segregations. But Cheryl has laid out the work we have to do—as workers for racial justice in America—how we have to include the experience and viewpoints of Black Americans in all our plays."

Lucina spoke softly: "What a blessing she has joined us. We have much to learn from…"

"Look, we're all more alike than different," Cheryl broke in, her face relaxed and smiling. "So I'll let you all know when I think the Black experience has been left out. And I'll share with you—books to read, activists to learn from. You know—change takes all of us wanting to see each other's truths. Anyway, yes—Black and white working together…" She closed her eyes, her lips moving as if saying to herself the thoughts she couldn't share.

Jim, next up to offer his concerns, nodded vigorously with a scowl on his face. "Well, what I'm going to say might sound like a whinny kid after Cheryl's revelation, but here goes. Look, I'm really bugged about a conundrum in *Eco-Drama*. Since I'm playing one of the Bills, who spills pollution all over the place, I feel I know of what I speak." Gesturing nervously with his hands, he continued. "It's about not adding pollution to our environment. That's what the play is about, but is our group thinking about how we might be adding to it? We have ten metal boxes of props for that play alone. Each bit with the Bills has stuff being thrown around on the stage that has to be collected at the end of every scene."

Courtney laughed. "Who needs all that shit? Jim's right. We're making work for ourselves." Jim relaxed, his hands now resting on his legs as he continued: "How can we not use all that junk? It's possible to show pollution another way. Say, projecting slides of it. It'd save a lot of space and muscle power. Also—I'm sure you all know—the three vehicles we're taking on our tour, including our station wagon, are gas guzzlers. We're polluting the air as we travel about protesting pollution. I suggest, by the way, that each of us limit what we bring for the three weeks to one small suitcase or backpack apiece. Otherwise we're not all going to fit in our wheelies."

Hands immediately went up. Marlene shouted out, "I've been saying that, too!"

Of course, Lucina thought, *it's much easier to speak to Jim's issue, than to Cheryl's revelation.*

Al spoke first: "My suggestion is that the Bills do asides to the audience. For example, instead of throwing lots of pine cones aka grenades around the stage, one Bill could say: 'You have to use your imaginations now. Imagine me polluting the stage with grenades—as our military saturates land, air, and water with poisons, agent orange, and napalm. Unlike the military, we do not want to pollute, so thank you, your imaginations will keep our pollution down.' Something like that might work."

Hans clapped enthusiastically. "I dig this! And slides can show a hell of a lot of pollution that goes way beyond the Bills throwing stuff on the stage. I'll work on that. And maybe even outside we could project pollution on a sheet—although that could be hard if we're in a demonstration situation. Have to think about that."

"That'll be great, Hans." Courtney added. "I'll help you, man. Or maybe we could use big posters carried on poles, with photos of all kinds of pollution for the different Bills to use. And maybe we can get the ten prop boxes of crap down to five." Everyone laughed.

Lucina thought: *Yes! And besides, everyone grumbles when it's their turn to carry the prop boxes on the subway to a performance.*

"About our gas guzzlers, Jim…" Now Jack was speaking. "Maybe someday some genius will invent the electric car. Then the whole country can be pollution-free."

"All industry has a polluting side to it," Marlene piped up.

"The electric car has already been invented." Al was back into the discussion. "Henry Ford and his pal Thomas Edison worked on one. Problem was, it was four times the cost of a combustible engine. Petroleum was easily available but electric charging stations weren't. So we're still waiting for the affordable, practical, non-polluting electric cars to appear."

"Okay, thank you, everyone." Jim, smiling broadly at his audience, waved his hand like a politician greeting his followers.

Again Lucina was fretting: *No one is speaking to Cheryl's words. I should say something!*

Donna rose to speak: "This is going to be a challenging experience for Jim and me—working with you all. We could make our puppets do anything we wanted them to do. With you guys and gals, we'll probably get pushed around a bit. Just kidding. But I want to say to Cheryl first—you're one gutsy lady, and you've already inspired me to find my courage. My angst is that I won't be able to act with the soul and heart you senior member actors show—I still have to learn to take up my space." Donna wiggled her hips playfully, before adding stern-faced: "But in the women's group I hope to find the support I need."

As Marlene and Marin stomped their feet in support, she cleared her throat nervously: "One more thing. I don't think this group has addressed yet—well, maybe in *DreamCatcher* it's come up. It's about people who don't fit into the norm. I'm talking about the mentally and physically disabled, and gays and lesbians. How do they fit into this theater troupe and our country in general? I don't want to be in a troupe that panders to 'normal,' the 'white normal.' I welcome any comments about what I've just said…" Donna sat down, sighing heavily, as if a weight had been lifted from her and nodded at Jim, sitting a few chairs from her. He was giving her a thumbs up sign and nodding.

"Welcome to our troupe, puppeteers Donna and Jim," Marlene piped up in a warm voice. "Maybe you won't miss your marionettes so much if we do a bit where actors become puppets activated by strings. You and Jim could teach us how to do that. But regarding your concern about disabled people and gays and lesbians—I'd like to add transgender people—that's a new word being used. People who feel they don't have the right body parts…"

"You mean, your prick is too small?" Hugh waited for everyone to laugh. No one did.

"No! You feel you shouldn't have a prick! Marlene snapped. "Anyway, as Cheryl has made clear, we need to be inclusive in every way we can. We just have to keep our repertoire growing and growing and make it a very conscious goal to include every ethnic group, every person that has been marginalized by a system geared to white middle-class men. Onward for the good of all."

Many cheers greeted Donna and Marlene as Lucina stood to speak. "Yeah, ever since Marin shared with us about the brutal treatment of her brother, I've been wondering—when are we going to do a play about same-sex love? Geez, we all know someone, I bet, who's gay. Can you imagine being treated as an outcast just because you love Robert and not Roberta? For a supposedly democratic country, I'd say this 'home of the brave' has an incredibly prejudiced track record around Blacks' and women's civil rights, mentally and physically challenged people's rights, gay, lesbian, trans—you name it. Why is this so? This is what makes me so goddamn sick! And our theater group has the responsibility to do something about it."

As if acknowledging the hard truth behind Lucina's words, they all stood again. Then Courtney turned to Cheryl and spoke: "I want to work with you on making our group more and more aware—and responsive to the systemic, endemic racism that exists here, but as a white person I haven't experienced and have been kept blind to it. Cheryl, we need you. So, I guess it's Dawn's turn to tell us how we need to do better. I pass the flame to her." He sat down again and the others followed.

Dawn seemed reluctant to be exposed in this way. She sashayed around the loft space for a while, as if looking for someone or something, or creating a persona who would speak out as a character. But it was soon obvious, this was Dawn: whimsical and quirky. When she stopped next to Cheryl, she started speaking. "I'm glad to be part of the Ghost Dance play because I was ignorant of how Native Americans have been treated by my country. Is that the right way to address Indigenous people?" She directed her question first to Cheryl before turning to the others.

After some silence, Louis responded. "That's good, Dawn. But the best way is to name the tribes specifically. Many tribes took part in the Ghost Dance Movement, but as you know, we mainly focus on what happened to the Lakota Sioux Tribe at Wounded Knee, South Dakota. But, yeah, I think it's okay to say, Native Americans."

Dawn nodded appreciatively and continued talking. "I still feel it's a country I want to be proud of, but not at the cost of staying blind to the truth. I'm so overcome by Cheryl's concern. Thank you for being with us white folk. I do want to be your sister and…" Dawn's shy, almost apologetic look made her seem vulnerable. She paused, catching her breath. "All right, what's my concern?" She glanced quickly at Lucina before continuing. "You know, when we're singing the chants and dancing in a circle, I feel it brings me closer to everyone here. I heard about the full moon ritual you all did at that mythical Yellow Farm. Well, I feel the Ghost Dance makes me become part of a tribe. I like that. But I don't understand the need for the holy sacred man, Wovoka. I guess you don't quite either, Hugh—at least, you seem to question how to portray him…? What happens to me is, it makes me feel like a child. And Wovoka is like my dad, a power figure I'm supposed to follow. So I'm really glad about the women's plays where each woman gets to tell her story and the rest of us will show solidarity to her by acting it out. That's all I have to say for now."

The women clapped first and then the men joined in. Dawn curtsied playfully. With Marlene's warm hug, she burst into tears and sped back to her place in the circle.

"So many different emotions have been filling up this loft space, comrades." Lucina enthused. "We've all been so present and so focused on what each of our newcomers has shared! And wow! I can't believe the exercise we've gotten, getting up and sitting down!" She laughed, letting her shoulders and face relax for the first time since the meeting began. "What I hoped for has been so much more—overwhelming! It's our responsibility now to really respond to each other's needs." Suddenly self-conscious, she looked at Louis for affirmation.

He gave her a thumbs-up and Marin chimed in her support: "Today, let's make a commitment to ourselves and to each other to do the work that has been laid out here by our new members. Amen. Ah, women!"

Louis suddenly produced a large bottle of Chianti. As they passed it around, Marin barked: "We fired-up Fire Dragons will be wheeling across America in a few days with a lot to think about. Just remember, playmates, limit your baggage—no more pollution of any kind!"

Acknowledgements/Appreciation

Fire Dragon Street Theater 1962-1969 is the first of four novels in my memoir-based *Rune Quartet*. During the forty years of its arduous construction, many people encouraged my writing. Isabel Miller (*Patience and Sarah*) wrote about my debut historical memoir novel, *Mari*, a cross-cultural lesbian romance, (New Victoria Press, 1991): "Admirers of Jeri Hilderley's music will be happy to see that she brings the same creative boldness and energy to this novel...heroic women...passion for justice...." Nancy Willard (*Things Invisible to See*, *A Visit to William Blake's Inn*) wrote: "Full of imagination ... a unique voice...."

And then I am most grateful for the enthusiastic responses to my many readings at women's cultural centers and from my readers, who gave me courage to write about my struggles to find my identity and voice as I integrated them into a larger body of inclusive, compassionate awareness.

I am also grateful for the generous support of fellowships from Cummington Community of the Arts, Virginia Creative Center of the Arts and Blue Mountain Center—where I wrote the early versions. I am appreciative of the tender and incisive critiques at the workshops: Writer's Voice with Marcia Golub (*I'd Rather Be Writing*); In Our Own Write with Jennifer Levin (*The Sea of Light*); Memoir Writing with Florence Howe (*A Life in Motion*). I shared writing for many productive years with the PEN Women Writers' Group. Novelists Jerome Badanes (*Final Opus of Leon Solomon*) and Padma Hejmadi (*Room to Fly, The School Master and Other Stories*) gave me vital suggestions over many years. Additionally, I am indebted to the members of my writers' group of recent years who have critiqued the recent iteration: Josephine Diamond, Caroline Thomas, Sue Elizabeth Davis, Janet Mayes, Loretta Goldberg, Sue Harris and Sarah Relyea.

Sarah Relyea (*playground zero*) has served as a careful, insightful substantive/content editor, copy editor, and proofreader of the final version. That I could discuss with her the complex issues that arise in this process has been precious. It was exhilarating to find common ground as we hashed things out.

A natural and necessary part of my relationships with my significant artist partners through the years has been the sharing and critiquing of each other's creative work. Jerome Badanes, Rain Bengis and Janet Mayes have been extraordinarily generous and supportive in reading and critiquing my work. Janet and I have been partners for seventeen years now; our writing projects have become as necessary and integral to our relationship as our love.

I am grateful for the supportive exchanges about our creative work over the years with many colleagues, partners, friends, collaborators: Diana Bellessi, Paul Bernstein, Joan E. Biren, Marianne Burke, Lynne Cooper, Verity Dierhauf, Julie Enszer, Vicki Felder, Merry Gangemi, Kay Gardner, Shelley Grabel, Avital Greenberg, Sorrel Hayes, Gail Kinn, Eileen Downey, Eric Lindbloom, Bruce Macpherson, Jodi Miller, Helen Pine, Jeffrey Rabkin, Marilyn Ries, Mei Mei Sanford, Jacqui Schnider, Elena Sheehan, Lois Sperakis, Ronnie Tuft, Fleur Weymouth. And to friends for their encouragement: Ginny Davies, Susan Elliot, Fran Israel, Linda Ito, Dee Livingston,

Nancy Myers, Dianne Oakland, Lynda Radar, Judy Winters. And to all my Facebook friends, too numerous to mention, but whose own creative works and support of my work have nourished me through the years, I thank you.

I extend appreciation to family members who have encouraged me to "get that book published!" as I described my efforts to take the reins and self-publish. I thank you: Johanna, Clifton, Laura, Clif, Andrea, Gioccomo, Brad, Parker, Cris, Beth, Lauren, Dylan.

My therapist Lynne R. Alterman continues to guide and support me through all the insecurities and obsessions we writers suffer.

I would like also to extend appreciation to the many dedicated activists in the International Action Center who have inspired and educated my revolutionary optimism and that of my characters.

And to all other dear supportive friends I failed to mention, I offer my apologies.

I am grateful for the patient expertise of Dave Bass, who designed the interior of the book and served as my self-publishing guide/facilitator. To Jodi Miller, my graphic designer friend, who artfully executed the cover for the book and accepted my feisty dragon drawing with enthusiasm, I give thanks.

Finally, how can I possibly list the endless writers who have led and fed me since I first visited my hometown library when I was five? Their impact is embedded in my writing.

Acknowledgement of people and organizations is not meant to imply that they endorse or in any way agree with assumptions put forth in my book. Those are entirely mine.

About the Author

I have been engaged in the intriguing and complex relationship between artist and activist for seven decades. With a first career as sculptor (after studying art at Smith College, University of California, Berkeley, and obtaining a Master of Arts in Sculpture from the University of Michigan Ann Arbor), I settled in New York City's artists' district in the 60s to construct large wooden female figures in action. The ritual-like sculptures, described in the *New York Herald* as "highly ingenious and mad," didn't fit into sedate New York galleries then, so I invented Sculpture Theater, incorporating dancers and musicians to accompany my work. Like protagonist Lucina Holzer in *Fire Dragon Street Theater 1962-1967,* I was soon propelled by the anti-war movement to use my artists' skills for political activism, working with collective street theater groups.

In the late 60s and early 70s, I co-founded the women's theater groups, Women of Burning City and Painted Women's Ritual Theater, to showcase our life stories, which played an integral role in building the Women's Movement. In connection with the Women's Music Network of the 70s, I founded the SeawaveRecordings label and recorded my original compositions for voice, marimba and guitar: *A Few Loving Women* and *Jeritree's*

House of Many Colours. Extensive performances throughout the United States allowed me to reach out to and be educated by other artists/activists, feminists, women of color, LGBTQIA+ audiences, and the many community activists concerned with building an inclusive culture of caring in a true democracy.

While teaching autobiographical and essay writing in Women's Studies Departments at SUNY Purchase, Empire State College and CUNY's Seek Program, along with language and music skills to Special Ed students in the New York City public schools for the next 3 decades, I continued to write fiction and articles about the creative process.

After retiring from full-time teaching, I built my own recording studio, producing original songs for *12 Meditations on Love* and *Talking Truth* with the trio, SeaWaves. (Janet Mayes, bass/vocals; Susan Ahlborn, guitar/vocals, composer, and myself.) With partner Janet Mayes, I produced the CD and accompanying booklet: *Time Traveling with Sappho,* a song-cycle of Sappho's poem fragments translated by Pulitzer Prize nominee Konstantinos Lardas, set to my original music. My CDs have enjoyed world-wide distribution.

Although I have moved through different media, I have always found a deep interconnection between the many art forms that fed my need to create collectively with other artists/ activists. My sculptures moved me into theater, where I began to compose dramatic, personal and political songs; my writing began with journaling to record the exciting drama of my street theater work. My fifty-page essay, "Burning City Street Theater: Analysis of a Theater Commune." Chicago Review 23, no 1(Summer 1971): 40-92, served as inspiration for much of the flavor of *Fire Dragon Street Theater.* Through the years, I have written sequels to this novel, following the major characters on their tour and then into the 70s, 80s and 90s as they and new protagonists seek unique ways to address complex careers, same-sex love, discrimination, the AIDS crisis and the Israeli-Palestinian conflict. So, I continue, at 85, to create and recreate my life; though *Fire Dragon Street Theater 1962-1967* is the first novel in *Rune Quartet*, the next three novels will be the latest recordings of my evolution.

Publications (partial list):

"To Be Extra-Ordinary", *Opyrus, Corona Silver Linings Anthology*, 2020.

Mari, Norwich, VT: New Victoria Publishers, 1990.

"The Alphabet Wedding." *Sinister Wisdom: Pleasure* 99 (Winter 2016): 104-108.

Badanes, Jeriann. "Burning City Street Theater: Analysis of a Theater Commune." *Chicago Review* 23, no. 1 (Summer 1971): 40-92.

"A Woman Remembers Her Music." *Heresies*, no. 10 (1980): 16-17. Women and Music. [http://heresiesfilmproject.org/wp-content/uploads/2011/09/heresies10.pdf]

"How to Find the Music in You." *Paid My Dues* III, no.1 (Fall 1978): 6,7, 38. [https://queermusicheritage.com/pmd3-1.html]

"Burning City Street Theater's Ecology Play." In *People's Theater in Amerika*, by Karen Malpede Taylor. 317-320. Drama Book Specialists/Publishers, New York. 1972

"I Was There and I Am Here." *Sinister Wisdom: In Amerika They Call Us Dykes: Lesbian Lives in the 70s* 82 (Spring 2011): 78-86.

Website:

https://jerihilderley.blog/